Praise for
Jane Goodger

Into the Wild Wind

"With this adventurous, passionate romance on the high seas, Goodger once again sweeps her fans away."—*Publishers Weekly*

"★★★★. Goodger provides what I most appreciate in the books I read: an entree into past worlds, accurately but romantically recreated. She has become a 'must buy' for me."
—*The Romance Reader*

"★★★★★. This book captured my attention from the very beginning. Once I started reading it, I couldn't put it down. This love story promises adventure, entertainment and passion: all of which Jane Goodger aptly delivers."
—*Affaire de Coeur*

"Ms. Goodger provides her audience with a fabulous Americana romance that will have the audience scampering for her previous works."
—Harriet Klausner, *Painted Rock Reviews*

"With exceptional characters, a fun array of secondary characters, and a story line that captivates, this is a definite keeper."
—*Under the Covers Book Reviews*

continued . . .

Dancing with Sin

"A deep, insightful portrait of late-nineteenth-century society and women's place within that world. Ms. Goodger's talents lie in presenting a different picture of the era and following through with themes that are as relevant today as they were a century ago."—*Romantic Times*

"Thrilling . . . exciting. . . . A novel you don't want to miss."—Lisa Kleypas

Anything for Love

"Simply wonderful. A beautiful, touching story of a second chance at life and love. Goodger has created a winner with *Anything for Love*."
—*Romance Communications*

The Perfect Wife

Jane Goodger

A SIGNET BOOK

SIGNET
Published by New American Library, a division of
Penguin Putnam Inc., 375 Hudson Street,
New York, New York 10014, U.S.A.
Penguin Books Ltd, 27 Wrights Lane,
London W8 5TZ, England
Penguin Books Australia Ltd, Ringwood,
Victoria, Australia
Penguin Books Canada Ltd, 10 Alcorn Avenue,
Toronto, Ontario, Canada M4V 3B2
Penguin Books (N.Z.) Ltd, 182–190 Wairau Road,
Auckland 10, New Zealand

Penguin Books Ltd, Registered Offices:
Harmondsworth, Middlesex, England

First published by Signet, an imprint of New American Library,
a division of Penguin Putnam Inc.

First Printing, September 2000
10 9 8 7 6 5 4 3 2 1

Chapter One

He already felt sorry for her and he hadn't even broken her heart yet.

Henry Owen looked across the crowded music room at Anne Foster and had a nearly overwhelming urge to run from the room, away from her, from himself, from the absolute certainty that he was a bastard. He could remember his father telling him, a sin is made worse when you know you are sinning. If that were true, the devil himself would be waiting at the end of the line for Henry James Owen.

Unless he received a miracle, something he considered highly unlikely given his fallen state, Anne would be his wife before year's end. She was perfect for his purposes and so imperfect in nearly every other way. Indeed, Anne Foster was everything that Henry disliked in a woman. She was blonde, blue-eyed, shy, vacant, and—putting it kindly—plump. And not pleasingly so, he thought with brutal honesty. He preferred dark-haired, dark-eyed beauties with slim waists and petite figures, women who sparkled with intelligence and wit. Conversations with Miss Foster were tedious affairs, punctuated mostly by her rather irritating habit of giggling in nervous bursts at nearly everything that came out of his mouth. But he suspected she was already half in love with him, so convincing her to marry him would be effortless. Anne Foster was indeed perfect.

He only prayed that she would never know the real

reason he had chosen her above all other women, because as callous as he tried to be in this matter, Henry was not a cold nor a cruel man. He was simply an obsessed one.

"So, when are you going to pop the question?" Alex Henley asked carelessly, lifting his chin toward Anne. Alex and Henry had been friends since they were boys in short pants. Where Alex was elegant, a stickler for proper dress if not proper behavior, Henry was rugged and dangerously handsome. Something about his careless elegance attracted women, made them want to straighten his tie and press his suit jacket. The fact that he'd been orphaned as a boy— even though he was now twenty-seven—only added to his appeal.

Giving his friend a look of sheer irritation, Henry said, "I'll consider proposing after I speak with my grandfather. There is still a chance he'll give me Sea Cliff so I can avoid this mess." As always, Henry felt his stomach churn uncomfortably at the thought of actually marrying Anne.

"You know he'll never do it," Alex said. "If only you would give up your obsession with the place."

Henry tightened his jaw. Of all people, Alex should know why Sea Cliff was so important to him. He'd give up his inheritance completely if only his grandfather would grant him that old summer home on Jamestown. His inheritance included the cottage, but it was out of reach until he turned thirty or married. In three years' time, when he celebrated his thirtieth birthday, Sea Cliff would be long gone, a certain victim of a New England coastal storm. Even now, the house teetered on the edge of disaster, clinging precariously to the bluff overlooking Newport, where it had been built thirty-six years ago in 1857. He must gain ownership immediately to save it, and that left him only one option: He must marry.

Henry, a severely practical man, could not begin to

rationally explain his driving need to save the cottage. If he spoke the words aloud, they would sound trite, ridiculous: "I want the house because I was happy there." But there it was, his reason for needing to save Sea Cliff. Simply put, he wanted to be happy again.

The summer cottage of his memory was a sort of paradise, a haven from all that was evil and dark. He knew his memories were those of a twelve-year-old boy, that all the days spent on that tiny island tucked between Newport and the Rhode Island mainland melded into one glorious summer's day of blue skies, warm, salt-tinged air, and little-boy toes digging into soft sand. He could not think of Sea Cliff without remembering sultry summer afternoons sitting on the porch with his mother as she read aloud to him, or prowling the woodlands with his father in search of a particular wildflower. The old cottage had been lost to him on the only rainy day he could recall, the day his parents died sailing on Block Island Sound—a day he hadn't even been on Jamestown. In one moment, he lost all that was good in his life. Including Sea Cliff.

Years of neglect had turned it into a ramshackle memorial to a time when he'd been young and completely, utterly happy. As the years passed, he watched in agony as the cottage slowly, horribly deteriorated, abandoned and neglected by his grandfather, who refused to do anything to save the old place. Ten years ago, Henry noticed that the bluff upon which Sea Cliff sat was eroding dramatically, and that was when he'd started his campaign with his grandfather to save it. He'd always known that marriage was an answer, but it was one he'd never seriously considered. He'd watched too many of his friends marry simply to expand the family fortune, and he'd vowed that he would marry only for love as his parents had. Money had never been an issue. Until now.

He could still remember his discussion with Alex when he'd finally decided that marriage was his only option if he truly wanted to save the cottage. He needed a quick marriage to someone who wouldn't question him about the haste, nor object to being abandoned to a solitary life. Henry had no intention of becoming one of those cowed men who made money only to satisfy their wife's vanity. Indeed, he had no intention of becoming a true husband at all.

"If you have to marry, marry an ugly girl, Henry. She'll be so grateful to be Mrs. Henry Owen, she won't question why she's been abandoned," Alex had said half-jokingly. "You'll avoid a lot of messiness, mark my words."

Despite the cruelty of such a scheme, Henry immediately thought of Anne Foster—shy, homely Anne, whose eyes peering from beneath thick banana curls of yellow hair followed him around the room at a dozen different Newport functions that summer. In his obsessive haze, Alex's suggestion made perfect sense, and Anne was the perfect target.

When he'd asked her to dance that first time, he'd felt so horrid, he'd nearly abandoned his ill-conceived plan right there. Anne had been so clearly delighted, so awed to find herself dancing with him, he'd wanted to fall to his knees and confess then and there what he planned. She was, he thought, so very unaware of how rotten he was. And that made his ability to follow through more difficult; she was making it all too easy for him.

Anne looked over at Henry again. She simply couldn't help herself. He was so beautiful and she loved him so much. Oh, please, God, let him speak to me again tonight. She drank in the sight of him, his strong, cleanly shaved jaw, his curling brown hair, his mesmerizing gray eyes. She need only look at him to feel all aflutter, quite unlike herself. For the first time in her life, Anne felt pretty. She thought her new blue gown made her appear thin. Well, thinner. God knew she'd nearly made herself and her maid faint by demanding that her stays be pulled beyond what she thought she could endure. It was worth the agony—and it was sheer agony to have one's waist squeezed so unmercifully—if she could again attract Henry's attention. She loved her thick curls, the way they bounced around her head whenever she moved quickly. She found herself turning her head quickly on purpose, just so she could create the effect of bouncing curls.

"Do stop that," Beatrice Leyden said after getting smacked in the face for the third time with one of Anne's errant curls. Beatrice was Anne's closest friend—her only true friend—and the only person to whom she confessed her love for Henry. Anne hadn't much cared for Beatrice's reaction. "Oh, Anne, he's a bounder in the extreme. He's nearly as bad as that Alexander Henley he's always with."

"Henry is a fine man. You don't know him the way I do," she'd countered.

Now Henry was on the other side of her parents' music room, and all she could think about was that he might ask to sit with her when the string quartet from New York began its concert. He looked her way and her heart pounded hard against her ribs. "Oh, mercy, here he comes," Anne said, letting out an uncontrollable giggle.

"Don't worry, I won't leave your side," Beatrice said, grabbing Anne's wrist as if she needed fortification.

"But you must leave. Oh, please, Bea, I hardly ever get a chance to be alone with him."

Beatrice cast an obvious look about the crowded room, but gave her friend a smile before moving away.

Nodding to his friends, Henry began making his way across the room, skirting behind a row of chairs set up for the small audience. To Anne's loving eyes, he looked magnificent in his black jacket, silver embroidered waistcoat, and crisp white shirt. His cravat was silver with the tiniest black polka dots, tied to perfection. Perfection, Anne sighed, like everything else about him.

"Happy birthday, Anne," he said when he reached her.

Anne giggled. It was about all she did in his presence, to her great annoyance. Anne, who disdained the silly, skinny, twittering girls who seemed to monopolize men like Henry, found herself acting just like them. It was a wonder Henry kept coming back, for certainly he'd no idea that she had a brain in her head with all that giggling she did. She couldn't help it. Whenever Henry talked to her, her brain shut down, and out of her mouth came the most inane, ridiculous things. When she recalled their conversations later, she found herself mortified by her complete lack of poise.

"I've a small gift for you," he said. "A small token of my esteem."

"Oh." She looked down at the small, rectangular wooden box. A gift. For her. From Henry. She swallowed a giggle that threatened to erupt from her throat.

Anne took the box and ran a hand over the smoothly polished surface, savoring the moment, her pulse racing. Never before in her life had a man other than her father given her a present. Slowly she opened the lid to reveal a pretty little gold heart on an impossibly delicate gold chain.

"For me?" she asked stupidly. Then giggled, hating herself.

"Of course, for you."

She pulled the necklace out of the box, hardly feeling the thin chain against her fingertips. "It's lovely. Thank you, Henry. Do you mind?" she asked, handing the necklace to him and presenting him with her back, all the time thinking she sounded like a woman who was used to accepting gifts from admirers.

Henry fumbled with the clasp and nearly dropped the necklace down her dress before she rescued it, digging for it as discreetly as possible. Her skin flushed so hot it prickled, but she handed the chain back to him for another go, pretending she wasn't dying of humiliation. Anne felt the cool gold chain go around her neck, pull tight, then loosen. His knuckles pressed against her nape as he worked to clasp the chain.

"One minute. It's . . . the chain's a bit short."

He tried again, Anne's cheeks flaming red in embarrassment, and she quickly prayed no one was looking. The longer he struggled with the chain, the more self-conscious she became. He mistakenly pulled the sensitive hairs at the base of her skull and she bit the inside of her bottom lip to keep from crying out. Disappointment filled her, that this moment she should have cherished in her heart would be simply another humiliation. The chain is not too short, my neck is too big, she thought, hoping that Henry would give up. She lifted her chin a bit, hoping to thin out her neck, and felt the chain again biting slightly into her.

"There," he said with obvious relief.

She turned with a forced smile on her lips. "I'm certain it looks lovely."

He gave her something like a grin that looked to Anne more like a grimace, and agreed it did. Anne found for the rest of the evening that whenever she spoke, the little heart would flip up and down, up and down. And when she laughed, which she did less and less as the evening wore on, it would flutter there like a butterfly with a damaged wing.

A soft knock sounded on the study door of Arthur Owen's New York town house a brief moment before the butler quietly opened it and cautiously poked his head through.

"His grandson is here," the butler whispered.

Williamson nodded and glanced back at his employer, who sat slumped and snoring in his wheelchair. "Give me ten minutes," he said softly.

Before the door clicked closed, Williamson was by Arthur Owen's side, a hand gently shaking the old man awake. "Sir," he said loudly into the old man's hair-tufted ear, receiving only a garbled mumble for his efforts. "Sir, Henry is here. He'll be up in ten minutes."

The old man's head snapped up. "Henry, you say?" he demanded, his words only slightly slurred. "On his way up now?" His tone held a hint of panic, and Williamson gave him a small reassuring smile.

"In ten minutes, sir. We'll get you together, all right." Even as he spoke, Arthur Owen's cadaverously thin valet walked briskly to a large cabinet at the far side of the darkened room. He removed a freshly starched shirt, cravat, tan waistcoat, and dark brown jacket, and draped them across one arm. In his free hand, he held a pair of stockings and the old man's brilliantly polished shoes.

Within minutes, the fragile-looking invalid was transformed into a sharp-eyed curmudgeon. His grandson would never know that beneath the lap blanket was only a pair of drawers, slightly stained from his breakfast that morning. There wasn't time to haul Arthur out of the wheelchair to tug trousers over his useless legs. Williamson wheeled Arthur behind the desk and briskly pulled open the thick velvet draperies that ordinarily remained closed, ignoring the old man's protest. On the desk in front of Arthur, Williamson placed a leather portfolio and a scattering of documents, gaining him a rueful smile of appreciation. Arthur's thinning, gray hair was swept back, his eyes sharp. He was ready to face the one person in the world he loved more than life.

Henry walked into the study without knocking, squinting against the bright sun that cast his grandfather into an imposing silhouette. He was shrouded in light and dust, which served to give the old man a menacing spectral quality. Even sitting in the wheelchair, even though it was obvious the stroke that had stricken his grandfather more than a decade before left him an invalid, Arthur Owen was the only man who could—and did—intimidate Henry. He hated that fact, almost as much as he hated the man himself.

"You didn't schedule an appointment," Arthur said loudly.

"I never do," Henry countered easily, even though his gut clenched. The old gent never failed to make him feel like the stuttering, skinny twelve-year-old boy he once was, standing before his grandfather to explain an unsatisfactory school report. Shutting out that memory, Henry forced himself to stride farther into the room.

"I'm here about Sea Cliff," Henry said, moving to the side of the desk so that the sunlight struck the side of his grandfather's face, fully revealing each line that crisscrossed his pale skin. My God, Henry thought, he's so old. Unexpectedly, his heart softened, something that surprised him as much as it would have the old man. For the first time he noticed how his grandfather's fine suit jacket hung limply on his shoulders, how thin his legs appeared beneath the blanket that covered him. He turned away to look out the window, not wanting to have his resolve weakened by the real evidence that his grandfather was old and frail and probably dying.

"Sea Cliff is not yours yet," Arthur said, gripping his wheelchair's armrests fiercely.

Henry spun around, all kind thoughts swept away by his grandfather's belligerence. "I am aware of who owns Sea Cliff. But perhaps you are not aware that the house is about to tumble into Narragansett Bay. That last storm stripped away the hill and exposed the foundation."

His grandfather sneered at him. "If it were up to

me, if I had the strength," he said as he fisted his thin, veiny hands, "I'd push that cursed place into the water today."

Henry's face tightened with anger. "You will get your wish, Grandfather. One more nor'easter, one more hurricane, and she'll be gone."

"Good riddance."

Henry took a deep breath and attempted a calm smile. "I know you don't like the old place. All the more reason to give it to me now. Why wait until it becomes official in three years when I turn thirty? I'll not ask for money, just the house."

"No."

Henry stood rigid before the man who had controlled his life from the moment his parents had died fifteen years ago. His grandfather had controlled the huge inheritance that awaited when he turned thirty, money that would free him from the tentacles his grandfather had wrapped around him, strangling him since he'd walked away from his parents' empty graves and into his grandfather's care.

"I could use my own money to shore up the cliff, if only you'll grant me permission." He could hear the pleading tone of his voice and it made him want to scream.

Arthur snorted. "What money? All your so-called money is tied up into that embarrassing boatyard."

Henry closed his eyes. It was an old argument, one he would never win with his grandfather, who'd made his vast fortune in the China trade. Henry knew that no matter how successful his yacht-building enterprise became, it would never be considered a socially acceptable way to make money. His name and his huge inheritance bought his way into New York's finest homes and nothing else.

"I could save Sea Cliff."

Arthur lifted his chin, his eyes blazing with intensity. "I don't want it saved."

Henry clenched his jaw so tightly, his teeth hurt. "Then sell it. But why let it waste away?"

"You're too damned sentimental, Henry. It's another weakness," he said, clearly inferring that Henry had many.

For an instant, Henry pictured himself putting his hands around the old man's sagging throat and squeezing the life out of him. Instead, he said, "Mother and Father loved Sea Cliff. They were happy there and would feel the same way as I. They would want to save it."

The old man snorted again. "No one was ever happy there. I should have had it torn down years ago."

"Then why didn't you?" Henry shouted, anger pulsing through his veins. "Why let it rot on that cliff? You're nothing but a cruel, vindictive old man who's blaming a house for his own sorry tragedy. Mark me well, Grandfather, if it's the last thing I do, I'll save that house."

Arthur gulped, his face growing a deep red, the veins in his neck clearly visible. "That house . . ." He gasped, his hands grasping at his cravat. "That house . . ."

Alarmed, Henry moved quickly to his grandfather's side, pushing the old man's shaking hands away from this throat. He deftly undid the necktie before rushing to find Williamson.

"He's having some sort of fit," he told the secretary, concern clear in his voice.

"I'm fine," Arthur managed to call out, and Henry turned with surprise to see that his grandfather did, indeed, seem fine. Or at least no longer in any danger of keeling over dead.

Henry, suddenly feeling deeply remorseful, moved quickly to the wheelchair, and knelt beside his grandfather. "I won't argue about this, Grandfather. I didn't

come to argue, but to inform you that I intend to save
Sea Cliff, one way or another."

"Sea Cliff is mine." That fact alone seemed to
soothe the old man.

"There is another way for me to obtain my inheritance, as you well know." Henry stood, a fist pressing
hard on the surface of the desk, as he outlined precisely how he intended to obtain the money that was
rightfully his. As he spoke, Henry sensed that his
grandfather tried to remain unmoved by his words,
and he would have believed Arthur unshaken if he
hadn't noticed the old man's gnarled hands clench
convulsively.

"Don't be an idiot," Arthur spat. "I may be stuck
in this town house twelve months a year, but I do
know you haven't seriously courted anyone. Or do
you plan to hire someone to marry you?"

"I have a girl in mind. She'll say yes."

Arthur cackled. "Who? Some desperate shriveled
old maid?"

Henry flushed at his grandfather's near miss. "She's
only twenty-one."

Slapping his hand down in triumph, Arthur shouted,
"I knew it! Who is the unfortunate girl?"

"Anne Foster."

Arthur drew his bushy eyebrows together in
thought. He'd been away from society for several
years, and Henry was counting on him not knowing
Anne. He was wrong. "The fat one? Good God,
Henry, you can do better than that. Certainly Sea Cliff
can't be worth a lifetime shackled to her." Then the
puzzled expression left his face. "You don't intend to
be shackled to her for life, do you, boy? That's why
you picked her." The idea seemed to delight him.

Henry's features hardened. "As I said, I will do just
about anything to save Sea Cliff. Even marry an ugly
girl," he said, being purposely coarse.

His grandfather closed his eyes for such a long time,

Henry began to think that the old man had fallen asleep. When Arthur finally opened his eyes, Henry saw something he'd never seen before on his grandfather's face—defeat. "You are more like your father than I thought."

His eyes blazing with new anger, Henry said, "Don't think it is an insult for you to compare me to my father."

His grandfather smiled blandly. "It is hardly that, Henry. I meant it as a compliment. The greatest of ones."

Henry turned away as if he suddenly smelled something putrid. "I know what you thought of my father."

"Do you?"

"I'll not have this discussion now. I bid you good day, Grandfather. The next time I see you, it will be to sign the necessary papers regarding my inheritance." Henry began walking from the study.

"Don't think this will be so easy, Henry," his grandfather warned.

Henry turned at the door, victory shining in his eyes. "The conditions upon which my father's money and properties become mine are quite clear. Since you will not free up any portion of the inheritance now, you have forced my hand."

Arthur slammed a fist down upon his wheelchair. "I will not allow this!" he shouted, sounding almost overwrought. Once again, his grandfather was cast in silhouette, making it impossible for Henry to see just how crazed his grandfather's expression had become.

"You have no choice, Grandfather. No choice at all." He walked from the room, nodding at Williamson, who rushed past him to Arthur's side.

Even after Henry closed the door, he could hear his grandfather's shouts, and the quiet tones of Williamson as he tried to calm the apoplectic old man. Henry had to chuckle. He'd finally triumphed over him, and he began to whistle as he let himself out of the town house and into New York's bustling Fifth Avenue traffic.

Inside the study, Arthur was calming down, though his entire body still shook with helpless rage. "My stationery, Williamson. And an empty journal. Get them now."

It was time to tell Henry the truth about his parents and the awful secret Sea Cliff hid. For weeks Arthur had felt death creeping ever closer, and he had dreaded that final end almost as much as he dreaded telling Henry the truth. He must not allow the boy to discover for himself the true reason he'd kept Sea Cliff from him. As he had done a thousand times, he cursed his own foolishness, and the crippling seizure that had prevented him from righting a wrong committed so long ago.

Williamson returned with the stationery and journal, poised to transcribe Arthur's words. Williamson, a loyal servant and dear friend, would soon be the only other soul on earth who knew about Sea Cliff and the horrible events of fifteen years ago. He sat, pen at the ready, on the far side of the gleaming desk.

"The letter first," Arthur said.

Williamson pulled out a sheet of rich, cream vellum. "To whom are we writing, sir?"

Arthur was silent a long time, his watery gray eyes boring holes into the cold fireplace. He'd be damned if he allowed this wedding to take place. He began dictating: "My dear Miss Foster . . ."

Chapter Two

Anne peered into her mirror and frowned. Today was not a good day, she thought, staring at her face until it became ugly and distorted. There were times when Anne would take a quick look in a mirror and think, I'm not so ugly as I think. And there were times, like now, when she wanted to cry at what she saw, when she saw with clarity what Henry must see. He had left for New York shortly after her birthday, and Anne feared he was gone from Newport for the season. She dared not ask anyone, for she realized that when it came to Henry, she was nearly transparent.

"Do stop mooning over Mr. Owen," Beatrice, who was fiercely protective of her, had warned her.

She couldn't help it. Henry had given her a gift, an intimate gift of jewelry, the kind of thing a girl got from a suitor. All told, they'd danced together four times, spoken perhaps twice that number. Did that constitute courting? Or was Henry simply being nice?

And he was so nice, Anne thought, sighing. If only she could be certain that he was paying her special attention. Anne had found herself writing her name over and over yesterday: Anne Owen, Mrs. Anne Owen, Mrs. Henry Owen. She'd torn the paper into the tiniest shreds, mortified that anyone might find it and realize how foolish she was. She'd been tempted to write a note to him, something light and flirtatious, but she feared she had no right to send him such a note. Anne put her hands over her face and squeezed.

"You'll wrinkle your face like that, Anne," her mother said as she walked into her room, knocking on the open door as she spoke. Francine Foster, dressed and coifed to painful perfection, stared at her daughter as if she'd never seen her before.

"Henry Owen is downstairs and is asking whether you'd care to join him in his carriage for an afternoon ride. Why on earth would Mr. Owen request such a thing?" she wondered aloud, completely unaware how cruel she was being.

"I believe he likes me, Mother," Anne said, suppressing the urge to whoop out a hooray. She turned quickly to the mirror and saw immediately that her reflection was much more pleasing now that she was smiling.

"No, no," Francine said absently. "There must be some explanation. The dances, that ridiculous charm he gave you . . ." She tapped a manicured finger against her chin, making the loose skin on her thin neck jiggle slightly. "Your father was thinking about having a yacht built. Perhaps that is what this is about. Of course," she said, sounding like a woman solving a mysterious puzzle. "That must be it, though I cannot say I care for his business tactics." She made a small clicking noise with her tongue.

Anne blanched. It explained so much. Henry's sudden interest in Anne corresponded almost exactly to the time her father had begun blustering about building a new, grander sailing vessel. Still, she said, "Perhaps he simply enjoys my company."

"Oh, Anne," her mother said, giving her a sad smile. "Now, I suppose you could wear what you have on. You do have a matching parasol for that gown, do you not? Stand up, dear," she insisted. "Let's see you." Her mother frowned and Anne felt her disapproval like a blow. "Oh, dear. I don't know why you are so very large when your sisters are so very small." She gave a light laugh. "There's nothing to do for it now, I suppose. If Mr. Owen asks about a yacht, you are to tell him that your father is considering several different boatyards. It wouldn't do for your father to appear too anxious. Owen Yachts are exorbitant enough, but we absolutely must have one."

Francine squinted her eyes at her daughter, examining her from head to foot, then threw up her hands in a light show of dismay. "Just be pleasant. You can manage that." She gave her daughter a quick kiss on her cheek. "Let's go, dear. Mr. Owen is waiting. Oh, I wish your father were here, so Mr. Owen wouldn't feel so obligated. Where is Clara?" she asked, casting about for Anne's maid. "I cannot accompany you, of course, and Clara will do as chaperon. I hardly think anything untoward will happen, but still it wouldn't do to have you be seen alone with him." She laughed gaily.

Anne trailed after her mother, a large lump lodged in her throat. Henry was the very last person she wished to see at this moment. Just the thought of him being pleasant to her made Anne ill. All for business. She should have guessed that rather than jump to the ridiculous conclusion that Henry was courting her. Thank God she'd not confided her hopes to anyone but Beatrice. Suddenly it all seemed so ludicrous. Henry Owen courting Anne Foster? Why, she would laugh this minute if she weren't so close to tears.

Henry waited for them in the formal parlor. When they entered, he was examining a portrait of Anne's late grandmother, a beauty whose face had enthralled a generation of men. Anne shared many of her features, and she'd often as a girl imagined growing up to look like the pretty lady in the parlor picture. Again Anne was painfully reminded of exactly what she must look like to a man like Henry, a man who attracted beautiful women effortlessly. A fresh rush of humiliation and anger filled her. How dare he use her simply to gain business? That anger washed away for the first time any shyness she'd felt in front of Henry.

"I understand you've requested my company," Anne said in a haughty tone.

Henry smiled despite the obvious hostility directed at him. He bowed politely, "If you would be so kind, Miss Foster." He turned to her mother. "Your mother has already granted me permission."

"How nice," Anne said. "Let's go then." She turned and walked from the room, ignoring her mother's entreaty for her to wait until Clara could be found.

Anne heaved herself up on the carriage, one hand clutching the handle, the other in Henry's large hand, brutally aware of how much the vehicle dipped when she sat down, its springs groaning loudly to her ears. Clara, found chatting in the kitchen by Anne's frantic mother, sat in the rumble seat behind them, looking quite pleased to be out of the house.

"I thought we'd avoid Bellevue at this hour," Henry said, which only fueled Anne's anger more. Of course the handsome Henry Owen wouldn't want to be seen publicly with her during the coaching, a time when all those who wanted to be seen paraded up and down Bellevue Avenue. Wasn't it bad enough he found it necessary to dance with her so publicly?

"By all means," Anne said.

Henry was about to slap on the reins when he turned to her. "Are you angry with me?"

"Why would I be angry with you, Mr. Owen?"

"Please call me Henry." He gave her a charming, lopsided smile and her heart fluttered a bit.

He started down the drive, and Anne opened her parasol. "I'll save you some time and effort, Mr. Owen— Henry. My father is considering buying a yacht but is uncertain of whom to contract for the work, so I'm afraid this little jaunt is quite unnecessary."

"What are you talking about?"

Anne looked at Henry uncertainly. Could her mother have been wrong? "Don't you want to discuss boats?"

Henry's brow furrowed. "I suppose we could if it pleases you. Do you know much about yachts?"

Anne laughed. "Not really. I've never even been on ours. My father says it's no place for a girl, though it looks rather fun if one likes being blown about a bit."

"Perhaps I should take you sometime."

Joy filled Anne and she hugged it close. He didn't have ulterior motives and was hinting at a future that now glowed with promise. "I'd like that."

They rode in silence for a time before Henry steered the carriage past an old stone wall and to a pretty little spot by a stream. The horses gave a huff at the scent of water, stamped a bit, then settled down. A windmill turned slowly in the distance and a handful of cows grazed nearby.

"If you don't mind, miss, I'd like to stretch my legs a bit," Clara said, a conspiratory smile on her lips.

"Certainly, Clara." Henry set the brake, jumped down, and helped Clara from her perch.

"It's pretty here," Anne said when he returned to his seat. "I'm always shocked to find myself in the country when Newport is so close by."

"Miss Foster, why did you think I wanted to talk about yachts?" Henry asked softly.

Anne flushed. "It was simply something my mother said. She . . ." Her hand fluttered in her lap. "She thought perhaps you were trying to influence my father into buying an Owen Yacht."

"And she thought that's why I took you for a ride?"

Anne looked at the scenery, deeply humiliated to discuss her mother's suspicions. "It's not as if I have many suitors, Mr. Owen. In fact, you are the first man who has ever asked me to ride out with him."

I can't do it, Henry thought desperately, I cannot. Then the sharp image of Sea Cliff sliding into the bay hit him, and cold seeped into his veins as if he were slipping into the icy depths of the sea. Get it over quickly, be done with it, say the words, suffer her happiness. Harden your heart.

"I suppose, then, that no one has asked you to marry him, either." He watched as her plump, pale cheeks turned crimson. She let out a small self-deprecating laugh.

"Twice a week, Mr. Owen," she said, turning to him, forcing him to look away. He'd realized weeks ago that if he didn't look at her, it would all be much easier. He didn't want to see the happiness in her eyes when he asked her to marry him, he didn't want her to be real, to know anything about her but that she would marry him. He pulled out a small, square, satin-lined box and opened it, grateful that his hand was steady.

"Marry me." He practically thrust the box in her hands, as if trying to get rid of the ring as quickly as possible. Take it, just take it and be done with it.

She let out a gasp, then a sob. Oh, Jesus, don't cry, don't you dare begin to weep. He closed his eyes and thought of Sea Cliff, but for the first time he was not soothed by the image. Henry nearly grabbed the ring back from her, but she'd already placed it on her finger, symbolically sealing his fate. He let out a long breath as he stared at her finger, which now glittered with a one-karat diamond surrounded by emeralds. He had purchased the ring without much thought, asking the clerk to pick out something appropriate, and he felt an unwanted stab of conscience at how pleased she seemed with it.

"Yes. I'll marry you."

Henry forced himself to kiss her cheek, realizing that the shrinking soft spot in his heart had been silently beseeching her to say no.

Never had Anne been as purely happy as she was in the weeks following the formal announcement of her engagement to Henry. If people seemed puzzled, even skeptical, it didn't bother her a bit. She knew without a doubt that Henry was not the fortune hunter that her mother had constantly warned her about. Everyone in Newport knew that Henry was heir to a vast fortune and had little need for money, never mind the rather modest dowry her parents had bestowed on her. Dozens of notes and letters arrived in the coming weeks congratulating her on her engagement. She was suddenly so popular among the cottagers, she hadn't come close to reading them all. Among those carelessly tossed aside was the letter from Henry's grandfather. Anne, floating on a cloud, living in a hazy golden world of love, never knew how very close she came to altering the course of her life.

More confident, Anne lost her shyness with Henry and discovered a man of generosity and good humor. They talked and laughed, and she relished the odd look he would give her sometimes, as if she'd purely surprised and delighted him. It didn't even bother her that Henry spent most of the remaining season in a sailing race to Bermuda. She was an engaged woman. She had a wedding to plan.

A wedding. No matter how many times Anne pinched herself, she still found she was not dreaming. Dear Beatrice remained worried about her. Anne found such concern endearing most of the time and only got sharp with Beatrice once, accusing her of jealousy. How could Anne remain angry at her best friend when all in the world was right and good?

Four weeks before the wedding, Anne stood in front of her mother's cheval mirror and grinned at her reflection. She'd vowed to lose some pounds for the wedding, but she was too happy to starve herself into misery. She thought she looked delightful in her pink-

and-white wedding gown, its bodice a clever swirl of shimmering seed pearls.

"Oh, Anne," Beatrice said, tears filling her eyes. "You look so pretty."

Anne started to cry as well. For the first time in her life, she felt pretty.

Henry vomited for the fourth time in three days, clutching the toilet as if it were a life preserver. He lifted his head wearily and swallowed down a surge of bile. Behind him, Alex chuckled.

"I'm so glad I amuse you," Henry said after spitting into the fouled water. He stood and yanked on the chain, flushing the evidence of his anxiety down the toilet.

"Oh, you do. You might think you're the first man to marry a woman he doesn't love," Alex said as he watched Henry splash water on his face and rinse his mouth.

"What I am about to do is the lowest thing a man can do. I feel like a goddamned coward."

"Then call it off," Alex said with remarkable fierceness.

Henry looked beyond tortured. "I can't. I wish to God I knew why. Hell, I'm this close, I might as well go through with it."

"Clearly you haven't the stomach for this kind of work," Alex said, laughing at his own joke, his good humor restored.

Henry grimaced, then dried his face with a soft cotton cloth. "I don't." He moved past Alex and into the room that he always took when staying in Newport. Alex had been his closest friend for twenty years, and his family—as disharmonic as it was—was the closet thing he had to a family of his own. Since his parents' death, Henry had spent his summers with the Henleys in their Newport cottage.

Henry moved to the window that overlooked Narragansett Bay. "I sailed past Sea Cliff yesterday. Last week's rainstorm stripped away even more of the hill." He wouldn't tell Alex that as Sea Cliff came into view, he'd broken out into a cold sweat and felt as if the wind had been knocked from his lungs. For one horrid moment, he'd thought he was dying.

Alex studied his friend for a long moment, taking in his drawn appearance, the lines around his eyes, the tightness of his mouth. Henry was the picture of a man being torn apart.

"You do what you have to do," Alex said softly.

Henry married Anne in New York on September 20 and abandoned her that same day, claiming an emergency had come up at his boatyard in Newport. Anne said she understood, and hid the terrible disappointment of returning to her parents' home after her wedding rather than to Henry's town house. It was for the best, Henry said, for he couldn't know how long he'd be and wouldn't she be more comfortable waiting for him in the home she knew?

Three weeks after her wedding day, on a cold and blustery October day, a strange man knocked on their West Fifty-seventh Street front door and asked for Anne. Her first thought was that a man so boyishly handsome could not possibly be the bearer of bad news, even though she felt the oddest sense of foreboding. He asked if she were Mrs. Henry Owen, and when Anne nodded, he handed her a large envelope embossed with the name of a legal firm.

Anne opened the document and read, at first confused by the legal words blurring in front of her. Then, slowly, as if thickened by fear, blood rushed to her head until she was nearly blinded. She fell in a heavy heap to the marble floor, her skirts spreading around her, and bent over in a pathetic effort to contain the pain that paralyzed her.

Henry had filed for divorce.

From the Journal of Arthur Owen

I am old and I am dying. And so, Henry, it is time to tell you the truth about Sea Cliff. I lied to you when I told you I hated that old place. I don't. I close my eyes sometimes and can breathe in that clean, cool salt air, the stink of the seaweed that settles on the beach in August. It is a fine perfume to me now. I remember each window, what I saw when I looked out across the bay to Newport. I can hear the wind blowing through the pines, the snap of a sail, the gentling sound of the waves against those rocks. You used to sit there, below the house, and fish for striped bass and blues. You didn't have any bait and your string only reached five feet into the water, but you'd sit there for more than an hour, clutching that string with a little boy's hope. If I close my eyes, Henry, I can still see you there, your hair reddened by the sun, your bare feet toughened by the slate and sand, toes dangling just inches from the water. I can still smell the heat of the summer sun on you.

Some of the happiest moments of my life were spent at Sea Cliff. I fell in love there, and perhaps that is why I long for the old place to crumble into the sea, to finally put an end to a story that began twenty-eight years ago. It has everything to do with your mother, the most beautiful, horrid, lovely woman I've ever met.

I will never forget the day your father brought your mother home to Sea Cliff. Elizabeth was lovely beyond words, the kind of woman who steals a man's breath away. I had just come back from a sail when I saw her standing on the second floor balcony gazing out onto the East Passage toward Newport. Her hair, long and free, and black as night, flew behind her. She looked like an angel standing there, her white dress brilliant, pressing against her form. Though I knew your father was bringing Elizabeth and her parents for a summer visit, I could not imagine Walter and this girl together. Walter, God rest his soul, was a weakling. He was my son, so do not think it pleases me to admit such a thing. When he introduced me to Elizabeth as his fiancée, quite frankly, I was stunned. Walter had always been attracted to a bookish sort of girl, not one with such obvious and flamboyant beauty. I suppose no man could have been completely unaware of Elizabeth. I wasn't. I couldn't even pretend to be. Not even that first night.

Elizabeth completely captivated me, as she had so clearly captivated Walter. He was lovesick, poor boy, doing her bidding like a puppy trying to please its master. It disgusted me, even as part of me understood how a man could become entranced by such a lovely creature. It took only a few days before I realized something evil lurked beneath that loveliness, but by then, I was completely infatuated. Obsessed, really. She was that beautiful, that charming. No other woman I'd met, or met since, had possessed such life, and such an unabiding awareness of how she drove men insane. At first, I found even that captivating. I was amused by her blatantness. She was, as I said, quite young. And I, well, if not old, certainly I was not young. I want you to know that I tried to resist her, with every fiber of my being, I resolved to never let her know she affected me. By the time she wrapped her web around me, I was a willing victim.

God help me, but I loved her so. And God help you if you ever love a woman like that.

Chapter Three

Two years later

Anne Foster had been invisible for most of her life, first a girl, then a woman, of no consequence. Now, thanks to one man, she was notorious, a woman all of Newport would be talking about tomorrow. And she feared none of it would be kind.

"They're all looking at me," she whispered to Beatrice.

"They're wondering who that beautiful woman is escorted by my very sought-after brother," Beatrice whispered back.

Indeed, Anne was beautiful. As she stood, seemingly poised and cool at the entrance to the Wetmores' ballroom, she looked exactly like the sort of woman who belonged among the richest of the rich. Only she knew, and perhaps Beatrice, who was kinder in her thoughts than Anne herself was, that she was a fraud. Her heart thumped painfully, her hands, beneath the pristine white of her elbow-length silk gloves, were wet with nervous sweat. She could barely breathe. She could barely swallow past the lump of fear growing in her throat.

She wore a white-and-silver gown that dipped low to reveal the tops of creamy and quite lovely rounded breasts. Her skin was flawless and unpowdered, her cheeks so flushed, they almost looked painted on. One look from any admirer would prove that the becoming blush was natural, as natural as every other beautiful part of her. Her soft blonde hair was pulled gently back from her face with diamond clasps, then gathered at her nape, shining pearls interwoven in an intricate design.

With her brilliant blue eyes she scanned the opulent ballroom. The walls of the large, rectangular room were of finely tooled gilded leather, and high above guests dressed in the latest fashions from Europe was a glass ceiling illuminated by gas jets. Two enormous mirrors—one on each side of the room—gave the illusion of greater splendor. Balls at Château sur Mer attracted hundreds, and this was no exception. Three hundred guests, considered modest by Wetmore standards, milled about in the ballroom and great hall.

"Is he here?" Anne whispered, unable to get a louder sound to come from her stricken throat.

Beatrice nodded toward one corner as discreetly as possible. "Near the waterfall," she said, quickly averting her gaze to make it appear she was searching for someone. Anne could not look that way, fearing she would faint dead away if she caught a glimpse of that maddeningly handsome, loathsome man.

"Ladies," Thomas said, his voice tinged with impatience, "I believe we have called enough attention to ourselves. Shall we enter?"

"No."

"Yes."

Beatrice squeezed Anne's hand. "If you cannot brave this evening out, we might as well forget our entire scheme," she said. "No one can know that you are afraid. No one can know that you still feel anything for him. Not even hatred. You know how important this evening is."

Anne took a deep breath. "I know." She closed her eyes briefly. "I know, I know, I know."

"Ladies, we are becoming obvious." Thomas stepped forward, forcing Anne and his sister to follow. She

would not panic. She would act as she always had in
the past. She knew the rules, knew nearly all of these
people who were staring at her so curiously. Some
she had thought of as friends. There was Christine
Eldred Shaw, standing by her new husband, Alfred.
Anne and Christine had come out within a week of
each other in New York. And there was Agatha
Cleves, finally back in society after giving birth—
rather vulgarly—to twin boys. And somewhere in this
room, standing by the waterfall the Wetmores had in-
stalled for the first of the summer balls, was Henry
Owen, the man she vowed would pay for ruining her
life.

Ruining.

Now there was a word, Anne thought as she
scanned the crowd, looking everywhere but toward
that gurgling waterfall. Girls were "ruined" every
summer in Newport. But few would bear the consequence of it their entire life as Anne was certain she
would. Money could repair most damage. Money, ac-
companied by a good marriage, could do wonders for
a ruined girl. Girls were "ruined" for a week, then recreated by desperate parents the next. And men, well,
they were never truly ruined, unless they went broke.
All it took was scads of money for them to be restored
to their rightful place.

But Anne Foster, once inconsequential fifth daughter of the fabulously wealthy New York Fosters, was
ruined forever. Anne was convinced that nothing
could truly redeem her. Beatrice had agreed. And that
was why revenge would be so very sweet. It had all
been Beatrice's idea, one that quickly became known
between them as "The Plan." It was to be executed
with finesse and subtlety, with grace and moral
strength. A large flaw existed in The Plan, one that
Beatrice dismissed with a cheerful wave of her hand,
but one that tormented Anne each day since its con-
ception: Anne needed to be beautiful for their plan

to work. Because if Henry Owen had a weakness, it was that, like most men, he adored beautiful women. He had been collecting them for years, Anne being his one and only deviation from a lifetime of having some willowy creature gazing up at him with devotion. Of course, Anne hadn't known that two years ago, having convinced herself and anyone who would listen, that Henry Owen was a man of fine character, a man who knew that a good woman wasn't always wrapped up in a pretty, willowy package.

What a lot of rubbish.

"I'm ready to see him," Anne said between her teeth.

Beatrice laughed, delighted. "Let's whet his appetite a bit more. By the time we make our way over to him, I want him to be biting at the bit wondering who the enchanting new girl is." Beatrice gave her friend a searching look. "I'm glad to see that you've fortified yourself."

"I've only reminded myself what a fool I was two years ago."

"Good."

Anne frowned a little, wishing Beatrice hadn't agreed so readily with her harsh characterization of herself. She had been a fool, the worst kind—a girl so lovestruck, she hadn't seen what was cruelly clear to every other person of consequence in Newport. Henry Owen had used her, coldly, brutally, and heartlessly.

"Let's go test the new you out on these two-faced devils," Beatrice said. She turned to her brother. "Thomas, we're putting step one of The Plan into place."

Thomas gave his sister an indulgent smile, took a bow, and gracefully left the two friends alone. "Mother's here somewhere, probably keeping an eagle eye out for us, so it's quite all right," Beatrice said unnecessarily, referring to their sudden lack of chaperon.

"Yes, we wouldn't want the new girl's reputation

tarnished this early in the season," Anne said, knowing her reputation was tarnished black.

Beatrice giggled and looked over potential victims. "We should pick someone who knows you well. That will be the true test."

Anne scanned the room. "Christine."

Beatrice nodded her approval. "If we pass this test, we can certainly fool that scoundrel for a time. Just don't talk too much."

Anne chuckled beneath her breath at Beatrice's name for Henry. She never referred to him as Mr. Owen or Henry, but simply as "that scoundrel." There had never been a more loyal friend than Beatrice Leyden. She knew, as well as Anne, that championing a ruined girl could in itself lead to ruination. But Beatrice had been stubborn and stalwart in her defense of Anne, who could only pray that when things worsened, which they certainly would, Beatrice would not be too harmed by the fiasco.

The two women made their way over to Christine Eldred Shaw, nodding now and again to acquaintances who could not quite hide their curiosity over the lovely blonde accompanying Beatrice. Everyone knew everyone in Newport's closed society, and the appearance of a new face always drew intense curiosity. Anne, beneath her nervousness, was secretly thrilled. No one had looked at her with even the slightest bit of recognition. Her courage grew with each step she took, with each curious glance from the men and women she passed—people she'd known all her life. Perhaps, she thought, this evening would not be the disaster she'd feared it would be. Even if their plan never reached fruition, she would have this night and the knowledge that she had made a fool of Henry Owen.

"Christine, I adore that gown," Beatrice said in greeting. "I feared that once you married, you would take to wearing matronly attire."

Christine flushed. "My husband spoils me," she said, instantly casting about for her new husband. "He must be off playing billiards." Christine gave Anne a questioning look, then turned pointedly to Beatrice, who was, by now, smiling brilliantly.

"How rude of me, Christine, but I didn't think to introduce you to someone you already know." Beatrice pressed her lips together to avoid laughing aloud at Christine's obvious confusion.

"It has only been a little over two years," Anne said, her voice low. "But certainly you haven't forgotten me, Chrissie."

Christine frowned and stared rudely at Anne's face, her brows coming together as if examining an interesting specimen of orchid. Then her eyes grew wide and she slapped a gloved hand over her mouth to stifle the loud squeak that emitted. "Oh. Oh, my goodness. Oh." She darted a look around the room, instantly becoming aware that she was standing exchanging pleasantries with *the* Anne Foster.

Anne's eyes grew steely, but she continued to smile. "What are you doing here?" Christine whispered frantically. "My goodness, Anne. It *is* Anne? Of course it is. Oh, goodness. You've, well, you've changed quite a lot, haven't you?"

"I have." Anne suddenly found herself amused by her old friend's dilemma. Clearly she was curious about Anne, but was painfully aware of the social consequences of chummying up to a ruined woman.

"Yes, yes. I hardly recognized you. I mean, I didn't recognize you at all." Again, she looked frantically about the room. "Does anyone else know who you are?"

"Only you. And Beatrice, of course." Anne's good humor evaporated as she watched Christine expel a breath of relief.

"Thank goodness." Then, as if realizing what she said, Christine, in her way, tried to explain. "It's just that, well, everyone here knows you. And knows what happened. So . . ."

Anne refused to let the girl off easily. "So?"

Pretty Christine flushed. "So you must know that I cannot openly acknowledge you. A divorced woman. Oh, my. And of course, you must let anyone who asks know that I hadn't the slightest idea who you were."

"Mustn't she?" That from Beatrice, whose brown eyes were glittering in unconcealed anger.

Anne lay a hand on her friend's arm. "Bea, it was what we expected, after all." She turned to Christine, whose cheeks had turned a brilliant pink. "I do understand, Christine. Self-preservation at all costs, right?"

To her credit, Christine did look rather miserable. "You know how it is," she said with real regret.

Anne felt tears prick at her eyes, but willed them away. She'd known what her reception would be, but living it was an entirely different thing. "Could you please keep my identity a secret for just a little while?" Anne knew it was hopeless. Gossip of this sort was too delicious not to spread thickly. She knew that by the time she was ready to leave, hardly a person at the ball wouldn't know her identity. It was time to confront Henry.

"I will try to keep your secret, Anne," Christine said, and Anne smiled at that weak promise. Then Christine turned to Beatrice. "I hope you will understand if I cannot—"

Beatrice interrupted her. "Don't worry, Mrs. Shaw. I never considered you a friend, so the loss of your companionship will not be a great one." With that, she grasped Anne's arm and led her away, her body stiff with anger.

"Bea, if you're going to get all in a huff each time I am cut off, this is never going to work. You said yourself we must act as if we do not care what people think. Or say."

Beatrice scowled. "That was before I witnessed such

horrid behavior. She was your friend, Anne. I wanted to scratch her eyes out, and I can't believe you stood there and allowed her to cast aspersions on your character."

"She did no such thing. She did precisely what we expected everyone to do. Precisely what we would have done in her place not too many months ago. She was actually rather polite about it all. Far more polite than I suspect most of these people will be when they learn who I am."

"I suppose you are right," Beatrice said mournfully. "Are you up for the rest of this evening? Now that Christine knows your identity, it is only a matter of time before someone goes hauling off to that scoundrel and tells him who you are. That would ruin everything."

"My thoughts exactly," Anne said briskly, to hide the real terror she felt in her heart. She would have to call upon every bit of self-control not to fall apart when she stepped in front of the man who had tormented her thoughts for two years.

Squaring her shoulders and lifting her chin, she said, "Let's confront the devil."

Chapter Four

"Hello," Alex said beneath his breath. "She's coming this way."

Henry downed the last of the sweet, warm champagne that lingered in his crystal flute, and grimaced. He truly loathed the stuff, but the Wetmores served only champagne, and surely there was nothing worse than being completely sober at one of these tedious events. "Who?"

"The girl I plan to marry," Alex said heartily.

Henry looked up to see Beatrice Leyden and her lovely friend making their way toward the waterfall. "I thought you couldn't abide Miss Leyden," Henry said, sounding nearly as bored as he was. "And I know you aren't talking about her companion. From here she appears to be quite beautiful, and you've sworn off beautiful women and marriage. Remember?"

"A girl like that could make me change my mind. Good God. She can't be real."

"She's mine," Henry announced, not for any other reason than to create a competition between the two men. It was only two weeks into Newport's summer season and he was already wishing time away. He would rather have been in his study working on his latest design for a single-masted sloop than at the Wetmores' lavish ball. He'd come as a favor to Alex, who still found Newport, if not exciting, then at least far better than languishing in the city and enduring the stifling heat.

Henry lost his taste for Newport last summer, when every eligible girl's mother suddenly became immensely interested in him. Or rather, in his considerable fortune. Having his inheritance in hand, rather than in probate, made a startling difference in his desirability among the single women of the Four Hundred—New York's social elite. He could no longer enjoy a ball at the Casino or a swim at Bailey's Beach without being pounced upon by some female. The scandal that had sent poor Anne into hiding had hardly touched him, a fact that had not eluded him.

The evening fetes, the lazy days at the beach, the concerts at the Casino left him feeling flat and annoyed with the shallowness of society. He used to enjoy the social round, but now he found it irritating. When the lovely ladies batted their eyes at him, when they turned their heads just so, he would think of Anne and her straight-eyed gaze. Anne might not have been pretty, but at least she'd made him laugh. He sighed, now thoroughly annoyed with himself for his hypocrisy. Who was he kidding? Poor Anne Foster never had a chance. None at all. She was doomed from the start, and his real remorse would not change what he'd done to her. The last he'd heard, she was still hiding away in a town house living quite alone, her parents having banned her from their residence.

The two ladies were just steps away when Henry forced his attention back to the present. Every time he saw Beatrice Leyden, he was filled with unwanted guilt over what he'd done to her best friend. She'd been cool to him ever since, and he was faintly surprised to see her walk so pointedly toward him and Alex.

He heard Alexander whisper, "I'll bet a box of my finest Cubans that she'll be swooning in my arms before the night is through. Or," he amended quickly, "at least dancing."

Alexander took a step toward the women. "Ladies. How lovely you look this evening."

Beatrice glared at Alex before turning her gaze to Henry, to whom she gave a dazzling smile. "Gentlemen, I was just telling my friend here how gallant the men of Newport are."

"Oh?" Henry's left eyebrow quirked up in disbelief.

Beatrice giggled. "Mr. Owen, all that business is water under the bridge." She gave his forearm a flirtatious pat. "Forgotten and forgiven, hmmm?"

Henry narrowed his eyes, but nodded his assent. Then he turned his gaze to the woman standing next to Beatrice, and found, to his great dismay, that he had a most difficult time drawing air into his lungs. Suddenly, those words he had uttered so casually, "She's mine," took on a stronger, and somehow prophetic meaning. For in that instant, Henry knew with every fiber of his being that he wanted this woman to be his—and only his.

Breathe. Breathe, you silly idiot. Slowly, with the utmost care not to gasp, Anne took in a breath of much needed air. Her hands were clenched together so tightly, she didn't think a team of horses could have ripped them apart. And still, she managed to smile at the men standing so expectantly before her, her eyes quickly darting from one to the other. She was vaguely aware that Henry was staring at her, that Alex had taken one hand she'd forced free from the other and said something that made Beatrice giggle. Beatrice, to her knowledge, never giggled. She must be as nervous as I, Anne thought, as she withdrew her hand from Alex's grasp.

As much as she prayed that Henry would not recognize her, part of her was a bit crushed that he did not. It only served to reinforce the fact he'd never cared about her, never truly looked at her.

"Dance with me."

Through the fog of terror that enveloped her, she suddenly became aware of that deep baritone she'd once loved sounding close to her ear. For a moment so fleeting she hardly recognized it, Anne was transported back two years to a time before Henry had broken her heart, to a time when she still foolishly believed in fairy tales.

"You will, won't you?"

She could hear laughter in his voice, and knew, if she dared look directly at him, that his gray eyes would be filled with confident amusement.

Anne shot a look of pure panic to Beatrice, whose eyes widened in unconcealed delight. "Of course she will," Beatrice said, nudging Anne away from her.

And then Anne felt herself being tugged toward the section of the ballroom reserved for dancing, Henry's hand warm on her naked upper arm. Never had he been so forward when they'd danced together before, never had he used such an intimate tone. It was, she realized with sudden clarity, the tone of a man speaking with a beautiful woman, a woman he intends to get to know far better. In an instant, the terror was gone, replaced with a hardened resolve. This man, this handsome, rotten-to-the-core man would pay for what he'd done to her, and he'd begin paying tonight.

Just before she slipped into his arms for their dance, she bestowed upon him a smile she'd been practicing in the mirror for weeks. It was one meant to bedazzle, though more often than not, Anne would reduce herself and Beatrice to helpless mirth whenever she gave clear thought to what she was doing. To her satisfaction, Henry appeared momentarily stunned, and the last vestiges of her nervousness fled.

He didn't recognize her; of course he didn't. The Anne Foster he knew was ugly. Fat and ugly, stuffing herself into gowns she had no business stuffing herself into, surrounding her chubby face and triple chin with large banana curls she'd once thought made her look pretty. The woman he now looked down so warmly at had a heart-shaped face other women envied, the requisite eighteen-inch waist—with only a bit of help from whalebone stays. Anne Foster, whose fat cheeks once nearly hid the startling blue of her eyes, who was made the joke of the Four Hundred, was now every man's fantasy. Power surged through her veins. Power and the certainty that if she wanted to wrap Henry around her finger, she could.

"Henry Owen at your service, Miss . . ."

She gave him an innocent look, another of the expressions she'd practiced with Beatrice. For hours upon hours she had pretended to be the beautiful stranger she saw in the mirror, not the shy, self-conscious woman she was. She'd practice so much, it wasn't long before she trusted that image not to dissolve away.

"We haven't formally been introduced," she said, tilting her head just so. "I believe it would be quite scandalously forward of me to introduce myself to a strange man."

Henry smiled, flashing white, straight teeth, and making Anne—for just the tiniest moment—wish she didn't loathe him quite so much. He was ungodly handsome. Henry had a way about him that made women want to stare—right before they fussed with his collar or pointed out a bit of lint. He was dashing and tall with a physique men envied and married women commented openly about. His deep-set gray eyes were heavily fringed with black lashes, a shade or two darker than the thick, wavy hair he kept tamed most of the time. Anne had always found him quite beautiful, even before she'd fallen hopelessly in love with him all those months ago, and she hadn't changed her opinion about the exterior attributes of this man she hoped to crush. She was slightly annoyed that he was handsome still. It didn't seem fair at all that he had come out of the scandal he'd created completely unscathed. He was handsome, rich, and one of the most sought-after men of the Newport season, and she was a pariah.

He was giving her his most charming smile, one that Anne hardened her heart against immediately. Part of her wanted to scream at him, "I'm the same person. It's me, Anne Foster, the girl you wounded irreparably." She had been brutally beaten down with the casual ease of a man with no heart.

"So, you intend to remain a mystery woman." He stared at her face with new intensity and narrowed his eyes, making Anne's heart race. Oh, he couldn't guess who she was yet, she thought frantically, dipping her head a bit.

They moved easily and gracefully around the nearly vacant dance floor, for few couples graced the gleaming parquet during the orchestra's first turn. Anne felt the curious looks from those who watched. Did any of them know? Surely some did, but she was too afraid to look at the spectators. Instead, she kept her eyes glued to a sterling silver button on Henry's stark white shirt. It was loose.

"Is this your first season at Newport?" His question seemed to hold more than idle curiosity, and Anne's pulse quickened.

"I spent the season here two years ago," she said, keeping her voice low in an effort to disguise it. Not that Henry would remember her voice or anything else about her, she reminded herself bitterly. She'd barely known Henry that summer, and yet she'd convinced herself that she loved him. Stupid, silly, desperate girl.

"You could not have been here in 'ninety-one. I would have remembered." The teasing quality was back in his voice, and Anne relaxed.

"Would you? Do you recall every girl you meet?"

He leaned forward until his mouth was just inches from her ear. "I would have remembered the most beautiful woman I've ever seen."

Instead of being flattered, Anne was filled with impotent rage. Anger made her bold. "We were introduced, Mr. Owen." She lifted her head to gaze directly at him, almost daring him to remember her.

"Surely not. You think I am one to give idle flattery?"

He was clearly trying to flirt with her, and the thought only served to anger her more. He'd never acted this way with her before, never graced her with that dazzling smile that made other girls sigh. He'd been polite and stiff and formal in the beginning, and later relaxed and friendly. They'd had wonderful talks, times that Anne still looked back on with begrudging fondness. But never had he looked at her this way. She realized, her heart wrenching just the tiniest bit, that for the first time Henry was gazing at her the way she'd always dreamed he would. She inwardly cringed, remembering the innocent girl she'd been, so in love and yet miserably hoping for him to kiss her with the passion she felt growing daily. He never did.

She instinctively knew that she could now get that kiss she so longed for—and from a man who thought her a stranger. As they danced, Anne trying to avoid his gaze, and he, trying to charm her into laughing at his wit, all she could think of was what it would be like to finally get that kiss. How humiliating it would be for him to find he'd finally kissed Anne Foster, the girl he'd ruined beyond repair without a second thought. Would he be repulsed? Angry? Repentant?

Anne suddenly didn't care. If she only had this night, she would make him kiss her. The ultimate goal of the plan might never be realized, but at least she would know that Anne Foster, ugly, fat little Anne, had finally gotten her kiss.

"Let's walk in the garden," she said, sounding overly bright. "It's so warm in here, is it not? And there's so many people out there, it wouldn't be entirely improper. Would it?"

"No. Not at all," Henry said, looking as if someone had just unexpectedly handed him ownership of the finest yacht in Newport. Anne sought out Beatrice and gave her a wide smile. She felt like skipping toward the door, so delicious was this moment. Before this evening was out, he would know whom he had kissed—and so would most of the people at this ball. Anne had to suppress a giggle, so delighted was she by her impromptu plan. She and Beatrice hadn't clearly sketched precisely what would happen this evening. They had only planned to present Anne to Henry, who would eventually realize to whom he'd been introduced. Never had she considered he would ask her to dance, and certainly it had not occurred to her that she would end up strolling about a garden with him, darkly anticipating a kiss that was sure to come. She simply could not wait to see his reaction when he realized whom it was he kissed.

The Wetmore lawn was strung with Japanese lanterns, making much of the lush green expanse almost as light as day. The air was tinged with the smell of brine and oil from the lamps, and Anne could hear the muffled sound of the surf crashing against the rocks below the Wetmore property. The air was cool, almost too cool to be out at night without a wrap, and Anne shivered. In an instant, she was enveloped in the warmth of Henry's jacket. The jacket, heavy and fine and smelling just faintly of expensive cologne and cigar smoke, felt wonderful draped across her back. Anne's first instinct was to thrust it off, but the truth was, she liked the feel, the smell of his jacket.

"Thank you," she said, disliking the soft sound of her voice.

They walked side by side, Anne intensely aware of the tall man next to her. Her mouth was dry, her mind empty of everything but the fact that she was taking a stroll with Henry Owen as if she were just an ordinary girl, as if this walk on a summer evening held the promise of something more. As if she didn't want to destroy him with every fiber of her being.

She turned abruptly when they reached the end of the light cast by the Japanese lanterns, her courage to exact a kiss from him waning. Until she looked at his wickedly handsome face. For in that moment, all she could think of was kissing him. Hard. And long. Oh Lord, she thought, if I am going to carry through with this plan, I must stop looking at him.

"Who are you?" he asked, with more than simple curiosity.

Anne gave him what she thought was a secretive smile and strolled away, farther into the shadows. She felt his hand, warm and firm on her arm. "Oh, no you don't. I'll not let you get away from me until I've had my answer."

Anne tilted her head and raised one finger to her lips. "For a kiss, I will tell you."

Henry swallowed convulsively.

"A kiss." His voice sounded odd, and Anne smiled again, her finger still pressed to her mouth, only partly aware of the devastating picture she made. Oh, she knew she probably looked charming, but Anne hadn't a clue what she was doing to Henry's blood—or other parts of him.

"Just one small kiss as payment for my identity," she said, almost laughing in delight at how easy this would be. Surely there were enough people about to witness this kiss, to report it with glee tomorrow, to completely humiliate Henry. Her own reputation was so far gone, she reasoned that one small kiss could not bring it down any more.

It was too dark for Anne to see the sudden heat in Henry's gaze. If she had, perhaps she would not have taken so lightly the thought of a kiss, and she certainly would not have allowed Henry to draw her farther into the shadows.

"I don't know if I want to know who you are," he

said, his voice low, making her shiver unexpectedly. "Perhaps it is your mystery I find so intriguing." He lay a finger along one of her cheeks, tilting her head toward the light. "No. It is your face, your remarkable face."

Again, his stare made Anne wonder if he somehow knew her game. His eyes swept over her features, lingering on the lips she'd offered so blithely. His gaze moved back to her eyes, and he lowered his head slowly, that single finger along her cheek holding her captive. He pressed his mouth against hers, lingering there, moving slightly, before he lifted his head. Anne wanted to be repulsed, wanted to at least suffer his kiss stoically. She was completely unprepared for the awful need for him to kiss her again.

"Perhaps two kisses," he said gruffly. This time, his entire hand spanned the side of her face, and he drew her to him. This time, when their lips met, it was more than a brief pressing of lips. He moved his mouth against hers, and let out a strangled sound as he pulled her close against his hard body. Anne was lost in a fog she didn't recognize, aware only that she was slowly forgetting everything but the feel of his mouth against hers. And then his tongue, skimming over her lips, making her gasp, swirled slowly, erotically against her tongue. She let out a sound that later she would insist was one of protest, as he pulled her even closer, as their kisses deepened, as she began to move her tongue against his, a sensuous exploration that made her knees turn to water. Her hands were at his neck, not squeezing out her anger, but caressing, moving to his nape, where she buried her fingers in his hair, pulling him harder against her already-swollen mouth.

It wasn't until he moved his hands beneath the coat to press lightly against her ribcage, his thumbs tantalizingly close to her breasts, that some sanity returned. She pulled away because she knew to her great disgust that she didn't want to stop. He let her go only after the slightest resistance. Anne stared at him, at that moment hating herself as much as she hated him, her breath shaky. He had the gall to stand there with an idiotic grin on his face, seemingly unfazed by a kiss that had clearly devastated her. Oh, how she loathed him!

"Now, my mystery lady, let's have your name."

Shaking with rage, she jerked his coat from her shoulders and spat, "Go to hell." She turned and lifted her skirts to allow her to run from him—and from her own traitorous self. She heard him call out, laughter tingeing his voice. Anne ran on, slowing only when she became aware of others on the vast lawn watching her. She reentered the mansion with as much poise as possible, stopping only to see if Henry pursued her. Spotting him sauntering toward the piazza, she spared him a sneer she knew he couldn't see before taking a calming breath and stepping back into the ballroom.

Beatrice was by her side in an instant. "What happened?" she asked, taking in her friend's flushed cheeks and overly red lips.

"We kissed," she said, defiance in her voice.

Beatrice pulled Anne aside, her eyes wide with delight. "You didn't. Oh, that's too delicious. And he never knew who you were?"

"He still doesn't," Anne said smugly, conveniently forgetting how that kiss had affected her. "I altered tonight's plan a bit. I hope you don't mind."

Beatrice could only clap her hands together and laugh. "How wonderful. Utterly wonderful."

"I thought so, too. Even if we never accomplish the full plan, at least we'll have tonight. My one and only triumph."

"Oh, no. This is too much fun."

"Perhaps for you," Anne mumbled. Now that she had a bit of time, she could look at the kiss for exactly what it was—part of a wonderfully devious plan to make Henry Owen fall in love with her. The beauty of

the plan was how sweet it would be when she publicly
spurned him. Beatrice was right, it would be fun driving Henry to his knees. If he felt only part of the pain
she'd lived with for the past two years, it would be
worth it.

Anne's elation was short-lived as she became
acutely aware of the stares and whispers around her.
"They know," she said woodenly, her cheeks flushing
bright red, her entire body rigid.

"I'm afraid so. Even I was surprised at how quickly
the news traveled. I'm so sorry, Anne."

Each eye felt like tiny pinpricks on her skin, each
whisper a loud, grating sound in her ear. "I think it's
time to leave," she said, willing the tears that pressed
against her eyes not to well over. She would not give
them the satisfaction of seeing her cry. She'd not done
it before, and she'd not do it now. Lifting her chin,
she plastered a polite smile on her face and began
moving gracefully to the ballroom door. Only after
the footman had closed the massive front door behind
her and Beatrice did she allow even the slightest emotion to touch her face.

"We knew it wouldn't be easy," Beatrice said, giving her friend a worried look.

Anne pressed the tips of her fingers against her
eyes. Hard.

"We've got the Casino tomorrow," Beatrice reminded her.

Anne shook her head until Beatrice dragged her
hands away from her face. "We've got to show them
you don't care what they think."

"But I do care," Anne said, her eyes finally glittering with tears. "I care with every breath I take."

"Then you've got to make yourself stop caring. You
did nothing wrong, Anne. You've got to tell yourself
that, over and over."

"I do, Bea," she said wearily. "It just makes it
worse, don't you see? If I'd really done something

horrible, I think I could stand before them defiantly, snub my nose at them. But to think they would turn on me for nothing. It's almost beyond bearing."

"But not *completely* beyond bearing?"

Anne let out a shaky laugh and lifted her eyes to the starlit sky as if asking for divine help with her insane friend. "No," she said softly. "Not completely. I'll give it one week. I'm quite certain I'll not last longer than that. I'm not as strong as I look."

Beatrice laughed aloud. If ever there was a person who did not look strong, it was Anne Foster. But she *was* strong—stronger than Beatrice had imagined. "Perhaps. But you're tougher than you think you are. Think about what you just did. You just kissed Henry Owen. You made a fool of him in front of all of Newport. Few people could have done what you just did."

Anne shook her head, wanting nothing more than to scurry off to New York and spend the rest of the summer roasting in her elegant town house. Behind them, footsteps sounded, and the women whirled around in alarm.

"Ladies, you certainly don't think to make your way home without an escort." Beatrice's brother grinned at them, before hailing a footman to fetch their coach. He looked down fondly at Anne. "You can take it from me, Miss Foster, your plan is an unadulterated success."

Beatrice clutched at her brother's sleeve. "What happened?"

"Let's just say that Mr. Owen's face turned the shade of a newly bleached sail a short time ago." Thomas let out a delighted laugh when Beatrice shrieked with happiness and gave Anne a hug.

"You see? You were a triumph. And this is only the beginning."

Anne managed a weak smile but her stomach twisted sickeningly. She was starting to think that revenge wasn't going to be nearly as sweet as she'd hoped.

Henry had slowly made his way back to the ball-room, confident that, not only would he find out the identity of his mystery girl, but would find the girl herself, coyly waiting for him. What a delightful turn this evening had taken.

No sooner had he stepped back into Château sur Mer, than Alexander gripped his shoulder hard. "Where the hell have you been?"

Not yet recognizing the seriousness of his friend's inquiry, Henry gave him a wide grin. "Falling in love, my friend."

"Sweet Jesus."

"Sorry, old friend, but I believe it's mutual. I'm afraid I've won this round at any rate."

"Good God, Henry. You cannot be serious."

Alex's mood finally cut through the hazy fog of lust and infatuation. "What happened?" Henry asked, slowly becoming aware that nearly everyone in the ballroom was looking at him. A bit of panic twisted his gut. Who the hell was that girl? The daughter of a well-placed family? Or, heaven help him, a new bride? He had the sudden and horrible image of an irate father bearing down at him accusing him of molesting his young daughter. He'd spent the past two years keeping clear of anything that remotely resembled scandal; he did not need to become the center of another ugly episode.

"Do you have any idea who that was you were dancing with?"

The sick feeling in Henry's stomach grew. "No. She wouldn't give me her name."

"That woman, you bloody idiot, was none other than Anne Foster."

Henry's tanned face paled visibly. "Anne?" The word came out choked.

"That's correct, Henry, old pal. None other than your former wife."

Chapter Five

Anne was silent during the short ride down Bellevue Avenue to the Leydens' twenty-four-room summer cottage. Her mouth still tingled from kissing her former husband's lips, a strange and foreign feeling and one she wished would disappear immediately. Henry had kissed her only once before, on their wedding day, and it had been quick and dutiful. Even now she flushed, remembering how she'd anticipated her wedding night, a night that never came.

Though people might think Henry a cad, they thought her a fool or worse. She'd been completely blind to the fact that Henry was marrying her only for money, and not even her money at that. She hated to think about the weeks following their sham of a wedding, how she had pathetically insisted to all who would listen that Henry loved her and of course he would return. But as days turned into weeks, even an eternally optimistic Anne had to admit that her handsome young husband had no intention of returning. The loneliness, bewilderment, and pain she suffered in those first few weeks after his abandonment were nothing compared to that excruciating visit from Henry's lawyer.

Perhaps worse was her parents' reaction. They had not been outraged, they had not even been miffed, except for the horror of having a divorced daughter. It was almost as if they'd expected such a thing to occur, as if a puzzle had been solved that had put their world off kilter, and Henry's request for a divorce put things right again. Henry had been kind, her parents told her. Not only did he accept blame for the divorce by admitting an adulterous affair—one Anne suspected never occurred—he'd granted her a huge settlement. How Anne had wanted to throw the money back in his face. But to her great dismay, her parents, in a polite and stiff interview, informed her that she was no longer welcome under their roof.

"Just think of the appearance of it all," her mother had said, her hands fluttering in her lap.

Her father, his expression implacable, remained silent as her mother informed her she would be disinherited because, "It is expected, my dear. Whatever would people think of us if we allowed you to remain under our roof? Anne, you mustn't be so selfish as to think you could stay here."

Never would Mrs. Randolph Foster do anything that might be unexpected, even if it meant breaking their youngest daughter's heart. Her mother, Anne realized, was likely unaware that they'd dealt her such a crushing blow, for their actions, as her mother had calmly explained, were the only ones to take to assure their place in society. Surely Anne understood that. Her mother had even kissed her tear-stained cheek before departing the salon, a reassuring, if vague, smile on her face.

Her parents hadn't shown their faces in Newport since, so ashamed were they. Of all people in the world, her parents knew Anne had been used terribly. To have them discard her so callously drove Anne into the depths of despair. For weeks and weeks, she did little more than sleep and wander about her lovely new town house, alone, alone. As alone as she'd be ten years from now, she told herself. She went days without talking to anyone but servants, she dared not leave the house for fear that with one look those walking by would know her shame. Her family, friends, her husband, had all abandoned her. She wanted to die but lacked the courage to do the deed herself.

Each time Anne recalled that happy, bubbling girl who'd fancied herself in love with Henry Owen, she wanted to disappear into the folds of her blankets. She tortured herself with memories of them dancing and laughing, of his crooked smile, his mesmerizing eyes. And all that time when she'd been falling hopelessly in love, he'd only been thinking of his money. What a fool she'd made of herself.

It took a visit from Beatrice, who was shocked by the condition she found her friend, to begin to feel the tiniest niggling of anger toward Henry. For weeks, the only anger she'd felt was toward herself. She'd been telling herself she deserved her awful fate. Even as part of her rebelled against such a thought, she'd gone far to convincing herself that a stupid fat girl didn't warrant the same dreams of other women. Beatrice, bless her golden heart, set Anne straight.

Her depression had taken a toll. Anne, once more than plump, lost a startling amount of weight in the first few months after she'd signed those hateful divorce decrees. So filled with self-loathing, she hadn't bothered looking in a mirror in months until Beatrice dragged her out of bed and forced her to stand in front of the glass. What she saw was shocking. Gone was the apple-cheeked girl she had been. In her place stood a wan, pale, almost-thin girl with matted hair, chapped lips, and dark bruiselike marks beneath lifeless eyes. It was almost as if she'd disappeared completely. She started to cry, and cried and cried until Beatrice, beside herself with concern, slapped her face.

"Oh, Anne, I'm so sorry. I didn't mean to," Beatrice had gushed, her pretty face filled with remorse and grief. Anne stared at her friend, then cried a bit more, before finally getting a grip on her emotions.

Slowly, Anne reentered the world. Beatrice and her dear mother practically moved in with her. The only time Anne was alone was at night, and by then she was so weary, she didn't mind. They forced her out of bed each day, forced her into pretty dresses, made her sit to have her hair done. Before long, she found herself laughing. A half day went by without crying. Then a full day. And then, eighteen months after she'd gotten married, she got angry. Full-blown, hair-ripping, teeth-gnashing angry. It hit her suddenly, like an unexpected summer storm. She ranted, she raved, she screamed out every curse word she knew, she threw things wishing they were Henry's head.

Beatrice and her mother clapped as if appreciating a grand performance at the Metropolitan Opera. Oh, it felt good to be this angry. And that was when Beatrice came up with The Plan. Once again, she dragged Anne in front of the mirror and forced her to look at herself. She never got over the shock of seeing someone beautiful peering back at her. Anne was not a girl who carried weight well. She turned rather piggy. But now she was quite lovely, and quite unlike the girl she'd been two years before when Henry first began his suit. Now, Anne looked precisely like the kind of girl Henry was always flirting with, the kind of girl Anne had always envied. The kind of girl who could get revenge and enjoy every minute of it.

Riding in that coach after her Newport debut as a divorced woman, Anne resolved to never forget those dark days she'd spent utterly alone.

Beatrice broke the silence. "So," she said, drawing out the word. "He kissed you."

Anne hoped her friend couldn't see her cheeks pinken in the carriage's dim interior. "Twice."

"Twice!"

"I thought I would gain the upper hand if—"

"Anne Foster, you liked it." The shock in Beatrice's voice was palpable.

"I did not. Don't be absurd. He is loathsome." Anne could hear the lie in her own voice. "Oh, Bea, you needn't worry that I will fall under his spell again." But she couldn't help adding, "If only he wasn't so very handsome, my task would be far easier."

Beatrice threw up her hands. "That's it. The Plan is doomed to fail. I never thought you would weaken so quickly. There was always a danger, of course," she said thoughtfully. "I've heard it said that hate and love are closer emotions than we'd like to believe."

"Oh, for goodness' sake, Bea, I do not love Henry."

"I never thought you did. Not now. But a few more kisses and . . ."

"Please have more faith in me than that. I can be as coldhearted as the next person. I plan to ruin him and I'll use whatever wiles I have to do so. If I have to suffer his attentions, I will. But don't you dare think I could be silly enough to fall in love with him again. I would never forgive myself."

Beatrice leaned over and patted Anne's hand. "I know, dear."

Anne let out a huff and crossed her arms. And tried to ignore the lingering feeling of Henry's kiss.

Mullaly's String Orchestra was sounding a bit off the next morning at the Newport Casino, its violin section short two men, its cellist also missing, victims of a bit of bad fish eaten the night before. No one truly noticed, for they were too busy buzzing about a certain former Missus, now Miss, who'd dared to infiltrate the Wetmore ball the previous evening.

People who had attended the ball insisted they suspected something odd about the beautiful woman immediately. "She had that look about her," said one newly married girl. "She looked . . ." and she paused as she sought the right word, "soiled."

The Horse Shoe Piazza, a meeting place of the "cottagers" each morning, was crowded with men and women wearing the summer uniform of whites and pastels. Most were taking delight in the latest scandal involving Miss Anne Foster, the girl whose existence was barely acknowledged before she had the misfortune of marrying Henry Owen. What a season this would be, they agreed. The season had barely begun and already there was all this excitement. Why, it was more than a soul could take. They were giddy with vicious delight, and secretly glad that every scathing remark was directed toward someone other than themselves.

"I hear Henry took the blame for their failed marriage to spare her," one woman said with a knowing nod.

"Oh, shush. Everyone knows he only married her to get his inheritance," another woman said, the only one who seemed to recall precisely what had happened two years ago. The others ignored her. Henry Owen was a delightful, handsome, amazingly rich member of the Four Hundred, and was certainly innocent of any misdeed. Who was Anne Foster, but an upstart, a woman who was allowed into Newport society only because she happened to be the daughter of Randolph Foster? And then there was poor, loyal Beatrice Leyden. Didn't she know how damaged her own reputation would become if she continued to champion a divorced woman?

Suddenly, the throng mulling about the piazza shifted, all eyes staring across the emerald expanse of lawn to the men's club where Mr. Owen himself stood. Even from a distance, Henry Owen was an imposing figure. He was tall, with broad shoulders that tapered to narrowed hips, and a face that made matrons and virgins sigh. He was well-liked by men—after all, he was a fine sailor, an excellent horseman, and knew how to make money—and coveted by women for nearly the same reasons. Henry Owen was one of those rare men whose shoulders were made of some slippery element that allowed scandal and ill news to slide right off. And so when he made an appearance at the Casino the morning following the Wetmore ball, it was curiosity, not censure, that made all eyes turn toward him.

"Hell." Henry felt like a fine cut of beef laid out on a platter with a thousand hungry eyes staring at him.

"Feeling brave, Henry?" Alex asked, a wide grin on his face.

"Not particularly. Tell me again why we are here."

"To show them you're not the complete ass you made of yourself last night."

"Ah, yes. A grand reason. The thing of it is, old friend, I truly don't give a damn what that load of gaping fish think of me."

Alex's grin widened. "Yes, but as your only true friend, I do care. It's a reflection on my good taste, you see. Can't go mucking around with that."

"Of course. I'd forgotten that this is all about you."

Alex gave him a small nudge and he stepped forward, pretending for all the world that he was unaware of the interest he was stirring. Damn these meddlesome people. He'd not go among them if it wasn't so very important to his business to do so. If he was anything, Henry was a practical man. He might not be dependent on his yacht-building business to live, but he was fiercely proud of what he'd accomplished. Owen Yachts built some of the most beautiful, luxurious sailing vessels in the world, the type of boats bought only by those with money to burn. And there stood his customers, drooling over his latest scandal, waiting to see how he would react. They would be disappointed, he feared, but at least he'd diffuse the gossip with his bored demeanor. He always did.

He and Alex strolled across the lawn, their shoes sinking deep into the thick carpet of grass. He could barely hear the orchestra over the din his approach was making. And then, it quieted, as if these fine folks noticed suddenly that they were acting common, that they were nearly shouting to be heard above the noise they were creating.

Henry smiled, giving the crowd that now pretended to ignore his approach a sweeping look. He nodded at a few acquaintances, and headed to a long side table where coffee, tea, and fine pastries were laid out. Henry stared blindly at the food, intensely aware that he was the subject of stares from people who were pretending with the greatest of grace not to stare. Still, he overheard some of what was said and found himself oddly surprised. He was evoking sympathy, not ridicule. The sheer hypocrisy of these people almost angered him as much as if they had openly shunned him, though he was human enough to be relieved that they had not.

"She's just come back to humiliate him," he heard one woman say. Ah, championed by the fairer sex. He couldn't help but smile at that.

And then an even greater buzz started up. Henry's first reaction was gratitude for whoever was taking attention away from him.

"My God," Alex said next to him. "What can she be thinking?"

Henry turned slowly, knowing in his gut whom he would see, and yet still surprised when he saw her. She was a vision wearing a deep blue skirt and a gold-and-blue shirtwaist, with matching parasol held above her golden head. A tiny, plumed hat was perched jauntily atop her head, the dark blue feather bobbing gently as she made her way across the lawn. Her sleeves, great puffy creations, only served to make the rest of her appear tiny . . . and vulnerable, despite what he saw as a determinedly serene look on her face. Nothing about her bespoke what certainly must have been a terrifying experience. Surely the shy girl he'd known two summers ago would have found it nearly impossible to walk into this seething den with a vague smile plastered on her face. He looked at her white-gloved hand tightly clutching her parasol, and realized she was as terrified as any young girl would be confronting such a crowd, but had become adept at hiding her feelings. What the hell did she think she was doing? For a moment he had to squelch the urge to go to her, to drag her away from this cruel throng. To protect her.

Henry swallowed at the wad of guilt that formed in his throat. He had done this to her. He had turned her into a woman people scorned and ridiculed. But for a just reason, he argued weakly. Sea Cliff had been saved, was still being saved because of his short-lived marriage. Shortly after Henry had abandoned Anne and begun working to save his family home, he had pushed aside the nagging guilt that had plagued him over what he'd done to a girl he had come to like.

"Marry an ugly girl," Alex had urged, only half jokingly. "She'll be so grateful to have a husband, she won't care if you abandon her." Why he had listened to that bad advice, he still could not recall. All he'd known was that he had to save Sea Cliff; it hadn't mattered what means it took. He needed to marry quickly and Anne was there, looking at him with an adoration that had been almost embarrassing to him before he selected her as his intended victim. Anne had been a pawn—and a willing one, he'd reminded himself a hundred times. He'd not lied to her. He'd not told her he loved her. Well, not until he'd taken those vows. Those words had shaken him to the core: "Do you promise to love her and honor her all the days of your life?" He'd said, "I do," and nearly choked on the words.

Because once said, he realized he'd no intention of living up to his part of the marriage. Henry determined a quick, quiet divorce would be the most painless way to end the marriage. He'd not given much thought to what it would mean to Anne, telling himself it was far less cruel to divorce her than continue to ignore her. He could now admit, with much regret, that he hadn't thought about much of anything during those months but his obsessive need to save his beloved Sea Cliff.

And now, she was here, back in Newport, the former wife who had never been a wife, bearing up under scathing scrutiny. Henry spared a look around him and saw that he was being given looks of sympathy and commiseration. Anne, on the other hand, if she was spared a look at all, was the subject of scorn. They were all waiting to see what he would do, what she would do when it became painfully obvious that she was being publicly cut by the entire Four Hundred. After today, Anne Foster would not be allowed in any of their homes or yachts or carriages. It was as if someone had taken a paintbrush and splashed it upon her, making her invisible. And Henry knew with painful clarity that he himself had mixed that paint.

Henry couldn't help it—he stared at the woman who was once his wife, the one he'd kissed with such mind-numbing abandon only ten hours before. She still smiled, while Beatrice seethed next to her, but Anne's cheeks were flushed, and the grip on her parasol was impossibly tighter. Again, that nearly overpowering feeling came to him that he should do something to make things right for her. He knew, though, that he could do nothing but watch her suffer and know that he was the cause of it. Going to her now would only fuel gossip and would do nothing to salvage her reputation.

"Got to give her credit," Henry said. "She's got gumption."

"That woman with her, too," Alex said, smiling at the way Beatrice was staring down those around them.

"Let's get out of here. My being here only makes it worse for her."

Alex gave Henry a long look before shrugging his shoulders and following his friend from the piazza, down the steps to the empty tennis courts. "You shouldn't be surprised," Alex said as they made their way to the locker room where they could exit the Casino.

"I shouldn't, should I? But I am."

Alex gave a snort. "If you're going to be a cad, Henry, you can't let a little thing like a wounded female get to you. You knew what you were doing when you married her."

"I don't think that I did," Henry said softly. "Hell, I don't believe I was thinking at all."

"Well, on that we agree."

Henry narrowed his eyes good-naturedly. "You are the one who convinced me I was doing the right thing."

"I never said that," Alex said blandly. "If you are going to quote me, please do so correctly, sir. I said marrying Miss Foster was the smart thing. No one with any conscience could say it was the *right* thing."

Henry let out a sigh. "What am I going to do?"

"There's nothing you can do, my good man. She's ruined. You ruined her. Just go on."

"And what about her?"

"What about her? She's learned a painful lesson and at an early age. Better that than be married for ten years only to discover you have three mistresses."

"Your perceptions of marriage have been unalterably warped, Alex. Not all parents are like yours. My mother and father loved each other. It does happen, you know."

Alex stared at the darkened entrance to the locker room, his brown eyes clouded with memories. "Not that I've seen." He blinked and cleared his gaze. "Believe me, as painful as this little episode has been for our now-little Miss Foster, it is a far lesser pain than she could have suffered at the hands of a true husband."

"Thank you for your confidence," Henry said dryly.

Alex shrugged again, ending the discussion. "Let's go to the Reading Room and get soused with the old men. Game?"

"You go on. Some of us have to work for a living."

Alex laughed, knowing Henry was one of the wealthiest men in Newport thanks to his inheritance and the intelligent investments made since he came into his money. But it was still his yacht-building business that was his first love—a business others in the Four Hundred called Henry's "hobby."

Henry watched as Alex made his way down Free-body Street, dodging horses and workers, a thoughtful expression on his face. He had no desire to head to Spring Wharf and the pile of new designs he had waiting for him. He felt slightly ill and knew it was his conscience gnawing at his stomach. It had taken two years for the guilt that was always with him to attack him this way, and part of him welcomed the pain. But another part realized Alex was right: If he was going to act the part of the cad, he should not allow himself to succumb to guilt.

If only she hadn't been so brave, so proud. So uncommonly beautiful. If only she'd stayed in New York, so he could at least pretend she was happy. If only he could do something to help, he thought as he turned onto Bellevue Avenue. He looked up and saw Mrs. Astor alighting from her carriage, her jet-black hair gleaming in the sun. He watched as Newport's all-powerful matriarch made her way into the Casino, a smile on his lips, suddenly knowing he just might have figured out a way to save this dismal summer season after all.

From the Journal of Arthur Owen

Elizabeth was an incomparable, a girl who could have chosen any man in the world and made him bow to her. Why she chose Walter, I still do not know. I told myself then that Elizabeth loved me, but she did not. She loved your father, something he—and I—discovered far too late. Elizabeth's love was a destructive thing, unnatural and corrupt, something I knew even then. What I am about to tell you about your mother is not meant to sully your memory of her, but rather to help you to understand how things could have gone as horribly wrong as they did. For years I have tried to understand your mother; why she did what she did to me and to your father. I can only conclude that she desperately needed to be loved but hadn't the vaguest notion of how to go about it. If only she had realized that she was loved, desperately so by Walter, she would not have followed such a destructive path. She needed constant reaffirmation of love, until even Walter wearied of telling her, showing her how much he loved her. Until the pure love Walter had for Elizabeth turned into something bitter and ugly.

They were not happy. Even in the beginning they were not. Walter was painfully shy and insecure and a bit bewildered that such a beautiful woman actually wanted to marry him. And Elizabeth, in her own twisted way, was just as unsure of herself.

That first night at dinner she flirted rather outrageously with me. Remember that your grandmother had been dead for ten years by then, so I was not immune to Elizabeth's blatant flirtations. Her behavior irritated Walter. I could tell by the amount of wine he had to drink that night, but he said nothing to her. I am ashamed to admit that I enjoyed Elizabeth's attentions, enjoyed the irritation I saw on Walter's face. Even that first night I realized I was jealous of my son. That he would marry such a creature! That jealousy turned into a monstrous thing, a consuming, debilitating disease that nearly destroyed us all. I could place the blame entirely on my own shoulders. I was, after all, far older than either one of them. But Elizabeth knew, she *knew* what she was doing to me, and she relished every bit of torment she subjected me to.

While she stayed with us on Jamestown, Elizabeth's parents visited friends in Newport, believing I would act as chaperon to the young couple. Even then I saw the irony of their trust in me to watch over the pair. Elizabeth got into the habit of sitting with me in the library as I worked. She would sit there gazing at me with those mesmerizing eyes, drowsy and suggestive, for nearly an hour. At first I thought it was my imagination, that no mere nineteen-year-old child could possibly be saying what those eyes seemed to be communicating. She'd been staying with us for nearly a week when she tore my world apart. Already I had trouble keeping my eyes off her. I was ashamed by my behavior, repulsed by the idea that I was attracted to my son's future wife. At the same time, she drew me to her with her laugh and voice and her very being. I became captivated by her and everything she did. She had a habit, I can still picture her doing this, of sucking on her pinky finger whenever she was deep in thought. It could have been an innocent gesture, charming, on any other girl. But on Elizabeth it seemed a blatant invitation meant only for me.

On that day she came up to me as I worked, standing beside me, making me patently aware of her. I could feel the heat of her as I tried to continue working. But she stood there for an eternity, just inches away, until I finally swiveled my chair around, angry that she had distracted me, that she was consuming my every thought. I was about to tell her to leave, in a polite but firm tone, when she knelt down before me. I, to my great shame, did nothing. I don't think I even breathed for fear I would stop her. With those eyes staring into mine, she spread my legs apart and pressed her mouth against me, between my legs. I'll never forget the way she smiled at me when she discovered I was not immune to her. It chills my blood

now, but at the time I was anything but cold. I was
consumed with lust in a way I wouldn't have thought
possible. I had lived forty-five years and never wanted
a woman more than I wanted her. I nearly broke my
hands, so hard did I clutch the chair's arms in an effort
not to reach out to her. I shook with it, but did not
touch her. Then she stood and walked from the room,
closing the door silently behind her, that smile still on
her lovely face.

I wanted to curse her. I wanted to run after her and
make love to her then and there. She was my son's
future wife and I had allowed her to touch me. I
wanted her to touch me again. Because I knew the
next time, I would not be able to stop myself. And I
knew I no longer wanted to.

Chapter Six

Beatrice and Anne made their way across the piazza to the side table, their skirts swinging gracefully, their heads held high. Beatrice's eyes shot daggers, but Anne felt surprisingly calm. So, she thought, this is it. This is the end of me.

Newport had judged her guilty and mentally excluded her from their set. Anne Foster no longer existed. It was almost liberating.

"The coward left," Beatrice hissed by her ear. "How they can accept him and shun you is beyond me. They ought to be ashamed."

"I'm certain some of them are."

Beatrice let out a humorless laugh. "They can all go to hell," she said rather too loudly, and Anne clutched at her friend's wrist.

"Don't be a complete idiot, Bea. Right now, you are simply misguided. But if you persist in championing me, you and your family will suffer. As supportive as your mother has been, I think it would crush her to have you cut."

Beatrice wrestled her wrist free. "She knows I am taking a risk and she has applauded me."

"I think the applause would stop if you were not invited to a single ball or supper this season. Please, Bea. I would blame myself if you were hurt," Anne said, appealing to her friend's charitable nature. "It would completely crush me to know I was the cause."

"You don't understand, Anne. I truly don't care what these people think of me."

"Anne is right, darling."

The girls whirled around to see Helen Leyden, Beatrice's mother. Helen was an older, slightly shorter version of her daughter. Her hair was still a deep brunette, though dulled a bit by a sprinkling of gray, and her eyes were the same deep brown as Beatrice's.

"Mother," Beatrice grumbled. "How can you say that?"

"Your father relies on these people, my dear. It is our responsibility as women to assure his place among society. Don't for a second think that his business dealings wouldn't suffer if you continue on this reckless track. I've lived among these people long enough to know we would all be hurt."

"But you said—"

"You tried your best. It was even a bit of fun. But Anne has suffered enough, and she is right. There is no need for you to continue as her champion. The cause, I fear, is lost."

"But our Plan," Beatrice reminded her mother.

Helen let out a musical laugh, then drew the two girls to a private corner. "Oh, Bea. You surely never thought it would work, not truly, did you? Henry Owen is a powerful man these days and could court any number of women who would advance his position even further. I don't mean to be cruel, but why in the world would Henry pay court to Anne, a girl cut from society, cut off from her own family? It is a practical world we live in. Anne has already learned that in the most cruel of ways."

"Mother," Beatrice said, clearly shocked that her mother could be so blunt in front of Anne.

"She's right," Anne said. "It was a silly plan, really. Just a bit of fun, and thinking about it did help to pull me out into the world. We will simply have to be content with last evening. I know I will never forget that I made a fool of him.''

Anne looked back to the piazza, to the wealthy, beautiful people she would never be a part of. She told herself she didn't feel the slightest bit sad that she would never be a part of them again. "I'm going home tomorrow.''

"You can't!'' Beatrice said.

"Of course I can. It's for the best, Bea. I don't belong here anymore. I don't think I ever did.''

Beatrice looked back at the piazza. "I think I hate them,'' she said, her voice filled with emotion. "I think I shall always hate them.''

"Oh, my dear,'' Helen said, her voice light and airy. "They hate themselves, as well. That's part of the fun.''

Beatrice gave her mother a look of bewilderment, then let out a laugh. "You know, Mother, I believe you are right.'' She turned to Anne. "Let's take a carriage ride this afternoon. It will be your grand farewell. We shall snub everyone. No! We shall give them evil looks.'' Beatrice clapped her hands together, pleased to have another plan.

Anne smiled at her friend. "No, Bea. We shall sit in your carriage like a pair of queens and we shall smile at them. Smile as if they are our greatest friends. We shall make them squirm in their seats.''

Beatrice gave her friend a quick hug. "It's a plan.''

Each day when the weather was fair, Newport's cottagers would dress themselves, their horses, and footmen in their finest and parade up and down Bellevue Avenue. Minutes before the "parade,'' a horse-drawn wagon was brought down the avenue and water sprinkled upon the road so that no dust would rise up and offend the ladies' nostrils. As the cottagers made their way tediously slowly down Bellevue, they would stop occasionally to leave cards at various homes, footmen formally presenting them at the gate. One was never home during the coaching hour, and if you were, you pretended you were not.

The women wore their best day dresses, being certain to carry matching parasols, and wear matching, feathered hats. No matter how hot it was, the ladies wore long white gloves and brought along an extra pair in the event they became wet with perspiration. The coachmen, with their formal livery and unsmiling faces, added to the solemnity of the event the locals thought quite silly. The horses, groomed to gleaming, tails combed and manes tightly braided, wore either a feather or boutonniere on their heads that matched those of the footmen.

One did not wave at acquaintances or smile at strangers sitting in passing carriages. A close friend received a smile and a nod, a stranger not a glance. And it was an unspoken rule in the peculiar hierarchy of Newport that a lesser member of the Four Hundred would never, ever smile or nod at one of the matriarchs—unless they were for some reason granted such a gesture first.

Knowing these rules, Anne and Beatrice were prepared to be completely ignored when they went coaching the next day. They would leave no cards, as Beatrice was quite certain none would be left for her. They would sit in their carriage looking regal, hoping to at least shame some of those who shunned Anne. It was a hopeless endeavor, but for Beatrice's sake, Anne went along with it. She cursed the thunderstorms that had prevented her from going coaching the day before. She would be home in her New York town house by now, away from Newport and its painful memories, if not for those storms.

A few puddles remained on the avenue, and Anne wondered that some nabob had not demanded they be soaked up for fear of muddying their fine carriage wheels. The Leyden coach was not as grand as some, but was pretty and comfortable. Green with gilt trim and rich brown undercarriage, its leather seats were soft, and the coach ran smoothly over the avenue behind four perfectly matched bays. Though Beatrice's brother sometimes took the reins, today the Leydens' coachman sat high in the seat, a tall top hat with green band and feather perched on his head.

"I used to look forward to this," Anne said to Beatrice and her mother. Though the coaches were meant to carry six passengers, it held only the three women, with Anne sitting on the far left so that all would be able to see her.

"This won't be too awful, Anne," Helen said. "And it is certainly better to be seen out here than to be found at home hiding."

Anne sighed and smoothed out her skirt of soft yellow silk before snapping open her matching parasol. She wished she could hold the umbrella over her face to spare herself and the Leydens more humiliation, but instead she held it firmly upright, not even allowing it to rest upon her shoulder. "Two hours," she muttered.

"It will fly by," Beatrice said cheerfully as the coachman drove the horses slowly from the Leydens' drive onto Bellevue Avenue. He'd had to wait several minutes before finding an adequate opening in the parade, for it never would have done to cut in front of another carriage.

The procession was slow, making the heat of midday seem even more oppressive. Anne tried to ignore the trickles of sweat that flowed between her breasts to soak into her stays, as she tried to ignore everything else. "If only there were a breeze," she said softly.

"It is hot for early July," Helen said cheerfully. Anne couldn't help but think darkly that the Leyden women were an irritatingly cheerful pair. "Too bad you are going back to New York, Anne. You'll miss the July Fourth festivities."

"I think I would have missed them this year regardless," Anne said, trying not to sound as wistful as she felt.

Next to Anne, Beatrice stiffened, and whispered, "Mrs. Astor."

It was only fitting that the young women be in complete awe of Mrs. William Astor, a woman who was known as the queen of Newport. Like a queen, she held court at her balls in her Beechwood cottage, her head and neck dripping with diamonds, her plump fingers covered with jeweled rings. She was almost always surrounded by a large group of lady friends, but with her jet-black hair and signature white satin gowns, she glittered far brighter than the rest.

Her carriage was full of women wearing frothy pastels, the ladies almost hidden by their expensively trimmed parasols. The great lady sat in the middle, her eyes straight ahead as she passed the carriage in front of the Leydens'.

"She once complimented me on my gown," Beatrice whispered from the side of her mouth. "I made a fool of myself thanking her."

The Astor carriage was nearly abreast of them when Mrs. Astor turned her head toward them. And then the most remarkable thing happened. Mrs. William Astor smiled and nodded at Anne. It was unmistakable. The other women in the carriage smiled and nodded as well, as if Mrs. Astor held some magical string that made them do exactly as she did. Anne stared unblinking until she felt a sharp jab at her ribcage. Only then did she find the presence of mind to nod back. She was too stunned to actually smile.

"Oh, heavens, Anne. Did you see? Did you?" Beatrice said in a hasty whisper.

"Of course I saw."

"And so did the occupants of the carriage in front and behind," Helen observed thoughtfully.

"Do you think she mistook me for someone else?" Anne asked, trying not to feel excited.

"I hardly think Mrs. Astor would make such a mistake. If she acknowledged you in such a public and obvious way, you can be assured it was not an accident."

Anne shook her head in confusion. "But why? I've never met the woman formally. How does she even know who I am?"

Helen let out an airy laugh. "My dear child, *everyone* knows who you are. But you are right to be confused. Mrs. Astor is not a stupid woman. She did not attain the position she has by making hollow gestures." Helen tapped a finger against her cheek in thought. "I believe you have a champion, Anne. A powerful one."

"You don't think Mrs. Astor could have formed her own opinion about Anne?" Beatrice asked.

"Oh, no. Someone must have spoken to her. The question is, who?"

They were still discussing the event when the Oelrich carriage passed by. Tessie Oelrich, Mamie Fish, and Alva Vanderbilt were each engaged in a power struggle in preparation for the inevitable day when Mrs. Astor abdicated the throne. The three women, known among the Four Hundred as the Great Triumvirate, yielded nearly as much social power as Mrs. Astor. When not one, but all three, nodded and smiled at Anne, her place in Newport society was completely secured.

Just like that, Anne went from shunned to accepted.

"I should return to New York to spite them," Anne said, not meaning a single syllable. She would stay. She would show them all that Anne Foster was as good as any of them. She would carry on with the plan and make Henry pay the price for all these two-faced jackals. She could play the game; she could nod and smile and pretend all was well when inside she felt like scratching their lying eyes out.

For all her venom, there was a part of her that rejoiced. This was her world, and despite herself, Anne did want to be part of it, no matter how mightily she protested to herself and others that she did not. For a girl brought up in the glitter of Newport, it had been devastating to suddenly be cast out—and it was wonderful to find herself not only readmitted, but welcomed by the grand dames of Newport society.

"Oh, Anne," Beatrice said, bubbling over with happiness Anne wished she could feel. "Isn't it wonderful? We'll be able to go to all the balls and dinners. You'll be all the rage now that Mrs. Astor and the rest have acknowledged you."

Anne frowned. "I suppose."

Beatrice shot her friend a look of disbelief, recovering in time to look serene as the next carriage passed. "You suppose?" she hissed. "Oh, no you don't. Don't you dare throw this chance away."

"Don't you think it would be a bit hypocritical of me to accept invitations from the very same people who publicly humiliated me?"

Beatrice waved a hand of dismissal. "Oh, that. Who cares? It's all water under the bridge. And, frankly, I think you are being terribly naive. You must jump at this chance. If they are silly enough to cut you and welcome you within the same twenty-four hours, then let them. They are the hypocrites, Anne, not you."

"Beatrice is absolutely correct, Anne," Helen said in her cheerful singsong way.

"So I should pretend nothing happened yesterday?" Anne asked Helen.

"Yes, dear. That's exactly what you should do. But might I suggest a certain cold reserve?"

Anne smiled. "They will turn to icebergs on the spot."

Beatrice let out a delighted laugh. "Oh, this shall

be fun. They dare not say a thing against you, not with the formidable Mrs. Astor and the Great Triumvirate behind you. You can tear them to ribbons if you wish, Anne." She clapped her gloved hands together.

"There is only one person I wish to tear to ribbons, and now I believe it may be possible."

"The Plan," Beatrice said. "I'd nearly forgotten. We already know the scoundrel is intrigued by you."

Anne blushed at her friend's obvious reminder of the kiss she'd shared with Henry.

"It must have been Henry," Helen said, startling Anne by speaking the name of the man who had just been on her mind.

"What are you talking about?" Beatrice asked.

"As much as I know you two loathe him, Henry Owen is not a complete wretch."

"Mother," Beatrice said, shocked to hear her mother defend the scoundrel.

"Think about it, darling. Who else would be able to get an audience with an Astor, an Oelrich, a Vanderbilt, and a Fish in a single day, and convince all those ladies to back your cause?"

"Any number of people," Beatrice said. "His friend Alexander Henley, for one. He certainly couldn't keep his eyes off Anne at the Wetmore ball. Or at the Casino, now that I think of it," she finished, sounding slightly disgruntled that her friend had garnered so much attention from the man.

Anne interrupted the bickering pair. "It couldn't have been Henry. He's never given any indication he cares a bit for what he did to me. And it would be completely out of character for him to do anything remotely kind."

"Perhaps he has an ulterior motive," Helen said thoughtfully. "Or perhaps he is feeling a bit of guilt. Guilt, Anne, is a powerful emotion."

"He ought to feel guilty," Anne said, unwilling to

spare a kind thought for him. "And you have not convinced me that he was behind the events of today."

The Leydens' carriage plodded along toward Ocean Drive, where the driver would turn the vehicle and head back to their cottage. The sun disappeared behind a bank of clouds, summoning a sigh of relief from Anne, who peeled off her sweat-soaked gloves and snapped her parasol closed. "Henry has never shown a single bit of kindness toward me," Anne said, bringing out a second pair of gloves. "Why would he start now?"

"Perhaps it was that kiss," Beatrice teased.

Anne flushed red. "He would not put his reputation on line because of a little kiss," Anne said firmly. "Honestly, can you picture that loathsome man bowing before Mrs. Astor and begging a favor? And Mrs. Fish? She'd just as soon filet me with her sharp tongue than bow and smile to me because of something Henry said to her."

Helen looked thoughtful. "I'll admit, when you put it in those terms, it *is* difficult to imagine guilt being the only motive behind a man like Henry kowtowing to Newport's ladies. What was this about a kiss?"

"It was nothing," Anne said, casting Beatrice a scowl. "It was part of the plan to humiliate him publicly—just in case the full plan could not be put into play."

"I see," Helen said, drawing out the words in a way Anne didn't like.

"You most certainly do *not* see," Anne said so harshly that Helen raised her eyebrows. Anne was immediately sorry and said so. "It's been a difficult few days, Mrs. Leyden. I think when we return home, I'll go up to my room and stay there until autumn," she said, sitting back against the cushioned seat for the first time. She was exhausted.

"This has been the longest hour of my life," Anne said wearily, garnering the energy to stiffen her back so that only the very base of her spine touched the cushion. Another carriage was passing and it would never do to be seen slouching, no matter how exhausted she was. Years of being taught proper behavior made the gesture as natural as breathing.

As soon as the threesome returned to the Leyden cottage, they were immediately confronted with Anne's newfound popularity. Anne was about to ascend the granite staircase to her room, when Beatrice stopped her.

"Oh, heavens, Anne. Look at this." In one hand she held a stack of calling cards, in another no less than five invitations to luncheons—all with "Miss Anne Foster" scrawled hastily as clearly a last-minute addition.

"It appears, Anne, you will have little time to rest this summer," Helen said. "You, my dear, have instantly become the most sought-after belle of the season."

Chapter Seven

"All right, my friend, it worked. Your ex-wife is again accepted in this capricious society of ours. What do you plan next?" Alex lounged in a worn cushioned chair on the Reading Room's porch overlooking Church Street. The men's club was contained in a modest yellow-and-white wood-framed house that gave no clue to its rabidly protected exclusivity. Women and other unwanteds were not allowed inside—a beefy doorman saw to that—and if a woman happened to stroll by on the sidewalk within feet of an old acquaintance lounging on the porch, she was not acknowledged. Ever.

Although the club was a haven for cigar-smoking, whiskey-drinking, wealthy men, Henry rarely found himself there. He found it ungodly boring as he didn't smoke and disliked heavy drinking, which were the two main activities of the members. But this time Alex had not allowed him to decline.

Henry knew that Alex was brimming with curiosity over why he'd humbled himself before Newport's matrons. He couldn't answer his friend because he was still trying to figure out for himself what had caused him to urge the women to save his former wife from banishment. Guilt, he realized, had only been part of the reason. "What do I plan next? Why, nothing. I've done what I set out to do."

Alex leaned forward, his cigar held casually in his right hand, which dangled between his knees. Cigar smoke rose up between the two men and was swept away by a soft breeze. "You're not going to pursue her, then?"

Henry was in the process of sipping his port, and nearly choked. "Good God, no. Have you forgotten who she is?"

Alex smiled at his friend's reaction, and taking a few puffs on his cigar, he peered through the smoke, his brown eyes narrowed. "Then you'll not mind if *I* pursue her?"

Henry, who was about to take another sip, froze for an instant before bringing the fine crystal goblet to his lips. "You're crazy."

"Why? She's beautiful. Available. And thanks to you, entirely acceptable." Alex took another puff before adding, "Besides, I've always wanted to marry a virgin."

Henry brought his glass slowly down and placed it on the white-clothed table with quiet deliberation. "You've gone too far, Alex."

Alex put his cigar between his teeth and smiled. "So, she is. I thought so."

Henry gave his friend a look of annoyance, telling himself he would not take the bait his friend had so temptingly cast out in front of him by losing his temper. "Whether she is or is not is none of your business," he said blandly. "Since I know you've no intention of marrying her, I'll have to insist, one friend to another, that you leave Miss Foster be."

Alex raised his eyebrows. "Oh, you're insisting, are you?"

Henry shrugged, pretending indifference, but feeling something uncomfortably like jealousy at the thought of Alex wooing Anne. "All right. Not insisting. You are correct. If you wish to pursue Miss Foster, you may."

"I wasn't asking permission," Alex said, laughing. "It *would* bother you, wouldn't it?"

It would bother him, Henry realized. And because it would, he said, "Of course not. I'll admit I was attracted to her at the Wetmore ball." More than attracted, he added to himself. Damned near obsessed might be a better description of his instant and overwhelming fascination with his former wife. Just thinking of her soft lips, her pliant little body, her sighs of contentment was enough to stir his blood. "But now that I know who she is . . . Let's just say I'll let my eye rove in other directions this summer."

"Oh? Anyone in particular in mind?"

Henry was suddenly inspired. "Miss Leyden looked lovely at the ball. And I must say I've been impressed by her stalwart defense of Anne. Loyalty is an admirable trait."

Henry nearly laughed aloud when he saw the expression on Alex's face, quickly concealed, but recognizable just the same. He'd suspected that Alex was attracted to Beatrice, and now he'd just had that suspicion confirmed.

"That sharp-tongued witch? Surely you're joking."

Henry admired Alex's ability to recover so quickly, and he couldn't help but wonder why his friend hadn't pursued a woman he so clearly liked, despite his protestations to the contrary.

"I find her witty and not at all sharp-tongued," Henry said lightly.

"Then you've not heard her speaking to me," Alex said, sounding much like a grumpy boy.

Henry laughed, then stood to leave. "They'll likely both be at the Casino for Friday night's ball. I'd say neither of us have much of a chance with those two ladies. I'm sure they enjoyed playing their little joke the other night, but I've a feeling they'd just as soon shoot us as dance with us."

Alex grinned. "I'll take the chance. You know, Miss Foster just might be the one I've been looking for."

Henry forced himself to smile and shrug, dashing

away the image of himself grabbing Alex's lapels and shaking the idea of Anne out of his head. "Then I'll see you Friday night. But I'd suggest you wear some armor."

Anne had never felt comfortable dancing at the Casino, for in no other place in Newport was she more aware that she was one of the privileged few allowed to attend the balls there. A gallery, supported by Corinthian pilasters, surrounded the room decorated in gold and blue, and for one dollar the "townies" would watch from above as the rich mingled and danced below them. The gallery was noisy and crowded, the ballroom itself even more so for the July Fourth ball. Afterward, there would be fireworks shot from a barge moored off Bailey's Beach, where the idle rich would gather in their formal dress, sit on fine cashmere blankets, and watch the show.

Anne wore a cream-colored gown from Madam Donovan and a beautiful new pair of shoes from Seabury's. Her honey-blonde hair was swept up and elegant, her face lovely and fresh. But inside she felt like that dumpy little girl with silly banana curls bobbing around her head. It didn't help that her acceptance back into society had been chronicled in the notorious gossip column, "Saunterings." "Miss F. has been readmitted into the sacred circle of the mighty Four Hundred. We shall all sigh with wonder at her miraculous recovery and speculate about its origin. Perhaps we should look to her past for answers."

It had been an exceedingly annoying entry, but far tamer than the one poor Miss Van Alen suffered. "Miss Van Alen suffers from some kind of throat trouble—she cannot go more than a half hour without a drink."

Anne could almost guarantee that the mortified Miss Van Alen would not show her face at the Casino this evening. And she wished she were not here, ei-

ther. In the instant she entered the ballroom, Anne
wished she were part of that rowdy crowd in the gallery, and not a member of Newport's elite. Entering
the room as a scorned woman had been easier, for
she'd known what to expect, even if it was painful.
This time, the buzz in the room when she entered
softened noticeably, then grew louder and louder until
she wanted to put her hands over her ears and drown
it out.

For the first few moments, Anne stood next to Beatrice, bracing herself as if for some terrible assault.

"Miss Foster. You intrigue me. And how lovely you
have become. Quite remarkable, really. Take care not
to disappear from us completely."

Anne looked to her right to find Mrs. Stuyvesant
Fish, known as Mamie to only her closest friends,
standing next to her and waiting for her to respond.
The older woman had the vaguest of smiles about her
thin lips and her eyes sparkled with good humor.
Anne immediately relaxed.

"Mrs. Fish," Anne said, giving the lady a gentle
smile. "I'm afraid if I disappeared completely, there
would be nothing left for this crowd to talk about all
season. I could hardly be so cruel."

Mamie Fish laughed, giving those around the three
women pause. Beatrice, standing silently next to Anne
as if frozen by terror, let out a nervous, false-sounding
laugh in response.

Mrs. Fish flashed a look of annoyance at Beatrice
before giving Anne a look of pure admiration. "Henry
was right about you. A remarkable girl."

Anne's stomach clenched and her smile disappeared. "Henry?"

Seeing the look of hostility on Anne's face only
made Mrs. Fish smile more. She looked very much
like a cat with a feather sticking out of its mouth and
an empty canary cage above its head. "Why, certainly
Henry. Who else?" She lifted her gaze away from

Anne. "Ah, and here is the knight in shining armor now."

"I'd hardly use such grand words to describe Mr. Owen," Anne said with venom, not caring if she alienated Mrs. Fish.

Again, Mrs. Fish gave Anne a piercing look. "No. I don't suppose you would." With that, the lady nodded her head and walked away.

"My goodness, Anne, do take care. You don't want to make an enemy of Mrs. Fish," Beatrice said in a flurry of whispered words.

"I don't care who I make an enemy of," Anne said, still seething about the information Mrs. Fish had imparted. Helen had been right—Henry was behind her being accepted back into society. She supposed he expected a thank-you. Well, he could wait until doomsday if that's what he wanted. "He's made a fool of me again."

"Who? Henry?"

"Who else," Anne said, looking across the crowded room at her former husband. "I'm quite certain everyone in this room now knows why I have been welcomed back in the fold. Pity! He pitied me. How dare he try to help, when he was the cause of all my misery."

Beatrice widened her eyes at the pure venom Anne was directing toward Henry. Anne had said a hundred times that she hated Henry, but it had simply been a word she used. Now Beatrice could almost see that black cloud of hatred surrounding her friend.

"Now, Anne, don't do anything rash," Beatrice said softly.

Anne shot her friend a quick look, closed her eyes, and took a deep, shaky breath. "I won't. But he will pay. I promise you, Bea, he will pay for ruining my life."

At that moment, a memory hit Beatrice, one that she had refused to think about because it was one of the few good thoughts she had about the man she referred to as "the scoundrel." Perhaps it was the venom in Anne's voice, or that this gentle woman could sound so fierce, but she found herself wanting to defend Henry. And so she did.

"Anne, when Henry was courting you," Beatrice began, ignoring the scowl that immediately formed on her friend's face, "I overheard something that at the time I kept to myself because I didn't want you to be hurt."

Anne kept her eyes pinned on Henry, the coldness in her expression not wavering. "Go on."

"Some of his friends were joking about his courtship, saying awful things about you and his motives for marrying you. He said that you were the only truly good person he'd ever met and they'd best keep their opinions to themselves. He said that if he ever heard any of them saying anything against you, he would thrash them."

"That doesn't mean a thing. He was trying to save his own pride by defending me," Anne said, but she didn't sound convinced. "And it certainly does not negate what he did to me."

"Of course not. I told you only so that you wouldn't think his motives behind helping you now are based on pity. He does not seem to be a man who would be moved by pity alone."

Anne nearly snorted. "Oh, yes, Henry Owen acted for purely altruistic reasons. Because he is so very kind and compassionate."

"Someone is certainly bitter," Beatrice said, raising both eyebrows.

Anne sighed, then laughed away her ill humor. "I am bitter. And angry. It feels wonderful."

"Warn me away when you feel dreadful, will you?"

"I think I shall never feel dreadful again," Anne said, eyeing Henry and relishing the time when he was brought down by her. She ignored that tiny flutter her heart gave when she looked at him, preferring to feed the anger that had lived inside her so long.

Alex was grinning at Henry, who was taking care not to appear to be looking for Anne among the Newport belles in silk, chiffon, and lace. "She's here. Already saw her with that friend of hers talking to Mrs. Fish."

Henry nearly groaned aloud. "Then she must know. I should have known they couldn't keep something like this to themselves. I did ask, you know, and Mrs. Fish laughed at me."

"Why keep it hidden? I'm certain when Anne realizes it was you behind her remarkable return to society, she'll be eternally grateful."

"I don't think so," Henry said, shaking his head as he stared at Anne. "I think I'm the last person on earth she wanted help from."

"Let's go test the waters, shall we? This is the perfect opportunity for me to gain acceptance. I'll express horror at what you've done, and she'll be in my arms before the end of the night."

Henry gave Alex a withering look. "You made that prediction one other time, if I recall, and she ended up in my arms."

"That was part of her plan to humiliate you. I'm certain she'll be more receptive to my advances now."

Henry clamped his mouth shut, knowing that if he allowed himself to speak, he'd let Alex know exactly what he thought of his "advances." He couldn't understand why he cared that Alex wanted to pursue Anne, but he did. Lord knew, he wouldn't have a chance with her. He suspected that she hated him—and with good reason, he reminded himself. It was that kiss that was so bothersome, a kiss he should have forgotten days ago, but one that had lingered rather gratingly on his mind. Had her response been pretense? At the time, she certainly had appeared to have been moved. Perhaps, though, it had simply been his ego that imagined those dreamy eyes, those softly parted lips, the way her hands moved to clutch at his neck.

Where had she learned to kiss that way? he wondered suddenly. If he could be certain of one thing, it was that he had not taught her.

"Come on, you coward. The orchestra is about to start and I intend to claim the first dance," Alex said, brimming with good humor. "You can ask the other one if you want."

Henry forced a smile. "Miss Leyden does look inordinately pretty this night."

Alex's gaze went from Anne to Beatrice, and he frowned. "She shouldn't wear pastels," he muttered before heading toward the two ladies.

The last thing Henry expected to see when the two approached Anne was a welcoming smile. It was as dazzling as it was false.

"You need to work on that smile if you expect people to believe it," he said close to her ear. She stiffened and he heard the slightest gasp, but when he moved back to look at her, the smile was still in place.

"You look lovely this evening, Miss Foster," Alex said grandly as he stepped in front of Anne, nearly pushing Henry out of the way. "You, too," he said, giving Beatrice a passing glance. Henry gave Alex a dark look before turning his attentions to Beatrice.

"You must forgive Alex, he's given to exaggerated flattery," Henry said.

To her credit, Beatrice laughed at Henry's sarcasm. "If I gave one moment's thought to what Mr. Henley thinks of me, it would be one moment wasted," she said.

Henry put a hand on Beatrice's elbow and led her slightly away from where Alex and Anne were standing, apparently enthralled with one another. "I see things are going well this evening," he said with meaning.

"Yes," Beatrice said. "Though I must warn you, Anne is not entirely pleased that you are behind her sudden acceptance."

"I thought as much," he said, unable to keep from looking at his ex-wife. She looked lovely in her cream gown, which only made her skin appear that more flawless. She had an almost luminescent quality, her skin gently reflecting the soft gaslight of the ballroom chandeliers. She was in profile to him and so was unaware of his intense perusal.

"It's hard to believe she's the same woman you met two years ago, isn't it?" Beatrice said.

Henry gave Beatrice a wry smile. "Yes. But is she still lovely on the inside, or have I destroyed that Anne Foster as well?"

He continued to stare at Anne, so was unaware of the thoughtful look Beatrice gave him. She smiled when she saw him scowl as Alex led Anne to the dance floor, his hand possessively at the small of her back.

Finally he turned toward her. "Care to dance?"

"You don't think this is awkward? I mean to say, won't people think the four of us odd dance partners?"

"I don't give a damn—pardon—I don't care what people think if me. But if you are concerned . . ."

Beatrice laughed. "Do I strike you as a person who is concerned about what people say about me?"

"No. Only what people say about Anne. On that matter, we seem to agree."

"Mr. Owen, if you gave one whit about what people say about Anne, you would not have betrayed her the way you did. Though I am grateful for what you did yesterday, I have not forgiven you for what you did two years ago. I never shall."

"Then again we are in agreement," Henry said. "I don't believe I shall be able to forgive myself."

Beatrice allowed Henry to lead her to the dance
floor, only because he had managed to stun her once
again. If she were not careful, she would find herself
not only forgiving Henry, but liking him as well. Again
and again she forced herself to remember what a complete cad he was.

They had gone around the dance floor twice before
Beatrice realized that Henry hadn't spared her more
than a glance. His eyes had been on Anne, who was
looking up at Alex with sickening attentiveness. She
wanted to pinch her friend to remind her that it was
Henry Anne needed to woo, not Alex.

"I believe it is customary to stare at the woman you
are dancing with now, not the one you wish you were
dancing with," Beatrice said with good humor.

Startled, Henry looked down, then blushed. The effect was entirely too innocent and boyish for Beatrice
to completely ignore. He was doing it again, she realized; he was softening her heart. How long would it
take before he softened Anne's?

Anne, her face flushed from dancing nonstop for an
hour, finally begged off and headed for the punch
bowl, Beatrice by her side.

"How does it feel to be the belle of the ball?"

Anne wanted to be disgusted by her newfound popularity, but she was having too much fun. "Wonderful," she said honestly. "I may be the most shallow
person in the world, but I don't care a bit that these
same men completely ignored me the last time I attended a ball here. I'll get on my high horse tomorrow.
Is that too awful?"

"Not at all. You deserve to have fun," Beatrice said,
giving her friend's arm a little squeeze. "I think every
man in this room is smitten with you."

"The new me," Anne said, forcefully reminding herself of her former life. Despite her good humor, she
couldn't help but remember what balls had been like

before, when she had stuffed herself into the latest styles in a desperate attempt to appear fashionable and modern. She had spent so many dances pretending to be jolly as she stood with other unwanted girls, she had become used to it. But she had never stopped being hurt by it.

And then she'd met Henry Owen. Good-looking, rich Henry, who'd made her laughed and who danced with her when no one else would. Henry, who made Anne fall in love with him the first time he laughed aloud at one of her witty remarks. She would never forget that fat little girl who was Henry's only ticket to his inheritance—a rake who she thought had agreed to settle down because he finally found someone he could talk to. He'd even said as much to her.

She could still remember looking up at him, loving him so much, she could barely contain it. "You're the only person I can talk to like this." He'd sounded bewildered and awed. He'd sounded like a man in love—at least to Anne's ears. Just remembering made Anne flush with humiliation and anger.

"Oh, don't you dare go getting all dour on me," Beatrice said, studying her friend's suddenly stormy expression. "Just when I was thinking I'd helped to create a truly flitty girl, you turn retrospective. Really, Anne!"

Anne laughed, pushing away her dark thoughts. She truly wished that for just this night she could forget about the girl she'd been and celebrate the woman she was now. "All right," she promised. "No more frowns."

"That's better." They each took a sip of punch before Beatrice brought up the one subject they'd avoided all evening.

"I noticed you danced with nearly every eligible man here. Except Mr. Owen."

"Don't you mean 'that scoundrel'? When did he

become *Mister* Owen? Besides, he hasn't asked," Anne said honestly.

"I've seen him approach you half a dozen times only to have you turn to someone else. You know, Anne, if you're going to make good on The Plan, you've got to at least talk with him."

Anne let out a beleaguered sigh. "I suppose."

"Don't you want to carry on?"

"Of course I do. I just find it entirely too difficult to be pleasant to him just now." It was only partly true, Anne realized. Despite her real animosity toward Henry, every time she felt his eyes on her, her skin warmed uncomfortably and she remembered how it felt to be held in his arms. He had the oddest effect on her senses.

"Here he comes now," Beatrice whispered.

Anne braced herself, then turned to him with her best smile.

"Better," he said, grinning at her. "But it's not quite reaching your eyes."

Her smile instantly disappeared. "If you are here to ask me to dance, the answer is no. We've already given these people enough to talk about. What would they think to see us dancing together? It's bad enough we attend the same functions. Do leave me alone, Mr. Owen. You are embarrassing me."

Something shifted in his eyes just before he gave her a bow, and Anne had the ridiculous urge to say she was sorry for being so rude.

"My apologies for embarrassing you, Miss Foster," he said, all good humor quite gone. "But I came over to you ladies to ask Miss Leyden to dance." He turned to Beatrice. "Will you?"

Beatrice's eyes flew from one to the other uncertainly. Finally, she held out her gloved hand and allowed Henry to lead her to the dance floor. Anne watched, unsure if she was angry at him for all his past transgressions, at Beatrice for dancing with him so willingly, or herself for wishing it was *her* being held in his arms.

On the dance floor, Beatrice once again found herself dancing with a man whose attentions were elsewhere. "Did you really come over to ask me to dance, Mr. Owen?"

He gave her a slight smile. "Promise not to be offended?"

"I promise."

"Then I must confirm your suspicions. Miss Foster was my target."

"She's very . . ."

"Angry. Yes."

Beatrice had the sudden urge to warn Henry away, one that she quickly put down. Something gave a little when she saw his expression after Anne had cut him down. It actually seemed as if the cold-hearted Mr. Owen had been hurt by Anne's words. More than ever, she needed to remember that Henry deserved what Anne planned to bestow upon him.

"I think you deserve her anger," she said, keeping her tone light.

"So do I," he said maddeningly.

Beatrice brought her brows together. "If you persist on agreeing with me every time I say something awful about you, it will be rather difficult to continue hating you," she said before realizing how silly she sounded.

"I hardly would want that, Miss Leyden."

Beatrice let out a huff of mock impatience. "So you would like to convince me that you are an angel, a man who deserves the forgiveness he seeks. Forgive me and Anne if we are a bit suspect of your motives. After all, you married Anne for money. You're no better than a fortune hunter."

Henry stiffened and said, "I should remind you that I married to gain access to my own fortune, not Anne's."

"I suppose that makes what you did acceptable,"

she said, all good humor wiped away by his chilly response.

"Hardly. But faced with the same dilemma, I would do so again. I might handle the end of the marriage differently. I do regret that she was socially hurt by the divorce, but there was no real affection between us. I hardly broke her heart."

To Beatrice's vast relief, she found herself loathing him once again. She pulled away from him and was jostled by a couple dancing by. "I beg to disagree. What do you think happens to a girl's heart when her parents throw her from her home? When all her friends abandon her? When all her hopes and dreams of marriage and children are dashed. You could have married anyone. Why Anne? Why her?"

A muscle ticked in Henry's jaw. "She was available. She was willing."

"But clearly you weren't. I've always wondered, why her? Back then, Anne wasn't even pretty. I'm her greatest friend, but even *I* know she . . ." Beatrice's face blanched when she recognized the guilty flush that stained his cheeks. "My God. You picked her *because* she wasn't pretty." She knew with one look that she was right. The muscle in his jaw bunched as he stared down at her, and his gray eyes flickered to Anne before coming back to rest on Beatrice.

"You didn't think she'd make a fuss. And she didn't, did she. Fat girls don't have feelings, is that what you thought? If she ever found out . . ." Beatrice shook her head, not wanting to believe what he had so clearly just admitted to.

"She won't."

Tears flooded her eyes. He'd married Anne, he'd picked her from the dozens of available women, simply because he knew she'd never make demands of him, simply because she was plain.

"You are loathsome," she said.

Henry looked away, as if unable to meet her eyes. "So I've heard."

And then, because she hated him with new fierceness, she said, "I can't believe she wants you still."

His head snapped up, and Beatrice wanted to shout in victory. "I won't tell her just how vile you are, but I will continue to do my utmost to make certain Anne stays away from you.'

She turned away, a pleased smile on her lips. Nothing intrigued a man more than knowing he would be denied the one thing he wanted most. The Plan would continue on course.

Chapter Eight

"I'm getting the hell off this island," Henry told Alex as they walked along Bellevue.

"Just when you were getting so cozy with Miss Leyden?"

"I've no interest in Miss Leyden. Or any other miss."

Alex chuckled, which further irritated Henry.

"Don't tell me you're going to New York."

"To Jamestown. The workers are expected to start on the foundation this week and I want to be there," Henry said, turning toward the waterfront where his small catboat was moored.

"Ho there. You're not going tonight, are you?"

"I am." It was only a short sail, and with the moon nearly full and lighting the bay, it would be an easy one.

Alex stopped in his tracks and watched Henry walk purposefully toward the harbor. "I'll visit," he called down. "Mind if I bring a guest?" He nearly laughed aloud when Henry halted abruptly and turned.

"If you bring Anne with you to Sea Cliff, I'll beat the stuffing out of you. I'm warning you, Alex."

"Would I do that?" Alex asked, all innocence.

Henry gave his friend a hard stare before turning and walking down the hill toward the harbor. He had to get away before he did something he'd regret. He had to get a certain woman out of his head. He had no business wanting her. It was insanity. But seeing her again tonight, watching her dance and laugh with every available man, had driven him mad. He didn't think Beatrice would tell Anne just how rotten he truly had been two years ago; she was far too loyal and good a friend to hurt Anne more.

"I told him you wanted him," Beatrice said between the sputtering cracks of a fireworks display.

Anne turned fully to Beatrice, her mouth agape, but her eyes dancing with excitement. "You what?"

Beatrice put on a smug expression. "I wanted to get this plan of ours back on the right track."

Anne was silent for a moment, not certain whether she should give her friend a hug or a slap on the arm. She bit her lip as she waited for the silence between explosions. "What did he say?"

"Nothing, but he certainly looked interested."

Anne tried not to feel disappointed. "He didn't say anything?"

Beatrice thought for a moment. "No. I'm certain he didn't. But believe me, I could tell he was intrigued."

Anne fingered the soft blanket beneath her hands as she secretly scanned the crowd for Henry. The moon cast the faces looking skyward a ghostly white, and when the rockets exploded, it was nearly as light as day. Here and there the glow of a cigar flared, but none were held by her former husband.

"Don't you think it strange that Alex seems, well, interested in me?" Anne said.

"He's doing it to annoy Henry. That man delights in making people annoyed."

Anne let out a laugh. "That's not very flattering. I suppose you never thought he could be truly interested in courting me."

Beatrice looked immediately contrite, but Anne laughed her expression away. "You're probably right. I've sensed a kind of ingenuineness about his attentions."

"You can be certain of one thing," Beatrice said. "Henry has absolutely no interest in me. He couldn't take his eyes off you all evening, and looked particularly annoyed when you were dancing with Alex. This is going to be like taking a lamb to slaughter."

Anne grimaced. "I wish you wouldn't be quite so graphic."

"He deserves whatever we dish out, Anne. That and more. I'll admit he's fantastic looking. Rather too handsome. But inside he's rotten. He has to be to have done what he did to you."

Anne wrapped her arms around her knees and cursed the fact that she could not maintain her anger for more than a few moments. Just hours ago she was ready to skewer the man, and now the fact that he was interested in her made her heart flutter. She was pathetic, Anne realized with disgust, to be so swayed by a handsome face.

"You have to keep me strong," Anne said. "Remind me again and again what a wretch he is."

Beatrice groaned. "You haven't a devious bone in your body, have you? The man ruined your life, Anne. He doesn't deserve mercy," she said forcefully.

For a while, Anne "oohed" and "aahhed" with the rest of the crowd as the fireworks exploded above them. A shift in the wind swept the pungent smoke from the fireworks toward the shore to blend with the strong scent of rotting seaweed, a combination that sent Anne into a state of melancholy. She had always so looked forward to summers and Newport, and nothing had ever come out the way she'd thought. Her sisters had been so much older, they rarely made time for her as they flitted from one event to another. Newport's harshness never seemed to touch her family until it pummeled her with a vengeance. Sitting on the beach, breathing in that summer scent, made her heart ache for a time when she was too young and too naive to even imagine the events of the past two years.

"Oh, it stinks all of a sudden," Beatrice said, wrinkling her nose.

"It's the seaweed," Anne said, sounding wistful. "I know it stinks, but I love that smell."

"Goodness, Anne. Your nose must be blocked." She swallowed heavily, the smell getting to her delicate stomach. "I think I shall be sick," she said, holding her hand over her nose.

"Come on, then. Let's find your brother and get you home. Do you know where he is?"

"Thomas is probably hovering over that Carlisle girl. That's as nauseating as this stench."

Anne laughed and helped her friend to her feet before bending down to retrieve the sandy blanket, taking care not to spread sand onto their neighbors. "I think the way your brother acts around Miss Carlisle is sweet," Anne said.

"It's disgusting."

"Now who sounds bitter?" Anne said lightly. "You've simply never been in love."

"What I've seen of love does not ingratiate me to it." Beatrice shook out her skirts and began trudging through the soft sand toward the spot where the Carlisles were sitting, Anne following in her wake. As they walked, the sky was brilliantly lighted by the final display. Nearly all eyes were wide and pinned to the fireworks, so it was for that reason that Anne noticed a man standing alone, his eyes not on the display at all.

Alex Henley stood at the edge of the crowd, his waistcoat undone and his tie loosened. He looked, at that moment, every bit as handsome as Henry, Anne thought, standing there, hands resting loosely on hips, eyes intense and almost angry-looking. Anne followed his gaze, curious about what held Alex's attention, and came to—Beatrice. Her friend was walking carefully among the blankets strewn on the beach with her head down and so did not see Alex until she was almost upon him. He spoke and Anne watched as Beatrice stiffened her back. She was too far away to hear the exchange, but it was clear that it was not a friendly one.

"What was that all about?" Anne asked when she caught up to her.

"He actually had the nerve to question my judgment about coming here unescorted. I pointed out that my brother was just a few feet away. Imagine him lecturing me on good moral behavior. Of all things. I think that man makes a point of harassing me."

"He does seem to enjoy antagonizing you."

"If he dislikes me so much, he should keep his feelings to himself," Beatrice said, and Anne was alarmed to hear her voice thicken as if tears were threatening. She was relieved when she peered at Beatrice and saw no evidence of any true distress.

"I don't think he dislikes you," Anne said. "Perhaps he was truly concerned." Anne saw hope flare before Beatrice put on a frown.

"The only thing that man is concerned about is himself." She marched through the sand to her brother, anger apparent in every step she took.

Anne looked back to see if Alex was still about, but he was gone.

Henry loved sailing at night. There was something healing about sailing on the bay when it was smooth, reflecting the moon and distant shore lights. The only sound was the sail snapping softly, the creaking of the lines, and the hull slapping against the calm water.

Sea Cliff was located on the southeastern tip of Jamestown, on what was more a bluff than a cliff. Henry had always thought the name of the house reflected his grandfather's ego more than the house itself, which was considered modest even when it was built in the 1870s. The rocky shore was topped by a sandy layer that had been scourged by years of hurricanes and nor'easters. The clapboard-and-stone cottage looked out over the bay toward Newport. A small protective cove with a sandy beach curved gently toward the house before abruptly ending at an outcropping of dark gray slate. Pine trees surrounded the property, making it look more like the coast of Maine than Rhode Island.

Though only a short sail across the bay, Jamestown was worlds away from Newport. The tiny island had just begun attracting the rich, but it was a different sort of wealth that moved here to build their summer cottages. Jamestown was the place for people who found Newport society pretentious and absurd. It attracted summer residents who were artists and intellectuals. The town boasted three luxury waterfront hotels and little more. Only one street was lit by lamps at night, and only during the summer months, as Yankee frugality dictated.

No roads led to Sea Cliff; the only way to access the cottage was by boat. It was a true escape from New York, a place where Wall Street and investments were not discussed or even thought about—at least for a few days. Henry always felt the world slip away when he dropped anchor in his little cove below Sea Cliff, and this night was no different.

The cottage was a dark, looming shadow but for a single light on the wraparound porch. Henry kept only four servants: a cook, two housemaids, and an all-around man, Peleg Brown, who, oddly enough given his name, had only one leg. When he was twenty-two, Peleg Brown lost most of his right leg during the War Between the States. Brown was already rowing out to him, the splash of the oars loud in the silence. The man was uncanny when it came to knowing when Henry was coming home, and he claimed he could smell him arriving. That this same man didn't smell a dead possum rotting beneath the porch one summer never stopped him from making such declarations.

"Mr. Brown. Good evening," Henry called.

"And to you, sir," Brown said as he pulled up beside the catboat.

Henry climbed into the boat and took the oars from Brown, who suffered from arthritis but would never admit to being in pain. The first time Henry took over the job of rowing back to shore, Henry claimed it was because he was getting soft and needed the exercise. Brown had glared at him, his beady brown eyes nearly disappearing beneath his bushy eyebrows. And then he'd handed over the oars without comment. That Brown didn't argue told Henry just how much pain the older man was in, and from that day on, Henry made it a habit of rowing himself to and from his boat.

"How is the work on the foundation going?"

"It's not going atall," Brown said. "Workers got pulled off the job for some emergency, so I was told." The way Brown relayed the information, it seemed he doubted the existence of an "emergency."

"Mr. Owen is here," he said without preamble, and Henry could swear the man enjoyed relating bad news.

"My grandfather is here? Perhaps I should return to Newport."

Brown let out a cackle. "He's here with a great bunch of people. A nurse, a doctor, and that skinny little weasel Williamson. He was sniffin' around the cellar. Probably looking for some hooch. Got that ruddy look about him."

"Williamson does not drink, Brown."

The older man sniffed in disbelief. Brown had no respect for a man who didn't work with his hands—or at least allow himself to get dusty once in a while, which Williamson apparently did not. Henry won Brown over only after coming back into the house, hands bleeding, body covered with dust, after helping workers build a bulkhead to stop Sea Cliff from sliding into the bay.

"Did he say why, after staying away from Sea Cliff

for nearly twenty years, he's decided to pay a visit?"
Henry asked.

"Didn't say a word to me, except to ask where you
were. To be honest, he has the look of a man with
one foot in the grave."

That sobered Henry up. As much as he told himself
he hated his grandfather, he did not want to see the
old man die. Without his grandfather to battle against,
it would almost be like a prize-fighter finally defeating
his greatest contender. He could admit that he enjoyed
their sparring of late, like the grudging respect he'd
seen in his grandfather's eyes the last time they'd spoken—or rather shouted at one another. The thought
that his grandfather might have come to Sea Cliff to
see it one last time—or worse, to die here—was unexpectedly crushing.

Williamson met him at the door holding an oil lamp,
looking macabre in the eerie light that cast his long,
thin face in shadows. "Your grandfather is here," he
said unnecessarily.

"So I heard. The old man doesn't believe in writing
before he visits?"

Williamson had no answer for that, but stepped
back as if condescending to allow Henry to enter his
own home. Henry gave him a sour look and purposefully strode into his home, casually draping his coat
and hat on the newel post. Already he could feel his
stomach clench nervously at the thought of his grandfather being in his home. He had not seen the old
man in two years; not since signing the papers that
sealed his ownership of Sea Cliff. They'd written to
each other frequently, however, and Henry suspected
his grandfather was keeping tabs on him—and on the
progress he was making on Sea Cliff's renovations.

In his letters, Henry refused to give Arthur any information about the old house. He'd long suspected
that the inordinate delays and setbacks he'd experienced could be attributed to his grandfather. As frus-

trating as it was, Henry was curious and a bit bemused
by the old man's antics. While he'd not resorted to
out-and-out sabotage, his grandfather had managed to
delay the project by at least six months. Work crews
quit without notice, two architects suddenly grew too
busy to design additions despite the exorbitant price
Henry was willing to pay, and building supplies would
mysteriously disappear en route. Henry met each delay
with a sense of fatalism and a tip of his hat to his
grandfather, who was undoubtedly rubbing his gnarled
hands together with glee. Now that the house was
safely reinforced, Henry found that he was in no great
hurry to complete the project. No hurricane would rip
it from its seating now. The rest could wait until his
grandfather was cold in his grave, turning over at the
thought of Henry happily living in the place Arthur
had so detested.

"Mr. Owen asked that he be awakened when you
return home. I've instructed the nurse to do so. If you
will follow me," Williamson said with a slight bow.

Henry worked his jaw a bit, not liking the feeling
that he was being usurped in his own home, but he
followed the elderly servant anyway, curious as to
what was so important, it could not wait until morning.
He idly wondered what his grandfather thought of Sea
Cliff. The place was a mess with half-finished projects
around every corner. Stacks of wood and tile filled the
large entry hall, ladders lay on the floor where a fine
apple-wood cabinet once stood, and the air held the
distinct odor of dust churned up after decades of lying
dormant. And this was a vast improvement over what
Henry had found when he'd first entered the house
two years ago—a family of raccoons and ten genera-
tions of mice scurrying about. Henry had concentrated
on the exterior, protecting the house from erosion,
replacing the cedar shingles on the sides and roof,
and repairing most of the windows. Progress had been
maddeningly slow.

Henry followed in Williamson's wake up the wide, carpetless staircase, their feet causing the steps beneath them to groan and creak. The thick forest-green runner Henry planned to install was rolled up in the entry hall waiting for a time when the house wasn't choking on its own dust.

Not surprisingly, Williamson led Henry to his own room, where he found his grandfather sitting up in bed, a red robe giving his pale face a hint of rosiness. The room was well-lit, Henry noted. His frugal grandfather was not frugal with other people's money, it seemed.

"The house looks wonderful," Arthur said, his words more slurred than usual, his tone hinting at nothing. But Henry knew his grandfather's dry sense of humor and smiled.

"I've had a terrible time keeping workers about," he said, just as straight-faced. "Have you come for an inspection?"

"No. I've come here to die."

Something in his voice or perhaps his eyes told Henry he was serious. His grandfather had acquired a flare for the dramatic, and Henry pointedly refused to be affected by his grandfather's pronouncement. "Why here? Good God, Grandfather, you've always hated Sea Cliff."

"I lied."

Henry gave Arthur a hard stare. "What if I don't allow it? This is my home, after all."

"Sea Cliff won't be yours, not truly, until I'm six feet deep in the cold earth. You know it as well as I."

"You're quite wrong," Henry said. "Sea Cliff is mine."

Arthur's hands moved restlessly over the white sheets. He seemed almost to sag into the pillow, as if he'd expended every ounce of energy he'd had. Instantly a nurse Henry hadn't noticed was by Arthur's side.

"You've overdone it, Mr. Owen," she said with soft authority. She was an older woman, plump and grandmotherly, with soft gray hair poking out from beneath a crisp white cap. Arthur gave the woman a tender smile unlike any Henry had ever seen, and he was momentarily stunned by it. "Now, that's quite enough. You can continue with this pleasant conversation tomorrow morning." There was a glint of humor in her voice, and Arthur's smile widened.

"She is a dragon," Arthur said with obvious affection.

Henry looked at the nurse and was surprised to see the glitter of tears there after she'd turned away from Arthur. After she'd left, Arthur said, "If I wasn't dying, I'd marry her." Arthur looked at Henry's stunned expression and laughed softly before growing somber.

"Everything I've done, Henry, *everything* was for a reason." Then he closed his eyes, dismissing his grandson.

Henry stood there for a moment, trying to understand what his grandfather had meant by that cryptic last statement. Was the old man trying to apologize for a lifetime of cruelties? Or was he simply trying to excuse his behavior?

When Henry let himself out of the room, the nurse was standing there, dry-eyed and obviously waiting for him.

"Is he truly dying?" Henry knew he didn't sound like a bereaved grandson and he didn't care.

"He is. He suffered a minor seizure about a month ago. The doctors say the next one will likely kill him. He's very weak. Much weaker than he appears."

"He gets strength trying to antagonize me," Henry said.

She gave him a look as if she couldn't quite believe he was talking about the same man she knew. "You are all he talks about," she said. "He's so proud of you."

"Nurse . . ."

"Mrs. Bradley. I nursed my husband for five years before the good Lord took him from me. After he was gone, I felt a bit lost and decided to become a nurse to other poor souls."

Henry suspected then that Mrs. Bradley was one of those people who is so good, they cannot see evil in others. "Mrs. Bradley, thank you for caring for my grandfather."

"It's times like this when I question my decision to become a nurse. Such a good man. But I suppose he's lived a good life. A long life. God willing we are all so lucky."

Henry tried as best as he could not to look completely stunned by her description of his grandfather. A good man? Arthur Owen? All his life he'd thought of his grandfather as one of the meanest, coldest, most ruthless men he'd ever known. Granted, his opinion of his grandfather had softened over the years, but he certainly never would have used the word "good" to describe him.

"It is late. I believe I will retire. I'll see my grandfather in the morning. If he's up to it."

"Oh, I'm certain Mr. Owen will be. You know, his doctors were opposed to his traveling here, but he'd hear nothing against it. Perhaps I'm overstepping my bounds, but I sense a bit of an estrangement between you and your grandfather?"

"A bit," Henry said wryly.

"I thought as much. I sensed a certain desperation to his need to come here. I think he means to make amends."

"Mrs. Bradley, I do appreciate your concern for my grandfather and his well-being. But the rift between my grandfather and me is rather large. The man you have come to know is not the man I have known my entire life."

The woman's dimpled cheeks drooped. "I see."

"I'm glad." Henry bowed a good-night and turned to go to the only other bedroom on the second floor with furniture in it, thinking darkly that Williamson better not have taken up residence there.

From the Journal of Arthur Owen

It must be difficult for you to hear such things about your mother from your grandfather, to know that such things happened, to know we both betrayed your father in the most horrid of ways. When I think back to those days, it is as if I am talking about another person. Certainly I could never have done the things I most definitely did. My only excuse is that I was temporarily mad and it is that madness I am trying to explain. Divorce yourself from the fact that the woman I speak about is your mother and perhaps you can understand my obsession. As I write, it is as if I am recalling something that happened yesterday. I can still remember with painful clarity the way I felt in those first days . . . and all the days to follow.

After the episode in the library, Elizabeth became increasingly publicly affectionate to your father. I realized, of course, that she was trying to make me jealous. She told me later, she laughed about the way I would turn from them as she draped herself around Walter. Poor Walter was embarrassed by his beautiful fiancée's sudden affection, turning beet red and stammering and finally pushing her away. He even apologized to me once, and I wanted to grab him and tell him then what she'd done, what she was doing to us both. She ignored me for three days and I was as relieved as I was annoyed. I missed her, you see. And I was jealous, horribly so, even though I was fully aware of her game.

Then, the night of the third day, she knocked on my bedroom door wearing only a thin nightgown and robe, claiming to have been frightened by a sound from outside. Her hair was down and was more beautiful than I imagined. She clutched at me, she laid her head on my chest for comfort, she told me how she only felt safe with me. And I stood there, one hand on the door frame, the other still on the doorknob, shaking. She kissed my chest through my nightshirt. She kissed my neck and I stood there like a man being tortured. I can still hear her voice, that throaty whisper, begging me to kiss her. So I did. And more, before pushing her away like a man gone mad. I told her I hated her. I begged her to leave me alone. I reminded her and myself that she would marry Walter. I shook her until her head snapped back and forth, until I thought I might kill her.

If she had laughed at me or even smiled, I would have slammed the door in her face. But when the storm was over and I told her to leave, she started to cry—soft, silent tears that fell from eyes filled with torment. She told me she loved me, that she was ashamed by her behavior. Didn't I love her even a little? Didn't I like it when we kissed? If you could have seen her. Oh, God, even now, knowing what I do, I don't think I could have resisted her. You cannot imagine.

I pulled her into my room, shut the door, led her to my bed, and loved her. She was a virgin and I loved her then so much, I was ready to tell Walter that it was I who would marry her, not him. When I told Elizabeth as much, she looked at me as if I had told her a great joke. That is when she laughed and told me I was soft, much softer than she'd thought. I'd given into a woman's tears, she said, and not even Walter had done that. She was quite delighted with me, but of course could not marry me. I was too old and much too serious.

She thanked me and left.

I vowed never to touch her again. Even as I made my vow, I knew I would break it. I was desperately in love and actually believed I could make her love me more than Walter. I didn't know she was incapable of love, I only knew I would die loving her. It appears, in at least that, I was right.

Chapter Nine

It would never dare rain on a Poole lawn party, and as she had most years, Mother Nature gave the powerful family a cloudless day and a soft breeze off the bay. Three hundred guests milled around the grounds, decorated with sterling silver pears and fourteen-karat gold apples dangling from Lester Poole's cherry trees. Servants were decked out in silver and gold, carrying silver trays laden with solid gold champagne flutes. It was the most lavish party of the season, one that the rest of the cottagers would spend thousands of dollars trying to outdo. Lester Poole, dressed in a silly white suit with a large gilt-and-silver embroidered crest, strutted about his lawn like some prized rooster among his lowly flock of hens.

Beatrice didn't think anyone was looking when she gave the man a disgusted look before placing a tart upon a tiny silver plate. When she heard a deep chuckle coming from behind her, she blushed crimson before peeking a look to see who had discovered her disdain for their host. Alex Henley leaned against a large beechwood tree, arms folded around his chest, legs crossed at the ankles.

"Don't tell me you aren't impressed by this show of wealth, Miss Leyden," he said, sweeping an arm at all the grandeur.

Hiding a smile, Beatrice turned fully toward Alex. "I prefer things a bit less . . . obvious."

He pushed away from the tree and walked toward

her, hands stuffed into his pockets, looking boyish and charming, an effect Beatrice was certain he was aware of. Beatrice hated it when he looked boyish and charming, because of all the men she knew, Alexander Henley was not boyish and rarely charming, at least in her opinion. He was a rake, a man a woman could never take seriously, a man who would break a girl's heart if she were ever foolish enough to fall in love with him. Since the day she'd met him two summers ago when Henry had been "courting" Anne, Beatrice recognized him for what he was and had made every effort to let him know exactly what she thought of him. Well, not all her thoughts, she amended. She would never tell him that her heart nearly jumped out of her chest every time she saw him, that she'd actually wondered—fleetingly, she insisted—what it would be like for him to kiss her. She'd even considered allowing him to court her, just for the fun of it, knowing her heart was protected because she knew what he was like. But the truth was, her heart was more vulnerable than she would have liked, for each time he said something unkind to her, it cut her far more deeply than she let on.

As always, the mere sight of him made her blush, which made her angry, which made her appear as if his company was unwanted. And, of course, it was unwanted, she insisted. Her heart, pounding ridiculously hard, told her differently, despite her fierce frown. His smile faltered a bit at the sight of her frown and a look of annoyance passed over his face.

"Where is your latest admirer?" he asked, making a great show of looking around.

"I haven't the slightest idea whom you mean," Beatrice said honestly.

"Henry. Have you seen him?"

Beatrice raised her eyebrows at the thought of Henry Owen admiring her. It was obvious that Henry only had eyes for Anne—as did Alex, Beatrice reminded herself.

"Mr. Owen is not an admirer, and no, I have not seen him. Perhaps if you are looking for him, you will do better to look for Anne Foster."

Alex flashed her a smile revealing his startlingly white teeth. "Jealous?"

Beatrice lifted her chin and continued frowning. "Mr. Owen and I had a disagreement, so I hardly think I would be jealous."

"A lovers' spat already?"

Beatrice wanted to groan out her frustration with his maddening taunts. "Go away." She tried to maintain her frown, but his smile and teasing were so disarming, she lost the battle and smiled back at him.

"If you continue to smile at me like that, I'm afraid Henry will get the completely wrong idea. Aren't you afraid he'll see us together?" he asked, raising his eyebrows suggestively.

"You're impossible. You know very well Mr. Owen has no interest in me romantically. And if he did, I would immediately redirect his attentions. I find I cannot stomach the man. His friends," she said with meaning, "are nearly as intolerable."

Alex gave Beatrice a shrug, accepting her assessment of him, but suddenly sobered. "Henry's not the man you think he is. His reasons for marrying Anne are complicated."

Beatrice nearly snorted her disbelief. "I know all about his reasons for marrying Anne, Mr. Henley, and they are not at all complicated. I believe greed and heartlessness sum them up quite nicely."

Alex rocked back on his heels and looked toward the sparkling blue bay just beyond the Poole lawn. "Perhaps you are right. But if you must blame anyone, blame me. It was all my idea, you see."

"All of it?"

Alex's face hardened. "All of it. Henry doesn't have

a mean bone in his body, so I lent him one of mine."
He let out a bitter laugh. "It was just a game to me,
a way to help my friend. A diversion. It made him
sick. Literally sick. He couldn't keep a thing down the
week before the wedding. He even claimed to have
feelings for Anne, said she was like a friend and how
could he betray a friend. I gave him the courage."

For some reason, Beatrice felt as if her heart was
breaking, not for her friend, but for Alex. She didn't
want to know he was capable of devising such a cold
scheme. "Henry is not a child. He has a mind of his
own."

"True. But I can honestly say that if it weren't for
me, he wouldn't have walked down that aisle." When
he finally turned his gaze back to Beatrice, his eyes
were filled with regret, but his jaw was clenched, his
body taut, as if he were bracing for a blow.

"Is that why you are pursuing her now? Because
you feel guilty?"

He smiled, wiping away any deeper emotion he
might have been feeling. Instantly the rake was back.
"I'm pursuing her because she's beautiful. I adore
beautiful women."

Beatrice had to look away for fear he would see the
jealousy and hurt in her eyes, and she almost died
right there when he spoke again.

"Not jealous again, are you?"

She gave him a scathing look. "Hardly. I'm simply
trying to decide who is more loathsome, Henry or
you."

The smile remained on his fine mouth, but his eyes
held no hint of emotion. Giving her a slight bow, he
said, "I assure you, it is I."

Beatrice watched him walk away and fought the ridiculous urge to call him back. Instead, she crammed
the forgotten tart into her mouth—whole. Placing the
small plate on the tray of a passing servant, Beatrice
went in search of Anne, feeling horrid. She had man-

aged to alienate Henry and Alex within three days, severely damaging their hopes of fulfilling The Plan. The two men were not stupid, and certainly they would suspect something if Anne suddenly became enamored with Henry. Perhaps, though, her obvious animosity toward the two men could be used in their favor. She could pretend to be outraged by Anne's attraction to Henry. Yes. That could work.

The lawn was crowded with people, many gathered around the tennis and croquet courts. The *thwack* of the tennis ball carried clearly over the softly playing orchestra and murmuring of the guests. Beatrice, feeling crushed in by the tennis courts, had left Anne with her mother watching a match between Poole's son and a college chum. When she returned, they were nowhere in sight. She made her way through the crowd and stopped short when she spied her friend sitting on a bench at the edge of the lawn and having what looked like an intimate conversation with her former husband. Beatrice smiled secretly to herself, congratulating Anne on her deviousness. She made her way closer to the pair, hoping to catch a part of their conversation or at least witness Anne's performance a bit closer. Anne was looking up at Henry, her lovely face animated, and Beatrice let out a sigh of relief. At least Anne was remembering their plan, she thought, and reminded herself to compliment Anne on her fine acting ability.

Anne wanted to leave the party. She was beginning to hate her new popularity, the subtle questions from the women, the not-so-subtle suggestions from some men. She'd been blatantly propositioned four times in the past two days, and each time by married men. The nerve of them to think she had signed away her morals when she signed that divorce decree. If she had been a more sophisticated woman, she would have laughed at the men, or flirted and rejected them with grace.

Instead, she turned beet red, stammered something—
she couldn't remember what had actually come out of
her mouth the first three times—and practically ran
from the scene. The fourth time she was better prepared and, still stammering, said, "No, thank you."
She cringed each time she thought about how very
polite she'd been.

It was all incredibly foreign for her to have men
pursuing her so openly, a sudden immersion into a
world for which she was completely unskilled and unprepared. Before she'd met Henry, Anne rarely had
the chance to flirt with boys. Now, these *men* expected
her to fully know a game that she hadn't been given
the rules to. The latest rumor, or so Helen had told
her, was that she was an ice queen, something that
made her even more desirable. She was becoming an
unattainable prize. It was as disgusting as it was heady.

"Are you telling me that these men actually expect
me to . . . to . . . carry on with them without the
benefit of wedding vows?"

Helen had given her a kind smile. "That's exactly
what they expect."

"Why, that's terrible. These men are all married."

"Oh, dear, what do you think goes on in those
yachts anchored off shore? All those husbands who
sail to Newport each weekend and never step on
solid ground?"

"I simply assumed they liked being on the water."

"I'm certain they do, given the activities," Helen
had said with good humor. "I don't know firsthand,
but I've heard that some men bring in girls from New
York. Chorus girls." She'd said this last in a whisper.

Anne's eyes widened in shock. She'd thought the
past two years had wiped her clean of naiveté, but
she was learning quickly that she was still impossibly
innocent. Perhaps it was her imagination, but as Anne
stood watching the tennis match, it seemed as if everyone present was discussing her. Her stuffy New York

town house was beginning to look like paradise. Anne slipped away from the crush around the courts and found shade away from the guests. She sat facing the bay on a wrought-iron bench placed beneath a leafy Japanese maple tree and tried to fight the strangest urge to cry. She'd not cried, not a good head-clearing cry, since leaving New York. The events of the last few days had sent her emotions plummeting one moment and soaring the next. And at the center of it all was Henry. She could blame every tear on him.

"May I sit with you?"

Anne was so startled to hear Henry's voice, she jumped and let out a little squeak.

"Sorry to frighten you," he said, and sat down before getting an answer from her.

"You may not sit with me," she said, even as she recalled that she was supposed to be encouraging him. Oh, their ridiculous plan would never work.

Henry ignored her and sat silently next to her, making her want to flee. Finally, she looked at him and wished she hadn't, for suddenly she was twenty-one again and being courted by the most handsome man in Newport. His dark brown hair was tousled by the breeze, his face tan, making his gray eyes appear even more brilliant. He gave her a tentative smile and Anne suddenly realized that he was nervous. It was a liberating thought.

He cleared his throat. "I'd like to talk to you. We haven't spoken since the wedding, really."

"We spoke at the Wetmore ball," Anne said coolly.

"Yes, well, I didn't know it was you, so that hardly counts." He examined his hands and Anne noticed— quite against her will—how strong they looked. Clean and manicured, they were not elegant as much as they were capable, and she had a startlingly clear memory of how they felt upon her ribcage just below her breasts. She should not have brought up the Wetmore ball.

"I should have made it a point to talk to you long ago. I handled things between us about as poorly as a man could. I would never expect you to forgive me, but I do want you to know how sorry I am for what happened."

Throughout his speech, Anne kept her eyes on a schooner, its crisp white sails stark and pure against the harsh blueness of the bay. When he was done, she turned to him, all thoughts of plans and games gone. "I don't know what you expect me to say. I would think you'd be sorry, but that doesn't change what happened. It doesn't give me back my family or my reputation. Or my life. If you feel better for having apologized, then I am glad, Henry. But it changes nothing."

He nodded, as if she'd said precisely what he'd expected.

"That's one of mine," he said, inclining his head toward the schooner.

"It's very pretty," Anne said automatically.

An uncomfortable silence grew between them, one that was foreign to Anne. She felt an odd heightened awareness that she could only attribute to knowing what it was like to kiss this man. She'd never noticed his hands before, never wished in anything but a vague way that he would touch her. Now she knew what it felt to be dragged against his solid form, to feel his kisses as if he were drugging her. At this moment, she wished she could sit beside him as she had before. If Henry and she had anything, it was that they'd felt comfortable with one another.

He finally broke the silence. "I want you to understand. I need you to know why I did what I did."

Anne swallowed the sudden thickness that formed in her throat. "There is no excuse . . ." She could not finish her sentence, mortified with the thought of weeping in front of him.

At that moment, Henry had never hated anything

more than he hated himself. He watched as Anne swallowed in a wretched attempt to stem her tears, the slim column of her throat moving in a desperate spasm. He knew he could apologize every day until he died, and it would mean nothing, for he could not change what he'd done. It was indefensible, and yet he sat on this bench and asked that he be able to explain. How could he, when at the time he'd been insanely obsessed? How could he make real for her the terror he felt at the thought of losing Sea Cliff? The answer was simple. He could not, though he desperately wanted to. He knew that if he wasn't careful, a new obsession would take over his life. Already Anne was on his mind far more than she should be. He watched as a silken feather of hair brushed her cheek, and fought the urge to run the back of his hand there. He could tell she was trying to ignore him. She sat erect, every muscle tense, likely wishing he would go away.

"Let me show you, Anne," he said in a rush of words. "I swear I will leave you alone forever if only you let me show you Sea Cliff." Suddenly, what had been unthinkable became the answer to what he sought. If she saw Sea Cliff, if he could somehow convey what it meant to him, she would understand why he'd done what he'd done.

Anne looked at him, confusion clear in her face. "Sea Cliff?"

He smiled. "It's the reason for all of this. Let me show it to you."

Myriad emotions passed through her face before she finally nodded, the tiniest hint of a smile on her lips.

"He apologized?" Beatrice asked, bubbling over from the news. The two women sat on Beatrice's bed, their skirts heaped negligently around them.

"Yes. I felt like a spider luring a fly into my trap," Anne said, trying to match the excitement Beatrice clearly felt. She'd never admit to her friend that she'd actually been tempted to tell Henry she'd forgiven him, not after all the help Beatrice had given her. It was preposterous to feel anything but animosity toward Henry, but when he'd said he was sorry, when he'd looked at her as if his world would stop if she turned away from him, she was the one who felt like a helpless fly.

After Henry had left her alone, Anne thought back to their brief courtship to forcefully remind herself he wasn't what he seemed. When he was out of sight, she could think reasonably again. She made herself think about every kind thing he'd told her when he was courting her, every laugh, every dance, every touch that made her feel as if she were the luckiest woman alive. Lies, every bit of it. It was maddening, for when she was with him, it was difficult to hate Henry, to see him for what he truly was. It was difficult not to think of that kiss that haunted her still.

There was one question, though, she had no answer to: Why was he trying to mend fences with her? Henry must have an ulterior motive. A man like Henry Owen did nothing on a whim, and she refused to believe it was simply guilt that drove him. Perhaps he regretted the large divorce settlement he'd agreed to and planned to renegotiate it. Money had driven him before and might be behind his newfound remorse. Whatever his motives, Anne was ready this time. She'd not succumb to him again. She'd not be made a fool of again.

"He certainly is making no secret that he is interested in you, is he?"

"What I don't understand is why," Anne said, frowning so severely that a little line developed between her brows.

"Shall I take you to a mirror? You are beautiful, Anne."

"Then I shall gain every ounce I lost. That will cure

his interest," Anne said bitterly. "Sometimes I wonder if we'd still be married if I looked then the way I look now."

"He married you for money," Beatrice said quickly and forcefully. "It could have been anyone he married. You were simply the one who said yes."

"Why didn't you warn me?"

"I tried to, remember? You accused me of being jealous."

Anne buried her head in her hands and laughed. "Oh, I forgot." She dropped her hands to reveal eyes filled with merriment. "You hinted that it was rumored that Henry went to his grandfather for money and had been rejected, and I defended his honor."

"Your exact words were, 'You're just afraid you'll end up a spinster and cannot stand the fact I am going to be married.' "

Anne shook her head and laughed. "I believe I used the words 'old maid.' I am sorry, Bea."

She waved a hand, dismissing Anne's apology. "Water under the bridge."

"Speaking of water, he wants me to sail with him to Sea Cliff."

"His house? Alone?" Beatrice's eyes widened with shock, but it was clear she thought the idea wonderful.

"I thought you could come along," Anne said, ignoring her friend's look of disappointment. As a divorced woman, Anne had far more freedom than she had as a single girl. Before, she never would have dreamed of stepping aboard a boat with Henry unescorted, but now she could do nearly as she pleased without raising eyebrows. It was Beatrice who took the largest risk by going along, making Anne feel guilty for even asking, for she knew Beatrice would dismiss Anne's concerns.

"But I'd only get in the way. Just think of the progress you could make if you were alone with him."

"I know it could be risky for you, but my reputation

would be inalterably shattered if I go by myself," she said, only half serious. The truth was, she was afraid to be alone with Henry, afraid her resolve would weaken beneath that charmingly lopsided smile of his.

"Ah, yes, what would people think of the ice queen going on a tryst with her former husband." Beatrice laughed so hard, she didn't even notice Anne grab a pillow until she had a mouth full of feathers.

"You've gone too far, Henry. Just what do you hope to accomplish by showing Anne Sea Cliff? Do you expect her to fall at your feet?"

The two men sat on the Reading Room's porch surrounded by other men who had sneaked away from the Poole picnic and wives who were taking gleeful note of the extravagance employed for the fete. More than one conversation centered on just how they could afford to outdo Poole, fully knowing that their wives would demand it. Alex lounged on one of the chairs, leaning back with his hands folded across his flat stomach. Henry sat, elbows on their small table, hands buried in his hair.

"I don't want Anne to fall at my feet," Henry said into the table. "I want her to understand why I did what I did."

Alex rolled his eyes. "What will you say to her? Point to Sea Cliff and say, 'This is the reason I destroyed your life'? Frankly, Henry, if I were her, I don't know whether I'd laugh or kill you. It's not as if that shack you so grandly call Sea Cliff is another Château sur Mer. And just what is this ridiculous need you have to extract forgiveness?"

"Damned if I know." Henry rubbed his forehead with the heels of his hands before dropping them to the table to curl around his brandy snifter. Why couldn't he leave well enough alone with Anne? For some reason, she was consuming him, or rather what he'd done to her was consuming him. For two years, he'd fooled himself into thinking that his farce of a marriage was over. It had been remarkably painless, an ugly episode endured with only favorable results. Sea Cliff was saved, he was wealthy beyond many a man's dreams, he was single and sought after by some of the most beautiful well-connected women on the East Coast.

Anne's return had jarred him far more than he would have believed, and forced him to realize that he wasn't the cold bastard he'd tried to convince himself he was.

Alex drummed his fingers against his waistcoat. "You know, Henry, I let things go this far because I figured you needed to ease your guilty conscience," he said in a tone that told Henry how ridiculous he thought that idea. "But if you continue to pursue her, you will make a laughingstock of yourself."

"I am not pursuing her," Henry said tightly.

"And roosters lay eggs. I've seen the way you look at her."

"Every man looks at her the same way. She's beautiful."

"And she was once yours. Is that what this is all about? You had her and lost her and now she's become an unattainable beauty?"

"Shut up, Alex," Henry said, not quite as good-naturedly as he'd intended. Alex was beginning to get on his nerves because he was hitting closer to the mark than Henry liked. He'd never intended to strike up any sort of relationship with Anne, but it seemed that he was continuously seeking her out. He knew he was foolish to bring her to Sea Cliff. "If I'm not mistaken, you are the one pursuing her."

"You know me better than that. I wanted to know how obsessed over her you were becoming. I fear I have my answer."

Henry gave Alex a hard stare. "You are a reprobate," he said quite seriously.

His friend smiled and shrugged. "Here's another question for you. We've agreed you are insane for asking her. But why on God's green earth did she say yes to going to Sea Cliff? Think about it. Here is a woman you married for nefarious reasons. A woman you coldly divorced. She must hate you. Any woman would. And yet, she's willing to sail to see the very summer house that started this all in the first place. I find that rather odd."

"I had thought that, as well. But I was quite convincing."

Alex raised an eyebrow. "Really," he said in a tone that conveyed he doubted Henry's charm was that potent.

"All right. Say she has ulterior motives for going. What could they possibly be?"

Alex sat up. "Money, my dear friend. Take a look around you. This city is dripping with money, and very little of it is hers. She has few prospects of getting more unless she marries, and that is highly unlikely given her status as a divorced woman. Certainly she cannot be content with the settlement you granted her."

"I was more than fair," Henry said, hearing the doubt in his voice. "In any case, Anne doesn't strike me as a gold digger."

"You've destroyed her world, Henry. Why is she being so friendly to you?"

"I would hardly characterize Anne's behavior as friendly."

Alex took a long pull from his brandy snifter and looked at Henry over the brim.

"I haven't figured it out yet, Henry, but that girl and her friend are up to something. Mark my words."

Chapter Ten

The maid, a girl borrowed from Beatrice, tugged sharply at Anne's laces, making her gasp.

"Sorry, ma'am," the girl said cheerfully. "Gettin' a bit harder to squeeze you down to eighteen inches."

Anne remained silent, but panic gripped her heart. Was she getting fat? After the maid left, Anne hurried to the mirror and examined her face. Was it puffier than before? She pushed her chin down, creating a false double chin, a graphic reminder of what she used to look like. That face that she'd lived with nearly all her life, a face she'd smiled at and sometimes liked, now made her stomach wrench. She never wanted to be that girl again, a girl who could only attract a fortune hunter. Hadn't her mother said as much when she gave her a hug after Henry had asked her parents permission for her hand in marriage?

"I was so afraid for you Anne," Francine had said. "Newport seems to attract all sorts of men looking to marry money without a care for the bride. But to attract a man like Mr. Owen, with all his millions, I must say you've done remarkably well for yourself. Far better than I dared hope."

At the time, Anne had glowed beneath what she'd seen as her mother's praise. Now that memory filled her with shame. How pathetic she'd been, how desperate for even a hint of praise from her mother. With five pretty and well-married older sisters, Anne had constantly come up short when comparisons were made. Now she was the black sheep of the family, but she was beautiful. Now she could have any man she wanted—any married or disreputable man, she amended to herself. Anne knew that if she gained back the weight she'd lost, those propositions she'd been getting of late, as distasteful as they were, would disappear. And she was also honest enough to admit that, along with shock and disgust, those overtures also brought a tiny bit of pleasure. For the first time in her life men desired her.

Fear made her sick as she looked at her face for the small signs that she had gained weight.

"What are you doing?" Beatrice asked from the doorway.

Anne turned sharply. "Am I fat?" she demanded, again looking at her reflection, which was becoming distorted by her frantic thoughts.

"No. And even if you were fat, you would still be beautiful."

"Oh, please, Bea. I am naive, but I am not stupid."

Beatrice thrust her hands on her hips. "I am completely serious. I'll admit you were a bit too, um, plump before. But you could stand to gain a few pounds. Sometimes you look downright skinny, and no man likes a skinny girl."

Anne drew in a shaking breath. "I don't want to be that other girl again."

"Oh, Anne. That girl was you, and she was my best friend. She was funny and bright, and, yes, she was plump."

"Fat. You must admit I look better now."

"Of course you do. But that doesn't mean that if you gain a few pounds you'll instantly become—"

"Ugly."

"You were never ugly," Beatrice said vehemently.

"People didn't recognize me at the Wetmore ball. Even you said I was like a different person."

"That was more because of your hair and clothes.

And your newfound confidence. You *are* a different person, Anne. But it's more than the way you look. Could you have walked into the Casino two years ago knowing you would be cut? Could you have walked up to a man who had destroyed you and had the courage to get a kiss from him?"

"No." The answer was given grudgingly, but Anne knew there was truth to what Beatrice said. Anne would never again be that shy girl who blushed if a man so much as looked at her. That Anne had been destroyed by all that had happened.

"Could the old Anne have agreed to go sailing with her former husband for devious reasons?" Beatrice asked, laughing and raising her eyebrows suggestively.

A wide smile brightened Anne's face. "Never."

"So, you see? Even if you woke up tomorrow fat as a cow, you would not be the old Anne."

The grin was still there, but Anne turned to the mirror again anyway and poked at her cheeks with the tips of her fingers. "So, you don't think I've gotten fat?"

Beatrice looked at Anne, willow thin and beautiful, and shook her head. "You're hideously obese. Don't eat a thing for a month. Now, let's go seduce Henry."

Anne widened her eyes in delighted shock. "We never said a word about seduction," she said, whispering the last word, even though no one else was within hearing.

"A simple oversight," Beatrice said, grabbing Anne's arm and pulling her out of the room. "Our carriage awaits, and so does our boat."

Spring Wharf was bustling with activity, clogged mostly with oyster and clam fishermen, many returning from a predawn trip. The air was heavy with the smells—most unpleasant—of brine, bait, and fish. At the end of a long dock sat Henry's small catboat, bobbing gently in the water several feet below the wood planking that made up the pier. The only thing visible from the dock was the boat's mast, looking much like a metronome ticking out a tempo against the sharp blue sky.

All the angst Anne felt earlier had fled, leaving behind a feeling of jubilation. It was because it was a beautiful day and she was furthering her plan, Anne told herself. If she was actually looking forward to seeing Henry, it was because Beatrice and she were making progress toward her ultimate goal of crushing him.

As she watched the mast move back and forth, she sang in her head, "I hate Henry Owen, I hate Henry Owen." The singing became almost frantic when she saw him standing near the helm looking so stunningly, flagrantly male. He wore a battered and salty old captain's hat of black wool, pushed back to reveal his handsome face; a rakish curl rested on his forehead. His cream-colored fisherman's sweater showed off his masculine physique in a way his suits never had. A mighty gale couldn't blow this strapping man from the deck, standing there, boots spread for balance, a sure hand gripping the boat's tiller. His brown trousers were casual and fit him perfectly. Too perfectly.

Anne took a deep breath. How could she be so attracted to a man she hated?

I do hate him. I do I do I do.

Then he smiled up at her, and Anne's toes curled. "Good morning, ladies."

Beatrice nodded rather coldly, but Anne found herself gushing out a hello.

"Permission to come aboard," she said gaily, feeling as if someone had given her a medicinal powder that caused giddiness.

Henry held up his arms to her, and Anne hesitated only an instant. Other than jumping from the wharf, the only way onto the boat was via Henry. Laughing, she half jumped down into his hands, knowing he would catch her.

"You're light as a feather," he said softly as her feet touched the gleaming deck. Anne, despite herself, beamed him a smile, remembering herself only when Beatrice coughed.

"My turn," she said rather testily.

"I'll do the honors," said a male voice from the hatch. Alex swung onto the deck from below in a fluid motion. Unlike Henry, who was casually dressed, Alex wore a light gray waistcoat, stiffly starched white shirt, and burgundy tie cinched up tight against his rigid collar. "I was in the galley looking about for something to eat," he said to explain his rolled-up cuffs.

"Alex thought I said 'boardroom,' when I told him we were going boating," Henry said dryly.

"Never hurts to always look your best, Henry. Unlike you, I have no delusions of being a common man. I am rich, and by God, I'll look rich. Now, then, Miss Leyden. Jump down and I'll try not to drop you."

Beatrice scowled and clearly wished she had another choice. Finally she stepped forward and, bracing her hands on Alex's shoulders, allowed him to swing her aboard. Though Beatrice was more petite than Anne, Alex groaned as if presented with some great weight. She stepped back immediately, her face flushed with anger.

"When we return, it will be high tide," Henry said. "We'll all be able to step right off the boat and onto the pier."

"Thank goodness," Beatrice muttered.

"I'll second that," a man said from below. Anne immediately recognized him as Reverend Mosely, a portly older man who was a frequent guest of the Newport rich. Retired as pastor of St. Joseph's in New York, the reverend was unobtrusively powerful, his words well-heeded by even the most jaded of his former congregation.

"Miss Foster," Reverend Mosely said easily. "So good to see you again." He nodded to Beatrice. "Miss Leyden." He pulled down his black waistcoat over his round belly before taking a seat. "A beautiful day for a sail."

Anne looked to Henry for an explanation, confusion clear in her expression.

"Since neither of us have parents in town, I thought the reverend would do for chaperon."

"Oh." Confound the man, Anne thought. Why did he have to be so thoughtful, so very considerate of her reputation at a time when no one else seemed concerned? All of Newport might think her a fallen woman despite their acceptance of her, but Henry still gave her the respect she was once due. That he had brought along a chaperon touched her deeply and again made her question the sort of man he was.

As the two younger men went about throwing off the ropes and raising the sail, Beatrice and Anne settled themselves on the softly cushioned plank seats that ran along the boat's stern. The boat's wood gleamed as if freshly polished, the brass winked brightly beneath the sun. Every bit of the boat was spotless, evidence of a well-cared-for craft.

"I feel as if I'm slumming it aboard this dinghy," Alex said, clearly baiting Henry. He owned a fifty-foot steam yacht that was anchored near his family's twenty-room cottage.

"Then you may swim for shore. We're not too far out yet," Henry said with a grin.

"And get my fine clothes wet? I'll make the best of it."

Once Henry maneuvered the boat out of Newport Harbor, the breeze picked up and pushed them quickly toward the Jamestown shore. It was a lovely day, the sky unmarred by clouds, the sun bright and warm. Reverend Mosely appeared to be taking a snooze, but Anne suspected he was trying to be unobtrusive to the young people surrounding him. He held his hat against his chest, and his nearly bald pate reflected the sun, reminding Anne fondly of her long-dead grandfather, who eschewed hats in the summertime.

Both ladies wore large-brimmed hats tied down with scarves to protect them from the sun. Their hands were covered with white silk gloves and no bit of sun was allowed to strike their skin. Though it had been warm by the wharf, it was almost chilly on the water, and Anne was glad she'd decided to wear a gown with a matching jacket. Still, she envied the men their wind-tousled hair, their tanned faces and hands. Feeling a bit defiant, she turned her face to the sun for a short time, but could only imagine freckles sprouting up spontaneously, so she turned away so that her brim once again protected her skin.

"I find freckles adorable on a woman," Alex said. Anne smiled and Beatrice immediately pulled her hat down farther. "So many bitter old maids might have been happier if they'd only tilted their faces up to the sun." Alex was so clearly trying to get under Beatrice's skin that Anne laughed.

"Why are you two constantly sparring?" Anne asked.

"Alex always does that to women he's hopelessly attracted to," Henry said. "When they ultimately reject him because of his boorishness, it reaffirms his belief that beautiful women are evil."

Alex laughed, but Anne could tell he didn't think Henry's comment was funny. And poor Beatrice blushed red beneath her hat.

"Whereas you toss aside beautiful women when they have served their purpose." Now Anne was certain that Alex was angry, and just as certain that Henry was about to thrash his friend. She watched with odd fascination as Henry's grip on the tiller tightened convulsively and his jaw clenched tightly.

"Poor show, Alex," he managed to say. Alex shrugged, then stretched out on his seat as if he hadn't a care in the world.

Anne grew increasingly uncomfortable as the tense silence in the boat grew. Both men were angry, Beatrice was mortified, and Anne was simply curious as to why everyone was being so mean-spirited. If anyone had a right to be mean, it was her, but she was the only person on the boat in good spirits.

"Frankly, I think you're both behaving poorly," Anne said. Then turning to Beatrice, added, "Bea, do you know how to sail?"

Beatrice looked startled until she saw the sparkle in Anne's eyes. "Actually, I do."

"Then what do you say we cool both of these hot-headed gentlemen off with a little swim in the bay?"

"I wouldn't advise it," Henry said darkly.

"No doubt we'd be the ones ending up in the drink," Anne said as she crossed her arms grumpily.

"And then they'd have to save us both," Beatrice said. "We'd sink like rocks with these skirts tangled about us."

"They don't look like strong swimmers to me," Anne said, tapping a finger against her cheek as if deep in thought.

"No, they don't. Likely, we'd all end up drowning."

"Food for the fishes."

Anne sneaked a look at Henry to find he was chuckling softly to himself. For some reason, she was inordinately pleased that she had the ability to make him laugh. She always had. Thoughts of the past instantly depressed Anne and reminded her that she was not on a friendly outing, but on a mission. It was becoming more and more difficult to equate this stunning man with the man who broke her heart. But then, Henry had always been likeable, even when he held the metaphorical knife in his hand ready to plunge it into her back. He had a way about him that drew people to him. She'd seen him work a crowd, seen his lopsided grin, his sturdy handshake, his ability to say exactly what the person he was talking to wanted to hear. She'd seen how women fawned over him, batting eyelashes, twirling parasols, and she'd seen how men respected his opinion on everything from sailing to investments. How could the man who'd sat next to her yesterday and apologized so sweetly have coldly married her, then cast her aside when he got what he wanted? Alex was right, she realized. He had used her. But what was he using her for now?

"If I am the cause of that frown, I am sorry," Alex said, putting a hand over his heart. Next to her, Beatrice let out a small snort of disgust.

"Is something wrong, Miss Leyden?" Reverend Mosely inquired. Everyone gave him a startled look, for they all had assumed he'd truly fallen asleep.

Beatrice assured the reverend she was perfectly fine, but her blush gave her away. "Is that Sea Cliff?"

All turned to look toward shore. Coming into view around a pine-covered peninsula was an enchanting gable-roofed shingled house with mullioned windows that reflected the morning sun. A large porch wrapped about the entire structure above a sturdy stone foundation. Trimmed in forest green, the house seemed to disappear into the hill behind it. If not for the sparkle from the windows, the house would nearly be invisible to someone sailing by.

By Newport's standards, the house was humble, but Anne found herself enchanted by it and slightly disturbed by the way her heart was responding. It was almost as if she was looking at home, as if hidden somewhere deep inside she had memories of being here, a place she'd never seen. It was a cruel thought, but there just the same and impossible to shake.

"It's pretty," Beatrice said, and Anne gave her a stunned look. Pretty? It was so much more than simply pretty.

"This is my home," Henry said quietly, and Anne looked at him as he looked at Sea Cliff. She saw in his eyes the emotions she'd been feeling and immediately looked away. She wished in that instant she hadn't come, because she didn't want to understand why Henry did what he did. There was no understanding, she'd told herself a hundred times. But there before her stood the reason, looking somehow alive as it rested on that rocky shore welcoming her home.

Henry seemed to snap out of his reverie and move into action. He pulled on the tiller as Alex dropped the fluttering sail, and then Henry moved to the boat's bow to drop anchor. On shore, a man was already rowing out to them.

"Good morning, Mr. Brown," Henry called.

"And to you, Mr. Owen."

Henry introduced Beatrice and Anne to the craggy-faced Peleg Brown, whose jaw and chin bristled with a two-day-old gray-and-black beard. The old man's eyes nearly disappeared when he squinted up at them into the sun.

"Pleasure," he said gruffly. "Good day to you, Reverend. Mr. Henley." He moved awkwardly to the back of the skiff, and that was when Anne noticed he had only one leg and his hands were gnarled with arthritis. Henry hopped down into the skiff like a man who had lived on the sea for years, then assisted first Beatrice then Anne from the catboat.

"Need help, my lady?" he asked Alex, holding up a hand.

Alex gave him a look that said what he thought of Henry's inquiry, and hopped ably down onto the skiff. Henry sat in the middle gripping the oars, his back to Beatrice and Anne in the bow, and the reverend, Mr. Brown, and Alex took up the stern. Henry pulled off his bulky sweater to reveal a short-sleeved, striped shirt that a seaman might wear, and Anne lost her ability to breathe. The shirt left nothing to the imagination, perfectly covering a perfect form. Anne darted a look to Beatrice to see if she noticed, but she was glaring at Alex for some remark he'd made.

Anne tried not to watch as Henry pulled the heavy oars effortlessly, but it was impossible. His forearms were corded with muscle, his hands sure and strong on the oars. His back was broad, his shoulders brawny. It suddenly seemed insufferably warm, and Anne unbuttoned her jacket and flapped it for a breeze. The others were talking as if Henry were not sitting in front of them half-naked, displaying more flesh and muscle than a gentleman ought to. She swallowed and forced herself to look away. When the others laughed, she did, too, though she hadn't a clue as to what she was laughing about.

Finally, the boat scraped along the sandy bottom of the beach that curved toward Sea Cliff, jarring the passengers slightly. Anne put out a hand for balance, only to find herself touching the very back she'd been admiring. He was solid and hot. Anne drew her hand quickly back and clenched her fist, realizing that her palm had become slightly moist from his sweat. In fascination, she moved her fingers against her palm. Oh, God, what is happening to me, she thought.

Henry turned, a smile on his face. "Is everyone all right?" he asked.

"We're fine," Beatrice said.

"Fine." Anne hardly recognized her voice, and when he looked at her, she didn't know enough to hide what she was feeling. She only knew that when Henry turned to her, he took one look at her face and his smile was gone, replaced by a look that seared her skin. He turned away quickly, his hands gripping his seat hard.

Brown waded through the calm water, his gait lopsided and awkward, and he began tugging the boat further onto the beach.

"Could use some help," he muttered loud enough for all to hear.

Within a second, Henry leaped off the boat with a splash and was beside the older man dragging the heavy skiff higher onto the beach. Alex helped the reverend and the ladies off, and when Anne turned to find Henry, he had put his sweater back on despite the heat.

Anne wasn't certain whether she was glad or not.

Williamson stepped back from the window. "Henry has returned. He has guests."

"Push me to the window," Arthur said, his hands working ineffectually at the wheels of his cumbersome chair. Williamson did as he was asked and pushed the curtains aside so Arthur could see the small group now gathering on the beach below. He squinted his gray eyes. "That's Henley. A disappointment to his father, I'm certain. And Mosely. Hope he's not here for my sake. Who are the women?"

Williamson, who had become as isolated as Arthur, shook his head. "I wouldn't know, sir."

"Find out." Arthur sat still for a moment, catching his breath. In addition to the strokes that had left him paralyzed, his doctors had informed him that his heart was failing. He had come to Sea Cliff to die and to stop his grandson from learning the truth while he still lived. He cursed his affliction and himself for waiting so long. For now he knew it was too late to shield Henry. He was dying and he was afraid. The thought of dying in his sleep drove him to try desperately to stay awake. He'd listen to his own breathing until he drove himself nearly mad, knowing each breath brought him closer and closer to the last he would take. During the day, exhaustion would overtake him and he would doze, only to awaken in a panic until he realized he lived still.

"Williamson," he said, his voice only a scratchy

whisper. "Get my journal." His chest heaved with the effort it took to take in oxygen.

Williamson, his droopy eyes filled with sorrow, slowly went to the bedstand and opened the draw to withdraw the well-used journal. For two years the old man had been telling his story. They had finished only the night before. It had taken hours to finish this last entry, for Arthur's strength was depleted, and the story he told seemed to suck the life out of him. For several nights, Williamson sat beside Arthur, scribbling down his life story, becoming more and more stunned by what the old man said. Last night, Arthur had turned his watery eyes to Williamson and looked at his friend for a long moment.

"So, now you know. What do you think of me now, Williamson?"

Williamson closed the book slowly. "I think you have suffered enough, sir."

Arthur had let out a weak chuckle. "Do you know why I am so afraid of dying?"

"Sir?"

"I shall sleep with the devil, Williamson."

"Oh, no, sir."

Arthur closed his eyes, his only comfort the thought that Henry would someday know the truth. "Take me to bed," he said, turning his head away from the window.

Williamson helped Arthur into bed. He combed his hair, ignoring the old man when he asked if he were preparing him for the coffin.

"Shall I bring Henry up?" he asked when he was finished.

"I've no plans to die just yet." He seemed in good humor when suddenly his face crumpled and thick tears streamed from his eyes. "Don't let him find out until I'm dead. Promise me, Williamson."

Williamson clutched Arthur's searching hand. "I promise."

Chapter Eleven

Reverend Mosely sat on the porch in an old wicker rocking chair that creaked and stretched to comfortably wrap around whoever sat in it. The porch was the perfect spot, he announced, to keep an eye on the young people, who at that moment were gathered on the front lawn and looking out across the bay to Newport. He rocked for perhaps ten minutes before his head sagged into his chest and he began to snore softly.

Henry had never been so nervous. He could not quite understand his driving need to explain himself to Anne. He looked at Sea Cliff now, not with his usual loving eyes, but with the eyes of a stranger, and saw an old clapboard house with odd angles and disproportionate dimensions. What he'd always thought was charming suddenly looked downright shabby, almost menacing, and he felt like a fool for bringing Anne here and pointing to this dilapidated old building as the reason behind his villainy. Alex was right: She would either laugh or want to throttle him.

"So, this is Sea Cliff," Beatrice said, looking skeptically up at the old cottage. "It's . . . well, I'd say it's . . ."

"It's perfect," Anne finished, smiling up at the old house and making Henry's heart nearly pound out of his chest. He turned, and suddenly that ugly old cottage was again transformed into the house that he loved.

"Perfect?" Beatrice said, clearly surprised at Anne's assessment. "Château sur Mer is perfect. Marble House is perfect," she said, referring to Mrs. Alva Vanderbilt's mansion. "This," she said, waving a hand at the house, "is . . ."

"Little more than a shack?" Alex offered.

Beatrice laughed aloud, quickly stifling herself when she saw the look on Henry's face. "Oh, Mr. Owen, I'm sorry," she said, trying not to smile too much. "It's just hard to imagine going to the lengths that you did to save this house. Do you really intend to endear yourself to Anne by showing her this?" She waved a hand at the house, and Henry bristled at her disdain.

"It's not so bad," Anne said softly. "It's rather charming, really. It's homey and welcoming and just lovely."

Henry gave her a sharp look, thinking perhaps that she was making fun of him, but nothing in her expression showed she was mocking him. He gave Anne a crooked grin. "I thought so, too."

"But certainly it's not worth destroying someone's life over," Beatrice persisted.

Anne looked troubled as she turned from him to again look at the bay, and he felt as if his life was draining away from him. She could never understand something that he was only coming to grasp.

"Would the two of you excuse us?" Henry said to Alex and Beatrice. "Perhaps a stroll down the beach?"

"If you could suffer my company, Miss Leyden." Alex offered his arm, which Beatrice pretended to take reluctantly, and the two strolled down the lawn and to the stairs that led to the beach.

Anne kept her back to Henry, allowing him to admire her slim form, the graceful curve of her neck, the soft wisps of hair that escaped from beneath her hat. He wished he had the right to come up from behind her and wrap his arms around her waist, to kiss her neck. He cleared his throat.

"Anne, this little trip was not meant to be a panacea for all that I've done. I wanted to try to make you understand just a little of what possessed me two years ago. What I did had nothing to do with you and everything to do with Sea Cliff." She stiffened and he grimaced. "I didn't mean it to sound the way that came out. What I mean is, I was so obsessed, I would not allow myself to think clearly about what I was doing to you. I only knew that by marrying, I could gain my inheritance and, most particularly, Sea Cliff."

She turned to him then. "You never had any intention of staying married, did you?"

"I realized soon after the wedding that the best thing for both of us was a quick divorce. I had thought to keep you in New York, living a separate life. I actually convinced myself that you wouldn't mind. Do you see how crazed I was?" He gave her an unknowingly charming smile and was surprised to find her smiling back at him.

"You're so pretty when you smile, Anne," he said suddenly.

Anne couldn't help but widen her grin. She told herself that she was enjoying trying to dupe him, but the truth was, when she was with Henry, it was impossible to hate him. Why couldn't he act like the villain she'd made of him? Why couldn't he be mean or gruff or inconsiderate? Somehow, the thought of humiliating Henry, of hurting him by breaking his heart, was becoming more and more unpalatable.

Their plan was supposed to have been fun. She still remembered giggling with Beatrice about how she would make Henry swoon at her feet, and then she would take a pointed heel and pierce his heart with it, laughing wickedly all the while. She had imagined a hundred different scenarios that all ended with her laughing gleefully as Henry looked on with hurt bewilderment. As Anne gazed at him now, she wasn't certain whether she should harden her heart or give it to him.

Shocked by her thoughts, Anne said briskly, "So, let's hear it. Let's hear about your Sea Cliff."

Henry's warm gaze drank in the sight of the cottage. "Two years ago, where we are standing now was part of the bay. The waves had ripped away the earth until the foundation was showing in that corner there," he said, pointing to the house. "It was only a matter of time before Sea Cliff was dragged into the water. I had another three years before I came into my inheritance, and I believed the house wouldn't last that long. I had to save it."

"So you went to your grandfather and asked him to free up your inheritance. I heard that much."

"Yes, I did. And he refused. The only other way to obtain Sea Cliff was to marry, and I hadn't any prospects at the time. No one but you. I knew you would say yes if I asked."

Anne's cheeks flushed. "I was that obvious?"

"I'm afraid so. Which only made me feel worse. I liked you, Anne. I cannot defend what I did to you, but I want you to know that I never pretended more devotion than I felt."

"You asked me to marry you. I believe that infers a certain amount of affection," Anne said coldly.

"You're right. God, I know you are right." Henry let out a heavy sigh and swiped a hand through his already wind-tousled hair. "I was deceitful. I let you believe I shared your feelings."

Anne looked up at the cottage, which was losing its charm by the moment as their discussion brought back every ugly memory she had of the past two years. Nothing was worth what she had suffered, and certainly not this bundle of nailed wood.

"I'm not going about this right," Henry said, correctly reading Anne's hardened expression. "I brought you here to explain, not to dredge up all that ugliness."

"Why? Why tell me now and not two years ago when your lawyers showed up at my door and handed me that divorce decree? I know you don't want to think about 'all that ugliness,' " Anne mimicked harshly. "But it was my life that was ugly. Pray tell, sir, what ugliness you are referring to regarding your own life. You got your house, your money, your freedom. Oh, you suffered immensely, I can tell." When Henry opened his mouth as if to explain, she cut him off. "It is too late for explanations. I want to go back to Newport. This was a mistake."

Anne began walking toward the dinghy that would bring them to the catboat, vowing to abandon the ridiculous scheme to make Henry fall in love with her. She hadn't the stomach for it, she thought as she lifted her skirts and made her way down the steep stairs to the beach. She was not unaware that just moments before, she had been ready to forgive Henry for all his sins. The man was driving her insane and she was glad he'd made her angry. How dare he try to charm her, how dare he try to "explain" his devotion to that ugly house with its absurdly pretentious name. Sea Cliff, indeed. More like Bay Mound, she thought smugly.

"Anne, come back. I've made a muddle of things," she heard Henry call. She ignored him.

"Anne, please." Then, "Aw, hell." She heard footsteps behind her and she hastened her steps, looking about for Alex and Beatrice so she could tell them she wanted to leave. They were nowhere in sight. As she looked for her friend, one of Anne's feet slipped, and she found herself sprawled face-first in the soft sand. Sand was in her mouth, up her nose, down her dress. She spit ineffectually, trying to rid her mouth of the grit.

"They should teach ladies how to spit decently," she heard Henry say. "Are you all right?"

Anne spit again just to show him she knew how. "I'm perfectly fine. You may leave now." She was sitting, her hat askew, her hair coming down, her lap full of sand. He hunkered down next to her and she pulled her skirt away as if he might contaminate it.

"I can't let you go, Anne."

She looked up, ready to give him another bit of her venom, and her heart stopped. She didn't like the way he was looking at her, with a strange intensity that made her entire body feel flushed. Don't do this to me, Henry. Don't make me like you, not when I'd just decided to hate you for the rest of my life. Never in her life had Anne felt as confused as she did at that moment, looking into those warm gray eyes, drowning in his gaze, wishing absurdly that he would kiss her and wishing just as much that he would do something to make her loathe him.

"What are you doing to me?" she said without thinking.

"Kissing you." He brought his head forward, ducking it beneath the broad brim of her hat, giving her plenty of time to back away if that was what she truly wanted. And she wanted to back away, she wouldn't kiss him, wouldn't dare let his warm lips touch hers. No. Not again.

Anne sighed as she moved just slightly toward him and let her mouth rest against his. Their mouths touched just briefly, just enough to tempt Anne to press longer and harder. She moved back, her troubled gaze meeting gray eyes filled with a heat that Anne wanted to deny.

"I hate you, Henry Owen," she said softly.

"I know." And he leaned in for another kiss.

"Do you think we've given them enough time to talk?" Beatrice asked. She and Alex had walked per-

haps a half-mile down the beach and around a bend
so that Sea Cliff was hidden from view by a thick
stand of pine trees. They had said little to each other,
treating their time together as an unwanted duty—at
least that was how Alex seemed to be treating it. Beatrice was intensely uncomfortable knowing that the
man she walked next to would rather have a tooth
pulled than be stuck chatting nonsense with her. So
she kept her mouth closed until she thought she
would burst.

"I suppose we could head back now," he said, pausing to see how far they'd walked. "We don't want to
be gone so long that your reputation is at risk."

Beatrice shrugged. "I know I'm safe with you, of
all people, Mr. Henley."

He gave her the oddest look. "Why would you
think that?"

"It is my experience that a man tends not to make
advances toward a girl he finds . . ."

Alex raised an eyebrow. "He finds?" he prompted.

"Unappealing."

"Ah."

Beatrice felt her throat ache just the slightest bit
when he didn't argue with her assessment. So, Alex
didn't find her appealing. She shouldn't be surprised
and she certainly shouldn't be hurt. But for some reason she was. Why did this man, a man she claimed to
have no liking for, have such a great ability to hurt
her and without even trying? Perhaps, she thought
reluctantly, she liked him far more than she was willing to admit.

"Well, you are certainly safe from me, and for the
same reason," she said brightly, a desperate attempt
to salvage some pride.

As she turned to go back to Sea Cliff, she missed
the fierce frown on Alex's face. He followed in her
wake, that frown still on his face for several minutes,

until Beatrice stopped so abruptly, he nearly ran into her.

"Oh, goodness," Beatrice said under her breath, a bright smile on her lips. By the time she turned to Alex to point down the beach at the kissing couple, she was scowling. It certainly wouldn't do to let Alex know she was pleased that Anne was successfully wooing Henry.

"How dare he?" she asked, pretending outrage.

"She doesn't seem to be pushing him away," Alex said dryly. Indeed, from their vantage point, they could clearly see that Anne had both hands around Henry's neck and she didn't appear to be strangling him. "For all we know, she's kissing him."

Beatrice balled her fists. "Well, we'll just put a stop to it right now."

"Whoa there, Miss Leyden. Just what do you think you're doing?" Alex put a large hand around her upper arm to stop her from interrupting the kiss, and Beatrice yanked it away, truly flustered now. Alex threw her a look of pure irritation at her dramatics.

"I'm going to stop a disaster," she said.

"For once, stop meddling."

"Me? You accuse me of meddling when just last week you were pretending to pursue Anne simply to make Henry jealous?"

Alex smiled, a teacher pleased that his student had gotten the correct answer to a complex question. "And what makes you say something so preposterous?"

"Oh, please, sir," she said, waving a hand at him. "You couldn't have been more obvious than if you announced your intentions to the world."

"Henry never suspected," he pointed out.

"So. I am right! Ha!"

Alex glared at her. "If I am not mistaken, I am not the only one with ulterior motives when it comes to those two."

A tingling of fear made Beatrice almost shiver. "I haven't the foggiest idea what you mean."

"You are up to something. Or Miss Foster is. Instead of kissing him, she should be clawing his eyes out. Good God, Henry's not that charming a fellow."

Beatrice pretended boredom. "As much as I detest the man, I must admit he possesses a rare amount of natural charm. It's not false and forced. Like some," she said, looking at him pointedly.

Alex raised his eyebrows in mock surprise. "I'll have you know I work quite hard to cultivate just the right amount of charm."

"Mr. Henley, you have never worked hard at anything a day in your life." Beatrice meant to tease him and was surprised when he immediately seemed to shut down, his expression growing remote. "Have I struck on a raw nerve?" Beatrice asked, smiling and batting her eyes. "So sorry."

He smiled and shook his head, as if not wanting to let her restore his good humor. "You have a rare talent for that, Miss Leyden. You know just where to shoot your poisoned arrow, don't you?"

This time, Beatrice sobered, suddenly hating that they were always verbally jabbing at one another. It was so tiring. She nodded her head toward the other couple on the beach. "They've stopped," she said. "I wonder what will happen now."

As they watched, Anne stood up quickly and shook the sand from her skirts. Henry remained where he was, one knee in the sand, the other bent and used to prop up his elbow. His back was to them, so they could not see his expression, but Anne appeared to be flustered. And then she kicked sand at him and stomped away.

"Henry seems to have lost his charm," Alex said, chuckling softly.

Beatrice nearly rolled her eyes in frustration at the display. Anne would never get it right. Just when she thought her friend was making inroads, she went and kicked sand in Henry's face. That certainly was not the way to endear him to her. At this rate, it would be the end of August before she had Henry declaring his love—if even then. For their plan to work, Newport had to be in full season. Everyone who was anyone had to be present when Anne rejected Henry.

"Thank goodness she came to her senses," Beatrice said for Alex's benefit.

"I'm certain Henry will try again. He's smitten."

Beatrice turned to Alex, managing to hide her pleasure at his words. "Is that so?"

Alex shrugged. "I've told him he's treading on dangerous ground. He'll not listen."

Inside, Beatrice was thrilled by what Alex had just admitted, but she remained impassive on the outside. "He might as well give up now. Anne cannot abide him. I don't even know why she agreed to come here today."

"Don't you?"

Beatrice didn't like the hard gaze Alex gave her. "No. I don't." But she turned away so he wouldn't see the lie in her eyes.

From the Journal of Arthur Owen

I began to pursue your mother in earnest and in secret. I still had enough sense to know that what I was doing with my son's fiancée was abhorrent, but at that point, I did not care. I had to have her, and forever. Elizabeth found me and my ardor amusing. Each time she draped herself around Walter and gave me that secret smile, I died a little. She enjoyed torturing me, she reveled in her power over me. I was a fool to have let her know how she was driving me mad. I woke thinking of her, I lay in bed at night wanting her, I spent the day listening for her footsteps, her voice, her laugh. She acted as if we had never spent that night together, and even when I confronted her, she pretended not to know what I was talking about.

And yet, I could not get angry with her. She simply managed to drive my obsession deeper, until, God help me, I contemplated telling Walter what we had done. Can you imagine a father telling a son that he has lain with his future wife? When I actually pictured myself doing just that, I wept. I was in the library, it was late, and I had been drinking. I sat behind my desk, tearing my hair from my scalp, and let the agony of wanting her overtake me. She found me like that, my head on my arms, weeping like a boy. She kissed my tears away, begged my forgiveness. I will not go into detail, but you can imagine what happened. I had so little control when it came to Elizabeth. She was a drug I craved, and one that was offered again and again. I could only refuse so many times before succumbing.

Afterward, I regretted my weakness, but I came to accept that I could not resist her. I planned to leave Sea Cliff, to return to New York. I packed my bags that night, announced at breakfast the next day that I would leave Jamestown after arranging for another chaperon for the young couple. When I returned to my room, she followed me. She begged me not to leave, she begged my forgiveness. You cannot know how her tears affected me. She told me she was ashamed of what she had done, that she would die if I left. We made love, Walter still at the breakfast table reading some scientific journal directly below us.

Who was that man who betrayed his son? I cannot imagine him. He is the lowest of men, a coward, and a fool. I was that man and it shames me to this day. Even now I do not think I would have the strength to resist her, even knowing what I know now. It is difficult to comprehend how completely captivated I was. I was not a child, infatuated and reveling in a

first love. I was a man grown. She ensnared me, intoxi-
cated me. But she never loved me.

We made love whenever and wherever we could. In
the library, on the beach, on my balcony, in the
kitchen at midnight. I began to think of Walter as a
fool. How could he not know? There were times when
he would walk in on us just moments after we had
fixed our clothing, and be completely oblivious to what
had just happened. Elizabeth would be flushed, her
mouth swollen and red, her hair slightly damp along
her hairline. I would be red-faced, my cravat hanging
loose, my shirt wrinkled, but he never made comment.
My God, I could smell the passion in the air sometimes. Elizabeth and I would exchange frightened
looks when Walter turned away, or she would giggle
and point to a button I'd forgotten. We would talk
about how silly my son was, how blind to what was
happening. I think now he didn't want to know. It was
too horrible a thought to contemplate that his father
was making love to his future bride, and so he told
himself it could not be. In the end, the anger he felt
was not something that suddenly erupted, but rather
a cancer that ate away at him until he exploded with
fury. He knew. He knew all along.

Chapter Twelve

Anne felt ill each time she remembered kissing Henry on the beach and it certainly wasn't because the memory was so abhorrent. On the contrary. Anne had the horrible, devastating, soul-ripping feeling that she was—oh, God!—falling in love with Henry. Again.

It couldn't be. It simply couldn't. Was she so controlled by lust that she couldn't see him for what he truly was? Or was she finally seeing the real Henry, all charm and warm looks and wonderful kisses meant only for her? That was why she kicked sand at him. She hated herself for being so weak, so ridiculous. Imagine falling for a man who'd ruined your life, a man who systematically planned your destruction. Imagine being a woman who, with just a few kisses, could be persuaded to not only forgive, but toss away her heart.

It was too horrid to contemplate.

Anne was quiet all the way home. She sat near Reverend Mosely, her hands clasped in her lap, ignoring the hard-edged banter between Beatrice and Alex. She wanted to shout at them to stop bickering, but they seemed to enjoy it so that Anne remained silent. She couldn't bring herself to look at Henry for fear every confusing thought she was thinking would be telegraphed to him. Even when she recalled her dark time in New York, the devastation of being cast from her own home, even then, she could not shake the feeling that she was falling in love. Never had she been more miserable.

Every once in a while, Beatrice would give her a searching look, but Anne just shook her head as if to say, "Not now." If she knew what was happening, Beatrice would be so disappointed in her. Bea, who had dragged her kicking and fighting from the grave, who had dedicated more than a year of her life to restoring Anne to hers, would never understand how Anne could feel anything for Henry but disgust.

She tried, oh, how she tried, to bring back the hate that had been so comforting to her. On that beach, Henry had told her about a little boy whose summers were filled with magic, and at the center of that magic was Sea Cliff. He told her about his beautiful mother, his scholarly father, about bonfires on the sand and long lazy days of nothing but pure little-boy happiness. And then he told her about that terrible day when his parents had died.

He had been in Newport visiting with Alex for a week. The two of them had such a grand time together, digging clams, fishing, and rolling about the surf like two seals. His grandfather appeared one day, looking as if he'd been terribly ill. His hands shook, his eyes were red-rimmed, his usually tanned skin sallow. His grandfather, in a cold and businesslike manner, informed him that his mother and father had been missing for three days, that their broken sailboat had been discovered floating upside down off Block Island. No bodies had been found and no hope given that the couple would be found alive.

Henry had refused to believe they could be dead and he held out hope for weeks that they'd somehow been rescued and unable to return home. He didn't go to the funeral and he hated his grandfather for arranging one. Finally, though, he accepted that they were dead. His father had not been a good sailor, though he often managed to sail to Block Island and back without mishap. It was a short sail, and one that even the most novice of seamen could make. But a squall had come up, ripped their sails, capsized their boat, and sent them to the bottom of the Atlantic. That was when his summers at Sea Cliff ended. His grandfather boarded the place up and expressly forbade him to step on the shore. A caretaker was hired to live in a small cottage behind Sea Cliff to insure that nothing was disturbed—and that Henry kept his distance.

Soon after Henry and his grandfather returned to New York, Arthur Owen suffered his first and most devastating stroke. Henry's childhood was over.

Anne had listened heart-sore over that little boy who had known such happiness only to have it snatched away from him.

He had let out a long breath at the end of his story, his eyes searching her face for understanding. And she had given it with her kiss.

Now, sitting in his catboat, pointedly looking anywhere but at him, Anne told herself that only the most hard-hearted person would not have been affected by what had happened to Henry. She still could not forgive what he'd done, but now she had a clear understanding of what had driven him. She wished she didn't. She wished he had never brought her to Sea Cliff and introduced her to the sad little boy banished from the only place he'd ever been happy. How awful it must have been, those first days after his grandfather had so coldly informed him that his parents were dead. There was no one to comfort him, to hold him, only an old man who didn't have the capacity or the heart to ease a little boy's pain.

She didn't want to feel sorry for Henry. She didn't want to understand. She wanted him to be a cad who had broken her heart, not an orphaned little boy, alone and unloved. That was why she so childishly kicked sand at him. He had ruined everything. He had found her heart and let himself in without permission. And now, Lord above help her, she was afraid she couldn't or wouldn't cast him out again.

Beatrice waited until they were in Anne's room that night before interrogating her.

"I saw the two of you kissing," she said. Anne buried her face in her hands.

"And then I saw you kick sand at him. Really, Anne, if you want to accomplish our mission, you've got to hide your animosity toward him better than that. I know you hate him, but he's supposed to think you're falling for him. Remember?"

Anne kept her face hidden and shook her head, letting out something that sounded like an odd mixture of laughing and crying.

"Anne?"

"I don't hate him," Anne said, her voice muffled by her hands.

"I beg your pardon?"

Anne dropped her hands and looked at her friend. "I don't hate him. I . . ." She swallowed, truly feeling sick.

Beatrice thrust out a hand. "Don't. Oh, no. Don't you dare tell me that you love him. Don't. You. Dare."

Anne grimaced in answer.

"No! You don't, Anne. You don't. He kissed you and you liked it. Of course you did. He's kissed a thousand women and he's had all sorts of practice. I can understand that. And he's handsome, more handsome than a scoundrel like him deserves to be. Fine. You are attracted to him. But what you are feeling is not love. It is not."

"It's not?" Anne asked shakily.

Beatrice gave Anne a gentle smile. "Of course not. You're simply confused, getting all wrapped up in a role. You were supposed to be pretending to fall for him, and before you knew it, you thought you were. But you're not. Believe me.''

''Oh.''

''You are not.''

Anne pursed her lips in thought. ''I really think I may be,'' she said, tensing up for Beatrice's reaction.

Beatrice threw up her hands in frustration and then took a calming breath. ''All right, then. What happened?''

Anne told her, even shedding a tear when she described Henry's sad boyhood. ''I cannot remain angry with him, never mind want to hurt him the way we planned.''

''And you fell for all that hogwash? Oh, Anne,'' Beatrice said, shaking her head sadly. ''Henry is perhaps the most duplicitous man I have ever met. He married you for a house.''

Anne studied her hands, which were fiddling with her skirt. ''I know why he married me.''

''No. You don't,'' Beatrice said, sorely tempted to tell Anne the full reason. If Anne knew she had been targeted because Henry thought her plain, certainly she would forget the notion that she was falling in love. But Beatrice couldn't do that to her, it would be too hurtful. ''You don't remember the pain. Your brain is all befuddled with the way he is treating you now. But do you remember what he did to you?''

''Of course I do,'' Anne said, flushing. She remembered, she was simply choosing not to dwell on it. How could she when all she could think about was how warm his lips were, how his kisses made her body feel as if it were charged with some strange energy.

''He used you. The same way he's using you now to clear his guilty conscience. For all we know, his next plan is to change the conditions of your divorce.''

''He wouldn't.''

Beatrice grabbed Anne's hands and gave them a little shake. ''Wouldn't he? He took vows to love you forever. Vows he broke the day he divorced you and left you alone. Is that the sort of man who deserves your love?"

Anne began to cry. "No."

Tears filled Beatrice's eyes, too. "You have to harden your heart, Anne. This town would tear you apart if it knew you'd fallen in love with Henry again. You would be the butt of every joke. And Henry would come out unscathed. Again."

Anne nodded. Beatrice was right. Henry had said nothing of having feelings for her. All along, he'd spoken only of his need to seek forgiveness, not of renewing their relationship. Now she could recall that Henry hadn't looked hurt or even angry when she'd kicked sand at him after their kiss. He'd looked bemused, as if to say, "Oh, well, thought I'd give it a try." She felt like an idiot, having confessed any feelings of love toward Henry. Thank God she'd not made a complete fool of herself by saying something to Henry.

She'd been so wrapped up in her own confused feelings, she hadn't thought about how Henry had acted when they parted. Looking back, she recalled he'd seemed relaxed, calling out a good-bye to Alex and Reverend Mosely, bowing grandly to her and Beatrice. As if his mission had been accomplished, as if he hadn't a worry in the world.

And there she'd been thinking she was falling in love when he'd probably been thinking how easy it had been for him to be absolved for his greatest sin.

"Oh, Bea, I cannot believe how weak I am."

"He can be charming," Bea said with a shrug. "And you were in love with him before."

"Bea, if I ever weaken again, hit me hard. Right on the head."

Beatrice smiled. "I think it's your heart we have to worry about, dear, not your head."

*   *   *

Henry took a swallow of straight whiskey. He'd started the evening drinking whiskey and water, but as each drink went down, the color of his drinks got darker and darker. "I hate this town," Henry said, leaning against a silk-covered wall. "Look at 'em, jush waiting for someone to stumble. Wouldn't they jush love it if I were to . . ." He took another drink and blinked his eyes slowly. "What was I saying?"

"You were saying you wanted to go home," Alex said dryly as he removed the drink from Henry's hand, grabbed his arms, and pulled Henry from the wall that was holding him up so ably.

"No, no, no," Henry said, shaking his head. His eyes widened suddenly as he tried to focus. "Good God, I'm drunk."

"No kidding."

"How did I get this drunk?" Henry asked, clearly baffled.

"It could have been the ten whiskeys you swallowed. I'm not certain."

"S'pose it could have been that." Henry grinned. "Never could hold m'whiskey. Think I might be sick."

"Oh, no you don't, old fellow. Let's get you out of here in some reasonable semblance of normalcy. Can you make it to the carriage?"

Henry swallowed. "Think so."

"Sober up, good fellow, we're going to walk now," said Alex, chuckling at the exaggerated care Henry took to walk toward the entry hall. "Mrs. Astor would not approve of you vomiting on her shiny floors, you know, Henry."

"Don't talk about it jush now, will you, Alex?" He swallowed again, tears coming to his eyes. They made it as far as the graveled drive before Henry bent over and lost a great bit of all that whiskey he'd done so well in drinking.

"Either drink more to gain resistance, or give up entirely, Henry."

Henry leaned his head against a carriage, ignoring the coachman who stood by tsk-tsking about his employer's vehicle. "Feel better now," he said, staring down at the mess at his feet with a grimace. "Remind me never to do that again."

"I do every time. But since it's a rare occurrence, I figure when you decide to get roaring drunk, there's a good reason behind it. So. What is it this time? Or should I say, who?"

Henry straightened and threw the coachman a sloppy look of apology. "I want to know what her game is. When I kiss her. Hell, when we kiss, it's like the whiskey. So damned good. And then I've got puke all over me."

Alex let out a sharp laugh. "I know just what you mean. What you've got to decide is this: Do you want to acquire a taste of that whiskey so you can drink more and more, or should you go on to other things and never touch the stuff again?"

"I like whiskey so damned much," Henry said softly. Then he laughed drunkenly. "But it always makes me sick."

"Then, my friend, I'd try some sweet and bubbly champagne."

Sweet. She was very sweet. And bubbly.

Henry yawned and looked about the Casino ballroom, telling himself that he wasn't looking for *her*.

"Oh, I'm boring you," Annette Bissette said, batting him playfully on his arm.

"Never," he lied, forcing himself to pay attention to the girl. She was lovely. She looked enraptured when he talked about his interests, tilting her head at just the proper angle to hide a large mole that had the unfortunate luck to sprout near her left eyebrow at her hairline. That mole was perhaps the most interesting part of this girl, he thought. She was too perfect, too polished, too self-assured. But for that mole.

"Oh," she said, brushing a self-conscious hand over the mole.

Apparently, he'd been staring at it.

"I'm having that removed."

"Don't," he said with his usual disarming smile. "It's the most unique part of you."

She smiled brightly. "Why, thank you. I shall keep it forever, then." Annette looked up at him through long lashes and Henry fought the urge to tilt her head back so that she looked directly at him. Good Lord, she was annoying.

He glanced around the room again, stopping sharply when he saw Anne. She was talking with a tall man with thick blond hair. She batted his arm playfully and looked at him flirtatiously. It was all Henry could do not to march across the floor and pull her away from that fortune-hunting varmint, whoever he was.

"Is that our Anne talking with Jake Morrison? Hear he's the catch of the season. Philadelphia new money and lots of it." Alex had sneaked up behind Henry simply to torture him.

Annette looked over to where Anne was standing with the catch of the season. "Oh. Her. I don't know how you can stand being in the same room. It must be awfully uncomfortable."

"I'm certain Henry is awfully uncomfortable every time he looks at her," Alex said meaningfully.

Henry nearly laughed at his friend's off-color double entendre, and would have if it hadn't been so nearly the truth. He certainly did not want to encourage more of the same.

"Alex, you know Miss Bissette? Miss Bissette, Alex Henley."

Alex nodded. Annette giggled.

"I thought you were the catch of every season, Mr. Henley," Annette said. She was so clearly flirting with Alex that Henry was momentarily a bit put off, until he remembered that the girl bored him to tears. She was more Alex's style, all fluff and no substance, though he thought his friend wouldn't appreciate Annette's little flaw as much as he did.

Alex bowed to Annette. "Yes, but I have to let the other fellows have a shot at one or two girls."

Annette giggled.

"Why don't you two dance," Henry said.

Annette was polite enough to pretend disappointment. "You won't mind?"

"Not at all."

Henry turned to look for Anne, but couldn't find her among the dancers. And he didn't see Jake Morrison, either. He was about to make a complete ass of himself by going off to search for her, when he spotted her swirling about the dance floor, waltzing rather too closely with Morrison. She flashed the man her best smile and Henry fought the urge to march amongst the dancers and cut in.

"What the devil," he muttered, more angry with himself than with Anne. He'd gotten what he wanted. He explained to Anne how he'd come to ruin her, and had even gotten the satisfaction of knowing she understood the forces that had driven him. Her kiss told him she understood, just as her angry departure told him she hated the fact that she did. He understood that anger. Hadn't he spent a lifetime battling hate and love and anger with his grandfather?

The dance ended and he watched as Alex bowed to Annette, flashing a smile that held the promise of another dance that would, in all likelihood, never happen. Alex moved from one female to the next without a second thought, leaving behind a trail of broken hearts. But it wasn't Alex's fault. He never was more than friendly, never promised anything more than a ride down Bellevue or a dance in the Casino. If he needed more than a dance from a woman, he had a few married lady friends who could accommodate him. That trail of broken hearts was entirely the fault of the women who fancied themselves in love with a man who counted himself lucky to remember their names. Thankfully, Alex had a rare gift for remembering names.

Henry had been much the same, which was why when he'd needed a bride posthaste, there was no one he could even think of seriously asking. Except for Anne. Disposable, inconsequential Anne Foster, the ugly girl who wouldn't mind being cast aside. Good God, how could he have thought such a thing?

Well, he had and it was over. He'd done his best to clear his conscience. He should feel as if a great weight had been lifted from his shoulders, but all he did feel was a growing sense of panic. It was the same feeling he'd had as a boy in late August when the fall semester was about to begin and the magic of summertime was about to end. He could remember standing with his toes in the water at dusk, fiercely dreading the inevitable day his parents announced they were returning to New York. It was as if he'd missed out on something that summer, that even with all the lazy days in the sun, he needed more and more and more.

"What a delightful girl," Alex said.

"Marry her, then. She's already half in love with you."

"Where's the challenge in that?" Alex asked, his eyes resting on the form of Beatrice Leyden. "Speaking of challenges, where is your former wife? Walking in the deserted tennis courts with Mr. Morrison? Or perhaps he convinced her to view his yacht tonight. You should see it, Henry, a monster anchored off Château sur Mer, even more luxurious than Vanderbilt's *Alva*. He's holding a party there Saturday night. A rather fast crowd, so, of course, I was invited. I'm certain he'd have room for one more."

Two years ago, Henry would have gone without a thought, but now the thought of being cooped up on a yacht with a hundred drunken people was not appealing.

"I happened to overhear Morrison ask a certain Miss Foster to attend."

Henry stiffened. "Of course she said no."

"On the contrary. I believe she giggled, batted her eyelashes, and said yes. No doubt she'll be dragging her friend along with her."

That panicky feeling surged. He couldn't fathom why Anne would agree to attend such a fete. Certainly she was not so naive that she didn't know it was entirely inappropriate for her to go to such a party without a chaperon. What the hell was wrong with Morrison for asking her? A girl like Anne didn't belong— His thoughts stopped abruptly. As a divorced woman, Anne certainly could go to such an event without a chaperon. She was just the sort of woman— if one didn't know her—that a man would ask to such a party. Henry gave Alex a sharp look, then smiled.

"Have you signed on as her protector, then?" Henry laughed, knowing he'd immediately seen through his friend's motives for attending the party. "Oh, this is rich. Alex Henley acting as surrogate chaperon for two unsuspecting girls. And who will protect them from you?"

It was Alex's turn to stiffen. "Anne is perfectly safe with me and you know it. As far as the other one goes, someone has to make certain she stays out of trouble."

Henry took pity on his friend, whose face had turned an uncharacteristic shade of pink. "Very noble of you."

"So. Are you going?"

"You know I am," Henry said with resignation.

Chapter Thirteen

It was, perhaps, the most daring thing either girl had ever done. They'd both heard of the parties held on yachts anchored off Newport. In the summertime, one could hear the music and laughter coming from them, traveling smoothly and cleanly across the water, hinting at decadence and sin. They had been warned away from such parties as a child is warned away from being naughty with threats of a visit from a boogeyman.

Jake Morrison was devilishly handsome and supremely rich. He had dimples in his lean cheeks, a cleft in his strong chin, eyes that were green and gray and blue, with a bit of gold splashed for even more dramatic affect. His voice was low and soothing, his manner polite, and yet Anne felt intensely uncomfortable with him. It seemed that every look, every touch, no matter how innocent, had some other darker meaning that apparently Anne was supposed to understand. He talked with her as if she were worldly and sophisticated, and Anne did her best to act the part. He was not insulting the way those married men who had propositioned her were. Oh, not so blatant as that. Truth be told, it was rather flattering to have a man of Morrison's renown pay special attention to her and treat her as if she were beautiful and special. Anne didn't think she'd ever manage to completely relax when she was with him; she felt a bit like a tiny animal being stalked by a tiger. But with Henry flirting with

Annette Bissette—a girl she decided she loathed—she couldn't help but to say yes to his invitation.

Beatrice, at first shocked at the prospect of attending such a party, warmed to the idea until she was so full of expectation, Anne hadn't the heart to tell her she wanted to send her regrets.

Jake sent her three dozen roses tied together with a string of pearls on the eve of the party. While Beatrice oohed and ahhed over the extravagance, Anne fretted about how inappropriate it was for him to have sent them to her. She would thank him for the flowers and return the pearls. Beatrice agreed, but sighed over the perfectly matched pearls that gleamed softly against her throat when she tried them on.

"Marrying Jake Morrison wouldn't be the worst thing in the world," Beatrice said as she pulled on Anne's laces, making her gasp. It was nearing midnight and the two had dismissed their maids for fear someone would discover their plan to attend such a forbidden event.

Anne rolled her eyes. "I thought our only goal this season was Henry."

Beatrice dropped a deep green silk dress over Anne's head, then proceeded to work on the tiny buttons at the back. "It wouldn't hurt to have Mr. Morrison waiting in the wings when all this was over. I hear he has a mansion in Philadelphia that takes up an entire city block."

"I like my town house."

"But Anne, Jake Morrison. Jake. Morrison."

Anne shrugged.

"My turn," Beatrice said, presenting her back and loosened stays to Anne. "There isn't a single girl in Newport whose mother isn't frothing at the mouth to gain an introduction to him, and he walked up to you and asked you to dance. Twice. And he asked you to his yacht."

"He really oughtn't have. Not if he has honorable intentions."

It was Beatrice's turn to shrug. "He's a modern man and you're a modern woman."

Anne snorted. "I'm no such thing. I'm about as old-fashioned as a girl can get. It's only my situation that is modern. Besides, I have no interest in getting married again. I'm perfectly happy in my own little town house living my own life."

"Alone."

"Yes. Alone and happy to be that way."

Beatrice smiled. "Liar. Two days ago you fancied yourself in love with Henry and I'll bet you were already dreaming of a wedding."

Anne flushed a burning red, turning away to fetch Beatrice's dress so her friend wouldn't see. It was half true. A few kisses and she made the giant leap to imagining herself falling in love with him. Would she do the same if Jake kissed her? For some reason, the thought of him kissing her made her slightly queasy. Still, she supposed it would do no harm to let him kiss her. Certainly Henry would have no qualms about kissing a girl other than her. It made her livid to see him give Annette Bissette his lazy smile, the very same smile he'd given to her. He'd danced with a half-dozen girls at the Casino and not looked her way once. Not once.

If Beatrice's entreaty hadn't worked to harden her heart, seeing Henry at the Casino certainly had. No longer did he seek her out, no longer was he hovering about, now that he'd gotten from her what he sought. It made her purely sick to think she imagined herself falling for him again. And she found it humiliating to admit that the reason she flirted so outrageously with Jake was in the hope that Henry might be jealous. He hadn't cared a whit; he probably hadn't even noticed her and Jake dancing so well together.

"Well, I'm certainly not in love with Henry now.

And I very much doubt Henry is in love with me. Did you see him at the Casino Friday night? He must have danced with every girl there but me, not that I care, mind you. But now that he's apologized, he seems completely disinterested in me. Not that I care. I don't."

"You said that."

"Well, I don't care. Not a whit. Only that our plan will suffer, you see."

Beatrice looked Anne straight in the eye. "Do you want to forget about The Plan? Is that what you're saying?"

Anne took a deep breath. "No. I'm saying it might be more difficult now that Henry clearly has no interest in me."

"Are you certain you want to continue?"

"Yes." Because Henry Owen had hurt her again, had used her almost as coldly as he had the first time. He'd kissed her and asked for forgiveness. And once he'd gotten that from her, he'd discarded her. Anne knew she was putting her heart in danger, knew she might get hurt even more by this man in the end. This time, though, she was going into the quagmire with her eyes wide open. This time, she'd not weaken, even if her heart broke.

The two girls looked in the mirror and smiled. "Who needs a maid?" Beatrice said, twirling her skirts a bit. "The only thing that has suffered is our hair."

"Oh, we'll be out on a boat anyway. The wind would destroy anything too elaborate." Anne glanced at the clock. "We'd better hurry if we're to catch the ferry."

Along with the flowers, Jake Morrison had included a note giving directions to a beach where several boats awaited his guests to ferry them out to his yacht, the *Aurora*. When they arrived, there were half a dozen people milling about, men and women dressed for-

mally and acting raucously. Scents of tobacco and li-
quor mixed heavily with the moist salt air.

"Do you recognize anyone?" Anne whispered.

"It's too dark. Isn't this exciting?"

It was exciting, and Anne felt an odd affinity to the
other people milling about the beach heading to a
yacht for a clandestine party. Never in her wildest
imaginings did she believe frumpy, fat Anne would
attend a party on a yacht, the special guest of one of
the most sought-after men in Newport. Such parties
were always reserved for the sophisticated, fast crowd,
for the urbane Europeans who inundated Newport
each summer, and the new rich, who didn't know
any better.

"I'm glad I didn't bow out," Anne said, giving Beatrice a quick grin. "Do you think there will be chorus
girls from New York?"

Anne could see Beatrice's eyes widen even in the
dark. "No," she gasped. "Oh, I do hope so!"

The splash of oars coming toward the small group
quieted the gathering. She overheard someone ask if
others had already gone aboard, and learned that
three boatfuls of people had already departed the
beach for the *Aurora,* whose lights were visible from
shore. Even now, the sound of music and laughter
drifted ashore holding with it the promise of dangerous pleasures.

Just as Beatrice was about to step aboard the long
row boat, Anne placed a hand on her arm. "Are you
certain? Once we're aboard, it might be difficult to
convince someone to row us ashore."

"Are you joking? I wouldn't miss this for the
world."

Henry leaned against the railing of the two-hundred-
and-fifty-foot yacht and watched as the final boat came
slowly into view, his eyes immediately going to the
lovely blonde sitting in the very middle. "Damn,"

Henry muttered. He was beginning to hope that Anne had found some good sense between the Casino dance and this evening. He felt right at home among these less-than-acceptable people, but Anne did not belong here. He couldn't recall the number of times he'd spent long weekends drinking and womanizing on yachts very much like the *Aurora*. There had been girls from good families, girls bored with proper behavior, who attended such events. They would drink for the first time and wake up, virginity lost, reputation in shatters. Some were smart enough to leave unscathed, of course, with wonderful racy tales to tell. He would make certain that Anne was one of the smart girls.

"There they are," he said, jerking his head to the rowboat.

"So I see," Alex said, frowning deeply at Beatrice. "Fool girl."

Anne daintily stepped from the bobbing rowboat onto a ladder that led up to the deck, lifting her skirts high enough to expose a good bit of calf. Henry gripped the railing hard to stop himself from beating to a pulp the man next to him who let out a low whistle at the sight.

"I'd like a bit of that, eh?" the man said, nudging Henry's arm.

"She's taken," he growled, then shoved past the man to make his way down to the main deck.

"I can see that," the stranger said, looking pointedly down at Anne and the man standing over her.

Jake Morrison stood less than a foot away from Anne, gazing down at her as if she were his long-lost love, holding both of her hands. Henry watched with impotent rage as Jake lifted one of her hands and brought it to his lips, a slow, suggestive move. Henry let out the sound of a man who's just stubbed his toe hard against a sharp corner. He shoved himself away from the railing, intending to rip Anne out of Morrison's hands.

"Hold on, Henry. Don't make an ass of yourself just yet," Alex said, grabbing his friend's upper arm. "What are you going to do, call him out for kissing her hand?"

Henry swiped a hand through his hair. "He's a snake."

Alex shrugged. "She's a grown woman, Henry. Unless you plan to stake a claim, which I note you so eloquently did with that gentleman back there, it's really none of your business who kisses Miss Foster's hand. We're here to observe. To make certain those two little fools don't get themselves into trouble. We are not here to propose marriage. At least I'm not."

Henry continued to glare down at the couple.

"What of you, Henry. Henry?"

"What?"

"Are *you* here to propose marriage?"

He hesitated long enough for Alex to let out a groan of disbelief. "Of course I'm not," he said. "But I'll be damned if I'll stand by and let Anne's virtue be taken by Morrison."

"You do know that Morrison thinks Anne was married and has no virtue to protect."

Henry grimaced. "I'm quite aware of that. Perhaps we should set Morrison straight."

By the time the two men made their way down to the main deck, Anne and Jake Morrison had disappeared.

Acting sophisticated was giving Anne a headache. Jake seemed never to say anything that didn't have some other meaning. It was confusing and tiring. Anne wished Beatrice had come along on the tour of the *Aurora,* but she'd bowed out with a secret smile on her face that Anne wanted to slap off. She found herself wishing she was anywhere other than on this yacht with these loud people as she walked beside Jake exchanging witty and meaningless remarks.

"I'd like to show you my private stateroom," he said, giving the hand that rested on his forearm a little squeeze.

"I hope not too private. My reputation, you know," she said, as if she truly hadn't a care in the world about her reputation. She wondered frantically if he planned to kiss her. Should she say no? Wouldn't she appear to be a prude or a bumpkin if she protested?

The yacht was nothing like she'd ever seen. With its fifteen-foot molded ceilings, rich, gleaming walnut paneling, carpeting so thick, she felt like she was floating down the hall, it was more of a floating mansion than a boat. Each stateroom had an adjoining bath, some with deep copper bathtubs. On a lower deck was a gymnasium and game room, complete with billiard table and roulette wheel. Each room was filled with men and women laughing and drinking. She even saw a woman smoking a cigarette, a glass of what appeared to be whiskey in her other hand. Anne felt as if she'd stumbled upon a world of decadence, a place where people were different creatures than those she'd known all her life.

They walked through the huge dining room with its dazzling chandelier, past servants bustling to fill a table with steaming pots and food-laden serving dishes, into a short hallway, finally stopping at a room near the stern of the yacht. Jake stopped, as if for effect, and opened a door with frosted glass bordered by floral etchings. The first thing Anne saw was a small, lace-covered dining table with two place settings. The second thing she saw was the bed.

Beatrice found herself backed to the railing with two angry men standing in front of her.

"You let her go off with Morrison alone? What the hell were you thinking?" Henry nearly shouted.

"Henry, let me handle this," Alex said in a calm voice. Then he turned to Beatrice. "What *were* you thinking?"

Beatrice looked from one man to the other belligerently. "I certainly think she is just as safe with Mr. Morrison as she is with either of you. At least Mr. Morrison hasn't made any untoward advances to her," she said, looking pointedly at Henry.

"My God, Miss Leyden, do you have any idea what goes on at these parties? Do you have any idea who half these people are?" Henry asked, sweeping a hand at the people milling about. "You are out of your element here."

Beatrice looked down, knowing that Henry was right.

"If you know where she went, you must tell us," Alex said so gently, Beatrice raised her head.

"I don't know. I only know he was to give Anne a tour of the yacht. You don't truly think Anne is in danger." Surely Mr. Morrison wouldn't make any unwanted advances to Anne. Would he? It dawned on her suddenly just how precarious their situation was. Mr. Morrison was new to Newport. His only information about Anne came from others and his brief meeting with her. Alarm grew as she realized Anne had used her best acting ability to convince Morrison she was a sophisticated woman, not the innocent, naive girl she was. She raised a gloved hand to her mouth, then clutched at Henry's arm.

"You must find her, Mr. Owen. Mr. Morrison doesn't realize Anne is not like other divorced women." She blushed at even hinting of the marriage bed—and the fact that Anne and he had never shared one. In her mind's eye, she recalled the hungry, possessive manner Morrison used with Anne. Before he'd seemed suave, but now in her panic, she envisioned his every action a calculated attempt to seduce a woman he had no idea was completely innocent.

* * *

Something wasn't quite right with this woman, but Jake would be damned if he could figure it out. Anne Foster was a wondrous combination of beauty, innocence, and worldliness, a completely refreshing sort of girl that he'd never had the pleasure of meeting before. In his experience, girls were either innocents looking for marriage, or married women looking for excitement in bed. Anne seemed genuinely uncomfortable in his private stateroom, something that amused rather than alarmed him. Certainly she must have known when he invited her to his party, then suggested they visit his stateroom, what he had in mind. Perhaps she was playing a part, pretending reluctance to save her good name. From what he'd heard, and he'd made it a point to hear all he could, Miss Foster had rejected the advances of every man who'd approached her. But Jake Morrison, he thought smugly, was not every man.

The son of a powerful steel magnate, Jake was used to getting his way. If put to the test, he would be hard-pressed to find a single thing he'd wanted and had not gotten—from women to this yacht, everything had been his for the asking. He was intelligent enough to recognize how lucky he'd been in life to be born the second son of an incredibly ambitious and fabulously rich father who had little interest in what he did. He'd lost his virginity at fourteen to his mother's best friend and had never heard the word "no" in his entire life. That was mostly due to the fact that he'd never tried to seduce a woman who he suspected might say that noxious little word.

"You look like a princess tonight," he said, keeping his voice low, and was gifted with one of her brilliant smiles. My God, he thought, what a man wouldn't do to make this girl smile. It almost made a man think about abhorrent things like marriage and children. He laughed to himself, thinking that perhaps he should leave this particular girl alone if that's where his thoughts were straying.

"Thank you, my fair prince," Anne said, curtsying. "What a wonderful floating castle you have." Her eyes kept straying to his ridiculously large bed, the satin covers pulled back invitingly.

"We could skip dinner," he said, a slow seductive smile on his lips.

"Oh, well. I'm not so hungry." She fluttered her hand toward the table and took a tiny step back, as if she were frightened of him. Jake frowned slightly, then smiled again to reassure her. *Acting* innocent was one thing, but he didn't want a skittish female on his hands.

"Not trying to escape me, are you?" he asked silkily.

Her eyes widened more and again darted to the bed. Damn, but she was acting afraid. What the hell was wrong with her all of a sudden?

"Escape?" she squeaked. "Whatever do you mean? Perhaps it's time to return to the deck. I'm sure Beatrice is missing me. I hadn't meant to be gone this long."

"If I recall, your friend encouraged you to have fun. Now, let's have some fun, princess, shall we?"

He gave her his best smile, his most reassuring, seductive smile, and she looked as if the very devil approached her. Jake was just about to place his hands gently on her shoulders, when she swirled around, smashing her head hard into the closed stateroom door. She let out a screech, and when she turned, blood was running heavily from her nose.

Henry was going mad. He'd followed their trail to Morrison's private stateroom both enraged and terrified by what he might find when he reached the room. He could now acknowledge to himself that he wanted Anne for himself, for the thought of Morrison touching her, kissing her, made him want to rip that new-monied bastard apart.

Henry was walking across the dining room and entering the hall that ended with Morrison's stateroom, when he heard a loud thump and then a scream. His heart stopped, his blood ran cold, his hands formed two large fists. He lunged for the door and pushed hard, thinking it might be barred, and was surprised when it opened easily—until crashing into something solid. Another scream.

He saw this: Anne. Blood. Tears. Morrison. He stood there, his entire body rigid, silently assessing what he saw, until all he saw was a haze of red. He took one step toward Morrison, who was trying to say something like, "It's not what you think." But it didn't matter, nothing mattered but that Anne was crying and bleeding in Morrison's private stateroom. It took only one punch, a hard, fast, brutal punch to Morrison's jaw, to bring the man down and put him out.

Henry stood over him, sweat dripping down onto his prone, moaning victim, fists clenched, daring Morrison to get up. Praying Morrison would get up. He breathed through his nose like a raging bull, his ears roaring for several long seconds, until finally something broke through the rage that clogged his veins.

"What the blazes do you think you're doing?" Anne said, ineffectually trying to stem the flow of blood from her nose. "Ugh, it won't stop," she complained. "And just look at my dress."

Henry looked from Anne to Morrison, who was still lying down, but with his eyes open and looking warily at Henry. "I heard a scream."

"That was me," Anne said.

Henry closed his eyes briefly. "Obviously. What the hell happened?" Henry asked, taking out his handkerchief. He went over to her, tilted her head back, and pressed the cloth to her nose, ignoring the glare of anger in her eyes.

"Perhaps, you should have asked before resorting to your fists," came the dry response from below.

"Shut up, Morrison, until I find out whether I owe you an apology or another beating."

Anne brought her head down. "You owe him an apology. I was leaving when I hit my face against the door."

"A rather hasty leaving "

Anne flushed. "Well. Yes. But it's not Mr. Morrison's fault. It's yours."

Henry raised his eyebrows. Jake had propped himself up on elbows to watch, in no hurry to get up.

"My fault? Do tell me how that can be."

To Henry's horror, Anne's eyes glittered with tears.

"I'm a divorced woman, Henry Owen. And that makes men think I'm a different sort of woman than I am. That's how it is your fault. Do you think poor Mr. Morrison is the first man to come to the wrong conclusion?" She turned to look at Jake, giving him a small smile. "I'm sorry, Mr. Morrison—"

"Jake, sweetheart."

Henry made another fist.

"I'm sorry, Jake," Anne continued. "I was trying to act worldly. The truth is, I didn't know what you were saying half the time."

Jake shook his head in wonder. "You were wonderful," he said, like a man completely smitten.

Henry rolled his eyes. "Are you saying this man made unwanted advances to you?"

"No," Jake answered. "But I was about to when she slammed her nose into the door. I can assure you I completely misread the situation and would never have continued with my, um, plans once it became clear Anne was not a willing participant." Jake stood, rubbing his jaw to assess the damage. He held out his hand. "Jake Morrison. And you are?"

"Anne's husband." He shook the man's hand reluctantly. Henry wanted to remain angry with Morrison, but the man was turning out to be annoyingly likable.

"My *former* husband," Anne said. "Really, Henry,

please do not make the mistake again of calling yourself my husband." She crossed her arms at her midriff.

"This is awkward," Jake said.

"Not at all. The only person who should be feeling awkward is him," she said, pointing a finger at Henry.

"Think what you may, Anne. But know that the reason I searched for you was because I was worried and I . . ." Anne looked to the ceiling, dismissing anything he had to say with a flippancy that sent a shard of something very much like pain to his heart. "To hell with you, then, Anne."

Henry turned and left the room, closing the door behind him with exaggerated care.

Anne kept her face averted until the door shut, refusing to feel guilty for rejecting his self-proclaimed heroism. Every time she hardened her heart against him, he found a way to chip away. Chip, chip, chip. She could not let him in again, no matter how noble he acted.

"Does he always do that?" Jake asked.

"What? Curse at me? No."

Jake smiled knowingly. "I meant, does he always come to your rescue like that?"

"Only recently. He feels guilty about ruining my life," Anne said, checking the handkerchief for new signs of bleeding.

"Ah. Do you think he perhaps is trying to win you back?"

"Win me back?" Anne asked with bafflement. "Goodness no. He's simply trying to ease his guilty conscience, to win his way to heaven, perhaps."

"He acts like a man in love," Jake said, but his smile told Anne he wasn't serious. "I think I understand him completely."

The look Jake gave her made Anne blush to her very roots. She couldn't help but think about what Beatrice had said earlier that evening. Jake Morrison would be a wonderful catch once this business with Henry was over with.

Chapter Fourteen

Beatrice leaned up against the yacht's polished railing, one arm crossed about the midriff of her bead-encrusted gown, the other holding an elegant champagne flute. She was pretending to ignore the man next to her, but he was making that difficult to do since he wouldn't stop talking. Or rather, criticizing. Her dress was too flimsy for the night air, she indeed needed a chaperon, she was a nitwit to have allowed Anne to go off alone with Jake Morrison, she was drinking too much.

She waited until he seemed to take a breath. "Are you quite finished? I'll have you know I have an older brother and a father. I do not need another of either."

"I disagree, Miss Leyden. You most assuredly do or you would not have come to this party."

Beatrice laughed. "Oh, Mr. Henley, this is rich. You sound like an old, prudish school master. And we both know you are not."

Alex stiffened, then he smiled and leaned against the railing next to her, close enough so that the sleeve of his jacket brushed against her bare upper arm. "Bad things happen to good girls at parties like this," he said softly.

Surprised by his concern, she turned to look at him and found herself gazing into his deep brown eyes like some moonstruck adolescent. She blinked, remembering who she was and who Alex was. He was a rake, a man who made a habit of gaining kisses from girls and then forgetting they existed. "I am a good girl," she said to remind him, and she watched with fascination as his eyes drifted to her lips. His jaw tensed and he swallowed.

"I know what you are," he said, his voice sounding strained, almost angry. He was so close, his breath, tinged with brandy, hit her face in little puffs. "You are the most dangerous of creatures, Miss Leyden."

She raised her eyebrows. "I wouldn't hurt a fly."

"Not knowingly." He inhaled audibly and turned his head so she looked at his strong profile. Alex was, she thought, a most handsome man. "I wonder if Henry found her."

She ignored his obvious attempt to change the subject. "Were you going to kiss me?" Oh, goodness, too, too much champagne. Alex was right.

He looked at her again, studying her, as if trying to slowly translate her words into English. "I thought about it, but decided it would not be prudent."

Something strange had taken over Beatrice. It was more than the champagne. It was this balmy summer night, this yacht, this man standing next to her, a man whom she disliked heartily, a man she wanted to kiss so badly, it was all she could do not to lean toward him with her lips pursed. "I've always thought I wanted to. Kiss you, that is. Simply to find out what all the fuss is about."

Alex looked heavenward. "Beatrice." His jaw tightened. "Miss Leyden, now I know you've had a bit much champagne."

Beatrice defiantly took another swallow, pushing it down her throat with an audible gulp. She shrugged. "It wouldn't mean anything. But girls do talk, and your name is mentioned from time to time. They say," she whispered, "that you can make a woman's toes curl."

Alex nearly choked. But then he smiled with masculine pride. "Good God, do they really? Toes curl?"

Looking at his smug expression, Beatrice wished she hadn't mentioned that part. He was too confident by far, she needn't add to his already overblown ego. She swayed just a bit even though the bay was calm. Oh my, she thought, looking at her empty glass, I do feel a bit tipsy. "One girl said as much. And I doubt you ever kissed her. She was just talking." She put on a grumpy face.

"I suppose I could indulge you in one kiss."

"I've changed my mind," Beatrice said, feigning boredom with the conversation.

"Oh, come now. Not a minute ago you were fairly begging me for a kiss."

"I was hardly begging you," she said, completely aware that she'd succeeded in turning him about so that he was asking her for a kiss.

He stepped in front of her, taking her empty glass and placing it carefully on the deck. "I could make your toes curl, Miss Leyden," he said teasingly.

She yawned. "Oh, very well. You may try."

Very slowly he lowered his head. Her eyes fluttered closed, her hands gripped the railing behind her.

"Open your eyes, Miss Leyden."

She opened her eyes and saw only the blurry image of his eyes descending toward her. He touched his mouth to hers so gently, she could hardly think of it as a kiss.

"My toes are still intact," she muttered.

And then the kiss became more than a kiss, it became every fantasy she'd ever had coalescing into a reality so profound, she nearly swooned. He let out a sound of deep male satisfaction as he deepened the kiss, as he teased her lips with his tongue. That sound alone made her toes scrunch up inside her shoes, but his mouth, his tongue, made her knees weak and her insides deliciously warm.

Beatrice was dimly aware that he had stopped kissing her and was drawing away. Oh, do come back, she thought. Do do do.

"I'm sorry. Um, excuse me. Oh my."

"Miss Foster. Henry has been looking for you," Alex said, his voice slightly lower than usual.

"Anne!"

Anne smiled weakly at her friend. "Hello, Bea."

"We weren't . . . I wasn't . . ."

"Of course we were," Alex said, slightly irritated. "Your friend wanted to see if I could make her toes curl. I believe I did."

Beatrice's mouth gaped open in outrage. "You did not." She looked at Anne, mortified by what Alex was saying, and that was when she noticed her friend's bloodstained dress.

"My goodness, Anne, what happened to you?"

"Good God, you look like you've been in a barroom brawl."

Anne smiled. "I very nearly was. This," she said, pointing to her red and slightly swollen nose, "is the result of walking into Mr. Morrison's stateroom door. However, Henry arrived soon after."

"And I can imagine what he thought," Alex said. "Is Morrison still alive?"

"His jaw is a bit sore, I believe," Anne said, laughing. "Have you seen Henry?"

They shook their heads.

"I suppose I should go look for him. He was quite displeased with me."

"Stay here, Miss Foster. If you're both roaming around this floating hotel, you'll never find each other." Alex lifted his chin to look over Anne's head. "There he is now. I'm glad I insisted Henry and I come to this party. Who knows what trouble you two could have gotten into."

"Yes, we are all safe with the virtuous Alex Henley protecting us," Beatrice said dryly.

Anne missed Alex's counterpunch in their verbal

battle to turn to Henry. His expression was stony, his eyes a flinty gray as he gave her a slight nod. He was angry with her and she didn't care except that his anger perhaps meant he had feelings for her that went deeper than mere concern. Perfect, she told herself. She would apologize, flutter her eyelashes, perhaps allow him to kiss her. Tonight he might even profess his love for her and this nasty business would be over with.

"Henry," she said, placing her hand on his arm, and leading him toward the relative privacy of a hallway. "I'd like to apologize. As misplaced as your concerns were, I realize you made an idiot of yourself because you were truly worried."

Henry gave Anne a crooked smile. "That's about the most backhanded apology I have ever heard in my life."

Anne gave him a sidelong look like she'd seen other girls do so effectively. "Am I forgiven, then?"

He frowned at her. "Of course."

She broadened her smile and batted him playfully on his forearm. "Oh, good. I would so hate to think things would be awkward between us. Are we friends again?"

His frown deepened. "I suppose we are."

Her eyes widening in what she supposed was a charming way, Anne said, "What a lukewarm response, Henry. Why, I do believe you are still angry with me."

"What the hell are you doing?"

She tilted her head. "I haven't the slightest idea what you mean."

"You're flirting with me. Stop it."

"I'm only allowed to flirt with other men, then?" Anne said, feeling as if she were losing control but not knowing why. She'd been practicing this flirting thing with Jake Morrison and others and thought she'd gotten it down quite pat. She was only acting like every other woman who'd captured Henry's attention. Perhaps, though, she wasn't doing it exactly right. Perhaps she looked ridiculous to him. She pouted, an expression that used to make her look even fatter, but one she now found made her adorable. At least that's what Jake told her. Maybe he was just being nice. Perhaps pouting *did* make her look fat. She drew in her lip.

"Men get the wrong idea when girls flirt with them," Henry said.

Anne tilted her head back and looked at Henry with drowsy eyes. "Maybe I want them to get the wrong idea. I am, after all, a fallen woman."

"That's enough, Anne," Henry bit out. "I can't change the past."

"I'm not asking you to," she said lightly. "I like being a fallen woman. Just look at all the wonderful attention I get. Do you think a man like Jake Morrison would have been interested in me before my divorce?"

"Jake Morrison and men like him are interested in you because you're beautiful."

Anger surged. "Is that why he invited me to his stateroom? Because I'm beautiful? Or because he fully expected me to share his bed?"

He put his hands around her upper arms and squeezed. "You'll not see Morrison again."

Anne snorted. "Of course I will. I like Jake," she said, purposefully using his given name. How wonderful, she thought, Henry is jealous. She'd never thought of using jealousy as a tool to lure him into her trap. Certainly she wasn't secretly thrilled to know he was jealous, simply glad he was so very easy to lead. "And he kisses far better than some."

Anne knew she had pushed him too far, so she tried a smile to convey she was joking. For some reason, that smile seemed to agitate him even more.

"You are purposefully trying to antagonize me," he said, stunned by the revelation.

"First you accuse me of flirting. Then you accuse me of antagonizing you. Really, Henry, you're not being very gracious this evening. And you can remove your hands from my arms," she said, looking pointedly at each hand.

"I'll be damned if I will," he said calmly. Too calmly.

Anne wasn't certain how she was supposed to go about getting Henry to profess his love without allowing him to touch her, but she wished she could figure it out. How was she supposed to coldly break his heart when every time he touched her, she felt as if she were on fire? She swallowed as she looked into his eyes and recognized the hunger in them. You hate him, she told herself. But I love it when he touches me, her traitorous other half screamed.

"Shall I kiss you, Anne? Shall I prove that my kisses are better than Morrison's?"

Anne widened her eyes in panic. "No need," she said quickly. "When I said Mr. Morrison's kisses are better than some, I didn't mean you. So, you see, there is no need to prove yourself." She knew that if she allowed this kiss, even if she really, truly, agonizingly wanted his kiss, her heart would melt on contact. It was impossible to remain unmoved when his lips were pressed against hers.

"You want me to kiss you. You presented me with a challenge, sweetheart, and I just love a challenge."

Anne pressed her lips tightly together, like a child refusing to take a dose of castor oil. He let out a chuckle, deep and seductive.

He leaned forward, dropping his hands from her arms and bracing himself against the paneling, a hand on each side of her head. "Now, Anne, let's not be difficult," he whispered against her cemented lips. He moved his mouth against hers as if he had all the time in the world, and Anne tried to remain passive. She clutched her skirts with her two fists and pressed herself as far back as possible against the smooth teak paneling behind her. He moved his mouth along her jaw, darting a tongue out at the curve just below her ear, and she let out a stifled little sound. He moved slowly back to her mouth, brushing her jaw along the way, making her legs feel boneless and the rest of her like mush. Hot mush. By the time he again touched her lips with his, her mouth was soft and pliant and begging to be kissed. He nipped at her full lower lip with his mouth, darting his tongue out to taste her.

And then he pulled back to look at her. For the longest moment, he simply stared, his gray eyes dark as Jamestown slate. Anne wasn't certain what he saw, but when he brought his mouth down again, it was with a hunger that thrilled her as much as it confused her. He buried his hands in her hair, bringing her hard up against him. Instead of pulling away, she realized that she had flung her arms around him, a woman drowning and wanting to be saved. His mouth ravaged hers; there was no other way to think about it. Anne responded instinctively, moving her tongue against his, wanting more and more, but not knowing quite how to go about it. She let out a sound of pleasure tinged with frustration, and he responded with a low rumble in his chest that she felt down to her toes.

Henry moved one hand slowly down her back to cup her buttocks, and pulled her closer still until she could feel something hard and . . . Goodness, she thought dazedly, that must be what I think it is. Suddenly what they were doing seemed so carnal, so base. So wonderfully scandalous. His arousal pressing against her intimately nearly made her forget that they stood in the hall of a yacht filled with people.

But Henry did not forget. With a soft groan, he pushed away so that their bodies weren't in danger of merging but not so far that they were not touching.

He brought his hand to her cheek and gave her another one of those intense stares that made Anne, for some strange reason, want to cry.

"I didn't intend this, you know."

Anne smiled lazily. "I did."

Henry grinned, gazing at her warmly. "You were hiding in there all along, weren't you?"

It was not the thing to say. Henry knew it the moment the words left his mouth. Idiot, to have reminded Anne of their ugly past, of *her* ugly past. Her eyes, which had been gazing at him with warmth, grew suddenly cold, although she continued to smile at him. He had the oddest feeling that she was hiding something. Probably, he thought, she is hiding the fact that she is annoyed with me.

Despite her smile, she dropped her hands from his waist, instantly building a wall of silk and lace.

He dropped his hands immediately and crossed his arms over his chest.

"Beatrice seems to think Mr. Morrison will ask me to marry him. He's a very nice man, you know, beneath all that irritating self-assuredness." She was using that tone again, a practiced nonchalance, a flirtatiousness he found disconcerting. Flirting was so unlike Anne.

"Do you want to marry him?" he asked, pretending indifference even as he fought the desire to make a fist.

Anne skirted by him and began walking, and Henry kept step with her, this time without offering his arm.

"I never thought I'd get an opportunity to marry. But Jake doesn't seem to mind about my past."

"I'm sure." His voice was heavily tinged with sarcasm.

Anne stopped and put her hands on her hips. "Are you suggesting that the only reason Mr. Morrison is interested in me is because I'm divorced?"

Henry shrugged. "It is a possibility."

"Not every man has ulterior motives," she said, yanking at her skirts and stalking away. Ah, he thought, the real Anne is back. How could she not think that Jake Morrison had ulterior motives? His scene of seduction, complete with turned-down bed, was evidence of that. Anne stopped suddenly, leaning against the gleaming teak paneling beneath a softly glowing lamp, and looked back to where Henry still stood. She'd never looked more beautiful with her golden hair haloed in the lamplight. She stood with her shoulders pressed against the wall, her arms tucked behind her back, her skirts lifting in the front just enough to reveal her white satin shoes. Henry stood in the very center of the hallway, his hands stuffed into his pockets, his head slightly tilted as he gazed at her.

"Do you think, Miss Foster, that you'll ever forgive me?" he asked softly.

She shook her head. "No."

He looked down at the carpet then back at her and nodded, a crooked smile on his lips. "I think I knew that."

He walked toward her and she didn't move. She watched him approach with half-closed eyes that would drive any man mad. Did she know what she was doing? She seemed a practiced courtesan one moment, and then the next she seemed so innocent, so very perplexed to find herself being kissed.

"Why do you let me kiss you, Anne. If you hate me, why do you kiss me back?"

"I don't hate you, Henry. I hate what you did to me."

He gave her a small smile. "I suppose that's something."

Something hard glittered in her eyes for the briefest of moments, and was gone. "It's everything, Henry. Everything."

She pushed away from the wall and ran down the

hall from him and he let her go, because in that moment he realized a horrible truth.

He had fallen in love with his former wife.

From the Journal of Arthur Owen

Your mother and her parents arrived at Sea Cliff right before the Fourth of July, and were to stay until the horse show in early September. Then they were to return to New York to prepare for Walter and Elizabeth's Thanksgiving wedding. Elizabeth would chatter on and on about the wedding at the dinner table, all the while casting long glances at me to gauge my reaction. She would ask Walter where they would honeymoon. Would they go to continent? Or to England? Or both? She bubbled over with enthusiasm, making Walter laugh, something he rarely did, even then. Elizabeth could charm Walter, could make him into a man I barely recognized, almost into a man who deserved her.

I didn't really believe any of it. In my mind, I would marry Elizabeth. No matter how many times she told me the opposite, I refused to believe she would marry Walter after what we'd shared. I threatened more than once to tell Walter about us, but she pleaded, begged, and shed pretty tears. How could I think of hurting Walter that way? she'd ask. In the end I couldn't, and it wasn't because of anything Elizabeth said. It was because he was my son and I loved him. And that was why my affair with Elizabeth was slowly killing me. Every time I touched her, I betrayed my son. And yet, even knowing that, I did not, could not stop. I didn't even try.

In August, it all ended. Elizabeth came to me, her face pale. She looked terrified and I thought at the time that I was finally seeing an honest emotion on her beautiful face. You see, Henry, Elizabeth was pregnant.

It was not as if I never thought of the possibility. I think a part of me wished it would happen, for then she would be forced to choose me. I underestimated her, as I had always done. She came to me not to obtain a marriage proposal, but to come up with a plausible explanation as to why they would have to move their wedding date up. I thought, at first, she must be joking. I told her that marrying Walter now was out of the question. God help her, but she laughed at me. She reminded me again that she'd never intended our relationship to be permanent. I wanted to kill her. I don't know what stopped me from squeezing the life out of her as she laughed at me. I can still hear it, endless and musical, full of cruel mirth. When she stopped laughing, she put a provocative pinky in her mouth and thought for a long moment. The only way to move up the wedding was to finally sleep with Walter. She announced it like a woman announces she'd like to throw a dinner party.

She left me sitting behind my desk filled with impotent rage, my heart shattering. I was crazed with grief and love. How could she do this? All the while a voice in my head told me it was only what I deserved. Of course, I could not warn Walter that his fiancée was about to trick him into believing the baby in her womb was his. Unless I was willing to confess everything to my son, I would be forced to allow Elizabeth to carry out her plan. I did nothing. I said nothing, even as I watched as Elizabeth seduced my son that night. I heard them giggling on the porch, I agonized through the long silences knowing they kissed. I stood near the window, hidden by the heavy curtains, and pressed my head against the wall until I thought I might crush my skull. Later that night, I stayed awake to listen for footsteps in the hall, and when I heard them, I followed her to his room. Right before she went in, she turned and waved down the darkened hall and threw me a kiss. Driven by madness, I made myself listen to them, to her pleased sighs, to his satisfied grunts. And I thought I would die.

That night, I gave away my son.

Chapter Fifteen

For the first time in her adult life, Anne donned a bathing costume with the full intention of splashing about on Bailey Beach. She hadn't been to the small, seaweed-strewn beach in years, not since she was fourteen years old. Though it had been nearly ten years, Anne still recalled, with a rush of fresh humiliation, the last time she'd gone.

Anne had been invited to be part of a large group of young girls headed to the beach. She could still recall her excitement when she squeezed on one of her older sister's bathing costumes. Never before had she been invited along on an outing, and the thought of finally being accepted by that particular set of girls left Anne breathless. The bathing costume, which covered her from head to foot, was too tight by far, but Anne remembered looking in the mirror, her chubby face hopeful, and thinking that she looked almost thin. She'd turned this way and that, oblivious to just how awful she looked. She knew only that she was going to the beach like any other young girl. She would have fun. She would giggle and splash and gossip. It promised to be a day she'd remember forever and she hugged tight the joy of it.

The beach seemed like paradise, filled with young, laughing people, and she couldn't wait to wade into the water. She was up to her waist when she heard one of her new friends say, "Why, look everyone. A whale." Anne had actually looked about her, excitement filling her at the thought of seeing a whale. "Oh," the girl said with an exaggerated laugh. "It's just Anne." Everyone laughed. And Anne, not knowing what else to do, laughed with them. She stood in the water, looking back at the girls who had gathered at the edge of the surf, laughing and hoping she'd die right there. She didn't cry until she was home and in her room, until she looked in the mirror and finally saw what they'd seen: a fat, ugly girl. She hated those girls. She hated herself more.

"You're such a good sport," one girl had said. Anne had wanted to slap her face, her pretty, perfect face.

Nine years later, looking lithe and graceful wearing a bathing costume of dark blue alpaca, drawers, and black silk stockings, she still hesitated to walk from the protection of the Leydens' tiny cabana. Anne looked down at herself, breathed deeply, and stepped out into the brilliant sun. Immediately she placed her large straw hat on her head to protect her nose from burning and started walking toward the blanket where Beatrice already sat with her mother and brother. As she walked by a neighboring blanket, she overheard a young girl say to her mother, "I wish I looked like that. She's perfectly splendid, isn't she, Mother?"

Anne flushed scarlet with pleasure. Oh, how heady it was to hear even a little girl's envy. I am pretty, she thought, still filled with wonder at the idea.

Anne sat down next to Beatrice, leaning back on her hands and crossing her legs at the ankles, content with the world. Beatrice was dressed much as she was, except that her bathing costume was trimmed with white piping and had white buttons down the front, whereas Anne's costume was plain. "Are they here?"

"Of course," Beatrice said. "I knew they would be when I told Alex, um, Mr. Henley we'd be here. He pretended we were mad to plan a beach outing so early, but they were here before us. I'm so exhausted, I fear I won't be able to argue with him much today."

"Oh, is that what you two were doing last night?" Anne asked with a smile.

"Shh," Bea warned, casting a glance toward her mother and brother. The two women had sneaked into the house in the wee hours of the morning, so full of excitement, they'd stayed up until the sun rose talking about their adventure . . . and the kisses they'd experienced. Both pretended, of course, that the kisses meant nothing. Anne insisted that kissing Henry was part of her ploy, and Beatrice protested that Alex had taken advantage of her inebriation. "Why, I hardly even remember it," she'd said.

"Where are they?" Anne asked, looking around the beach.

"Alex is sitting in the sand chatting with some woman. Probably boring her to tears." Beatrice gave him a hard look before continuing. "Henry is swimming. See him? He's been out there swimming back and forth for about an hour. I hope he doesn't drown," she said without a hint of real concern.

Anne squinted her eyes and made out the form of a man swimming several hundred feet from shore, the flash of his arms the only thing she could see above the cresting waves. "He's awfully far out," she said.

"As I recall, he and Alex Henley used to swim across the bay in their youth," said Helen, who sat in a wooden ladder-back chair perched atop the blanket. "I doubt he's in any danger, Anne."

"Oh. I wasn't worried. Only concerned that he'd drown and someone would have to risk their life to go out and save him." Anne grinned at Beatrice and lay her hands over her heart. "His dying words would be to me, begging my forgiveness. And I would bend down close and whisper in his ear: 'Never.' "

"Oh, you are a hard woman, Anne," Helen said, laughing like a young girl. Anne joined in her laughter, but her eyes strayed to the flash of Henry's arms just to make sure he was still out there and doing well.

It was several minutes before Henry turned and
began swimming toward shore. When he emerged,
Anne's eyes were on him, peering surreptitiously from
below the wide brim of her hat in an effort to shield
her interest. Anne nodded to something Helen was
saying, but her entire focus was on Henry as he slowly
emerged from the water, his striped swimsuit clinging
to his body like a second skin. Oh my. Anne swallowed
with difficulty, for her mouth had suddenly gone dry—
perhaps because it was hanging open and she was
breathing so rapidly. He stood at the edge of the water,
his feet and ankles still submerged, and he shook his
head like a dog, water spraying like crystal pearls in the
sun. With one hand, he swept his hair back from his
forehead and strode onto the sand and toward Alex.

Anne watched his every movement, completely mes-
merized. Never before had she looked on the male form
with such utter fascination, never had she thought of
muscles and glistening skin, and soft, slippery-wet hair,
of bare feet, and of touching every wet part of him
she saw. Oh mercy.

"Anne. Anne!" Beatrice nudged her arm.

"What?"

"I asked if you wanted to go for a walk that would
take us past a certain blanket."

Anne leapt up. "Yes."

"Mother, Anne and I are going to take a stroll,"
Beatrice said as she stood.

"Good luck."

Beatrice bent down and gave her mother a kiss.
Anne smiled wistfully, thinking of her own mother,
with whom she'd never shared anything more important than a box of chocolates. "You are so lucky,
Bea," she said.

"I thank God every day for a mother like her. Did
you know that Mrs. Vanderbilt has vowed Consuelo
will marry into a title when she's of age? She's only
sixteen and her entire future is decided for her."

"Maybe she'll marry a handsome young prince," Anne said.

Beatrice snorted. "More likely some doddering old baron or duke or some such thing. No, thank you. I'd rather remain unmarried for the rest of my life than be forced to marry someone I didn't love or who didn't love me." Beatrice, realizing what she'd just said, laid a hand on Anne's arm. "I'm sorry, Anne."

Anne laughed. "No one forced me to marry, Bea. You've nothing to be sorry about."

The two women walked to the edge of the water far enough away from Henry and Alex so that they didn't look overly obvious, and got their silk stockings wet. "Oh, it's cold," Anne said, moving back as another wave approached.

"You get used to it," Beatrice said, working her way in so that the waves lapped up as high as her knees. Anne stepped in as far as her ankles and again retreated when her feet began to ache from the cold. Beatrice was up to her thighs, laughing with delight when a large wave splashed up and got her stomach wet. Anne, seeing how brave her friend was being, forced herself to step farther into the surf. Already, the water felt warmer to her feet, so she walked in slowly, the icy cold water creeping ever higher, her hands clutched together at her neckline.

"It's n-not s-so b-bad," she said, shivering.

A large wave loomed. Beatrice pointed at it, laughing. Anne stared at it in horror. With an ease born of long days at the beach wading in the surf, Beatrice jumped up just as the wave crested around her, getting no more wet than she already was. Anne, though, decided retreat would be far better. She turned in an attempt to outrun the wave, only to find herself struggling against an undertow just strong enough to hamper her advance. It was tantamount to running in place. Just when she broke clear of the sucking water, the wave slammed into the back of her legs, slapping her forward, down and into the sand. She let out a scream as water rushed past her. Then the water receded, leaving Anne kneeling in the drying sand feeling incredibly foolish.

"It's difficult to drown in six inches of water."

Anne looked up past the brim of her drooping hat to see a pair of masculine, sand-covered bare feet in front of her. She struggled to get up, her water-soaked bathing costume weighing her down, and ignored the large hand Henry held out to her.

"I wasn't afraid of drowning. I was simply startled," she said, adjusting her hat. "I haven't been to the beach in years and I don't know how to swim." Anne looked behind her to see that Beatrice had made her way to shore and was sneaking back to their blanket.

"We're alone," Henry said.

"Hardly alone," Anne said, looking about at the crowded little beach. She felt conspicuous, in fact, as if every eye was on her and Henry. As if everyone on the beach knew he kissed her, knew he'd pressed himself against her in the most intimate of ways. She was glad her hat brim shielded her face from his, for a telltale flush was creeping up her face.

"Would you like to go for a swim? I could hold your hand."

He didn't sound serious, so Anne shook her head, suddenly feeling incredibly shy.

"You know, Miss Foster, you look absolutely adorable in your bathing costume."

Look, everyone, a whale.

Anne's heart did a flip-flop. "I feel quite exposed," she said for lack of anything else to say.

Henry laughed. "You're covered from head to foot. I saw a girl once who got a hole in her stocking showing about a silver dollar's worth of skin. She was so mortified, she didn't show her face about town for days. Frankly, I would stand for a bit more exposure. Besides, you can hardly swim with all those clothes on. They're much more conducive to drowning than swimming."

Anne gave him a curious look and he went shy all of a sudden.

"I'm blathering. Aren't I," he said in such a charming way, Anne's heart did another of those little flips.

"A bit."

Henry squinted his eyes and looked out onto the water. "It's a very curious effect you have on me, Miss Foster," he said blandly, looking at her askance as if she were somehow to blame for his strange behavior.

Henry leaned slowly toward her, his hand outstretched, and Anne stiffened, her heart pounding with anticipation. He's going to kiss me. Right here on the beach, in front of all these people. And I'm just going to stand here and let him do it. Yes, I am. His hand touched her shoulder and her breath became shallow. Then he stepped back, a large piece of brownish seaweed in his outstretched hand.

"Oh," she said, and flushed.

"Did you think I was going to kiss you in front of all these people, Miss Foster?" He had that lopsided grin of his on that Anne found so distracting.

"Of course not. Don't be ridiculous."

His grin grew. "I think you did. I think you wanted me to."

Anne looked down the beach, knowing her eyes gave her away. "You're flattering yourself."

He bussed her cheek with his lips, and she turned, her eyes wide and filled with something that looked suspiciously like pleasure.

"There. See? I knew you wanted me to."

Anne looked frantically around to see if anyone had noticed. She nearly groaned when she spotted the rapt audience at the Leyden blanket. "People are looking," she whispered frantically.

"And that should matter because . . ."

Anne flashed him a look of incredulity. "Because

it's not seemly. It's not done." She spotted Jake Morrison in the distance and smiled wickedly to herself. "And because I don't think Jake would like it." She looked at Jake and prayed he would spot her so that it would appear they'd had an assignation planned. She nearly jumped for joy when Jake lifted his hand in greeting, flashing her his most winning smile.

All good humor vanished from Henry's face. "Who the hell let him on this beach? I'll have to talk to the watchman." Bailey's was guarded by a uniformed watchman whose job it was to turn away those unfortunate souls who were not members of the Spouting Rock Beach Association, one of the most exclusive clubs in Newport.

"Yoo hoo. Over here, Mr. Morrison," Anne said, waving her hand unnecessarily to the man who was already striding toward them.

"Ah," Alex said, sidling up next to the couple. "I see Mr. Morrison has finally arrived."

Henry shot Alex a dark look. Alex simply smiled. "I only thought it polite to return the favor for last night's party and invite him to Bailey's. Is there a problem?"

Henry looked at Anne in a way that made her want to run back to her blanket. Turning to Alex, he said, "So, Morrison is *your* guest."

Anne wrinkled her nose and gave a little shrug, knowing the ruse was up. "I never said I invited him."

"Do me a favor, Alex. Keep him away from me. And Anne." As if following orders, Alex departed to greet Morrison and steer him away from the couple.

Anne narrowed her eyes and put her fists on her slim hips. "You've no right to make such orders. If I want to see Jake, I will." She began to walk toward Jake with a smile on her face, but was stopped by a hand on her arm. "You must break this habit of manhandling me," Anne said, looking at his hand.

"And you must break this habit of purposefully antagonizing me. You know I don't want you to see Morrison."

Anne shook her head in disbelief. "Tell me, Mr. Owen, what gives you the right to dictate whom I may or may not see?"

He loomed over her, making her crane her neck to look into his eyes, and Anne knew that the moment she'd prayed two years for was about to happen. Henry was finally going to proclaim his love for her, right here in the middle of Bailey's Beach. It could not have been more perfect. He swallowed and clenched his jaw and his eyes were filled with the strangest light, it made Anne's insides turn to mush.

"I'll tell you what gives me the right, I think I'm . . ." To Henry's great frustration, he found himself looking at the back of Anne's hat.

A loud commotion at the beach entrance had saved Anne from a moment she'd thought she'd wanted for months. She was certain Henry was about to fall into her trap and declare his love—or something close to it—and for some reason the thought of crushing him here and now was unconscionable. Perhaps it was the pain she herself had suffered here, but she could not allow Henry to proclaim his love.

Not now, not yet.

Not with him looking so vulnerable in that silly striped swimsuit, not with his hair tousled, his face dotted with salt spray, his cheeks reddened by the sun. Anne refused to think why she'd turned away from him, panic flooding her, she only knew that she hadn't the stomach for it just now. Why ruin a perfectly glorious day by breaking someone's heart?

Henry took a step toward the entrance. "It's Peleg," he said.

"Who?"

"Sea Cliff's caretaker. If you'll excuse me."

Henry moved toward the entrance, leaving Anne nearly shaking with what she'd just done. She felt like a warden giving a prisoner a stay of execution—a jumbled mix of relief and anxiety.

"Are you certain Mr. Owen is no longer a part of your life?" Jake Morrison asked softly, startling Anne from her thoughts.

"Not a large part," she said, beaming at him. Then her mouth opened in shock. "Oh, look at your face." Jake's jaw was slightly misshapen and covered with a dark bruise from his chin to about midway to his ear.

"Yes," Jake said, touching his jaw tenderly and with a bit of self-consciousness. "I was hoping it would make me look dashing, but I can see by your expression I have fallen short of the mark."

Anne gave him a look of sympathy. "Oh, no. You're quite dashing still, Mr. Morrison. It's just that it looks rather painful. Is it?"

"Nothing that a sweet kiss from a pretty girl won't cure."

Anne made a great show of looking around for a pretty girl before saying, "I'm afraid I don't see any about just now, but for Beatrice, and I think someone might object to her kissing you. I wouldn't want the other side of your face getting all bruised."

Jake smiled in that predatory way that made Anne slightly uneasy. "I was thinking you would do."

Anne darted a look to where Henry stood with Alex talking to his caretaker. When she looked back at Jake, he was frowning.

"Miss Foster," he said. "Are you available or not?"

"Of course I'm . . ." she started, then stopped. "I'm afraid I don't really know."

"I see."

"No, you don't. I don't even see," Anne said with frustration.

He let out a soft chuckle. "Let me know when you do." He gave her a little nod of his head and sauntered down the beach alone. Anne knew she should not let him go and was about to open her mouth to call him back when she again looked to where Henry was. She would never be truly free until she'd finished with Henry once and for all. Oh, why hadn't she let him finish his sentence? She refused to allow herself to think that she was still falling in love. It was only that weak part of her that showed itself whenever Henry was around. She was such a pushover for that smile of his, she thought with a wistful smile of her own.

She watched as Henry headed toward his surrey with Peleg Brown. He hadn't come back or even waved good-bye. Perhaps she'd completely misread his intentions, she thought as Alex made his way toward her. It certainly wouldn't be the first time.

"Henry was called to Sea Cliff on a personal matter," Alex said. "He sends his apologies."

Sea Cliff. Like a bucket of cold water, just hearing the name of Henry's summer home washed away all tender thoughts of him. Remember, you idiot, remember what he did to you. He deserves what you're about to do. Her eyes followed the surrey as it rode away from the beach, her heart aching. What she needed now was a good dose of Beatrice.

It took only about a minute for Beatrice to once again fuel the fire of revenge that burned in Anne's heart.

"Thank you," Anne said with a sigh, after Beatrice quickly and scathingly enumerated Henry's misdeeds. She would have to act soon, while the soft part of her heart was properly subdued.

"I'm going to do it, Bea," Anne said, making a fist.

"What are you going to do?" Beatrice asked, breathless.

"I'm going to go to Sea Cliff. What better place to crush him than the scene of my ruin?" It wouldn't be the public humiliation she'd hoped for, but it would be entirely satisfying just the same. Henry would finally pay.

Chapter Sixteen

Anne took the first steam ferry to Jamestown, then hired a boat to take her to Sea Cliff. She determined she'd have about two hours to take care of business before asking Mr. Brown to sail her back to the East Ferry landing so she could catch the last ferry to Newport. If all went as planned, she'd be back at the Leydens' before sunset and in time to dress for the Vanderbilt ball.

Anne blocked out all emotion as she stood at the ferry railing, her face buffeted by the wind. She'd practiced all her life how to hide her emotions, and that talent would come in useful this day. Anne refused to think about the end result, that she would hurt a man who, if she were completely honest, she had come to like quite a lot. But good men did bad things all the time and had to answer for them. Henry had never paid for his crime against Anne. Now he would.

Henry was at the beach barefoot and with his pants rolled to his knees when the small sailboat she'd hired scuffed the bottom of the small cove. He waded in without a word and lifted her from the boat, his large hands strong around her waist. His only words were a thank-you to the sailor who'd brought her as he flipped the man a silver dollar.

"I already paid him," Anne said.

Ignoring her, he unrolled his trousers, frowning at a wet spot on his left pant leg where water had splashed. Anne fought a sudden surge of nervousness, realizing suddenly how risky her little jaunt to Jamestown was.

"What are you doing here?" he asked finally.

Anne looked up at Henry, her heart in her throat, for he didn't seem at all pleased to find her here standing upon his beach. Then she threw back her head and smiled at him.

"Now, what kind of a greeting is that?" she asked lightly.

"I asked you a question, Anne."

This was not going quite the way she'd imagined. Not only was Henry not pleased to find her standing on his beach, he actually seemed annoyed. Had she completely misread the situation? With dawning horror, Anne realized that was very possible. Hadn't her experience with Henry before painfully proven how badly she could misread him? She frantically recalled that terrible moment on Bailey's when she'd thought him about to declare his love for her. What had he said? Something about how he had the right to be angry about Jake Morrison's attentions. But that didn't mean he *loved* her. If only she had as much courage in front of Henry as when she was safely apart from him.

Anne looked down at the sand and bit her lip. What to say, what to say? She felt foolish beyond measure, as foolish as she had looking about for that whale all those years ago at Bailey's Beach. And as devastated.

"I thought . . ." she began, then stopped with a helpless gesture of her hands. Certainly she could not say that she'd thought he loved her, for she could not face the kind of humiliation that would follow when he looked at her with pity. "I should go. Do you think Mr. Brown could sail me back to the ferry landing?"

Henry looked at her incredulously. "You've come all this way only to turn around the minute you arrive?"

Anne looked back toward Newport, wishing with all her heart that she was there now. *Oh God, of course he doesn't love you. Why would he?* And why was the fact that he did not make her feel so entirely awful? Anne closed her eyes briefly, acknowledging just how foolish she truly was. She'd even convinced herself this was about a silly plan, when all along, in that secret place in her heart she refused to see, it was about Henry loving her. She wanted him to love her, not to exact revenge, but to prove she could be loved by him.

"Let's go into the house," Henry said, looking at a sky that was heavy with clouds. "It's a mess inside. I'm still renovating, which is why I didn't invite you and Beatrice in that last time you were here. That, and my grandfather is here and he's quite ill. His nurse thought he was dying, hence the urgency of my departure from Bailey's, but he's rallied since."

Anne murmured an expression of concern, then followed him silently as he walked into the darkened house, past piles of construction debris, and into a study that appeared to be one of the few rooms with furniture. A large table strewn with what appeared to be blueprints dominated one side of the room. The other side was set apart by a large couch and two overstuffed chairs that faced a charming stone fireplace. On the mantel was a model of a clipper ship in full sail. Though the curtains were open, the overcast day made the room dim, and Henry went about lighting a few oil lamps before giving Anne his attention once more.

Anne crossed her arms and fiddled with the yellow lace that trimmed the puffed-out sleeves of her mint-green summer gown as she looked out the bank of windows.

"Anne," Henry said softly. "Why are you here?" He stood just behind her as she struggled to breathe.

Like a woman prepared to thrust herself upon a

knife, Anne lifted her chin and faced Henry. "On the beach, you were about to tell me something. It's silly, really," she said, letting out a self-deprecating laugh. "But I started to think about it, wondering and wondering what you were going to say, and it drove me quite to distraction. So, Henry, what were you about to tell me?"

He became very still, and Anne felt as if that knife were pricking her heart already. Finally, he let out a curse beneath his breath and put his hand to the back of his neck in a weary gesture.

"I was about to tell you—"

"Don't tell me," Anne said quickly. "I don't want to know. Really." She laughed. "How silly of me to let it get to me so. I'm certain it was nothing, but I kept thinking about it and thinking about it until it loomed ever larger and then I could think of nothing else. 'What was Henry going to say,' I asked myself. 'What, what, what?'"

"Anne."

"What?"

"I was going to tell you I've fallen in love with you."

Her eyes immediately filled with tears. "You see? That's what I thought," she said angrily. "And now I'm supposed to . . ." She shook her head and blinked her eyes hard to rid them of the tears and let out a huff of breath. "Beatrice is going to be so angry with me." She swatted him on the arm and he took a startled step back. "It wasn't supposed to happen like this," she said desperately, and gave him another swat.

He smiled his lopsided smile.

"See there? You're doing it again, Henry," she said, pointing an accusing finger at him.

"What am I dong?"

She was sobbing now, fighting herself, driving herself mad. "You're making me fall in love with you."

Mortified, she covered her face with her hands. "Oh, God, I can't believe I just said that."

"Is it really so awful?"

She sniffed. "Yes. Because I really don't want to, Henry. I really don't. Oh, God."

"Why not?" he asked, putting his large comforting hands on her shoulders.

She narrowed her eyes. "Because you don't deserve my love. You don't."

"I know."

"Oh, Henry. I hate you too." She sniffed. "The thing of it is, I think I love you more."

He hugged her fiercely, bringing his mouth to her ear. "I'm glad."

Anne let herself go, let herself love him even as she realized a frightening truth. He loved her because she was beautiful. Anne remembered the fat girl she'd been, already half in love with him long before the miracle of his courtship began. He always had a beautiful girl next to him. And Anne feared she might not always be beautiful.

She hugged him against her as if he might slip away, hating the doubts that assailed her.

"Kiss me, Henry," she said, lifting her face. Kiss me and make me believe you truly love me, she beseeched silently.

Henry looked down at her and smiled. "You're so damned pretty," he said, before bringing his mouth down upon her soft lips. Heaven, he thought drunkenly, I've died and gone to heaven. He couldn't believe she was here at Sea Cliff in his arms and in love with him. After torturing himself for weeks, she was his. He'd never been so afraid in his life when he finally told her he loved her, because Anne never did seem to react the way he thought she would. He'd half expected her to laugh in his face. Instead, she'd gotten angry.

And now she'd asked for his kiss, as if he might say

no. As if he hadn't lain awake at night torturing himself with thoughts of her lying next to him. With a groan, he deepened his kiss and she responded in a way that made his blood run fast. Her full breasts pressed against his chest, her hands were threaded through his hair, her thighs pressed up against his. Sweet God, it was more temptation than a man could bear.

He lifted his hand to her breast, a tentative caress, and was rewarded when she gasped, then pressed herself closer. Through her gown he could feel her nipple harden beneath his hand. He tore his mouth away from hers, nipping her jaw, her neck, then he placed his mouth on her hardened nipple and gently bit her. She let out a sound of such pure pleasure, it was all he could do not to yank down her bodice.

The next thing he knew, he was sitting on his couch looking up at a panting, wild-eyed woman.

"What was that?" she demanded, her cheeks becomingly flushed.

He paused to catch his breath. He swallowed. "Nothing. I was . . . it's perfectly acceptable."

Anne looked down at her still-hard nipple clearly showing in the wet spot on her gown.

"Anne, it's what men and women do."

Looking adorably uncertain, she said, "Truly?"

He smiled. "Truly."

"Oh. I've made a muck of things." She bit her lower lip. Henry stood and she took a step back.

"I've pushed you too fast. I'm sorry, Anne. I didn't mean to frighten you."

"You didn't frighten as much as surprise me." Her eyes were riveted on his shirt. "I haven't much experience at this, you see. You're the only man I've ever even kissed."

"Really," Henry said, surprised. "Well, you're certainly good at it."

"Am I?" She looked so hopeful, Henry thought his heart would melt down to his toes.

"Yes."

"Then let's try some more of that and see what happens," she said with a decisive nod.

"That sounds like a splendid idea," Henry said, moving close again.

Anne melted beneath his embrace, thinking she now knew what it must feel like to be butter sitting in the hot sun. They kissed until the only thing that was holding her up was Henry's strong arm across her back. This time when he touched her breast, her head fell back, her entire body tingling, especially that spot between her legs. It was almost as if he were caressing her there.

"Oh," she gasped. Somehow Henry had managed to undo enough buttons of her gown to slip her bodice below her breasts. Her nipples, hard and aching, showed clearly through the thin fabric of her lacy chemise and corset cover.

"Beautiful, Anne," he said softly, moving his mouth down her neck and to her exposed skin. Then, with gentle urging, he scooped one breast, exposing it to the air, his gaze, his mouth. His mouth. Oh, God, his mouth was on her . . . it was there on her nipple.

"Henry," she whispered.

"Hmmm?"

"Don't stop."

He let out a sound of pure male satisfaction, then drew her hard nipple into his mouth, sucking gently as he moved his tongue over the tip. Then he moved to the other breast, caressing it until Anne thought she would explode from the pleasure of it.

"All right, are we?" he asked, pausing to kiss her swollen, pink lips.

"No. I think I'm going to faint."

He chuckled, and pressed himself against her, letting her feel his arousal against her, so foreign and so very provocative. As innocent as she was, she knew what it was she felt, what it meant to have him move against her.

"Anne. I believe it's time to stop."

"Oh, no, not yet."

He pressed against her again, letting out a moan. "Yes." He gently covered her breasts, his eyes filled with regret. "Because I want to make love to you and I'll not shame you again. This time, sweetheart, everything will be perfect."

Anne drew her brows together in confusion. "This time?"

"When we marry this time, I plan to have a wedding night." He kissed her quickly. "You will, won't you? You will marry me?" He laughed. "Again?"

"You want to marry me?" she asked, stunned.

"Of course. I love you. Say yes."

Anne stared at him, her mouth slightly open in wonder, then she frowned, her brow furrowed. "I don't know what to say."

"I think 'yes' would be appropriate."

Anne felt as if she were suffocating, because more than anything in the world, she wanted to say yes. But the thought of marrying him should not fill her with fear, and that's what Anne felt when she thought of saying yes. She began shaking her head.

"Don't decide now," he said quickly, growing endearingly alarmed when it appeared she would say no. "I know it's sudden. I know I've confused you and we've a rather horrible history together. I've thought of nothing else for weeks now and I realize the idea of remarrying is new to you. To me, that is. What I mean is that remarrying me is new to you. Hell." He stopped, knowing he'd ceased making much sense. "Just say you'll think about it."

"I'll think about it," Anne said, her eyes filled with misgiving, but she managed a smile anyway.

He looked at her with relief. "I'll make it my life's

work to make you smile like that at me every day of our lives. You're so beautiful when you smile, Anne. So beautiful.''

Henry kissed her again, so he didn't see the flicker of raw fear in Anne's eyes. For the first time in her life, she wished she wasn't beautiful.

Chapter Seventeen

By the time Anne got back to the Leyden cottage, it was time to dress for the Vanderbilt ball. In a flurry of blue silk and pale yellow chiffon, Beatrice entered her room, clearly dying to know what had happened with Henry.

With a pointed look to her maid, Anne shook her head. She'd not have a word of what had happened between her and Henry show up in *Town Topics'* "Saunterings," a notorious gossip column written by the brutally scathing Colonel William d'Alton Mann. Anne had been the topic of his column more than once—he'd described her as "looking like a bit of overstuffed pastry in her white-and-pink gown" in his column following her wedding—and she hoped never to see a hint of herself there again. Even the servants the wealthy vowed were the most loyal could be bought by the colonel's correspondents.

When they were finally free of the maid, Beatrice's mother entered the room, and the frustration Beatrice experienced was nearly palpable. Though Helen knew of Anne's pursuit of Henry, she never would have approved of Anne going off to Jamestown alone, so no discussion could take place with her in the room. Such a jaunt, even for a divorced woman, was highly improper and Anne was thankful that, thus far, no one knew of her adventure but Henry and Peleg Brown. Henry had assured her that Mr. Brown would never, even upon the threat of death, reveal that she'd been to Sea Cliff.

Anne felt as if she were floating on a cloud. She refused to let anything remind her that her happiness could be a fleeting thing. Again and again she wondered if she should have said yes to Henry. It was only when she forced herself to remember the pain of her past that she had any doubts at all, and her stomach would give a sickening lurch and all her misgivings would rush to her in dizzying force. He loved her and she loved him and that was all that should matter, but it wasn't enough. She'd heard such stuff all her life and had stubbornly and romantically clung to the thought that love alone would make everything perfect between a man and a woman. Yet, even though she knew better now, Anne couldn't bring herself down from the heavens where Henry had left her after his searing good-bye kiss.

"Something happened," Beatrice whispered, her eyes dancing with excitement.

Anne smiled broadly. "Perhaps."

"Let's go, ladies. Our carriage awaits," Helen said, clapping her gloved hands together. "Your father is downstairs prowling about the entry hall getting grumpier every minute."

"Tell Father, if he plans to be bad-tempered each time he comes to Newport, he can stay in New York all week," Beatrice said haughtily.

"I'll let you be the messenger of that directive, my dear," Helen said dryly.

When they walked into the foyer, Jonathan Leyden looked up from the pocket watch he was scowling at, snapped it closed, and stuffed it into his waistcoat. "You all look lovely," he said by rote. "Now, into the carriage. Hup, hup. I've got a meeting with Van Alen at ten."

"Oh, really, dear, must you conduct business tonight?"

Jonathan raised his eyebrows. "Of course. Only rea-

son I'm going to this affair is to capture Van Alen."
At his wife's look, he smiled, and said, "And to have
a dance with the most beautiful lady in Newport."

His flattery did little to soothe Helen's temper.
"Once your business is done."

"Of course," Jonathon said grandly. "Where the
dickens is Thomas, anyway?"

"He's going with the Carlisles."

"He's mad about Josephine, Father."

"Oh?" he said, his interest piqued. "Good family,
the Carlisles. Coal interests. Railroad." Anne could
almost see the dollar signs clicking away inside Mr.
Leyden's head. Like so many men in this town, if they
weren't talking horses or yachts, they were talking
money. How to make it, keep it, invest it. Their wives,
they joked, worried only about spending it—something that was not far from the truth.

Anne sighed, wondering what life would be like
with Henry—should she be insane enough to actually
marry him. Would he stay in New York while she
whiled away the time like so many other Newport
wives? No, not Henry. He would spend the long, lazy
summer days at Sea Cliff or at Owen Yachts, coming
home each evening to play in the surf with his children, who would run down to the beach to greet him.
His pant legs wet from the surf, he would lift them
high into the air and they would shriek with joy and
she would watch from the porch, a soft, warm breeze
caressing her face, and smile when he looked up and
stopped to stare, overcome with his love for her. Anne
sighed. Beatrice poked her in the ribs and widened
her eyes as if to say, "What is going on?"

"Later," Anne whispered, as she put her hand on
the footman's arm to steady her way into the Leydens'
carriage.

A heavy fog had descended on Newport, oppressive
and damp, giving the air a mystical quality that only
heightened Anne's feeling of anticipation. Marble

House was bathed in light, its white facade appearing like a fairy castle in the clouds. The portico was ablaze with new electric lights, and servants in maroon livery lined the way from the drive to the ballroom, so if a person so much as sneezed, they would be on hand to assist. It was the first time Anne had been in the astounding house, for it had been completed just the year before, and she couldn't help but stare. Alva Vanderbilt had hired Richard Morris Hunt to design the grandest, most opulent home in all of Newport, and he'd succeeded in grand style.

"Oh, my," Anne said as they crossed the threshold into the ballroom, which fairly glittered in gold. From the walls of gilded wood to the mirrors that reflected the massive gold chandeliers suspended high above them, Anne found herself surrounded in gold. Her gown of the deepest red velvet was a perfect choice, for it complemented her surroundings perfectly. Her gloves of light-weight velvet had cuffs of gold silk that folded down at the elbow. Though cut for summer wear, the gown was insufferably warm, but had looked so lovely, Anne wore it without complaint. With her golden hair piled in an artless style that had taken her maid nearly an hour to create, she felt nearly as beautiful as she was. She wished she could bottle this night and save it for the next time she felt like her old self, unsure, ugly, unwanted.

"Anne, I shall die in this very spot unless you tell me what happened at Sea Cliff," Beatrice said, eyes laughing.

Anne bit her lip. "Oh, Bea, he told me he loved me."

Beatrice's eyes widened in delight. "And what did you say? I want to hear it word for word. Did he cry?" It was then that Beatrice realized that she no longer had Anne's attention. She frowned at her friend's face, then looked to see what it was that was making Anne appear as if she were gazing at the kingdom of heaven.

Henry approached Anne, his eyes seeing only her, as if the entire room had become enshrouded with fog, as if she alone stood in the one clear spot in a room swirling with mist. He held out his hand and she took it, her eyes brilliant, her lips curved up. In a dream, he led her out to the ballroom floor and took her in his arms just as a waltz began, though the truth of it was, he would have danced without the music.

They danced, unaware as they did that they were the picture of two people in love. It wasn't long before people were nudging each other and looking their way. How perfect they looked together, like an actor and actress paired together simply to make the audience sigh with longing. How perfectly delicious that the former Mrs. Owen was dancing with Mr. Owen.

Beatrice stood at the very edge of the dancers, her mouth slightly open as she looked from Henry to Anne and back. "Oh, dear God, no," she whispered, her heart breaking. For it was as clear as day that Anne loved him. It might have been written across her forehead. It didn't matter that Henry had much the same expression on; she knew him already to be the consummate actor.

Helen's mother smiled when she saw the couple, and whispered to her dear friend Mrs. Forrest, "I knew it would happen when he went to Mrs. Astor."

Annette Bissette, who had flirted so well with Henry less than a week ago, said, "Look at her, making a fool of herself again."

Her friend next to her sighed. "I wish I were that beautiful."

The newly married Christine Eldred Shaw, who found herself quite alone yet again, frowned wistfully, and thought, Alfred used to look at me that way.

And Mamie Fish, a gleam in her eye, leaned over to Mrs. Herman Oelrichs and said, "Tessie, dear, do look and see what we've accomplished. How very charming they are."

Anne and Henry were unaware of anything but each other. They danced too close for convention, they stared too long into each other's eyes, they looked entirely too happy, too beautiful, too much in love to be part of this staid Newport crowd. In step with a Strauss waltz, they glided together, swirling around the ballroom floor as if they'd danced together a hundred times.

"I missed you," Henry said and was gifted with one of Anne's smiles. The curve of her lips, the line of her jaw, the perfection of her eyes. If she disappeared from him this night, he would never forget her face tilted up, eyes so bright, it was as if they were lit from within, one curling strand of hair waving in the wind of their movement.

"We just left each other."

"It's been an eternity." He smiled at his own absurdity and at the truth of what he said. Anne gave him a disbelieving look.

"Do other women fall for such rubbish?"

"All the time."

"Those poor women who succumb so easily. You'll find I'm not such an easy target," Anne said in a teasing manner.

He tightened the hand that rested in the soft velvet at the small of her back, pulling her even closer, unable to stop himself. He'd never felt this out of control, this entirely reckless. He was a hairsbreadth away from kissing her right in the middle of the Vanderbilt ballroom floor. Surely if he did, half the matrons of good taste in this city would faint dead away.

"I want to kiss you," he said low, his eyes ablaze with emotion.

Anne's eyes widened. "Do it, Henry. Right here. In front of everyone!"

He threw back his head and laughed. Oh, she

pleased him so. He never could predict what she would do. He'd expected her to look mortified, as she had at Bailey's Beach, not encourage him. When he looked down at her, he had the sensation of being pulled into the blue depths of her eyes. He stopped dancing and stared. "Marry me, Anne."

She bit her lower lip, drawing his eyes there. "I'm still considering your offer," she said, all business.

His expression tightened and he looked almost angry. "Come with me," he said, grabbing her hand and hauling her off the dance floor. The people along the side parted for them, tittering in their wake like a flock of terns. He brought her to the cloakroom, waving away the footman who stood like a sentry at the door.

With a quick look to make certain no one saw them enter the room, he silently led her to a shadowed corner. "I've thought of nothing but kissing you since the moment you left me," he said, his hands at her neck, his thumbs caressing the sensitive underside of her jaw. "I want to make love to you, Anne."

Her eyes widened. "Now?"

Henry shook his head and let out a low rumbling chuckle. "Actually, yes. But I didn't mean now."

"Oh," she said, and immediately realized that one word held a note of disappointment. Anne feared he would see her scarlet-tinged cheeks even in the dark. He kissed her burning cheeks, pressing his mouth against her heated skin in a way that was somehow more sensuous than if he kissed her lips. His hands were about her waist, and Anne knew he must feel how quickly she was breathing. She brought her hands to his neck, loving the thick, strong masculine feel of it, the slight prickle of his imperfect shave. Anne moved her face against his, her delicate skin scraping gently against the carved curve of his jaw.

"Marry me, Anne. You must."

"Why?"

"Because I'm broke and you have all my money."
She pushed him away and shot him a look of pure
mortification. Henry laughed. "Oh, sweetheart, I'm
joking."

Instead of mortified, she now looked downright
hurt.

He kissed her quickly, still laughing at her reaction.
"I never would have said such a thing if I thought for
a moment you would take me seriously."

"Henry, that only shows that you don't know me at
all," she said, sounding so sad, Henry wanted to kick
himself hard for joking about such a thing. He'd been
feeling a bit desperate for her to say yes, and when
she didn't, he thought he'd add some levity to save
his own sanity.

He cupped his hands around her face gently. "I love
you, Anne, and that's why you must marry me. Surely
you know that."

Anne closed her eyes, willing herself to ask the
question that was like a great wall blocking her way
to happiness, willing herself not to cry as she asked.
"Why didn't you love me before?"

A guilty flush stained Henry's cheeks and his jaw
tightened.

"It is not a difficult question. Surely you know the
answer."

"I married you for money. It could have been anyone," he stressed brutally. "I'll regret it the rest of my
life." He softened his voice, the lines in his face. "I
hurt you, Anne, and that kills me a little each time I
think of it. You didn't deserve it. I was desperate and
you were willing. It wasn't even real to me."

Anne took a step back, anger replacing the hurt.
"It was real to me." She turned to leave, but was
stopped by his voice.

"Don't go. Anne, I'm sorry. I've handled this badly.
Hell, I handle everything badly. Frankly, I wonder that
you speak to me at all."

She stood still, willing herself the strength to leave, but in the end, she turned back to him, her heart turning into a puddle at her feet when she looked at him. Why, she thought with self-disgust, was it so difficult for her to remain angry with him? Why did she have to *understand* him?

His eyes moved over her face as if looking for a sign that he still had a chance to convince her. "Marry me and I promise you'll never hurt again."

She gave him the smallest of smiles. "I'll think about it, Henry."

Anne hurried away from Henry, away from her doubts, away from the heart she'd given him long ago. She found herself on the mansion's second floor, where a footman nodded. "Guests are welcome to rest here, ma'am," he said.

Rest. Yes. Suddenly, Anne was ungodly tired. "Thank you." She found herself in a large L-shaped femininely appointed bedroom, the small sitting area tucked around a corner, and gratefully sank down into an overstuffed chair of salmon silk. She couldn't face Beatrice now with her questions, her disappointment, her lecture on how she must resist Henry, her reminders of what Henry had done to her. Her feelings were so jumbled, she wanted to scream them out. Perhaps then she could make sense of them. She grimaced when she heard the door open and female voices chattering, for she so wanted to be alone to think.

"I wonder what will happen when she gets fat and ugly again." One of the girls tittered.

Anne's face burned. She knew with humiliating conviction they were talking about her. Anne sat still as stone and prayed with all her might they wouldn't see her. She wanted to shrink into the chair, she wanted to disappear, her fragile confidence swept away with one malicious sentence.

"She will, you know. They all do. Frankly, I don't know what he sees in her." Annette Bissette, Anne realized with a jolt, the girl who'd been flirting so expertly with Henry not a week ago.

"You must admit she's pretty now. All the boys are crazy about her."

"But you didn't see her before. She was a cow. Or rather, a sow," Annette said, making a snorting sound, a fair imitation of a pig. "There, I knew my hair was lopsided. She'll go back to that. They all do. And then he'll be stuck with a fat, ugly wife and be forced to find a mistress. That's what Mother told me men do, you know, which is why I never eat pastries, even though I absolutely crave those chocolate tarts Cook makes so well. You remember that woman . . ."

They left the room, so Anne missed the rest of the conversation. But she knew that they'd repeat what they'd just said to anyone who would listen. It shouldn't bother her, but it did and for one reason: She feared it was the truth.

For the first time, Beatrice felt comforted having Alex nearby, so troubled was she by Anne and Henry. She wanted to believe Henry was sincere, and even suspected he thought himself sincere. But she was able to see what Anne, in her fog of love, could not. Henry had inflicted terrible pain and had suffered only a brief bout of regret. For Anne to not only forgive him, but to give him her love was so unjust, it made Beatrice crazy thinking about it.

"Alex," Beatrice said. "Would you ever fall in love with an unattractive woman?"

"I love you," he said with a flourish, his dimples showing rakishly.

"Oh, your wit astonishes me. Now. Truthfully, would you? Could you?"

"No."

Beatrice looked crestfallen. "No?"

"No. I'm afraid I'm that shallow. All men are."

"That's not true. Why, if it were, then no unattractive women would ever marry."

"You misunderstand," Alex said. "The question is, could I fall in love with a woman *I* didn't think was beautiful. A far different question, don't you see?"

"As in, 'Beauty is in the eye of the beholder'?"

"Precisely." He turned to her. "For example, some men might find your hair too dark, your eyebrows too pronounced, your skin too pale, your cheeks too red."

Beatrice's red cheeks grew more red beneath his scrutiny.

"But I find your face," he thought for a moment, "lovely beyond words."

Beatrice swallowed heavily and tried not to take his words too seriously. Alexander Henley was a charmer and he was trying to charm her. That was all. Still, a smile bloomed and stayed, making her feel foolish and wonderful.

"It's your sharp tongue that keeps men away, not your face," Alex said dryly, turning back to watch the dancers. Beatrice's smile instantly disappeared.

"Do you know you are beyond insufferable?"

"See what I mean? A viper's tongue. It's enough to keep any man away." He gave her a mock shudder.

"You think yourself amusing, don't you? You think yourself incapable of hurting people. 'Oh, that's just Alex, being charming and witty.' Well, I say you are mean and . . ." She turned away, mortified that her throat had closed up.

"Hey, what's this?" he asked softly. "It's bad manners to weep at a ball." He ducked his head to see her face, his eyes filling with real regret when he saw tears glittering in her lashes. "I'll let you in on a secret, Miss Leyden."

She swallowed thickly and flicked her eyes to him in question.

"Whenever I find myself in danger of falling in love, I'm absolutely cruel to the girl. I say the most terrible things. I've even been known to make girls cry at balls with my stupidity."

She looked him straight in the eye. "A terrible habit," she said in a near whisper.

"But one I will try to break." He tilted his head in that charming Alex way of his. "Forgiven?"

Beatrice blinked and frowned. "Are you admitting to almost falling in love with me?"

"I'm afraid I am."

She lifted her chin imperiously. "Then you are forgiven."

Chapter Eighteen

Anne's hands began to shake uncontrollably as her eyes scanned the gossip column "Saunterings." "It can't be," she whispered. "Oh, God, it can't be."

Beatrice looked up from her tea. "Heavens, Anne, what is wrong?"

Anne read in a trembling voice: "Miss F, the newly readmitted belle of Newport, has fallen back to scandalous ways with a solitary trip to a certain island cottage to visit a Mr. O."

Beatrice gasped, then turned a guilty look to her mother, who was stepping into the morning room like an angry school matron, a copy of *Town Topics* rolled up like a whipping rod in her hand. "What," she said, purely angry, "is this?"

Anne shrank into the sofa. "I didn't think anyone would find out," she said in a small voice. "It was all part of The Plan, you see. Henry was there and—"

"I cannot support this behavior," Helen interrupted. "You are a guest in this house, Miss Foster, and your actions reflect upon all of us. And you," she said, pointing the scandal sheet at her daughter, "should never have allowed this."

Beatrice looked about to argue, then hung her head dejectedly.

"I don't know what we can to do deflect this," she said hopelessly, tossing the offensive gossip sheet onto a small table.

Anne stood, clutching her skirts painfully. "I'm so

sorry, Mrs. Leyden. Truly I never would have dared
such a thing if I thought it would turn up in the colonel's paper." She shook her head. "I cannot begin to
think who would have told him. I was quite careful."

"Bah," Helen said loudly, making Anne wince and
giving a clear clue as to just how angry she was. "You
know the colonel has spies everywhere. Oh, Anne,
you are the center of all gossip this season. To do
something this reckless at a time when you are just
becoming accepted again, it is incomprehensible."

Anne closed her eyes and groaned. "The man who
took me to Sea Cliff. He must have told someone. He
seemed so nice."

"Money, my dear, is a powerful persuader. If only
we'd known about this piece, we could have bribed
the colonel and kept it out. Worse things than this
have never seen the light of day because of deep pockets and a willingness to buy his silence." Helen paced
in front of the two girls, tapping the rolled-up paper
lightly against her chin. "There's only one way to
save you."

Anne looked at Helen hopefully.

"You must convince Henry to marry you."

Anne nearly giggled, then put on a serious face.
"That might take some mighty convincing," she said
innocently.

"He has no choice."

For some devilish reason, Anne chose to keep Henry's proposal a secret for a bit longer. "It's not as if
I'm a single girl. I am a divorcée, and that gives me
much more latitude in how I behave. I'm certain society will forgive me."

Helen widened her eyes in shock. "Not even a divorcée can visit a man alone and not be susceptible
to retribution. Henry has more honor than you believe. He will marry you."

Anne smiled. "I know. He's already asked."

"What?" mother and daughter asked in unison.

"Last night at the ball. He asked at Sea Cliff, as well."

Beatrice glared at her. "Anne."

"I cannot share everything, Bea. I was afraid you would convince me to say no."

"You're already engaged, then?" Helen asked, well pleased. "Well, that solves our grand dilemma, though I am still angry with you for inviting such scandal. Even an engagement will not silence the whispers."

Anne bit her lip. "I haven't said yes. Yet."

"Then you must."

"Then you mustn't."

Helen looked at her daughter sharply. "Beatrice, enough. You've painted Henry Owen as the devil. He is not. It is clear he loves Anne to distraction. Any fool watching the two of them last night would know that."

Beatrice looked sullen but remained silent. Even Anne was beginning to question Beatrice's stubbornness regarding Henry. How awful it would be to marry and love a man her best friend openly disliked.

"I believe I would have said yes regardless of the column," Anne said. "It simply forces me to give Henry my answer sooner than I would have liked."

"Because you have misgivings, don't you, Anne?" Beatrice stood and rushed to her friend's side. "You mustn't marry him if you have misgivings. He was so cruel."

Anne's face tightened. "I know what he was. I also know what he is. I love him, Bea. Can't you understand that?"

Beatrice closed her eyes as if pain. "Of course I understand. It is only that you don't know . . ." Beatrice clamped her mouth shut.

"I don't know what?"

"You don't know him well enough," she finished lamely.

Anne laughed. "I know Henry, flaws and all. Before

I loved him because he seemed so perfect to me. Now I love him in spite of his imperfections."

"Yes, but does he love you in spite of yours?"

Beatrice's last words to Anne—she hadn't spoken to her in two days—drove into Anne's head like a persistent drop of water against her skull. The more she thought about them, the deeper they penetrated the haze of love Anne found herself wrapped in. Would Henry love her if she reverted to that ungainly girl she was? She didn't want to think about the answer and was too much a coward to blatantly ask him. Surely he knew there was more to her than a pretty face.

Then why didn't he fall in love with you two years ago?

Anne stared at her reflection without vanity. Am I the same girl I was? She closed her eyes and remembered her, that awkward pudgy girl, shy, quiet, and painfully in love with one of Newport's finest catches, a girl no one, not even her parents, wanted. So, now she was beautiful, the belle of Newport, according to the colonel. All because she'd lost a few pounds of flesh?

"No," she said aloud to her reflection. She had lost so much of herself in those months after her marriage, and not only in pounds. She had been stripped of everything, her soul left naked and exposed. She had lost that awkward girl and become a woman who could walk into a den of lions and pretend she belonged. She could stand up to Mamie Fish and hold her head high as daggers of disdain were thrown her way. Anne smiled into the mirror, liking what she saw. She had become the woman she'd dreamed of being: confident enough to believe Henry loved her for who she was, flaws and all.

"Miss Foster," her maid interrupted. "Mrs. Foster has arrived."

The woman in the mirror who had been smiling so blissfully looked suddenly like a woman about to be thrown over a cliff. "My mother is here?" she said, grimacing.

"Yes, she is, and you'd better have a good explanation for this," Francine said, waving yet another copy of that hated gossip sheet. "Haven't you put your family through enough already? I had to wear a heavy veil to hide my identity, so shamed was I. But I do have a duty as your mother."

Francine Foster was dressed entirely in black as if in deep mourning, and Anne felt a rush of guilt seeing how exhausted she looked. Her mother had never liked traveling, and for her to have arrived in Newport just two days after the appearance of the item in "Saunterings" was just short of remarkable. Anne had not seen her mother in more than six months, not since a painful and brief visit at Christmas. Francine visited Anne's town house in defiance of her husband, who, to Anne's surprise, was the one behind her banishment. It had been a tearful and entirely uncomfortable meeting that left Anne feeling irrationally guilty.

"I must say you look good for a girl who has brought such scandal down upon her good name," Francine said.

"Please, Mother, you're giving me a headache."

"Do not be rude to your mother," she said, talking to Anne as if she were still twelve. "I demand an explanation for Colonel Mann's article."

"Why don't you ask Colonel Mann, Mother?"

Francine glared at Anne. "You have become coarse, Anne. Perhaps you deserve what you get, but our family does not."

Anne massaged her temple. "I'm sorry. These last few days have been harrowing."

"Yes, I'm sure they have been. I know I have been quite beside myself," she said, collapsing gracefully into a nearby chair. "We must repair the damage of that item. Tell me, Anne, was it true?"

Anne looked at bit sheepish. "Yes. But I went there with the best intentions and never thought I would be found out. You see, Mother, Bea and I had concocted a perfectly glorious plan of revenge on Henry," she said, and went on to outline their outlandish plan. "I went to Jamestown to exact a proclamation of love from him, then break off. But things went a bit awry and I'm afraid I told him I loved him, too."

"Do you?"

"Yes. I do. Henry has asked me to marry him and I believe I'll say yes."

Francine smiled uncertainly, as if weighing whether or not Anne's remarriage to Henry boded well for the family or not. "Well, then, all is well but for that horrible Colonel Mann. I shall talk to your father. I'm certain that when he discovers you are engaged, all will be forgiven. Write me, dear."

"You're leaving?"

"Of course. I still can't show my face in this town." She sighed dramatically. "I do so miss Tennis Week. Ah, well. Perhaps next season when you are married and our good name is restored. Please try to be good, Anne. Oh, and I shall send you some of your things to help you prepare for the wedding. I do hope your father allows us to attend." With that, she left, leaving Anne feeling as if she'd been trampled by a line of lacquered coaches.

Henry's Spring Wharf office overlooked his boat-building enterprise, a partitioned section in a loft that scraped the ceiling of the large warehouse he'd been renting for four years. The air inside was heavy with the scent of sawdust, teak oil, and low tide, for the warehouse rested on pilings in Newport Harbor. His crew was putting the finishing touches on a fifty-five-foot sailing yacht commissioned by a Philadelphia man who'd never sailed a day in his life and likely would use this boat as a men's club. At least he had opted for the purer sail, rather than steam, Henry thought with reluctance. He was making modifications to his latest design when a knock on the door frame of his open door disrupted his work.

"Henry Owen?"

Henry lifted his head and stared at the man standing boldly in front of him. He wore a lime-green waistcoat beneath a chocolate-brown suit jacket, and his cream pants were short enough to show his bright red stockings. His handlebar mustache was well-waxed and perfectly symmetrical, his hair precisely parted in the middle and heavily coated with hair tonic.

"Andre LeClaire. I work for—"

"I know who you work for. Now you may leave. You are trespassing," Henry said, casually tamping out a cigar that smoldered in his ashtray.

LeClaire smirked and took a step into the office, faltering when Henry granted him a gaze that held a warning only a fool wouldn't heed. And Andre LeClaire was no fool. He backed up a step and held out his hands, palms up, in entreaty. "I came here outta the goodness of my heart. See, I knows something about something that just might interest you. A little bit of gossip that will appear in Colonel Mann's next column."

Henry stood and pressed his fists against his desktop. "I don't give a damn about Colonel Mann or his column."

"Oh, I think you'll care about this," LeClaire said, examining his fingernails.

"I don't. Now leave."

"Okay, okay," LeClaire said, backing out. "But if a little slip of a girl was making a fool outta me, I'd want to keep it between me and the man in the moon, if you get my meaning. Imagine, setting you up like that."

Despite himself, curiosity won over his disdain for LeClaire. Clearly the man was referring to Anne, and he'd be damned if another word appeared in Mann's column castigating her good name. Inwardly he winced, sensing that the damaging article that appeared in the last "Saunterings" about Anne's visit to Jamestown would pale in comparison to whatever Mann was now planning. Henry suspected that the disreputable Mann was going to attempt to extort money for his silence.

Sitting, Henry said, "Go on."

LeClaire pulled a chair that sat against the wall and made himself comfortable in front of Henry's desk. "Colonel Mann got himself a visit from a Mrs. Foster two days ago. That'd be Anne Foster's mother. She's all upset about that mention of her little girl visiting you on the sly. Wanted some positive mentions like we did for that D'Amber girl last summer."

Henry had heard all about the D'Amber girl, who'd been spotted by one of Mann's men out alone with her fiancé after midnight. The girl's father, so the story went, paid a king's ransom for three positive mentions about his daughter in hopes of soothing her future in-laws. It was common knowledge that for the right sum, Colonel Mann could be convinced to leave his journalistic integrity at the bank's door.

"Seems Miss Foster has been playing you for a fool." LeClaire smiled greasily, clearly enjoying his assignment.

"Oh?"

LeClaire's smile widened, revealing a gold incisor. "She's been battin' her pretty eyes at you all the time just to make a sucker of ya. Just wanted a bit of revenge for what you done to her. According to her dear mother, Miss Foster went to Jamestown to obtain a proposal so's she could throw it in your face." LeClaire's glinty eyes narrowed. "Now, you tell me, Mr. Owen. Did the girl accept?"

Henry stood so quickly his chair upended. "Get the hell out of here," he growled.

"Now that's just cruel, Mr. Owen, a girl doing that to a fine upstanding gent like you. Why, the colonel just might shed a tear when he sends the story off to the printer Tuesday." LeClaire paused, clearly enjoying himself. "Colonel Mann's torn, you see. He doesn't want to bring a man like you down but he feels he's got a duty to expose—"

"How much?"

LeClaire flashed his gold tooth, his smile faltering a bit when he took in Henry's expression. He stood like a man ready for battle, hands fisted by his side, eyes like steel shards impaling LeClaire.

"Why, I'm not certain what you mean," LeClaire said, squirming in his seat.

"How much does Mann want to keep this item from appearing in 'Saunterings'?" Henry asked silkily.

"Ten thousand."

Henry appeared to think about it. He even pulled out a bank draft. "Ten thousand, you say?"

"A real bargain," LeClaire said with a knowing smirk.

Henry wrote out the bank draft and handed it to LeClaire with a steady hand. LeClaire took it and glanced down, then paled. Where the money amount should have been written were the words, in elegant scrawl, "Go to hell."

By the time LeClaire lifted his head, Henry's fists were curled around his green waistcoat and he was being hauled from the chair as if he weighed no more than a child. Henry slammed him so hard against the wall, he saw stars. With his nose just inches from LeClaire's, Henry growled, "You give that little note to Colonel Mann. You tell him if I see one word of that piece of trash, I'll see that he never writes another word as long as he lives. I swear to God I am not threatening, I am promising."

Henry released him and wiped his hands against his pants legs as if trying to rid himself of something foul.

LeClaire jerked on his waistcoat in an attempt to retain some dignity. "I'll relay the message."

"You do that." Henry gave him a quick, ugly smile that spoke volumes of his distaste, and watched as the man slinked away. Then he sat down behind his desk, his hands folded in front of him, his thumbs warring with each other. He decided, after a long moment of painful contemplation, that he believed every word LeClaire uttered.

Once again, Anne had surprised the hell out of him.

Chapter Nineteen

Four days after Henry's proposal, Anne still had not given him a definitive answer even knowing she hung on to her place in society by a thread as flimsy as a dust rope swaying from a ceiling. Beatrice's words haunted her and her own misgivings plagued her. To make matters worse, she hadn't seen Henry in days, giving her hours and hours to doubt the depth of Henry's love. He was, apparently, giving her the time he thought she needed to make a decision. A persistent ache had settled in her heart of late, a need to see Henry, to hold him, to look into his eyes and see again the love that shined so clearly there. He'd sent only a cryptic note yesterday saying he was going to stay in Jamestown for a couple of days. He wouldn't be back in Newport until Friday—and today was only Wednesday. It seemed like forever to live with her misgivings.

Anne eyed the trunk her mother had sent, blaming it for her melancholy mood. It was the very same trunk she'd stored her wedding gown in, her bride's things, a bundle of well-wishing letters she'd never answered. Why her mother thought she'd want it was beyond her. She supposed for frugality's sake she could make use of some of the items, but any clothing it contained, including her wedding night dressing gown, would be far too large for her now. She should burn it without even opening it, she thought, then sighed and knelt down by the shiny black lacquered trunk. Inside was the girl she'd been, inside was proof of her broken heart.

She opened it and found, neatly wrapped, her pink-and-white wedding gown. Touching it with her fingertips, she recalled with burning heat to her cheeks how hopeful she'd been the morning of her wedding, how blindingly happy. She'd looked into Henry's eyes and convinced herself he loved her. So many little signs she ignored—the fact he never kissed her, touched her, looked at her. Even on their wedding day, with her heart full, he barely glimpsed at her. Now she knew why.

Anne put the gown and its painful memories aside and dug through the other items, silks and lace, a carved ivory mirror and comb set, an empty crystal perfume atomizer. She let out a small gasp as she recognized another item. Tied to a pink ribbon was her wedding ring. Eyes burning with unshed tears, Anne pulled on the slippery satin ribbon and freed the ring and laid it in the palm of her hand.

"Oh, Henry," she whispered, curling her fingers around the cool metal.

Was this why her mother had sent this trunk? Was she far wiser than Anne imagined, or unaware of what seeing these things would do to her already battered heart? The need to see Henry was almost overwhelming. She wanted to banish this ugliness, to make believe it had never happened.

At the bottom of the trunk lay two stacks of letters. One bundle was those letters opened and answered, and another sizeable stack of letters whose seals remained intact. She picked up the unopened stack she'd negligently put aside two years before, a wistful smile on her face as she began flipping through them, recognizing some of the names and wondering if these same people would wish her well this time around. In the middle of the stack a name jarred her: Arthur Owen.

"Henry's grandfather," she said aloud, her brow furrowing. She couldn't recall seeing the man at her wedding; Henry's side of the church contained almost no family. She was suddenly glad to have kept the letters and notes of congratulations, remembering that Henry's grandfather was quite ill and he might want to read his grandfather's kind words. Snapping the old wax, Anne pulled a rich piece of vellum from the envelope and began reading.

My dear Miss Foster,

    My grandson, Henry Owen, has informed me that he intends to offer for you. I feel it is my duty as a man of honor to warn you against such a marriage. Though I love my grandson, I despise his plans for you, an innocent girl who deserves better than to be misused. It is with the greatest regret that I must tell you that Henry has no intention to abide by his vows. Indeed, he has confided in me a plan so devious, it shames me. Henry is courting you because you are unattractive and will be no threat to his plans to obtain his fortune. To put it bluntly, he picked you from all the other Newport debutantes because you are plain—those are his words, my dear, and certainly not reflective of my opinion. As I recall, all of the Foster girls are quite lovely.

    Please take this in the manner it was intended, as a kind warning.

    Respectfully yours,
    Arthur Owen

The letter dropped silently to the thick carpet from a hand gone limp. Anne stared blindly at the empty trunk, tears flowing down her face, her neck, and soaking into the soft white lace of her gown. He'd picked her because she was plain.

Her grief was too much to bear, too much to contain, and she began sobbing into her hands, shaking her head in futile denial. "It's not true, not true," she said thickly, all the while knowing it was. "Oh, God, not true."

Her throat burned as she tried to stop crying, but it was as if an old wound had been brutally torn open, leaving her more damaged than before. Memories assaulted her, humiliated her, made her want to scream out her agony. A whimper escaped her constricted throat, then the damn broke loose in a rush of tears and body-wracking sobs. She heard the rushing sound of a woman's skirts coming to her, but she didn't care. It hurt too much to care about anything.

"My God, Anne, what happened?" Beatrice knelt beside Anne, her gaze taking in the opened trunk, the discarded ring and wedding gown. "Oh, darling, you should have had me with you when you opened this trunk."

Anne shook her head. "It's not that," she said in a tear-clogged voice.

"Then what?"

Anne sniffed and wiped her face with the back of her hands. "This," she said, flicking the note from Henry's grandfather toward Beatrice.

Beatrice picked up the note and gave Anne a worried look before reading it. In bitter resignation, Beatrice shook her head. "I told you he was a scoundrel."

"But he's much worse than that. He's a terrible person and . . . and . . . I love him," she wailed, collapsing against Beatrice's shoulder.

"You'll get over it. He doesn't deserve you. He never did."

"I know. I *know*."

Beatrice pulled a handkerchief from one of the deep pockets of her simple gown and handed it to Anne.

"I can't marry him now, can I?" Anne asked in such a pathetic little voice, Beatrice's heart nearly broke.

She shook her head. "I don't think you can. And I don't think you want to. Not really."

Anne was silent for a long moment, twisting the soggy handkerchief in her hands, her big blue eyes red-rimmed and swollen from her bout of tears. "I thought he picked me because I loved him. I never dreamed it was because . . . because I was ugly."

"You weren't ugly. You were sweet and trusting."

Anne's face grew taut. "And now I'm not any of those things."

Henry was more rumpled than usual, so much so that even Alex was alarmed when he visited him in his office.

"I thought you were staying in Jamestown until Friday," he said, eyeing his friend carefully.

Henry turned from the small, dusty window that looked out over Newport Harbor. "I can't stomach the place now that my grandfather's there," he said, then sat heavily down into his chair. He opened a deep desk drawer, pulled out an engraved silver flask, and took a small sip.

"You're drinking at this hour?" Alex asked, then held out his hand to take the flask and took a sip himself.

"Just a bit. It's whiskey and you know how I feel about her—it," he corrected himself.

Alex sat on the edge of Henry's large oak desk. "What happened?" he asked like an indulgent father.

Henry clenched his jaw, not quite willing to spell out clearly exactly how stupid and blind he'd been. Even if it was only Alex who knew. "Anne and I are not getting married," he said finally and with forced nonchalance.

"So that's why you look like hell. Don't tell me she said no."

Henry wet his lips and held his hand out for the flask. "Not yet. But she will." He took a drink.

"What makes you so certain? The last I saw, she was quite under your spell."

Henry let out a grunt. "One would think so. However, I've had it on good authority that Miss Foster is a consummate actress. I'm actually half inclined to respect her more for it. After all, it's not as if I don't deserve it. I do. Oh, I do." He chuckled morosely.

"What in blazes are you talking about?" Alex said, his patience clearly waning.

"It was revenge, pure and simple. She set out from the beginning to lure me into her trap, get me to propose, then say no."

Alex had the gall to smile. "Well, I'll be goddamned."

"I'm impressed by her resolve as well," Henry said dryly.

"Are you certain?"

"I'll be certain in a half hour. She's coming here to visit. It should be rather entertaining if you'd like to stay. I suppose I should clean myself up," Henry said, rubbing a hand against his beard-roughened jaw. He extracted a comb from a drawer and dragged it through his thick hair.

"Give me a hand with this tie, will you?" Henry said, lifting his chin.

"If you'd use my valet, you wouldn't look like you slept in your clothes all the time," Alex said, quickly undoing the mess of cloth at Henry's neck.

Alex eyed his friend curiously. "What are you planning?"

"You forget that she doesn't know that I know. She'll come in here thinking she's about to break my heart." Henry swallowed. "She won't get the satisfaction. Her plan will fail."

"Did it, Henry?"

Henry worked his jaw. "She'll sure as hell think it did." He would never let her know that she had perhaps ruined him forever. When Anne walked into his office, he had a plan of his own, one that would steal from her any satisfaction she hoped to gain by crushing him. Even as part of him knew she was due her revenge, he couldn't let her see that she had, indeed, broken his heart.

He'd returned to Sea Cliff following LeClaire's visit needing to be soothed by the old place, hoping to remind himself that everything he'd done was worth whatever the consequences. But he found himself instead haunted—not by his parents, but by Anne. Everywhere he looked, she was there, reading in the library, standing on the balcony, lying on their bed. Playing with their children. He realized he had built a vividly painted future around her, one that now would never exist. Without even knowing he'd done it, Henry made Sea Cliff their home. The thought of returning to Sea Cliff alone was highly depressing. He didn't miss the irony that Sea Cliff was now ruined for him by the very woman he used to restore it to him.

When he sailed away from Sea Cliff, he did not look back.

"How did you find out about her plan?" Alex asked.

"Apparently, her mother, in an attempt to explain Anne's visit to me, went to see Mann and he in turn tried to extort money from me to keep the whole mess out of his blasted gossip column."

"Hell, Henry, you can't believe a degenerate like Mann. You didn't pay, did you?"

"No. But his man LeClaire knew about my proposal and that Anne hadn't said yes." Henry toyed with the flask before shoving it toward Alex. "No one knew I'd asked her to marry me but for you and Miss Leyden."

"Miss Leyden," Alex said thoughtfully before finishing off the whiskey.

"How do I look?" Henry asked, glancing down at himself. Though his shirt was a bit wrinkled, it was mostly covered by his suit jacket and waistcoat—and his tie was at least neat.

"You don't look quite as mussed," Alex said with a critical eye.

"Unless you want to witness the final act, you'd best get your arse out of my office," Henry said with as much cheer as he could manage. "I believe Miss Foster has arrived."

From the Journal of Arthur Owen

You are my son, Henry. How I wish I'd had the courage in life to tell you. I watched Elizabeth's belly grow with my child, knowing I had forsaken any right to claim you when I allowed her to seduce Walter. From that moment, the future was cast.

Walter, embarrassed and ridiculously proud, told me in a private meeting that he and Elizabeth would be forced to move up the wedding date. He put it just like that, too timid to clearly say why such a change was necessary. I was the one who forced him to say it, to punish him, to punish myself. I wanted to hear it, to drive it into my heart, to force myself to believe that the child Elizabeth carried was not mine.

But of course, I knew it was mine. You were mine.

In those first years following their hasty marriage, Elizabeth and Henry lived in the same New York mansion as I, though in a different wing. Your mother was as beautiful with child as she was before. I think now that Walter chose to live in the mansion to torture me. It actually comforts me to believe that he was intelligent or wily enough to have at least suspected that something had gone on between Elizabeth and me. Sometimes I would catch her looking at me with a strange expression, and she would place a graceful hand on her rounded stomach, a silent acknowledgement that she would never forget who the real father of her child was. It was a cruel gesture and yet each time she did it, I rejoiced.

I yearned to feel you move within her, to share the

joy I tried so hard to deny. I wanted you. You were my child, my baby, my blood. I suffered as Walter had all the privileges I was denied, comforted only in knowing he did not share her bed. I know this because in a rare moment of frustration, Walter confessed that his surly mood was over Elizabeth's delicate condition. I was so relieved, I nearly wept. Do not forget for a moment that, despite what your mother did, I loved her with every breath I took. And I wanted her still.

When it became too much for me, I became insufferable, rude, cruel. I became the man you know. It hurt too much, Henry, to love her and know I could never have her. To see her belly grow big, to know I could never claim the child I loved even more than I loved Elizabeth, was more than I could bear. I threw them from my house, I made Elizabeth cry. I promised myself I would stay away. You know I did not. In the summer, I would return to Sea Cliff when I could no longer stand to be away.

I remember you as a small boy, so perfect and healthy and full of life. God, Henry, you were a wonder to me. I would watch you for hours at a time, afraid to touch you, afraid Elizabeth would finally say something and the walls would crash down upon us. I cannot say that Elizabeth was ever truly happy, but after she married Walter, the light went out of her. She was always cruel, but after the wedding, her cruelty held a harder, sharper edge. Oddly enough, Elizabeth took her vows seriously, for once they were said, she never again tried to seduce me or any other man. She was wholly committed to your father, and that drove her to the brink of an abyss only she could see.

The only thing that made her happy was you.

Chapter Twenty

Anne stepped into the cavernous warehouse, her nostrils assaulted by myriad scents that she recognized as the subtle cologne Henry wore—a rich and masculine combination of the sea, teak oil, cigar smoke, and sawdust. The rhythmic rasp of a worker sanding wood was the only sound in the room—other than her madly beating heart pounding in her ears. In front of her was a sleek sailing yacht, nearly finished but for the masts and rigging, which she assumed would be done outside the building. High above her, a bank of windows let in the early-morning sun, shafts of light cutting through the dusty air. At her feet was a wood-planked floor, sawdust imbedded between the boards.

"Hello?" she called out.

She turned toward footsteps and spotted a set of stairs leading up to a loft.

"Miss Foster. How are you, besides looking lovely," Alex said, walking toward her. In her nervous state, Anne didn't note how distracted Alex seemed.

"Hello, Mr. Henley. Could you tell me where I might find Henry?"

"Just up those stairs," Alex said with a nod in the direction he'd come from. "Do you happen to know if I might find Miss Leyden at home?"

Anne tore her gaze away from the stairs that marked the final steps in a journey begun two years before. "I believe so. If you'll excuse me, Mr. Henley."

She didn't know if he replied or if he left the building. She only heard the sound of her expensive shoes hitting the planking, the pounding in her ears, the rasping sound, the scream inside her head. At the base of the wooden steps, Anne paused and took a deep, shaking breath. Oh, why did this have to hurt so much? Why couldn't she simply march into his office triumphant and blithely tell him he had failed. No, I won't marry you, Henry Owen, because you are the cruelest man God created. That's what she should say, what she *wanted* to want to say. Instead, she was afraid she would break down and cry and run from the room after telling him she would not marry him.

She made it up those steep steps and faced the only door on the landing. Fisting her gloved hands she gave herself a silent speech of courage before knocking on the frosted window.

"Come in."

Anne gripped the doorknob with new determination, ready to face him and the certainty that if he did indeed have a heart, she was prepared to break it. The moment she opened the door, Henry was there pulling her to him.

"God, I missed you," he said, enveloping her in an embrace so tight, she felt her breath leave her. She refused to think how good it felt to be held by his solid warmth, and forced herself to put her hands on his shoulders. He pulled back and examined her face with such open want that Anne was momentarily stunned. "If you knew how much I love you, Anne . . ." He kissed her as if he would die if he didn't, wrapping his big hands around her head and pulling her to him. "If only you knew," he said against her lips.

"Henry, I—" she managed to say before his mouth muffled her words. She forcefully pulled her head away. "Henry, please." As his warm mouth moved against hers, Anne fought a battle she feared she would lose. He was doing it again. The minute she was with him, he stole her resolve, he wiped away everything with a single kiss. Not this time, she told herself as she realized her hands were no longer pushing him away but clutching his suit coat and dragging him closer. Oh, not this time. Not. She sighed. This. Oh, he kissed so well. Time.

"Oh, Henry," she sighed, and nearly collapsed against him.

"Please, please," Henry said, his voice raw with emotion, his hands moving over her slowly, skimming from her shoulders down, down to her hips. One hand stole behind her, kneaded her buttocks, pulling her against his arousal, thick and intoxicating. The other hand moved to her breast, cupping her soft fullness, moving his thumb with agonizing precision over her nipple until it was hard.

"Waiting for you will be sheer agony," he said, moving his mouth down the column of her neck.

Waiting . . . Something entered the fog that enshrouded her passion-drugged brain. Waiting, waiting . . . Oh, God, Henry was waiting for their wedding night.

Anne forcefully disengaged herself from his embrace. She couldn't think straight when he was touching her, kissing her, looking at her like he was a hairsbreadth away from ripping off both of their clothes.

"So," she said, stepping back on shaking legs. She looked around his small office. "This is where you work."

"I love you, Anne."

Anne inhaled sharply and walked jerkily about, pretending interest in the models of yachts he had displayed on his walls.

"Anne, look at me."

She didn't want to. She wanted to conjure a picture

of him in her mind of a man with horns, cloven hoofs, and a pointed tail. She didn't want to see the hunger in his eyes, the love, but she looked at him anyway, hardening her heart the way he must have when he asked her to marry him because she was ugly.

"I love you," he said simply. She looked away.

"Henry, I—"

"Marry me." He reached out, grasped her gloved hand, and brought it to his lips. She pulled her hand away, staring at him beneath a furrowed brow.

"I can't marry you."

Her words had seemingly no affect on him, or rather turned him from a besotted man into an emotionless, curious one. He had shut down. "Why?"

"I don't love you. And . . ."

He raised on eyebrow. "And?"

"And that's it. I don't love you, so I can't possibly marry you. I hate to break your heart."

He flicked a bit of lint on his suitjacket. "Oh, I'll be fine."

"I know this is sudden—"

"Not really."

Anne blinked. Just a moment ago, he was professing his undying love, and now he acted as if she'd told him they would have ham instead of fish for dinner.

"You knew I had misgivings."

Henry smiled. "I know, Anne. It just didn't work out. So. Is it to be John Morris, then?"

"Who?"

"That Morris fellow."

Anne widened her eyes. This was not at all going as she planned. He was supposed to be devastated, not glib. "Jake. Morrison."

"Ah, yes. Fine fellow. Takes a good punch."

"Indeed," Anne said softly, confusion written almost comically on her face. "You're all right, then?" Wasn't this the man who'd just been trembling because he was so filled with desire for her?

Again that smile. "About your refusal? Right as rain."

"I see. Good." Well, Anne thought, this is rather disconcerting. "I . . . I hope things won't be awkward between us. We will be attending some of the same events this summer. Tennis Week and all that."

"Not at all. Save a dance for me at the next Casino ball," he said, taking her elbow and escorting her from his office.

"Of course." Before she knew it, Anne was outside his office staring down the stairs, the office door clicking quietly behind her. She looked back and could see his shadow through the frosted window as he moved back behind his desk. As if he couldn't wait to get back to work, as if her marriage refusal didn't matter at all.

"You were in on this little plan, weren't you?" Alex said the moment Beatrice entered the morning room. She'd practically run down the stairs when her maid had informed her Mr. Henley was waiting for her downstairs, her heart singing, but the smile that glowed her on face faded swiftly, replaced by wariness.

"Plan?" she asked. But she knew, and dread filled her.

"The plan to break Henry's heart."

Beatrice looked at him, standing there so elegantly, dressed to perfection in his cream-colored pants and waistcoat and white suit jacket. He looked so very Newport, the picture of a wealthy man just stepping from his yacht or extravagant coach. A wealthy, angry man.

"Yes," she said. "I knew. It was my idea." She lifted her chin for good effect.

"That's all I wanted to know," Alex said, grabbing the hat he'd put on the couch and shoving it onto his head.

"How dare you!" Beatrice said, marching after him.

He ignored her as he made his way to the door. "And what of your plan to hurt Anne? What of your plan to find an ugly girl for Henry to marry? It was your idea, wasn't it? You told me so yourself."

He stopped in his tracks.

"I never participated in Henry's plan. I never pretended to like what he did. And Miss Foster never knew his true reason for marrying him."

"She knows now."

His eyes narrowed. "You told her?"

"Oh, don't look so shocked, as if you're some sort of saint. But no, I didn't tell her. I wish I had, though, for I think my telling it would have been more kind. She found a note from Henry's grandfather warning her away from him. He'd intended for her to receive it before their wedding, obviously. He was cruelly blunt about Henry's reasons for picking Anne."

Alex closed his eyes briefly. "Christ."

Beatrice shook her head, that he should be so unsettled by the letter Anne found. "The note was cruel, but Henry's act was monstrous. And you didn't stop him."

"No, Miss Leyden, I didn't stop him."

He was about to walk out the door and Beatrice couldn't let him do it, not without her stating their case. "Breaking his heart is only what he deserves," she said vehemently. "And to think she was actually going to say yes."

He turned. "Henry has been on the brink of hell his entire life. I'll not excuse what he did, but I can damn well say I understand it. He'd thrash me if he knew I was saying this, but I feel sorry for him. I have for years. He is the loneliest man I've ever known. For some reason, he thought that damned shack would make him happy. Yes, Miss Leyden, I wanted that for him. I wanted Henry to have one single bit of happiness. You and Miss Foster should be doubly pleased to know that obtaining Sea Cliff didn't make him happy. But loving Anne did. Sleep well tonight, Miss Leyden."

Beatrice, stricken, watched him walk out the door, her mind battling with what he'd just told her. Nothing justified what Henry had done to Anne. Nothing, nothing. Then why did she want to stop what she'd begun with Anne? She flung open the door and ran after Alex, not caring if every servant in the house reported her desperation to Colonel Mann.

"Are you happy, Alex?" she shouted to his re-treating form.

He stopped by the sweeping staircase just before he reached the entrance hall. Heartened, she ran to him and placed a trembling hand on his upper arm. "Are you?"

He dipped his head and sighed, the muscle of his arm where she clung to him contracting. "I don't like what you did, Bea," he said softly. "Henry isn't as strong as he seems."

"I don't like what you did, either. We're both hor-rid people."

He looked at her, his eyes sweeping her face. "Per-haps we deserve each other, then."

"Perhaps."

Alex turned fully toward her and placed a hand on each of Beatrice's wrists. "Was I part of your plan?" he asked finally, unable to look her in the eye.

"You were a complete surprise."

He smiled, his dimples creasing his lean cheeks. "A good one or a bad one?"

"I don't know yet," Beatrice said seriously.

He chuckled softly. "Me neither." He pulled her to him and rested his chin on the top of her head.

"What about Henry and Anne?" Beatrice asked, unwanted guilt filling her. She knew she'd been a large piece of a plot that would drive apart two people who loved each other. Any pleasure she might have had over their success was gone, replaced by the knowledge she might have committed a terrible deed all in the name of revenge. For the first time she wondered if Anne would be better off now that she'd exacted her vengeance.

"There is no Henry and Anne," he said.

Anne pulled off her be-ribboned straw hat and slightly soiled white gloves and handed them absently to a maid, still reeling from her encounter with Henry. When she'd first stepped into his office, he seemed almost desperate for her. By the time she left, she felt as if she'd be surprised if he spent a single moment missing her. The entire encounter was entirely unsatisfying.

"Susan," Anne called to the departing maid. "Do you know where I might find Miss Leyden?"

"In her sitting room, miss, attending to her correspondence."

Anne walked wearily up the staircase, feeling like a wet rag. Outside, the cool, damp morning was giving way to an intolerably hot and humid day, which did nothing for her already sour mood. She found Beatrice diligently working on a pile of responses to invitations and letters. Beatrice turned when Anne entered and a bit of ink dripped from her pen onto her morning gown.

"Oh, fiddlesticks," she lamented, dabbing ineffectually at the blossoming spot.

"I see your day has not been much better than mine," Anne said, propping herself at the edge of a nearby chair.

"Anne, he knows," Beatrice said, looking up from her attempt to save her gown.

"Who knows what?"

"Henry knows about our plan."

Anne blanched, her mouth opened slightly. And then came dawning comprehension. "That rat," she said, eyes narrowed, lips compressed. "Oh, I could just strangle him."

"Why? What happened?" Beatrice asked, completely forgetting about her ruined dress as she turned fully toward Anne.

Anne shook her head in disbelief, still reliving the confusing scene in Henry's office. "Once again, he's made a fool of me. It's so unfair."

"Tell me," Beatrice begged.

"When I got there, he was quite happy to see me," Anne said with a telltale blush. "And then, when I told him I couldn't marry him, he was completely blasé. Never in my life have I met a man with so few scruples." Anne flushed even more when she recalled how she'd almost abandoned her resolve when Henry began kissing her. He'd been playing with her emotions, testing her, all the time knowing—or at least strongly suspecting—that she would refuse his proposal.

"I think Alex was angry enough for them both," Beatrice said. "He came over here all in a tither about how horrible we were to concoct such a mean-spirited plan. Can you imagine? After what they did?"

Anne knitted her brows. "What do you mean, after what 'they' did? Was Alex in on this, too?"

Beatrice suddenly looked as guilty as a little girl who's lost her mother's favorite earrings. "It was his idea," she said reluctantly.

"Does anyone not know?" Anne said, clearly mortified that her humiliation was so complete.

"Oh, no one knows. Everyone mostly just thought Henry married you to get to his inheritance," Beatrice said, her voice trailing off when she realized what she was revealing.

"You suspected even then?"

Beatrice swallowed. "Well. Yes. Yes, I did. But I didn't want to hurt you, and at the time I couldn't be absolutely certain that Henry was using you. If it makes you feel better, I think you really did crush Henry, despite his pretending otherwise."

"Oh, Bea," Anne said, her eyes welling up with tears that had been threatening all day. "Why on earth would that make me feel better?"

"You still love him?"

Anne could only nod her head. She thought back to the way he'd held her, the sound of his voice, the near-desperation in his tone.

"If you knew how much I love you, Anne . . . If only you knew."

At the time, Anne had been proud of herself for not bending to his will. But now she felt ashamed. For both of them.

"Do you remember when we put this plan together? It wasn't supposed to hurt, Bea. It was supposed to be fun. This isn't fun. It's awful. I don't feel vindicated, or happy, or any of those things I thought I'd feel. I just feel alone and . . ." Her throat closed up with tears and she swallowed. "He loved me, Bea. I've just thrown away the only man who's ever loved me."

"No, Anne," Bea said fiercely. "Henry threw you away. Don't ever forget that it was his cruel indifference that started all this."

"Do you want to know something, Bea? I don't care who started what anymore. I'm just glad it's finally over."

Henry stared unseeing at the ledger in front of him for several long minutes before realizing it was upside down. The blackness that he'd fought for much of his life was threatening, and he feared that this time he wouldn't have the strength to battle it back. He'd trained himself to think: Things will be better when . . . And he'd have something to fill in that blank. But now, he could think of nothing that would make his life better, and that nearly paralyzed him. He shook his head to rid himself of such damaging thoughts, but he couldn't shake away the burning in his throat, the coldness in his heart.

When he heard footsteps, he knew Alex had returned.

"She knows," Alex said, his face grim.

Henry felt as if all the blood in his body pooled with sickening suddenness, in his stomach. He waited for Alex to explain what he meant.

"Anne knows that you picked her because she was plain, Henry."

The breath left Henry's body, leaving him weak. "Aw, damn." He shook his head and clenched his jaw, refusing to allow the full extent of his grief to show. He'd not do that, not even in front of Alex. "How?"

"Your grandfather apparently wrote to Anne in an attempt to stop the wedding. Somehow or other, Anne missed it. The letter was, by all accounts, rather blunt. She found it three days ago."

Henry kneaded his temples.

"She was going to say yes, Henry, until she found that letter."

Henry turned his head sharply to look out his window and prayed Alex wouldn't see the moisture gathering in his eyes. "You tell her for me, Alex, that her plan worked," he said, his eyes still trained on the harbor.

Alex took a hesitant step toward his friend, then stopped. He'd never been very adept at giving comfort. "You'll . . . be all right? Alone here?"

"Of course."

Alex stood there a long moment studying Henry. "You're certain?"

"Alex," Henry said, turning to his friend good-naturedly. "Just get the hell out of here, will you?"

When he was certain Alex was gone, Henry rose from his chair and stood by the window at the view that had always given him such solace. His movements were like those of an old man, as if something had stiffened his joints, thickened his blood. He told himself he would not cry even as tears traced his cheeks, even as his chest convulsed in a silent sob.

Indeed, Anne had gotten her revenge.

Chapter Twenty-one

A lex, bringing with him the scent of the raging storm outside, shoved his way past the Leydens' butler and began shouting for Beatrice. His boots left dark splotches on the carpet, which the butler looked down on with something akin to horror.

"I say, you can't come barging in," the affronted man said, hastily running after him.

Normally, Alex was a strict adherer to polite protocol. But today was different, for never in his life had he been as frightened as he now was.

Henry had gone missing. Just like before.

"Beatrice," he shouted, striding into the library, the parlor, the dining room. "Goddamn it, where is that woman?"

"Sir," the harried butler shouted, trailing after the madman prowling the Leyden household. "Sir, I insist you come with me and . . ."

Alex barreled past the man, ignoring his entreaties, trying to ignore the howling wind that could be heard even through the thick granite walls of the Leyden mansion. Rain, sounding like handfuls of sand being thrown against the windows, came down in torrents, battering anyone or anything unlucky enough to be caught outside. He could only pray—and the Lord above knew He hadn't heard from Alex Henley in quite some time—that Henry wasn't one of those unlucky souls.

"What is all this ruckus?" Helen said from the stairway. Beatrice trailed behind her mother, her eyes widening when she saw Alex. His hair was wet and plastered to his head, his clothes wrinkled, wet, and disheveled. Truly, something must be horribly wrong. "Mr. Henley, I demand to know what you are doing in my home unannounced and uninvited," Helen said.

Beatrice winced at her mother's tone, fully knowing that Alex's reputation preceded him and that she had no idea that her daughter was madly in love with one of the best-known rakes in Newport. Or that he was, perhaps, in love with Beatrice.

Alex, bless him, actually took the time to give Mrs. Leyden a small bow, before rushing past her on the staircase. "Bea, have you seen or heard from Henry? Has Anne?" His brown eyes suddenly snapped to the landing where Anne stood clutching the banister as if to keep herself from falling.

"What has happened, Mr. Henley?" Anne asked in strangely even tones.

"Have you heard from Henry? Has he sent a note or—"

"Perhaps we should retire to the parlor," Helen said calmly.

"But I just want to know—"

"The parlor, Mr. Henley. Now."

All three young people trailed after Helen like chastened children into the main parlor where a cheerful fire danced in the hearth. With maddening calmness, Helen went about the room and raised the flames on three lamps. With an imperial nod, she silently told the three to sit on the sofa. Beatrice sat between Alex and Anne, Helen sat, back straight, on a Chippendale chair directly across from them.

"Now, Mr. Henley, perhaps you can explain why you have barged into my home."

Alex, despite his rather public search, suddenly seemed ill at ease to have such an audience. Moving to the edge of the sofa, he leaned forward so he could see Anne. "Have you seen Henry, Miss Foster?"

"I saw him two days ago," she said softly.

Alex cursed beneath his breath and didn't bother apologizing. "He's missing. His catboat isn't at Spring Wharf."

"Perhaps he's at Sea Cliff," Beatrice said, still baffled as to why Alex would be so disconcerted about Henry's absence.

"I plan to go there as soon as this storm's abated. I was hoping he'd sent word to Miss Foster. Hell, I don't know what I was thinking."

Anne's cheeks flamed red, her heart seemed to contract painfully, at the thought that Henry might have tried to reach her. So many times in the last two days she had fought the urge to seek Henry out, to beg his forgiveness. Then, self-respect and sensibility would return and she'd silently chastise herself for even thinking about forgiving Henry. Yes, he'd told her he loved her and he probably believed it himself. He'd get past it, as quickly as he'd gotten past the guilt over marrying an ugly girl.

But there were moments when she'd remember his smile, his kiss, the way he'd gazed at Sea Cliff with a longing that was nearly tangible, when she missed him so much it hurt. Part of her was filled with disappointment that he hadn't sought her out to win her back. Certainly, she would rebuff him, but she ridiculously wanted him to try.

Anne swallowed, refusing to give in to the tears that once again threatened. The past two days she'd walked around with a lump in her throat the size of an egg, all because she'd finally dealt to Henry what he richly deserved.

"Is Henry in trouble?" Anne asked.

Alex threaded his fingers through his hair, leaving behind unkempt spikes. "I don't know."

"Why are you here, Mr. Henley? Surely there is a

reason you thought he might contact Miss Foster," Helen said, her voice far gentler than before.

Alex studied the Aubusson carpet beneath his feet for a long moment before he answered. And when he did, he spoke into the carpet, his eyes seeing not the intricate pattern, but a vision from the distant past.

"Henry is quite good at hiding his true feelings, he always has been. After his parents died, he never talked about it. We were just kids and I suppose I didn't see what was right in front of me. Now that I look back, I can see how sad he was that summer." He sighed. "He left a note addressed to his grandfather. All it said was, 'I've gone to find my mother and father.' He went off in his little boat, not much more than a dinghy, and sailed into a hurricane."

Anne gasped and turned to the rain-lashed window.

"He got picked up by a fisherman before he got too far, before the storm hit full force. Henry never talked about it, never admitted what he was trying to do."

"Then you don't know for certain he was trying to end his life," Helen said. "Perhaps he truly had convinced himself that his parents were alive."

Alex shook his head. "By then, he knew they were dead."

Beatrice put a hand on his arm. "He wouldn't have this time, Alex. Anne told me he hardly even reacted when she broke off."

Alex stood abruptly. "No. Henry wouldn't have reacted. He never would have let Anne know what leaving him did. But he did tell me one thing, Miss Foster," he said, turning his hard gaze to Anne. "He told me to tell you that your plan worked. You did intend to break his heart, did you not? So, congratulations, Miss Foster," he gave her a slight bow, "you have succeeded."

Something was tightening Anne's chest. "He acted like he didn't care," she insisted. "I would have known if . . ." Guilt, like a knife thrust into her breast, struck

hard. She'd actually been disappointed that he'd been
so blasé. "Oh, God," she said on a sob. "How did
this become so hideous? I'll never forgive myself if
something has happened to him."

"Everyone calm down," Helen said. "We don't
know anything right now other than Henry's boat is
gone. He might have sailed before the storm hit. In
all likelihood, he's safe and sound and licking his
wounds at Sea Cliff."

Alex sat down heavily. "You're probably right, Mrs.
Leyden. And, Anne, I apologize. You are not to
blame. Not entirely. I stupidly told him you were planning to marry him until you found that letter from
his grandfather. If anything, he's gone to Sea Cliff to
strangle him."

Anne tormented herself by recalling their last meeting. She could almost hear Henry's voice telling her
he loved her. She'd been proud of herself for remaining strong, telling herself over and over that
Henry deserved whatever pain she caused him.

"Oh, we're all despicable. Every last one of us,"
Anne said. She stood and walked to the window, torturing herself by looking out at the storm.

"Henry started this all," Beatrice said.

Anne whirled around. "Stop it, Bea. I don't care
who started it, who ended it, who was hurt, who was
not. No. I take it back. I do care. Henry is guilty of
being an insensitive lout. But I set out to purposefully
hurt him. If anyone is to blame, it is I."

"No, Anne," Bea said. "Henry is the one—"

"Who said he loved me," Anne nearly screamed.
"And I threw it back in his face all because of some
ridiculous plan." Anne turned back to the window,
wrapping her arms about herself as if struck by a sudden chill. Her fingertips dug deep into her upper arms
in a punishing grip.

Anne's last words hung in the air until the room

grew silent, with only the hissing of the lamps and the crackling fire breaking the quiet until Helen spoke.

"I think you are all wrong about Henry Owen," she said. "He strikes me as a man who would not go rushing off into a storm simply because he'd been spurned. I beg your pardon, Anne, but I think Henry far more practical than that. Henry was just a boy when he sailed into that storm, Mr. Henley. A lonely boy who had just lost both his parents."

"Now he's a lonely man who's just lost the only woman he's ever loved," Alex said softly.

At the window, Anne clutched her arms impossibly tighter, hating herself and thinking over and over how ugly she'd become on the inside.

Across the bay, Henry stood, safe and dry, looking through his hotel window at the same storm that tortured his friends with thoughts of his certain demise. He watched as the wind and current tugged relentlessly on his sailboat, moored in the limited protection of the harbor. The seas, usually calm, were dark and menacing with foam-whipped whitecaps heaving upward to crash against the hulls of the anchored boats that dotted the harbor. With almost fatalistic calm, Henry watched as a much larger sailing vessel lurched free from its mooring and headed directly toward his little catboat. Before his helpless gaze, the freed vessel careened, bobbing and swirling, toward his boat, inevitably smashing into its stern. For one long moment, it appeared as if the mooring would hold, as if the little boat fought against the larger vessel in a valiant attempt to stay grounded. And then, it broke free.

"Damn," Henry muttered, his lips pressed tightly together. What else could go wrong? He turned away from the window, cursing events that would likely force him to hire a horse to get to Sea Cliff overland.

Henry had hastily left Newport with a weather eye to the west, knowing he would have to leave immedi-

ately to beat the storm. The urge to leave had been
strong, as had the urge to gleefully murder his grandfather. So Henry had headed to Jamestown, his sails
filled and snapping with the precursor of the storm,
only to tack to Jamestown center, away from Sea Cliff
and his grandfather. He couldn't trust himself to speak
to the old man just yet without doing him bodily harm,
no matter how close he was to death. Curse that man
for meddling where he didn't belong. For the hun-
dredth time he wondered what it was about Sea Cliff
that his grandfather would go to such extremes to
keep it from him. Could it simply be a matter of spite
that led the old man to write that letter to Anne?
Henry had a difficult time believing his grandfather
was being vindictive simply to hurt him.

Henry thought he'd given up on trying to understand his grandfather, a man so cold and distant, so
unlike his own father, it was a wonder they were re-
lated. He missed his father even now, missed their
walks together, their long philosophical talks. Sometimes they would sit on Sea Cliff's porch and watch
the sun rise, breathing in the beauty of another day.
Neither would speak until the magic was over, until
the sky turned from deep blue-black to rose to yellow,
and finally, finally hinting at full-day blue. Henry
couldn't look at a sunrise without thinking of and
missing his father.

The window of his hotel room rattled, reminding
Henry where he was and why. The Thorndike Hotel,
while considered exclusive by Jamestown standards,
would not have as guests those who rented or owned
cottages in Newport. Hotels were not the thing, no
matter how elegant they were. Thorndike, only three
years old, was built on a bluff overlooking the East
Passage, and boasted a castlelike tower and ten pricey
shops on the bottom floor to attract the idle rich.
Though the hotel was crowded, Henry knew he was
almost guaranteed anonymity here. Thank God.

Henry needed to lick his wounds, to regroup, to stop himself from confronting his grandfather until his emotions were well in order. Lately, Henry had found it disconcertingly difficult to harness his feelings.

Anne. Just thinking of her hurt a startling amount. He was not angry with her. Indeed, he was somewhat proud of her backbone. Imagine concocting a plan so bold, his shy girl. Not shy anymore, was she, he thought, thinking back on how skillfully she'd flirted with him and Jake Morrison. If only she hadn't learned the truth behind his proposal. If only. If only.

Henry chuckled bitterly, thinking of their last meeting. He'd thought to confuse her, to convince her with kisses, with declarations of love, never knowing she'd walked into his office with the resolve of a general. After everything, he still thought he had a chance to change her mind. She had a plan? Well, so had he. He'd planned to prove to her that she loved him. But that was before he knew she'd found his grandfather's letter, before she discovered just how loathsome he was.

Henry pressed his forehead against the cool window and closed his eyes, hating himself and thinking that, all along, he'd been the ugly one.

Just when Alex had convinced himself that he was overreacting, he receive more proof that Henry had sailed off alone into the storm. A telegram to his town house in New York was answered by Henry's butler. No, Mr. Owen had not returned to New York. And then Henry's catboat had been found, badly damaged, on Prudence Island. No body had been found, but Alex knew that it sometimes took days—if ever—for the bay with its strong currents to return the bodies it stole. It was possible that the catboat had been torn from his anchor and that Henry was safe and sound at Sea Cliff. Alex had but one choice: visit Henry's grandfather.

Alex had never liked the man, probably because he'd been so cruel to Henry. Though Alex would describe himself as a man with few attachments, he had appointed himself Henry's guardian the day his grandfather came with word that his parents were missing and presumed dead. It didn't matter in the least that Henry was actually ten months older than Alex. From that day forward, Alex had unknowingly been watching over Henry like a mother hen. He would, quite simply, die for him. Certainly he could face Henry's grandfather.

Alex sloshed ashore, shoes and stockings in hand, from his rented centerboard sailing skiff, unmindful that his pants were getting a good soaking. He dragged the boat as best as he could to the sandy beach, then tied it off to a piling spiked into the beach for just that purpose, his eyes trained on Sea Cliff. No one came from the old place. Surely Henry would have seen him by now and come down to the beach. A curtain fluttered on the second floor, no doubt Arthur's man spying on him.

"Henry," Alex said aloud, "where are you?" His chest felt as if a heavy weight were bearing down on it. He'd convinced himself that Henry would be here. But now his gut told him he was not.

"Mr. Henley," Peleg called from his tiny cottage behind Sea Cliff. "What brings you to the island?"

"I was hoping to find Henry here," Alex said, slipping on his shoes. "His boat was found scuttled up on Prudence."

"That so?" Peleg said with little alarm. "Storm likely ripped it away. There's boats scuttled all 'bout the place."

"Yes, Well, I can't seem to locate Henry." Alex stood and squinted his eyes as he looked back across the bay in an effort to stop himself from sliding into despair.

"Check New York?"

Alex could only nod.

"Not in Newport, I take it," Peleg said, his voice for the first time taking on a note of worry.

"No. He left right before the storm hit."

"That so. Found his boat, you say? You're certain it's his?"

The weight against his chest was nearly suffocating. "Saw it myself earlier this morning. Had a gash in the hull, its mast was torn away."

Peleg grunted. "No way to tell if she was under sail or anchored, then."

Either way, it didn't much matter, Alex thought, studying the sand. Henry was not on that boat when they found it, and it was impossible to know whether he'd been on it when it was torn apart. He lifted his head and nodded toward the big house. "Is the old man up to a visit?"

"Wouldn't know," Peleg said. "I stay to the main floor to make sure that cadaver he's got for a valet stays out of mischief. Found him snooping around once." Peleg sniffed. "Figure he's still breathing, though, the old coot. Imagine they would have told me if he'd gone belly-up."

With his heart thudding somewhere down by his shoes, Alex trudged through the flotsam-strewn sand and up the steps to Sea Cliff's lawn. Before he could knock, the door opened and he found himself greeted by a chubby-cheeked woman with a wide smile.

"Mr. Henley," she said, as if he was an old friend. "Mr. Owen is so pleased you stopped by."

Alex stared at the woman for so long, her smile faltered. "Oh, forgive me. I'm Mrs. Bradley, Mr. Owen's nurse."

Alex nodded to her. "Mrs. Bradley. I take it Mr. Owen will see me?"

"Oh, yes. He's having a good day today, thanks be praised."

"If you will show me the way," he said, in the reserved politeness of the upper class.

The nurse, either too obtuse or too friendly to take a broad hint, chatted all the way up the stairs before showing Alex to a darkened room that smelled surprisingly fresh, given that a man lay dying in the massive bed. There on the bed was the emaciated figure of a man who, in his prime, could strike terror into a young boy with the glare of his eye. Alex had been the recipient of that glare more than once, often being blamed for putting the man's grandson at some sort of imagined risk. But today, Alex could place the blame squarely on this man's shoulders. If he hadn't sent that note to Anne, Henry would still be alive and planning to marry the only woman beside his mother he'd ever loved.

Alex walked directly to the bed. "That letter you wrote to Anne Foster hit its mark, Mr. Owen," Alex said without preamble. "She received it two years too late to prevent her marriage to Henry. But I'm certain you'll be pleased to know that it prevented a second marriage."

"What are you talking about?" Arthur said, sounding as if he had a large mouthful, his words barely discernible.

"Henry sailed off into that storm, Mr. Owen, the day after Miss Foster rejected his proposal of marriage because of your letter. His boat was found scuttled on Prudence Island. Henry is missing."

Henry is missing. Suddenly, Arthur was swept back thirteen years, holding in his trembling hand the carefully written note from his grandson: "I've gone to find my mother and father."

Arthur, who had suffered a mild stroke the year before, was in his New York mansion when he received that note. Within twelve hours, he was in Newport, raging against anyone who would listen that his grandson must be found. Gripping a cane like a sword, he'd slashed the rod through the air as if he could command God to return Henry to him. Alex's father, quite drunk at the time and of little use, tried to calm Arthur down by offering him a large snifter of brandy, which Arthur promptly threw into the fireplace. Mr. Henley's only comment was that Arthur had just wasted some damn fine brandy.

Like a man driven to madness, Arthur had paced in his odd thumping manner, one side of his face slightly drooping from the stroke, and questioned Alex until the boy was sobbing. Arthur hadn't been proud of himself, but the thought that Henry had taken his own life filled Arthur with a fear so consuming, he was nearly demented.

When a fisherman brought Henry, looking ragged and miserable, to the Henley front door, Arthur, in his terror, struck Henry hard on the shoulder with his cane for putting him through the most excruciating pain and horror he'd ever known. As soon as he hit him, Arthur wanted to pull Henry to him and never let him go. But Henry, as if he didn't even feel the blow, turned away from him and walked up the stairs to his room, Alex trailing behind him. Alex stopped at least three times in that trip up those stairs to look back and cast Arthur a glare of such unadulterated hate, it was almost amusing.

"Haven't you anything to say?" Alex demanded.

Arthur finally turned to look the young man in the eye. "Henry wouldn't be so foolish as to kill himself over a woman," he said quite clearly. "No doubt he was on his way here to finish me off." He tried to chuckle, but it came out sounding oddly like a sob. "By God, I wish he had."

Alex shook his head in disgust. "What did he ever do to you, that you hate him so?"

"Hate Henry?" Arthur peered at Alex. "My boy, I love him like a son." Thick tears fell from Arthur's eyes to roll unheeded, following the creases of his wrinkled cheek.

"If he's alive, if he shows up here, tell him I was looking for him, will you?" Alex said, trying valiantly not to be moved by the old man's tears.

Arthur closed his eyes and nodded wearily, hoping hell was not as lonely as he now felt.

Chapter Twenty-two

"Newport steel baron Henry James Owen, one of the richest men in this country, is missing after the storm that swept through this area Sunday night. He is presumed dead."

Henry, who'd been sitting in the Thorndike Hotel's crowded dining room drinking some good strong coffee, was suddenly beset by a choking fit.

"Are you quite all right, sir?" asked a young waiter, who hurried to his side and took the liberty of pounding upon Henry's back.

"Apparently," Henry said dryly, "I'm very likely dead."

The waiter backed up a step. "I beg pardon, sir?"

Henry shook his head, dismissing the waiter. "I'm fine." He scanned the article, a wry smile on his face, as he read the details of his supposed demise. Henry frowned when he read that his sailboat had been badly damaged. Damn good boat lost, he thought. But when he read that the article was apparently precipitated by the frenzied search of one Alexander Henley, he nearly choked on his coffee again.

"You idiot," he whispered fondly.

No doubt Alex had all of Newport sporting black armbands and placing black wreaths on their front doors. He couldn't help his next thought: I wonder how Anne is taking the news. Not that it mattered, but he wanted her to feel a little sad at his untimely passing. With a certain masochistic bent, he imagined

her celebrating, gleefully telling Beatrice that he'd finally gotten what he deserved. She would raise a glass
of champagne, urge everyone in the room to do the
same, and toast his death. Or, he thought, she would
collapse in a fit of tears, walk down to the shore, and
throw herself into the surf to join her one true love
in his watery grave. Hardly likely, he realized, given
that she'd announced not three days earlier that she
didn't love him.

Henry sat back, resting his chin on his thumbs, and
wondered just how long he should remain dead. It
would be cruel to prolong Alex's agony for too long.
Still, it would be just punishment for leaping to the
erroneous conclusion that he was dead simply because
his boat had been found without him in it. No doubt
Alex thought Henry so bereaved over losing Anne
that he'd sailed into that storm purposefully. While
Henry understood Alex's panic, he was slightly irritated that Alex still thought of him as that rash young
boy, that tragic romantic who'd gone off in a hurricane
to search for his long-dead parents.

Henry's decision about how quickly to let the world
know he was alive and well was made for him when
a wide-eyed hotel manager practically ran to him in
an odd lunging manner, a copy of the *Daily News* in
his hand.

"Mr. Owen, have you read the newspaper?"

"I have, Mr. Penney. Indeed I found it quite interesting."

"I will dispatch a telegram immediately, sir, with
your permission," the man said, eager to please his
prestigious guest.

With a look around the room to make certain no
one was paying undo attention to them, Henry
crooked his finger to urge Penney closer. "If you
would wait," Henry took out his pocket watch and
noted the time, "say, twelve hours before you send
that telegram, I would be very grateful, Mr. Penney."

Seeing dollar signs, Penney smiled. "Oh?"

Henry slipped him a hundred dollars.

"I will personally see to it that your message will be sent at the appropriate time," Penney said, stuffing the money in his suit jacket pocket.

"Thank you, sir. I shall recommend the Thorndike to all my friends."

He would count himself lucky if Penney made it through half the day without spilling the exciting news that Henry was alive and staying at the Thorndike. He'd bought himself at least six hours with that hundred-dollar bill. Now, Henry thought, I believe a visit to my grandfather is in order.

Anne looked up from the *Daily News,* fresh tears in her eyes. Henry couldn't be dead, he couldn't be. Guilt washed over her like molten lava, slow, hot, and suffocating. Anne's eyes were red and swollen from fierce bouts of crying, her nose hurt from blowing, her head ached. She wanted to believe Helen and others who couldn't conceive of a man like Henry taking his own life over a broken love affair. But Alex had painted such a tragic picture of Henry, it was difficult to remain optimistic as the hours passed with no word. It was near impossible to reconcile her knowledge of Henry with the lonely, sad man that Alex said he was. Henry, always so self-assured and infallably cheerful. Was it all pretense?

"Won't Henry have a good laugh when he reads this," she said, determinedly chipper even though her voice was soggy from tears. Before her sat a breakfast of poached eggs and sausage gone cold, untouched but for a bit of egg she'd managed to choke down. How could she possibly eat when Henry had killed himself over her, she thought dramatically.

Beatrice, who had handed Anne the newspaper, nodded briskly. "Yes. I'm certain he will."

Anne stared blindly at her plate. "He's not dead.

He's not. They're wrong to presume he is." She looked up at Beatrice. "Oh, Bea, even if it was an accident, how can I live with the fact that one of the last things I said to him was that I didn't love him?" She twisted the napkin in her hand. "But I do love him, Bea. I never stopped loving him. I was angry and hurt and I wanted to hurt him. I did want to. But I never stopped loving him. And now . . . And now he could be . . ."

Beatrice stood and rushed to Anne's side, gripping her arm and giving it a shake. "He's not dead. He wouldn't have the audacity to die leaving you behind with all this guilt to shoulder."

Anne choked on a laugh. "Well, that's certainly true. He has put me through enough."

"More than enough." Beatrice bit her lip.

Anne sat there, strangling her napkin, and thinking that she'd give up almost anything to be able to see one of Henry's careless lopsided smiles, to touch his lean jaw, to kiss his firm lips. If he walked into the room this moment, she didn't think she'd have the strength not to throw herself into his arms and promise to marry him a dozen times.

As if reading her mind, Beatrice said, "Anne, after this is all over, you're not thinking the two of you will make up. Are you?"

After blowing her nose, Anne took a deep, shaking breath and lied. "I just want him to be all right. I don't care if he marries a hundred girls."

Henry secured his rented horse and looked up at Sea Cliff, waiting for the familiar feeling of warmth that told him he was home. But this time, something vital was missing. Gone was that heart-filling sensation he'd had each time the grand old home came into view. Sea Cliff had simply become a house—and one that needed major renovations. Sea Cliff needed a family, boys tussling about the porch, girls wading in the surf, their bright gold curls dancing in the sun. Henry shook his head to rid himself of those sentimental images. His grandfather had been right about one thing: Henry had been a sentimental fool over Sea Cliff. He'd tied up his memories with his need for his family. And somehow, that need had turned from his parents, to Anne. He knew she would be the only woman who could fill that empty spot in his life, in his home.

With a sigh and a gentle pat to the horse's muscled neck, Henry strode to the porch and opened the door, only to be met by the strange sight of a grinning Williamson.

"Sir, you're safe," Williamson blurted.

"Quite."

Henry felt like the prodigal son returning home. Even Williamson, whom he'd never seen smile, managed to pull his lips up in something that some would consider a grin. It was rather frightening.

Mrs. Bradley, the nurse, was embarrassingly enthused at his arrival, burbling on and on about how pleased his grandfather would be to see him. She pushed forward, her apple cheeks so cheerfully red, they looked ready to pick. "But your boat was found badly damaged and we all thought—"

"That I was dead. Yes, I know. But as you can see, I am not. If you'll pardon me," he said, moving past the odd couple to the stairs.

"Oh, but sir, let me announce you," Williamson said, hurrying after Henry.

"No need," Henry said, waving the older man back. He stopped and gave Williamson a smile. "I want this to be a surprise."

Henry paused at his grandfather's door, debating whether he should knock, then decided to walk in without warning. He wanted to catch the old man off his guard for once. He quietly opened the door and saw that Arthur sat by the window looking out at the bay. Without turning, he said, "Any word, Williamson?"

"It's Henry."

Arthur jerked as if struck, then turned slowly toward Henry. And then he did something Henry had never seen his grandfather do—he started to cry, hard, body-wracking sobs. Something in that moment unfurled in Henry's chest. He swallowed heavily and walked to his grandfather, who hung his head—either ashamed or overwhelmed by his tears—and he grasped his grandfather's hand to comfort him. Arthur, his head still bowed, clutched Henry's hand and arm to his chest, his bony fingers moving convulsively, saying Henry's name over and over in his slurred voice.

"It's all right," Henry said softly, bending down so that his grandfather could give him a proper hug. "I'm here." His face was taut with emotion as he allowed the old man to pull him down for an awkward embrace.

After a few moments, Arthur withdrew and his eyebrows snapped together. "What fool thing did you do this time, that everyone thinks you're dead?"

Henry let out a chuckle, inordinately relieved that his grandfather had returned to the man he'd known his entire life. Henry put his arms out to his sides, palms up. "Nothing but look for a bit of privacy. I was staying at the Thorndike. In fact, I was at the window looking out when my boat was ripped from its mooring. In hindsight, I suppose I should have immediately dispatched a letter to Alex."

"Henley was here looking for you. He's likely already picked out your burial plot."

Henry let out a puff of irritation. "Alex apparently jumped to the conclusion that I tried to kill myself. And you, too, it seems."

"Bah," Arthur grumbled, wiping at his face with his lap robe. "It's not as if you hadn't tried such a fool thing before."

Henry shook his head. "I was a boy."

Arthur turned to look out the window. "I've lost a wife and two children. I almost lost you that day."

"You didn't."

Arthur grunted an acknowledgement. "What's this about that Foster girl? Henley said something about the two of you getting married or some such nonsense. But she jilted you."

Henry scowled. "Alex talks too much."

"Broke your heart, did she?"

"You don't have to sound so damn cheerful about it."

The old man actually let out a cackle. "Serves you right. Poetic justice for marrying like you did."

"So it would seem."

Arthur peered up at Henry, his chest heaving from the exertion of talking. "Get her back."

Henry ran his hand through his hair and turned away from his grandfather's sharp gaze. "It's too late. Thanks to you, I might add," Henry said, remembering suddenly why he'd traveled to Sea Cliff in the first place. "I came here to throttle you, old man, for writing that note to Anne. It hurt her badly. Is that what you intended?"

"I intended for her to get it before you married. I intended for her to call the wedding off. To save her some of the grief you've given her."

Henry shook his head, denying his grandfather's words. "No. You did it to stop me from getting what was rightfully mine. You had no consideration for Anne. I didn't think even you would go so far to keep Sea Cliff from me. Tell me why you tried so hard. I've a right to know."

Arthur set his jaw stubbornly. "You'll know."

Henry closed his eyes and prayed for patience. "When?"

Arthur remained silent, clamping his mouth shut like a child being forced to eat an unwanted vegetable. "Tell Williamson I want to go to bed."

Henry stared at his grandfather, his hands on his lean hips, almost admiring his stubbornness. "It had better be a damned good reason."

Arthur mumbled something Henry couldn't understand, then said clearly, "Get Williamson."

With one last exasperated look, Henry turned to do his grandfather's bidding.

"Henry."

He turned reluctantly.

"I . . ." Arthur played with his robe, pulling at it, bunching it together in his lap. He shook his head. "Never mind. I was about to get maudlin."

Henry smiled. "Thank God you came to your senses," he said, turning to go find Williamson. For a minute there, Henry thought his grandfather was about to do something irrevocable—like tell Henry he loved him.

From the Journal of Arthur Owen

I used to pretend that she loved you because you came from me. But I think she loved you because you were the only being who ever loved her without question, without demands. For hours you would lie on the porch swing, your little head in her lap, and she would stroke your forehead even after you'd fallen asleep. I would watch the two of you, the woman I loved and my son, dying a bit every day.

To torture me, Elizabeth would say things aloud that only I would understand. She'd comment on the color of your eyes, a soft gray, so unlike Walter's brown eyes and her vivid blue. You were so much like me, I lived in fear that Walter would somehow guess the truth. One night at dinner, she suggested a portrait of you and me, and Walter agreed. I stared at her for a long moment, so angry, I couldn't immediately trust myself to speak. I refused, of course. Perhaps you remember. I told your mother I wouldn't pose with you, that I didn't have time for such nonsense. She knew, of course, that I would refuse. It was just one of her subtle tortures. You were crushed. I think that was the first time you started to dislike me. Can you imagine having your son, a little boy you love more than life, look at you that way? My son. My son. It was a song in my heart, it filled my soul. It broke my spirit.

I should have stayed away, but could not. You were my son. Until you have a child, you will not know the bond that exists. It is difficult to imagine the sort of love a father has for his son. Elizabeth must have known this. But she drove us apart in a hundred different ways. I think she lived in constant fear that I would reveal her secret, that I would destroy the only thing in her life that was real to her. And yet, she would look at me sometimes and I would swear I saw love and regret. Perhaps I only wished it, for I never stopped loving and wanting her. I am old enough now to realize I could have done things differently. I could have fought better for you even though I could never claim you.

After your parents died, I planned to tell you. But each time, I lacked the courage. I could tell you already hated me, or at least feared me. How would you feel to learn that I had lied to you all those years? You mourned your parents' death so heavily, I could not add to your sorrow, I could not let you know that your mother was not the angel you thought her. I know you thought me cold, but I mourned their deaths as well. I loved your father, in my way. And you know I loved Elizabeth. She haunts me still.

Chapter Twenty-three

Henry found Alex at the breakfast table, moodily looking out a window, no doubt wondering what he should wear to his best friend's funeral.

"I have one question for you, Alex," Henry said from the door. "Are you trying to make me look like an idiot?"

Alex whirled around, a look of unadulterated joy on his face. He shoved his chair back and strode across the room, giving Henry a hearty embrace, then clasping him almost painfully about the upper arms.

"Where the hell have you been?" he asked, a broad smile still splitting his face.

"Certainly not at the bottom of the Atlantic where you thought I was," Henry said, forcing himself to scowl.

Alex looked a bit sheepish and began to explain but Henry stopped him.

"Don't worry about it," Henry said, making his way to the sideboard and piling food onto a plate. "In hindsight I suppose I can understand why you went off the deep end."

"Where were you all this time, then?" Alex said, his good humor gone now that the joy of finding Henry alive and well was wearing off. He sat back at the dining table and shoveled a large bit of egg into his mouth, his appetite suddenly restored.

"At the Thorndike trying to avoid people," Henry

said dryly. "Unfortunately, once the news of my death was out, my privacy suffered."

Alex shrugged. "Did you stop by Sea Cliff?"

"I did. My grandfather is getting sentimental in his old age. He actually seemed glad to find I was still alive." Henry waved away a maid and brought his plate and coffee to the table, sitting across from his friend. He didn't want to ask, but he couldn't quite stop himself. "I suppose everyone thinks I'm dead. And Anne, does she believe I would have sailed into the eye of a storm for her?"

Alex grinned into his plate, but looked solemn when he raised his head. "Actually, no. She's been carrying on as if all is well. I believe she went to the Phillips' musicale last night with Jake Morrison."

Henry stabbed an unfortunate piece of ham with his fork. "Glad to know the news of my death didn't interrupt her social schedule," Henry said, the muscle in his jaw bunching.

Alex began to chuckle. "Henry, you are a fool."

Henry shot daggers at his friend, until it slowly dawned on him that Alex was playing with him. "You ass."

"Anne, my good friend, was the epitome of a woman in deep mourning. When I visited Beatrice yesterday, she came down looking like she'd been crying for a week, all red-eyed and puffy. She is not a graceful weeper, apparently." Alex gave a mock shudder.

"Really," Henry said, a silly grin on his face. "What did she say?"

"Oh, only that she hoped you weren't dead or some such thing."

"And she appeared upset?"

"I've said so." Alex stopped eating for a moment. "See here, Henry, go see her yourself. Surprise her." He took out his pocket watch. "I'm due to meet Beatrice at the Casino in about fifteen minutes. I'm certain Anne will be there."

Henry let out a chuckle. "I can see just how very upsetting my disappearance was to you all. Did you plan to cry on each other's shoulders as you listened to Mullaly's Orchestra?"

"It was Anne's idea. She thought we could dispel some of the gossip if we appeared at the Casino as if nothing was wrong."

"How clever of her."

Alex sighed. "She has refused to believe you are dead. I thought it rather touching. Come with me to the Casino. Surprise her."

Uncertainty struck Henry hard. Of course Anne would be upset if she thought him dead, but that didn't mean she still cared for him. He ought to know how guilt could wear a person down. He felt that now-familiar squeezing sensation in his chest at the thought of seeing Anne again. It was over. She'd told him to his face that she did not love him, and he believed her. What possible good could come of seeing her again?

"Why not?" he said. His heart was already so battered, what would one more pummeling do?

Anne hadn't suspected how difficult it would be to face people at the Casino and pretend not only that she believed Henry alive, but that they were still a couple. Anne hadn't the heart to tell anyone that the pair they'd seen dancing together at Marble House was a fraud. Of course, the colonel's column about her jaunt to Jamestown did not help matters. In their minds, Henry and Anne were a couple torn apart once again. She thought she would scream if one more person came up to her and offered condolences. How many times would she have to smile and say that of course Henry was fine? But too many days had passed without a word. If Henry was alive, he would have let Alex know.

Yesterday she'd waited in anticipation for word of him until her entire body ached from the tension of such a vigil. Each time she heard a carriage or the footsteps of a servant, she was certain it was someone bringing news of Henry. She'd thought that if she prayed hard enough, if she pretended convincingly enough, that Henry would, indeed, return to Alex's home.

But now she could only conclude that he was likely dead and she was to blame. It didn't matter how many times Beatrice or Helen tried to comfort her, she would always know in her heart that Henry had sailed into that storm to escape his pain. Perhaps he really did love her, after all.

"I don't know if we accomplished anything by coming here today," Anne said through a throat that ached with unshed tears. Every time she saw a man with wavy brown hair, she thought, for a fleeting second, that it was Henry. Poor Henry, who was at the bottom of the bay because of her. "All anyone is talking about is when the funeral should be held." Anne looked out at the crowd darkly. "They don't give a fig about Henry, not a one of them. They're only wondering if they have to go out and buy a new black gown."

"If he is alive, he'll be glad you stood by him," Beatrice said.

"When did you begin to care about whether Henry was glad or not?"

Beatrice blushed. "He is Alex's dearest friend, so I suppose I must learn to like him."

"But it didn't matter when I loved him?" Anne asked with a bit of hysteria in her voice.

Beatrice bit her lip. "It's entirely different. Henry hurt you. I'd feel the same way if he hurt Alex. I certainly didn't wish for Henry to come to harm."

"I know," Anne said grumpily. "Truly, I don't know what I feel. If Henry walked in this very moment, I haven't the slightest idea . . ." And then she saw a familiar dark head. ". . . what . . ." Suddenly, there wasn't enough air in all of Newport to fill her lungs. ". . . I'd . . ." Her heart, goodness, her heart was beating madly, madly. ". . . do." Her knees felt weak and her stomach seemed to collapse inside her. Anne reached out desperately to grasp at Beatrice, her mouth gaping open and closed, her hand clutching her friend's arm until Beatrice let out a cry of pain.

"Anne. Anne, what's wrong?" Beatrice asked, and then followed her friend's eyes to Henry Owen, who was smiling and laughing and shaking people's hands. A man back from the dead being welcomed back by his peers.

Anne began to tremble. Not a delicate quivering, but a quaking, a shaking that she couldn't control, until she knew that if Beatrice wasn't there to hold her up, she would have dropped to the ground in a dead faint. Anne was dimly aware of people around her murmuring words of concern, but it was all she could do to hang on. She turned her head so that it rested against Beatrice's shoulder.

"I—I th-th-think I-I'm going to-to f-f-f—"

"Faint?" Beatrice guessed, giving Anne a look of alarm.

Anne nodded her head jerkily and squeezed her eyes shut as she clutched Beatrice's arm even tighter.

"Ow."

"S-s-s—"

"I know you're sorry. But don't you dare faint now," Beatrice whispered frantically. "I was with a girl who fainted once, and do you know what she did? She peed. Right there on her new Worth dress. She had to walk about with a stained dress until the carriage was brought round and was so mortified, she left for the season. She'd had quite a lot to drink, apparently."

As she hoped, her story made Anne chuckle and

distracted her enough so that she stopped breathing in great gulps of air and her shaking nearly stopped. Anne stepped back and loosened her hold on Beatrice's arm but did not let go. She dared look to search for Henry.

"Where is he n-now?"

Beatrice scanned the piazza. "He's been besieged by Annette Bissette."

Anne craned her neck, finally finding him, his wonderfully familiar form inches away from Miss Bissette's fluttering eyelashes. Next to him, Alex was searching the crowd, and Anne watched as a remarkable smile split his face when he found Beatrice. He took a step forward, then stopped, apparently remembering that Henry was with him. Anne watched with detachment as he nudged Henry, as Henry raised his head and looked in their direction, as he stared at her without smiling, without even a hint of the love he claimed to feel.

Anne's heart plummeted. Of course he wouldn't be pleased to see you, you ninny, she told herself. What had she thought, that he would rush over and swoop her up into his arms and . . . Anne let out a sigh. It is over, over, over. She watched with yearning and dread as the two men made their way to them. Beatrice, as lovestruck as a girl could be, couldn't wait for them to make the slow trip, and rushed to greet them both. She even kissed Henry's cheek in greeting, Anne noticed darkly. No doubt they would be great friends, the three of them.

When they reached her, Alex smiled. "See what I've found?" he said. It struck Anne that Alex seemed like almost a completely different man from the cynical, calculatingly charming fellow he'd been at the Wetmore ball. Jealousy over her friend's happiness rose hotly and then almost as quickly dissipated. Beatrice deserved to be happy.

Anne looked Henry straight in the eye and offered him the smallest of smiles. "Henry."

He nodded. "Anne."

It was clear that Alex and Beatrice felt terribly uncomfortable witnessing that cool greeting. Beatrice bit her lip, Alex went about straightening cuffs that didn't need straightening.

Henry looked over Anne's head as if something interesting was occurring there. "So glad to find you carrying on."

Anne's face tightened in anger. "So glad you are unrepentant about causing so many people to worry."

"I have apologized to Alex and Miss Leyden," he said.

Anne glared at him, recalling vividly that she'd nearly collapsed with relief when she spied him walking across the Casino's lawn. She pressed her lips together and narrowed her brilliant blue eyes.

"It's a beautiful day, don't you think?" Anne asked with false cheerfulness, carefully overpronouncing the word "beautiful." "I simply adore beautiful things. Why, the sight of something ugly makes me want to turn the other way. No one likes ugly things, now, do they? Just the other day, I saw this vase, quite hideous, and the clerk tried to—"

"Stop it, Anne," Henry hissed. Anne was so angry, she missed the raw pain that flickered briefly in his eyes.

Anne looked at him as if startled. "Whatever is it about this conversation that offends you, Mr. Owen? Or is it that you, too, disdain ugly things."

He took a step forward, a muscle in his cheek ticking madly, his eyes holding a promise of violence. "I said that's enough."

Anne's eyes glittered with tears. "You're right," she whispered. "This is supposed to be a happy day."

She turned and pushed her way through the crowd, tears coursing down her face. People stared but she didn't care about anything except getting away from Henry and his anger. She reached the cool, dark hall that led to Bellevue Avenue when she felt a large, strong hand on her arm. Letting out an outraged gasp, she turned ready to confront Henry.

"Do you love him?" Alex demanded.

Anne leaned up against the dark-green wall and swiped with the back of her hand at the tears still on her cheeks. "No."

Alex stared at her with an unreadable expression. "That's all I needed to know," he said. He began walking back toward the piazza.

"Yes." Anne clasped a hand over her mouth and cringed when Alex stopped dead in this tracks.

"Yes, you love him?"

Anne pressed against the wall so hard, the back of her head hurt. She shook her head even as she said the words, "Yes, I love him."

In two strides, Alex was by her side. That grin of his was back. "That's all I needed to know."

"Don't you dare tell him. It's my choice to let him know or not, Mr. Henley."

Alex waved in acknowledgement, and Anne wasn't certain whether he planned to obey her wishes or not.

Arthur Owen sat as he had since returning to Sea Cliff at the window looking out over the bay. It was nearing sunset, a time when the water was its bluest, when the sun lay golden in the west, painting Newport and the sailing ships with a soft patina of gold. All his life, Arthur never looked west at the setting sun, but preferred looking east and watching the reflection of the sun glitter like fire in the distant windows.

He was inordinately weary this evening, but happier than he'd been in years. Yesterday, for the first time in his life, he had held his son to his breast. If he lived another year or two or three, he would cherish that moment when he'd clutched Henry's arm and his son

had bent low to embrace him. But Arthur knew he
wouldn't live another year or two or three. He could
almost feel his heart winding down. He was not afraid.
He was at peace.

That night, just before he breathed his last, Arthur
Owen dreamt he was young and standing on the front
porch, his face buffeted by a salt-scented breeze that
carried with it the sound of a laughing boy.

Arthur Owen's well-attended funeral was held in
New York on a stiflingly hot August day. Henry did
not cry, but felt a sadness deep in his heart for the
man he mostly hated and, he realized at last, loved.
All his life, his grandfather had been a shadow, a person who had not quite been part of his life. Even
when his parents died, his grandfather saw him only
during school breaks. Oddly enough, as a boy he'd
craved his company only to be rebuffed time and
again until he learned to stay away.

Henry was the last to leave the grave site, watching
impassionately as the workers finished the job of filling
the grave. It hadn't rained in days, so each shovelful
released a puff of dust as it fell upon the mahogany
casket. After he was alone, Henry knelt on one knee
by the mound and lay a hand on the warm dark soil,
leaving an imprint there. "Good-bye, Grandfather,"
he whispered, seeing in his mind his grandfather standing on the porch at Sea Cliff, silent, frowning, watching, as he walked along the beach or fished on the
rocks. He'd never understood the man and now it was
too late to even try. With a sigh, Henry stood, not
bothering to wipe the dirt and grass from his knee.

"Mr. Owen." Williamson had apparently been hovering somewhere nearby and he came forward now.
His face, always solemn, looked particularly sorrowful
as he held out a leather-bound book to Henry. "Your
grandfather wanted you to have this upon his death."

Henry took the book and nodded. "Thank you for

your loyal service to my grandfather, Mr. Williamson. I know he left you well-cared-for in his will, but if you wish to continue working, you may stay on with me."

Williamson shook his head. "Thank you, sir, but I believe I shall retire."

Henry watched as his grandfather's most loyal servant walked to a hired hack and heaved himself up, keen grief in every movement he made. Henry glanced down at the book in his hands, opened it, and flipped through a few pages, not recognizing the neat penmanship. He closed it without reading and headed to his coach, the weight of his solitude suddenly unbearable. He'd told Alex to remain in Newport, thinking he was doing his friend a favor, but now he wished him in New York.

Henry stepped up into the well-sprung coach that his grandfather had used on his rare trips out of his town house and stared at the empty seat across from him. He tossed the book Williamson had given him onto the seat so it wouldn't look quite so uninhabited. He was twenty-eight years old and wealthier than a man had the right to be. But he realized he'd give it all up, his money, Sea Cliff, everything, if he could have Anne for the rest of his life. It was hopeless. Seeing her at the Casino told him that. All the hurt and betrayal had risen to the surface the instant they saw each other. Gone was the flirtatious, witty girl he'd fallen in love with, replaced with someone bitter and angry. And it was all his doing.

He tried to imagine a time when thinking about Anne wouldn't hurt quite so much. But all he saw was himself as an old man sitting on Sea Cliff's porch. Alone.

Chapter Twenty-four

Colonel Mann's column was quite interesting the Wednesday following Arthur's funeral, containing not one, but two titillating tales about Henry James Owen. First was the colonel's rather long-winded thanks that Henry had not been killed as feared, as well as a heartfelt expression of sorrow at the passing of his grandfather. Many a debutante dabbed at her tear-filled eyes with monogrammed lace handkerchiefs upon reading it.

Second was the colonel's detailed account of a certain Mr. O who'd been duped by a particular Miss F into proposing marriage, only to be spurned. Anyone who had been at the Casino when Henry made his triumphant return from the dead and seen the two sparring knew without a doubt that this particular bit of gossip was true.

What great fun.

The colonel's column, well-read and well-dreaded by those cottagers in Newport, was the talk of the town—just as the good colonel intended. The column was misogynistic in nature, chastising the devious mind of Miss F, and pretending pity and commiseration with Mr. O.

Henry, tight-lipped and seething, had a vivid and decidedly pleasing mental image of the colonel sinking into the East River with a bag of rocks tied about his ankles. Then he ordered *Town Topics* burned in the fire grate.

Anne, who'd become numb to the scandal that kept swirling about her, let out a groan of half despair, half disbelief. She immediately dispatched a stinging letter to her mother—for who else could have been responsible for such gossip?—that no doubt would make the woman swoon.

Beatrice, who read the item with Alex at the Casino, gasped in outrage for her friend. Alex, oddly unaffected by the scandalous sheet, comforted her.

And Helen Leyden smiled that secret smile she reserved for the times when she knew something no one else did.

It was a glorious ending to a perfectly scrumptious bit of drama that had fueled conversations at otherwise dull parties for weeks. There was little doubt among the vast majority of the cottagers that they held in their hands the end of the story of Anne Foster and Henry Owen. How cunning of her, many married women exclaimed, while others thought her devious. Poor Henry, the single girls cooed while they sharpened their talons, hoping to get their claws in him.

Whether they thought Anne awful or courageous, cruel or avenged, wasn't really the point at all, many of the savvy knew. The point was that Anne had held the queen in her hand all the time, ready to proclaim checkmate, and no one ever knew it. Not any of the Four Hundred, and certainly not Henry. They waited with anticipation for the final outcome. Would Anne Foster be banished once and for all, or applauded for creating such an interesting summer?

As it turned out, Mamie Fish read the column and had the best laugh she'd had in years. She invited Anne to a luncheon. It was official. Anne was still welcome in the midst of the cottagers.

Henry held the note from Anne in his hand a long moment before crumpling it in his fist. He hated that his heart beat harder simply because he held something that she once held. She wanted to see him, the note said. No doubt she wanted to discuss the colonel's enlightening column, though he couldn't imagine what there was to talk about. It was all there, laid out bare for all to see. Christ, what a mess.

He wanted to say no to her request for a meeting, but he knew he wouldn't. He longed to see her until it was nearly a physical thing. And so, after pretending to debate the issue for at least thirty seconds, Henry grabbed a bit of his stationery and dashed off a quick note to Anne telling her he'd see her. With a wry grin, he signed the letter, "Mr. O."

Anne sat in Mrs. Leyden's parlor at the appointed hour, feeling nearly ill with nervous anticipation. She had dressed with care, donning a pale yellow silk two-piece day dress with a wide waist, braid trim, and knotwork about the bodice. The waving neckline was modest, revealing only her slim neck and a small amount of her creamy bosom. Her hair was done in a simple braid, pinned to the back of her head. She hadn't the slightest idea what she would say to Henry when she saw him, though she had rehearsed a hundred different conversations in her head. Perhaps she should let him know how happy she'd been when she'd seen he hadn't died. Or perhaps she should again extend her sympathies regarding the passing of his grandfather. Anne had written a short note of sympathy, her heart aching that she had no right to do more. She'd told herself a hundred times that she had sealed their fate at the Casino by allowing her pent-up anger to erupt. Beatrice had consoled her, telling her that her emotions were so frazzled by Henry's unexpected appearance, she couldn't be held accountable for anything she said.

It was true. Her emotions were still so jumbled, Anne wasn't certain what she felt for Henry. Mixed in the love she felt was anger and hurt and pain and joy. She wanted to embrace him as much as she wanted to slap him. Oh, but she did want to hold him, to feel his breath against her neck, to absorb his wonderful warmth. To touch his lips with hers, to smooth his hair from his forehead, to . . . Anne gave herself a mental shake. Even though she'd seen him at the Casino, she was still not over the fear and loss she'd felt when she thought he might be dead. That was how she explained her continuing need to see him, to touch him, even though she'd walked into his office and rejected him.

In just a few minutes, Henry would stand in this very room, alive, oozing health and vitality, and she would have to stop herself from throwing herself at him. For she feared if she did, he would stand there like a rock, impassive and perhaps even disgusted by her hypocritical emotional display. Hadn't she told him less than two weeks ago that she didn't love him? She'd almost convinced herself that she meant it. Part of her still wanted to throw her pride to the wind and let it scatter like thistledown. For now, she simply wanted to feast her eyes on him one last time and then she could go on with the rest of her life.

The door opened and her heart nearly burst, only to slowly return to a normal beat when she saw that Beatrice's mother, Helen, was walking sedately through the door. It had been Helen's idea to write that note to Henry requesting to see him, and Anne, her silly heart hopeful and aching, had readily agreed.

"While I appreciate your being here, Mrs. Leyden, I hardly think Henry and I need a chaperon," Anne said, kindly but firmly.

"I'm not here to chaperon," Helen said. She was at her imperialistic best at the moment, and Anne hadn't a clue why. But she did know enough not to argue with her. Helen walked slowly to a chair much like a queen, and sat, adjusting her skirts about her with care.

"Then why are you here?" Anne asked hesitantly,

her gaze going again to the door, where she expected
Henry to appear at any moment.

"I'm here to offer a solution to your dilemma."

Anne frowned. "What dilemma?"

"Why, the dilemma of how best to proceed, my
dear. I'll admit that an invitation from Mamie Fish
goes a long way, but you're still mired in scandal and
that can only harm Beatrice and her prospects for a
good marriage."

"I believe you needn't worry about Beatrice much
longer, Mrs. Leyden," Anne said softly.

Helen lifted her chin. "If you are referring to that
scalawag Alex Henley, then I must most assuredly
worry about Beatrice."

Anne nearly winced from her tone and instantly felt
sorry for her friend, who was so obviously in love with
"that scalawag." A sound from the door interrupted
the women.

"Ah, here you are, Mr. Owen. Please sit beside
Anne," Helen said.

Anne drank in the sight of him, so handsome, so
stern, standing in the doorway. He was dressed in a
perfectly fitted blue suit jacket with a cream-colored
waistcoat beneath, and Anne wondered idly if Alex had
counseled him on the dashing attire. His hair was neatly
combed; not a curl was errant. His jaw was clean-
shaven, his eyes clear and piercing. He was, Anne
thought, very, very alive.

Henry gave Helen a small bow before doing exactly
as the older woman instructed. He didn't acknowledge
Anne, not even with a passing glance, and her heart
plummeted even as it raced to have him so near. He
sat no more than a foot away from her and she didn't
dare touch him. But she took a carefully deep breath,
trying to catch his scent, her eyes fluttering closed momentarily when it came to her, every smoky, salty,
woody, male bit of him.

"I assume I am here because of the colonel's amusing column," Henry said.

"Precisely why," Helen said in a clipped tone. "Before we begin, I have something to say to the two of you." She stood before them. "Never in my life have I met two people more mendacious, more cruel, more careless of another's feelings than the two of you."

Anne gasped, but Henry fought a smile of admiration for this woman.

"I have come to the painful conclusion that the two of you deserve one another. The only way to reconcile this unpleasantness is for the two of you to get married and as quickly as possible."

"No!" Anne shouted.

"Fine," Henry drawled at the very same moment.

Anne turned to him, a look of disbelief on her face. Henry's look to Anne was must less pleasant.

"I won't marry him," Anne said, moving a bit away from him on the couch, all the time wondering why she was protesting against something she'd not moments ago in her heart of hearts wished might still come true.

Helen's face softened. "You cannot say you do not love him Anne, can you?"

Anne darted a look at Henry, then focused on the carpet at her feet. "I love him," she whispered.

Henry let out a grunt of laughter.

"I do!" Anne said.

"Good God, can you believe she has the nerve to say this to me?" he asked Helen, thinking the woman would clearly be on his side.

"I count her a fool for loving you, but I do believe Anne does, Mr. Owen."

Henry's smile slowly faded.

"Now," Helen said, ignoring the belligerent look on Anne's face. "Do you love Anne, Mr. Owen?"

Henry worked his jaw for a long moment. He cracked the knuckles on his left hand. He swept a hand through his well-combed hair. "With all my heart," he said.

"Hah," Anne let out in an explosion of sound.

Henry turned to her. "Now, why wouldn't you believe me? Or course I love you. I wouldn't have asked you to marry me if I didn't."

Anne gave him a knowing smile. "Oh, really?" she said, drawing out the last word, obviously referring to Henry's first proposal.

"That time didn't count. I didn't even want to get married, I just wanted Sea Cliff."

Anne turned triumphantly to Helen. "Do you see? How am I to know whether he loves me this time?"

"I never said I loved you then," Henry pointed out.

"That's not the point. The point is I can't trust you. I can't believe you. You lied to me to get a house, Henry. Wood and brick and mortar."

"Then this is an exercise in futility. I can only say I love you, I cannot prove it."

Anne stared mulishly ahead. "You don't love me. You love my eighteen-inch waist."

Helen smiled, as if glad the two were finally getting to the point of things.

"What are you talking about?" Henry demanded.

Anne stood and began pacing. "Oh, just admit it, Henry. You didn't love me before because I was fat. Ugly and fat."

Henry looked at her, stunned. "I'd be lying if I didn't say I find you more attractive now," Henry began carefully.

"See!" Anne pointed an accusing finger. "I knew it. Well, perhaps you don't realize it, but someday, I'm going to be old and wrinkled, maybe even fat. And then where will your love be?"

Henry closed his eyes and hung his head. When he looked up, his gray eyes were dark with emotion. "Anne, I can say I'll love you when you're fat, when you're old, when you're more wrinkled than a prune, but you won't believe me, will you?"

Anne clutched her arms around her as if suddenly cold. "No, I won't." Then her face crumpled and she began to cry.

Helen stood and drew Anne into her arms.

"Perhaps you should go, Mr. Owen," Helen said kindly.

Henry stood uncertainly. "Is this what you had hoped for this meeting, Anne?"

"The meeting was my idea, Mr. Owen," Helen said above the suddenly louder sobs from Anne. "And it is exactly what I hoped to accomplish."

Henry's expression became stony. "Then congratulations, Mrs. Leyden."

Helen let out a laugh. "You stupid man," she said as she continued to pat Anne's shaking back. "I've given you the answer."

"What the hell was the question?" Henry asked, angry, frustrated, and not at all in the mood for riddles.

Helen smiled. "Look inside your heart."

Anne broke away and, keeping her back to Henry, went to a window to stare blindly into the Leydens' garden. Henry took both hands and rubbed them into his hair, completely ruining in one sweep his polished look.

"If the two of you don't want to be the subject of gossip for the rest of your lives, you should set a date," Helen announced in her singsong, cheerful way.

Anne whirled around, quite recovered from her bout of tears. "I'm not marrying him!" she shouted.

Henry, who had been staring at the carpet deep in thought, suddenly raised his head, a strange light in his eyes. "I've got some business to attend to," he said. "Good day, ladies. Oh, and Mrs. Leyden, I owe you my deepest gratitude." Helen smiled and waved his thank-you away.

"But that date, Mr. Owen," Helen called after him.

"Pick whatever she wants, Mrs. Leyden. I'll be there," Henry called back as he left the room.

Anne looked agape from Helen to Henry's departing back. "I don't believe the two of you. Didn't either of you hear me?" And then she shouted, "I'm not getting married!"

Calmly, Helen sat down and picked up her knitting. "Yes, you are, Anne."

"You can't make me marry. Not even my mother could make me marry."

"You'll do it quite voluntarily," Helen said, a serene smile on her face.

Anne threw up her hands in frustration, letting out an "Ugh!" before stomping out of the room to find Beatrice. Certainly she would be able to talk some sense into her mother. Helen had gone insane if she thought she could manipulate her into a marriage that would doom her to even more heartbreak. And Henry! He seemed to believe they'd get married as well. Had the world gone mad?

Chapter Twenty-five

It was as if the emotional, maddening scene had never occurred. As if she dreamt it all. For in the two weeks that followed Henry's visit, she heard not a word of weddings or proposals, or even of Henry. Helen had taken herself off to Portsmouth to rusticate in the country with an old friend, and so could no longer badger Anne about how she was obligated to marry Henry because of that horrid gossip column.

"My dear," Helen had said after Henry had left that day, "do you truly want to go through life as the woman who humiliated Henry Owen?"

Belligerently, Anne had crossed her arms. "I thought I was the woman who would go through life having been humiliated by Henry Owen. He has come off of everything quite unscathed."

"Except for his heart, dear, except for his heart."

Anne had nothing to say to that and ignored the little wrench her own heart made when she thought about it. How she wished she could forget the past, but she could not. The woman she had been—awkward, shy, unwieldy—still lived inside her and she could not ignore her. She was the one pushing Henry away, the wounded animal who doubted his love-filled eyes, who remembered crumpling to the ground with the divorce decree in her hand. Who read those harsh words his grandfather had written in hopes of avoiding this entire affair.

Beatrice was little help. Anne hardly recognized her

feisty and often cynical friend. She had become A Woman In Love, one of those creatures whose every utterance, every waking moment, is about the man she adores. Anne had little doubt that Beatrice would eventually return to earth, but for now she was simply impossible to be with—especially for a woman so torn about her own romance.

Anne, in a position she knew well, became the third wheel on all their outings. The two women would arrive together, but Alex, as if having some sixth sense, would appear by Beatrice's side within minutes. Anne saw only fleeting glimpses of Henry. She told herself before each supper, each ball, that she would not look for him, but she did. And when she found him, as she always did, her heart would pick up a beat, her cheeks would flush, and a lump would immediately form in her throat. It did not help matters that Alex and Beatrice were so obviously and publicly in love that everyone knew it was only a matter of time before a formal announcement was made.

Anne was not the wallflower she'd been before, but she found no joy in her popularity now that Henry wasn't around to see it. She tried to recall what he'd said at their last meeting. Hadn't he said yes when Helen suggested they marry? She brutally reminded herself that she had said no, that she had angrily shouted to his departing back that she wouldn't marry him. Perhaps he finally believed her. She should be glad. Instead, she wished back that moment a hundred times and just as many times told herself she'd done the right thing. There were times when she tossed and turned for hours vacillating, wanting to tear her hair out, hearing his words over and over in her head. *"Anne I can say I'll love you when you're fat, when you're old, when you're more wrinkled than a prune, but you won't believe me, will you?"*

She whispered, "I believe you" into her pillow, her heart breaking when she realized she might never be able to say those same words to Henry. He had hurt her so very badly, more than even she had realized. She couldn't listen to her heart anymore because it had been wrong so many times.

Henry knew it was best to stay away from Anne, for he couldn't trust himself to be near her without making a complete idiot of himself. He had to bide his time and be content with the knowledge that she would be his. Eventually.

But damn if it wasn't near impossible not to get all hot under the collar when he saw her talking and dancing with other men. He couldn't count the number of times he'd taken a few steps toward her before coming to his senses and retreating.

Precisely fifteen days since their meeting, he could take it no longer. It was Tennis Week, a time when the cottagers held even more balls, more picnics, more suppers than at any other time of the year. For if one was to be in Newport at all, it was for Tennis Week when appearances were nearly mandatory. By the end of this August tradition, everyone was so weary, the thought of heading back to New York was a relief. Henry sat with the Henleys and listened to Alex's parents bicker incessantly, a match far more interesting than the one being played on the court in front of him. If he leaned far back and to his right, he could just make out a bit of Anne's slim, graceful neck where she sat with the Leydens. She wore a large, flat-rimmed straw hat to shield her nose from the sun, as parasols tended to block the view of spectators. As he watched, perfectly aware he was making an utter ass of himself, she and Beatrice stood and carefully made their way down the steep grandstand, heading, Henry guessed, to the women's convenience. Like a thief, Henry stalked them, waiting until they had disappeared down a shadowed hall before pursuing them. Anne emerged first, waving a fan vigorously in front of her, for though the day was overcast, it was unbearably muggy and warm. She stood in the shadows looking toward the court where the match continued, Henry standing close enough to see a bead of perspiration make its way from her hairline slowly down her neck. As if sensing his presence, she became suddenly alert, turning just enough to know that it wasn't Beatrice standing behind her.

Henry moved closer, placing a hand lightly, tentatively at her waist. "Anne," he said, his mouth close to her ear. "Let me."

In answer she moved imperceptibly against his hand.

Henry placed his lips against her neck, tasting her salty skin, breathing in her feminine scent, growing hard from that simple touch. Slowly, he pulled her against him until her buttocks were firm against his arousal. Sweet Lord above, he was in heaven. He could feel her breath quicken as he kissed her sensitive neck, then moved down to kiss the small bit of shoulder exposed by her gown.

"I want my wedding night," he said, tightening his hand slightly.

"Henry," she said, but he could hear a note of denial in her voice.

Behind them, a door opened and Henry immediately moved away. Anne turned to him, and he saw the desire in her eyes, stunning him with its intensity. He grew impossibly harder and swallowed painfully.

"Hello, Henry," Beatrice said, then darted a quick look to Anne to gauge her friend's mood.

Henry nodded. "Miss Leyden."

Beatrice stood uncertainly for a moment. "Should I go on ahead?" she asked Anne.

Anne seemed to give herself a mental shake. "No." Then she gave a overly bright smile. "Of course not. Henry and I have finished our conversation."

Henry's eyes glittered dangerously. "Our 'conversation' has barely begun," he said to the women's departing backs. He learned up against the wall, arms crossed, and admired his future wife from behind. She would be his wife, he vowed. For the first time since their heated meeting with Helen, he actually believed himself.

Henry stayed away from Anne after that, realizing he hadn't the strength to not maul her if he saw her again. It took only a few hours of cooling down before he realized how foolish he'd been to nearly make love to Anne in a public place. He counted himself lucky that she hadn't turned and slapped him for his forwardness. Still, it didn't sit well with him to watch passively, to wait until the time was right. A few days, a few weeks. Surely it wouldn't take longer than that before he could go to her with proof that he loved her, that he would do anything to win her back.

A trip to New York would help, he realized, looking forward with relish to his confrontation with a certain colonel. He planned to make good on his promise to make Mann pay for that damaging bit of drivel he'd published. He was leaving just as Alex was returning from a night of dancing and wooing his lady love. The man still had a silly-looking grin on his face.

"Good morning, old friend," Alex said cheerfully, amazingly chipper for a man who hadn't slept in twenty-four hours. "Want to join me at Bailey's in a few hours?"

Henry shook his head. "I'm off to New York on some unfinished business."

Alex moved past him and began pounding up the stairs when he stopped mid-stride. "What business is that?"

"I promised Colonel Mann a visit," Henry said, a wicked gleam in his eye. "I've been looking forward to it for days."

Alex worked his jaw for a moment before slowly

descending the stairs. "You ought to reconsider," he said meaningfully.

Henry folded his arms and narrowed his eyes at his friend. "And why is that?"

Alex slowly let out a puff of air. "It may be that, upon your sage advice, the colonel didn't plan to print that column,"

"Don't tell me."

"And then he was persuaded that he should. Perhaps even promised that no ill would come of it."

"I told you not to tell me," Henry said, his large hands curling into fists.

Alex held up his hands as if to ward off a blow. "It wasn't my idea."

"Whose?" he demanded. And then Henry had the answer himself. "Mrs. Leyden." At Alex's expression, he knew he was right.

"Things did seem rather hopeless between the two of you, and Beatrice's mother thought you both needed some stirring up."

"My God, we've been stirred up so much, neither of us knows which way is up."

Alex shrugged. "The two of you weren't speaking, Anne was crying all the time. You were a royal pain in the ass. Hell, I would have done anything to get you out of the misery you were in."

"Even humiliate me?"

Alex flushed. "Well, you have to admit, the whole story is rather amusing. Just think of it. You marry her because she's ugly. She becomes beautiful, you fall in love. She plans revenge, but falls in love instead. Then she finds out how wretched you truly are and refuses your proposal. And it's all chronicled very nicely in *Town Topics*. Someday you'll look back on this and—"

"Still want to murder you," Henry said without rancor. "I may if she doesn't say yes."

Alex grinned. "So, you haven't given up."

"I've already asked twice and been rebuffed. She thinks I'm such a scoundrel that I can't possibly love her. But this time, I'll have proof."

"Proof?"

"Sea Cliff, Alex. I'm selling Sea Cliff."

"My God," Beatrice whispered as she looked at the item in the newspaper's classified section. "He truly does love you."

Anne tilted her head so she could see what Beatrice was talking about, and let out a startled gasp. Staring before her was proof of Henry's love. Sea Cliff was for sale.

"That is the most romantic thing I have ever seen," Beatrice said.

Anne read the notice again, not quite trusting what her eyes clearly showed her. She was not mistaken; there could only be one summer cottage named Sea Cliff on Jamestown. And there could be only one reason Henry had put the old house up for sale—he wanted to prove his love. Just as she'd demanded he do. She felt simply awful.

"He loves that old place," she said.

"Apparently, he loves you more," Beatrice said on a sigh. Having fallen hard herself, her view of Henry had softened considerably, Anne noted. How bad could he be if Alex considered him his greatest friend?

It had been two weeks since Anne had seen Henry. The summer season was winding down, Tennis Week had come and gone, and talk was now of returning to New York. Anne realized with more distress than she would admit to herself that returning to her town house was a thoroughly depressing thought.

She'd heard no more of marriage, of setting dates, and told herself she was glad. As each day passed and it became more and more clear that they were through for good, that Henry had simply given up after she'd been so cold to him at the tennis match. How she had

managed that, when her insides had felt like a raging
volcano, she couldn't be certain. But she hadn't seen
or heard from Henry since. Whatever she'd done,
she'd done it well. Henry appeared to be gone for
good. Following that tantalizingly brief moment when
she melted against Henry, savoring his firm lips on her
fevered skin, Anne's heart grew heavier and heavier,
until it felt like ball of lead in her chest.

And all along, Henry had been planning this, a
grand sacrifice. She couldn't let him do it.

"Mr. Owen, Mrs. Leyden and Miss Foster are here
to see you," Alex's butler announced. "What shall I
tell them?"

Henry handed the deed to Sea Cliff to his lawyer,
a grim expression on his face. "Show them in," Henry
said. Then, turning to his attorney, he said, "Good
day, Mr. Dunn. If you could file the proper papers in
the Town Hall today, I would appreciate it."

"Good day, sir." Dunn shook his hand and bowed
to the two ladies as they were escorted in before he
left.

The second the lawyer was out of the room, Anne
said, "I demand that you take Sea Cliff off the mar-
ket, Henry."

Henry, who had just moments before been again
questioning his decision, knew instantly he'd done the
right thing in selling the old place. God, how he loved
this woman standing before him, arms akimbo, expression fierce and lovely. How many women could have
done what Anne had done, risen from the depths of
humiliation and despair to become this spitfire before
him? She was the strongest, most amazing creature
he'd ever met.

He walked calmly to a tea service. "Tea, ladies?"

"No, thank you," Helen said brightly.

"Did you hear me, Henry?" Anne said harshly.

He smiled. "It's too late. It's been sold."

Anne dropped down onto the nearest chair. "Oh."

"Don't look so crestfallen," he said blithely. "It went to a very good cause, I assure you." A click of the door sounded as Helen made a discreet departure, leaving the two alone in the Henleys' study.

"I never wanted you to sell it. I never dreamed you would."

Henry shrugged. "It would have been there between us always. I couldn't think of another way to prove to you how much I love you."

"But Sea Cliff, Henry." Anne searched his face as if looking for signs of regret.

"It was just a house."

Anne began shaking her head, refusing to believe that's how he felt about the house that had so obsessed him not two years before. Standing, she stood before him but could not meet his eyes.

"Anne, look at me," Henry said, putting his hands on either side of Anne's face. She lifted her face, but kept her eyes trained on his chin, noticing for the first time the tiniest cleft. "It was just a house. I realized it wasn't Sea Cliff I wanted. I thought if I got that old house back, I'd be happy again. But in all these years, I've never been happy." Her eyes lifted to meet his. "Until I loved you."

Anne felt her heart expand, felt her love grow tenfold, as she looked at the truth in his eyes. "When I'm old and wrinkled?"

He smiled that lopsided grin of his. "I'll love you."

"If I get chubby?"

"More to love." He scrunched her face up between his hands, mushing her features comically. "I love you," he said, kissing her distorted lips. He calmly mussed her hair until it was a bird's nest of curls. "I love you." He reached to the tea set and scooped up a bit of jam and smeared it on her cheeks, her nose, her chin. "I love you." And kissed a bit of jam away.

She was a mess, but she was laughing. "Stop it," she said, overcome by mirth. "I believe you!"

"And you'll marry me?"

Anne looked at this man before her and knew her heart had only one answer. "Yes."

Henry let out a whoop of pure happiness then crushed her against him in a breath-stealing embrace. He kissed her hard and long, letting out a low moan as if he could not contain the joy bubbling inside of him. He drew back and gazed at her. He had a bit of jam smeared on his chin.

"God, you are so beautiful."

Anne knew she was not. Her face was covered with jam; her mussed-up hair was sticky with the stuff. But she felt beautiful, and that's all that really mattered.

Chapter Twenty-six

A rthur Owen's leather-bound journal lay on the coach seat for weeks in the deceased man's carriage, collecting dust and tiny red mites. It lay where Henry threw it after the funeral, until a cool, crisp day in October when the carriage was brought out to be spiffed up for the young master's wedding. It was perhaps good fortune that the footman who found the book was recently from Germany, for while he could speak English, he could not read it well enough to learn the secrets of his former employer. He brought the journal to the butler, a man of high discretion, who brought it to the study and laid it upon the desk, where again it sat for several days. Twice weekly, a maid entered the room and swiped her feather duster over the journal's smooth brown surface.

Arthur's secrets remained hidden for far longer than he would have suspected when he told Williamson to deliver the journal to Henry upon his death. But finally, they were about to be revealed.

The Owen coach pulled up in front of the opulent and gracious Fifth Avenue mansion, a footman dressed in the Owen colors of red and gold stepping smartly from his perch to snap open the door. Blushing crimson at what he discovered when he glanced inside, the young man stood at attention and waited for the couple inside to disengage themselves.

Breathless, Anne smiled up at her husband. "We're home, Mr. Owen."

"Mmmm," Henry said, nuzzling her neck. Having waited for this moment for months, Henry was finding it inordinately difficult to release his new wife from his clutches even long enough to step from the coach. He heard Anne let out a giggle as he sucked on her earlobe. "Laugh at me, will you?" And he lunged at her, playfully pushing her down onto the leather seat. Anne looked up at him trying not to laugh, and he looked down at her with a huge grin before giving her cheek a chaste kiss and letting her up.

"Really, Anne, now that you are my wife, you are going to have to learn to control your baser side," he said loud enough for the footman to hear.

Anne gave Henry a look of exasperation, smacking him playfully on the arm.

"This is not the time nor the place for such carrying on," he said with wicked sternness.

"Henry," she said with warning and a quick glance filled with apology and embarrassment to the servant, who was pretending not to hear.

Henry, oblivious of his formal wedding attire, hopped down from the coach with the exuberance of a twelve-year-old boy and immediately reached back and plucked Anne off the coach, carrying her in his arms, her skirts and petticoats frothing up to mid-calf, revealing her white silk stockings. Laughing, Anne tried without success to cover herself, then gave up and wrapped her arms around Henry's neck, laying her head against his shoulder.

"There's a good wench," Henry said, marching up the four steps to the intricately carved front door. The door opened just as they reached it, a smiling butler standing at the ready.

"Harlow," Henry boomed cheerfully. "Meet Mrs. Henry Owen," he said, still holding Anne in his arms.

"Madam," Harlow said with utmost solemnity, bowing his head of shockingly white wavy hair. Then he looked up at Henry and gave him a wink.

She whispered in Henry's ear, "Put me down, please."

He ignored her. "And this is Mrs. Craft, the housekeeper."

Feeling ridiculous, Anne tried to maintain an air of dignity, a failing effort, it turned out, for at that very moment, Henry, his hand quite hidden in the folds of her dress, gave her behind a squeeze. Her greeting to Mrs. Craft, a dower-looking woman, came out as a screech. She could feel the rumble of laughter in Henry's chest. Who this man was carrying her, she hadn't the foggiest notion, but she found she liked him a great deal. Anne knew she was seeing Henry truly happy for the first time, and knowing she was responsible was intoxicating.

"Send supper up when we ring," Henry called, as he carried Anne up a flight of stairs. His breathing only slightly labored, he reached the top and turned right to head down a long hall illuminated by gas jets burning brightly in their etched glass globes. Stopping at a door at the far end of the hall, Henry finally put her down. He suddenly seemed uncertain.

"You may change whatever you want in this house. I have only one condition for our marriage," he said, so seriously that Anne's heart slowed a beat. "You may have your own sitting room and dressing room, but I want you to share a bed with me, Mrs. Owen. I don't want to have to request a visit. I want you by my side every night."

Anne was so relieved, she nearly laughed aloud. "I agree," she said with a quick nod.

He opened the door and their eyes went immediately to the large canopied bed at the far end of the decidedly masculine room. The furniture was large and bulky, wood and leather, all browns and reds, including the ornately carved walnut bed, covered with a deep red quilt. A large and cheerful fire had the room quite warm, making that quilt unnecessary, Anne thought, trying to think of anything other than what they were about to do.

Henry stepped farther into the room. "Are you hungry? I can ring the maid."

Anne shook her heard, suddenly so nervous, her knees were shaking. "I will need to . . ." She cleared her throat. "Get undressed. Perhaps a maid could assist me?" She looked everywhere but at Henry. "And I suppose you'll need a valet." Again she cleared her throat. "To get, um, ready for . . . sleep."

With the most loving expression she'd ever seen on his face, Henry walked up to her, enveloped her head with his wonderful hands, and kissed her softly. "I think, for tonight, we can manage." Anne's eyes widened and she swallowed. She shouldn't be this nervous, she told herself. In the past few weeks whenever they could get alone, she and Henry had kissed and touched and nearly died from wanting to consummate their love. But this was different. This wasn't the frenzied, all-consuming lustful thing their kisses had been. This was planned. They were going to do It. Now.

Oh, goodness.

"You start," Henry said, lifting his chin. "Undo my cravat."

Anne frowned as she looked at the intricately tied bit of cloth. "Who did this?" she asked.

"Alex's valet. Why? Is it incomprehensible?"

"Nearly," she said, bringing fingers that trembled slightly up to tackle the knot. After a few moments, it slipped free and she sighed with relief.

"Now me," Henry said. "Turn around." He trailed a finger down her back following the long line of buttons. "Now, this is quite an endeavor." With agonizing slowness, Henry began to undo the tiny buttons down the back of her gown. "Why, look at what I've done," he said softly, as if in wonder. He brought his lips against the first bit of exposed skin, a caress that shot a shard of unexpected feeling to Anne's breasts and between her legs. She let out a shaky breath to gain control of her body.

Every few buttons, Henry would pause to kiss her, to place a hand on her naked skin, just above the soft material of her combination and stays. Finally, the row of buttons was undone. If she wanted to, Anne could have shrugged her shoulders and her gown would have fallen to her feet. But some wanton, wicked part of her turned to Henry, the sleeves slipped down slightly, exposing the tops of her stays and laced combination and a good deal of her breasts. His eyes slid from her face to rest on those creamy mounds, and she watched as he took a deep breath and swallowed.

Feeling brave, Anne moved her hands inside his jacket and pushed his suit jacket from his shoulders, tugging it off with relish. Then, biting her bottom lip, she tackled the buttons on his waistcoat. He stood still, his body rigid, his breath growing harsh as she moved to his shirt, finally, finally, revealing a muscled chest lightly covered with soft, curling hair.

"Oh." She had never seen a man's naked chest before and she found the sight rather startling. She lay her hand on him, moving her fingers, watching with fascination as the muscles beneath her hand jumped at her touch, surprised to find the hair there soft. Anne smiled, staring at him, pleased beyond measure by what she was discovering. Suddenly, Henry covered her hand with his, stopping her caresses.

"My turn," he said, his voice rough.

He kissed her neck as he pushed her dress from her shoulders, moving his mouth to her lips as he expertly tackled first the laces at her back, then the hook to her petticoat. When she was free of her corset and petticoat, Henry stepped back, keeping one hand on her wrist. He brought her forward so Anne had to step from the dress that lay crumpled at her feet.

"The game is over," he said, then pulled her to him, his eyes hot and greedy on her, and with a groan, kissed her deeply. It was a kiss filled with longing, possession, frustration, and love. With a movement filled with raw strength and fueled by need, Henry lifted her up against him, his hands going to her buttocks, her legs wrapping about him. Anne could feel him hot and hard between her legs, a new rush of sensation flowing through her veins. He lowered his head, nuzzling the top of her breasts, letting out a moan when she wriggled slightly against him. Anne's elbows rested on his broad shoulders, her hands were buried in his thick hair as she pressed him wantonly against breasts that ached for his touch.

Anne felt herself dropping and clutched Henry even tighter, only to find herself safely falling on the bed. Her legs were spread and he was still nestled there between them as he stood looking down at her. Swiftly, he removed his shirt, then he bent down to give her a searing kiss before stepping back to remove the rest of his clothing as quickly as possible.

Uncertain once more, Anne wondered if she should take off her combination, but modesty stopped her. Her mother, the night before her first wedding to Henry, had told her it was perfectly acceptable, if not preferable, to keep as many clothes on as possible when allowing one's husband his rights. Perhaps Henry would think ill of her if she stripped herself completely. So she lay there, her eyes closed, and waited.

"Anne."

She opened her eyes and couldn't help it when she darted a look from his face to the glorious rest of him, stark-naked and standing next to her, his member jutting out splendidly. Oh, goodness.

"What are you doing?" he said, and she could hear the humor in his voice.

"Waiting."

Anne was unaware that she lay stiff as a board, her teeth clenched, her hands balled into tight little fists. Even her feet, still inside her slippers, were clenched.

"It looks as if you are awaiting execution," Henry said with a loving grin.

"Oh. Sorry."

Henry in all his naked glory lay down beside her, and she squeezed her eyes shut. All Anne could think of was: There is a naked man next to me. A naked man. A naked man.

"Anne."

She opened her eyes.

"It's just me. Henry."

"But you're naked. I've never seen you naked. It's quite disconcerting."

"It's still me." And he kissed her burning cheek. "Would you feel better if you were unclothed as well?"

"No," she said quickly. "I'd feel better if you were clothed."

He chuckled, but Anne frowned. She wasn't finding this at all amusing. "That would make what we are about to do rather difficult," he said.

"I suppose it would," she said uncertainly, again thinking back upon her mother's advice.

"Sweetheart. It's just us. Henry and Anne. After all we've gone through, this should be easy." He kissed her again, this time putting one large, warm hand on her abdomen. Anne tensed, then relaxed as she centered her thoughts on his wonderful lips, his tongue that darted out to lick her. Slowly, she melted beneath his kisses, until she was moving to embrace him, until she wasn't even aware in any real sense that his hand was moving to her back so that he could pull her even closer.

He felt smooth and warm and firm beneath her hand, his muscles hard and yet not. Naked, she decided, was a good thing.

"Undress me, Henry," she whispered against his ear, instantly mortified that she'd made such a request.

Without a word, he complied, untying the satin ribbons that held the top of her combination together. She heard him inhale sharply when her breasts were finally revealed to him, a gasp she echoed when she felt his mouth on one hardened nipple. He spent long moments sucking, licking her there, first one breast, then the other, all the while with one hand between her legs to caress her thighs, to brush tantalizingly against the material that lay against the spot where all sensation was centered. He knelt on the bed and drew the material down, past her slightly rounded stomach, past her hips, and down, down until he was pulling it past her toes. And then, Henry did something unexpected. He gazed down at Anne, his face tense, his eyes filled with love, then he lay down and pulled her to him, embracing her so she could feel him, all of him. Never could Anne have imagined how wonderful it would be to feel his warm flesh pressed against her, to feel hard and soft, smooth and rough all at the same time.

"I love you," he whispered. She hugged him tight against her in answer. Anne could feel his arousal, foreign and wonderful, pressed against her thigh. She'd always known men and women were built differently, but could not have known how delightful their differences would be. With a boldness she didn't know she possessed, Anne moved her hand from his back to his firm buttock, smiling when she heard a hiss of pleasure erupt from his mouth. She felt his thick arousal jerk against her thigh, and moved her leg, slowly, erotically against him.

"Anne," he said on a laugh. "If you don't stop that, I'm afraid things will progress a bit quicker than I planned."

In retaliation, he brought his hand between her legs and, within seconds, had her gasping and writhing and laughing in sheer joy. But when he again moved his mouth to her breasts, all the laughing stopped, replaced by gasps and small noises of pleasure that she tried to stifle but could not. Because suddenly, she was filled with more sensation, more pleasure than she thought she could contain.

"Oh," she gasped, moving her head back and forth. She didn't even realize she was driving him mad by jerking her hips against his hand, she didn't realize anything but that she was spiraling to a place she'd never been before. When she reached it, she let out a sound that would later make her blush just thinking about it.

Before she could completely return to earth, Henry had moved on top of her. "Anne," he said. "I'm going to hurt you, sweetheart, when I go inside."

"No," she murmured, unwilling to believe anything could hurt at this moment.

She was wrong. It did hurt when he entered her fully. But it felt wonderful, too, to feel him slide deep inside her, to know that they were finally, finally, husband and wife.

"Good God," Henry said, his body strained and shaking, his shoulders slick with sweat, as he began moving. His head was against her skin as he moved faster, harder, his hands at her hips, guiding her until she no longer needed a guide. Suddenly, he lifted his head and arched his back and let out a sound that later would make him blush.

Henry withdrew slowly, wincing as Anne winced. "Sorry, love," he whispered, and kissed her. He lay by her side, one leg still holding her close, unwilling to move away, a feeling of overwhelming protectiveness and tenderness flooding him. They stared at each other, eyes bright with love and spent passion, and smiled.

"It wasn't too horrible, was it?" he asked.

Anne fought to remain straight-faced. "Not too."

Henry pulled her close, tucking her head under his chin. "I could have a bath run, if you like."

"That sounds like heaven," Anne murmured sleepily.

Henry turned his head just enough to check the time, and he chuckled. "Don't fall asleep on me yet, wife," he growled. "It's only six o'clock."

"You wore me out, husband," Anne said, smiling against his chest.

Reluctantly, Henry rose and pulled the bellrope that would call a maid. When she arrived, he called his instructions through the door. Turning back to Anne, he found she had snuggled under the covers, modesty returning full force. He stood there and stared, his heart overflowing, at his sleepy wife, her honey-blonde hair spilling over the pillow, her drowsy eyes smiling at him. His body responded instantly, blood surging with startling quickness. He wanted to make love again, something she would have known instantly with a single look. Embarrassed that his desire was so blatantly evident, Henry snatched up his drawers and pants.

"You're shy," Anne said, sounding pleased to have discovered this about her husband.

Henry grunted something as he fastened the final button of his pants, before he sat at the edge of the bed. "I'm not used to being around a woman all the time."

"I thought you had a bevy of mistresses," Anne teased.

Looking shy once again, Henry studied the quilt. "I never had a mistress. Just, hmmm, acquaintances."

Anne scowled, apparently not wanting to hear any more about his former lovers. A knock sounded on the door and a maid called out, "The bath's been drawn, sir."

Henry called out a thank-you, and nodded his head

to a door at the far end of the chamber. "Should I leave you to your privacy?" he asked.

Anne seemed unsure, then nodded, scrunching the blanket even higher. Henry smiled down at his wife. "I've already seen every lovely inch of you, Anne. I promise not to ravish you until after your bath."

Anne bit her lip, a distracting little habit of hers, and her eyes sparkled. "Lord, woman, but you tempt me," he growled, before kissing her soundly.

Henry pulled on a robe and gave his new wife the privacy she wanted, though he knew he would count himself a saint if he didn't accidentally stroll into the bathroom and interrupt her. Just the thought of her sitting in his deep tub, all sudsy and warm and slick, was more than enough to tempt him. Already, Anne delighted him, gave him more than he would have expected of someone as innocent as she. He knew that if he should return early to find her lazily enjoying her bath, she would go willingly into his arms. He grew hard instantly, and was grateful for the robe that hid his state from the servants. Hoping to distract himself from ravishing his wife, Henry headed to his grandfather's study, making mental notes along the way about changes he would make to the mansion. The study was dark and cold when he entered, and he lit a lamp on his grandfather's desk. That is when he saw the journal.

For a moment, he eyed the volume curiously, not quite remembering when he'd seen it last. Then he recalled Williamson solemnly handing it to him the day of his grandfather's funeral, saying something about how his grandfather had wanted him to have it.

Henry sat down in the leather chair and leaned back, the journal on his lap. He opened it and read: "To Henry." And then he turned the page and began reading, "I am old and I am dying. And so, Henry, it is time to tell you the truth about Sea Cliff."

From the Journal of Arthur Owen

Elizabeth never allowed the two of us to be alone.
Even as years passed, the passion that flared up so
briefly between us was still there, a raging hot ember
that needed only the smallest of breezes to turn into
a flame. I stayed away as much as I could, seeing her
in the end only at Sea Cliff, and then only for a week
or two. It was inevitable that one day we would be
alone.

You were visiting with Alex in Newport, and I,
angry that she had shuttled you away when she knew
I would come, remained past the time I planned. I
wanted to see you and she knew it and so she sent
you away. It was that kind of cruelty that I could
never understand. Walter had grown more and more
distant the longer I remained at Sea Cliff, taking himself off for long walks into the woodlands. Elizabeth
must have been beside herself to know that at any
given time, she would find herself alone with me. I
was aware of her discomfort, and enjoyed it. I con-
spired again and again to be alone with her, only to
have her immediately leave the room or ring for a
servant the moment I entered a room. I didn't know
that I was wearing her down, I didn't know she felt
anything other than annoyance over my persistence. I
didn't know she burned for me as I did for her.

It was a hot, heavy day with a storm brewing to the
south. Dark clouds built ominously on the horizon, a
thick wind bringing tropical air. I found her in the
library gazing out the window at the clouds. She'd
been weeping. When I came up behind her, she leaned
back into me. I can still remember the joy that washed
over me, to have her in my arms again. Finally, she
turned in my arms and kissed me. I had wanted her,
yearned for her for so long, I lost my head. I forgot
we could be discovered, I forgot everything but that
Elizabeth was again in my arms.

You must have already guessed what happened next. Walter came into the room and discovered us. It was a nightmarish scene. He went quite mad, tearing me away from her and thrashing her soundly again and again, beating me off when I tried to pull him away. I will never forget that Elizabeth made almost no sound even as he struck her, accepting her punishment, almost welcoming it. I went to my desk and removed my pistol, cocking it loudly, not even knowing if it was loaded. I told him to release Elizabeth, and he refused. He held Elizabeth by her dress, his other hand poised to strike her, when she sealed our fates. It is then she told him, with him already mad with rage, with him poised to deal her a blow, that you were not his son. He looked from her to me, horrified, shaking his head in disbelief, finally screaming out his denial, even as it became clear he knew she was telling the truth. He shook her and demanded she name the father. He already knew. He must have known, but he demanded it anyway. And that's when I told him. And that's when he struck the final blow. And that's when I pulled the trigger.

You wanted to know why I didn't want you to have Sea Cliff . . . I will tell you. I buried my son and his wife in the wine cellar and there they lie still. I did it in a haze of madness, but once done, I could not undo it. I convinced myself that it was better for everyone, particularly for you, that their bodies never be found.

So, Henry, now you know why I tried to keep Sea Cliff from you. And you know I love you. I am so very sorry.

Chapter Twenty-seven

Henry closed the journal, walked to the fireplace, and shoveled a good amount of coal onto the grate. When the fire was dancing and hot, he threw the journal into the flames and watched it burn. Bits of charred paper fluttered up the chimney to rise and fall as ashes upon Fifth Avenue. Memories assailed him and his heart broke knowing that nearly everything he'd held to be true about his childhood was not. He felt betrayed, as if something vital had been ripped from his soul.

He sat, cross-legged as he had as a boy, and watched the journal burn until nothing was left but the hard leather binder, black and curled.

"Oh, God," he said, his voice rough. His throat convulsed as he tried with all his strength not to give in to the emotions that scraped him raw. "You sorry bastard," he spat, his eyes boring into the journal's remains. "My father," he whispered harshly, shaking his head. "My father."

And then he wept.

Anne found him sitting in the library on a sofa staring into the cold fire. "I waited for two hours," she said cautiously, knowing something was not right that her new husband would be sitting in the darkened library alone on his wedding night. She searched his face and saw a grief so piercing, her heart wrenched. "Henry, what has happened?"

Without saying a word, he drew her to him, pulling

her against him hard, embracing her in an almost desperate way. And then he released her and told her the story his grandfather had written.

"All my life, I thought I hated him. And he was my father. It was all a lie. All my memories, all lies."

"No, Henry, you mustn't think that way. Oh, I wish your grandfather had just kept that horrid story to himself. I do not believe in deathbed confessions," Anne said fiercely. "What harm would it have done to keep it to himself?"

"Don't you see, Anne? He was afraid that I would find the bodies when I was renovating Sea Cliff. He must have lived in constant fear I would learn the truth before he had the chance to die. It wasn't that he was hiding my parents from me, it was that he was hiding himself. I always thought he was the toughest, strongest man I'd ever know, but he was a coward. He could not risk that I might find out who he was. The truth is, I've been in that wine cellar a dozen times and saw nothing amiss. I never would have discovered them."

Anne hugged him to her. "Am I being awful to say I'm glad you sold Sea Cliff?"

"I don't think I could have kept the old place anyway, knowing what I know now." And then Henry began to laugh, so hard, tears formed in his eyes.

"What is it? Tell me, Henry."

"Colonel Mann," he managed to say between laughs.

"What about him?" Anne could hardly think that the colonel would find out about Arthur's sordid story. The man couldn't find out all their secrets.

"He bought Sea Cliff," Henry said, wiping his eyes.

"But I thought—"

"It was a ruse. The man bought Sea Cliff, then immediately transferred ownership to Mann. Apparently, he became enthralled with the place when he learned how obsessed I'd been with it. Bought it sight unseen."

"Oh, goodness," Anne said. And then she burst out laughing. "You have to tell him."

"The hell I do."

"Oh, Henry, we must."

"The only thing we must do, Mrs. Owen, is go back up to our bedroom. I don't want to discuss this anymore." Henry was suddenly serious. "The only thing I want right now is you. I want to forget about Sea Cliff. Just for a while. Can we do that?"

Henry was kissing her again, so it was easy to forget that there was a world outside. "Henry?"

"Hmm?" he said against her lips.

"Let's build our own memories. Happy ones."

He kissed her and smiled. "I think we've already begun."